LESSONS FROM
A SORCERER!

"For convenience, we classify our demons by power and station. Not all the demons imprisoned in days of yore were leaders and priests of demon hordes, see. The vast majority were, oh, common laborers: secretaries and assistant librarians and such. The big dangerous types got all the attention, and everyone believes all demons are equally powerful. Suunwaduun's a nobody, practically an apprentice demon."

"Oh," said Polijn. "Then he isn't dangerous?"

"Well, he's no one you'd care to have over for dinner. . . ."

ROUSE A SLEEPING CAT

Dan Crawford

ACE BOOKS, NEW YORK

To STEPHEN D. LAMPE,
who died while this book was going to press,
and had better not do it again
if he expects a Milk Bone

This book is an Ace original edition,
and has never been previously published.

ROUSE A SLEEPING CAT

An Ace Book / published by arrangement with
the author

PRINTING HISTORY
Ace edition / May 1993

ISBN: 0-441-73553-3

Ace Books are published by The Berkley Publishing Group,
200 Madison Avenue, New York, NY 10016.
The name "ACE" and the "A" logo
are trademarks belonging to Charter Communications, Inc.

PRINTED IN THE UNITED STATES OF AMERICA

10 9 8 7 6 5 4 3 2 1

PROLOGUE
Nimnestl

THE morning was white: cloudy without being dark, but bright without being warm. The brittle air held no hint of spring. Those who could afford them were glad for the heavy robes of state.

Yet spring was mere days away. Its arrival would no doubt be announced with the traditional cloudburst on the Feast of Arghast. Nimnestl, near the head of the parade, hoped so. The King would be back by Arghastfeast, and torchlight parades were safest during the rainy season. Pity to mark the King's triumph by burning down his capital.

The procession wound back behind Nimnestl for nearly half a mile. Its tail, a ragtag assembly of scavengers hoping the mighty lords ahead would drop something saleable, was barely out of the gates of Malbeth. Along the procession's length, banners proclaimed the presence of the more important participants. Nimnestl herself was represented by no banner, but farther overhead sailed the sharp black form of Mardith. This sight held little interest for those in the parade, who were used to the bird's attendance on the big Chief Bodyguard. Taking advantage of the crowd's inattention, Mardith swooped to the road for a lump of slush and ice. Rising again, he let this fall against the bare neck of Culghi, riding next to the Mayor of Malbeth.

Culghi's loud, fluent commentary choked off as the bodyguard recalled that he was riding in solemn procession. He glanced at his superior and, seeing her mouth twist, asked, "Ma'am, may I

1

shoot him just once, just a little? One tail feather is all I ask."

Mardith fluttered to Nimnestl's shoulder. "What the fault with him, Missy?" the bird demanded. "I think him look too hot so I help out."

Nimnestl bestowed the same amiable sneer on her bird and her lieutenant. "You shouldn't have left the back of your neck open," she pointed out.

"I should have roasted the lintik bird," muttered Culghi.

The King, who had been following this, laughed and nudged his horse toward Nimnestl's. "You will have to do better," he declared, all dignity, "if you wish to be part of our escort."

Culghi bowed his head in a show of deference that was only part mockery. Nimnestl braced herself for what would come now, for the seventh time. She tried to think of something new to say.

The King urged his horse still closer and said, "What do you think of my escort, Nimnestl? Really?"

Suppressing the second sigh, she told him, "It's perfect: a few too many for a friendly visit, but many too few for an invasion."

Nurse, also for the seventh time, injected the opinion that a mighty robber baron would sweep down from the hills and carry away the entire mismatched company. Nurse had not been chosen to go along.

Nimnestl did not quite let the remark pass unheeded. "The important thing," she told the King, "is not to try to be invincible. Just be strong enough to make the fight a long one. The wise will then realize you aren't worth the trouble, and the fools you can generally defeat."

He glanced at the hammer that showed under her robes, but Nimnestl couldn't tell whether this indicated agreement or disbelief. The Chief Bodyguard was popularly considered invincible. She had so far found only three men brave enough to duck under the hammer; most beat a retreat if she so much as reached for it. Small children not yet versed in politics screamed and ran when she approached. They had heard so much about Nimnestl from their parents that they knew she was the next thing to evil incarnate (the Regent).

Nurse was unimpressed. Before the monarch could escape, she had pushed her horse in front of Nimnestl's, and around to where she could rearrange the brooches on the King's collar again.

"You're wearing enough gold to tempt the very rabbits," she rumbled. "Why you choose to wear half the Treasury around your neck . . ."

Conan III, Lord of All Rossacotta, the Mines of Troppo, And Anything Else He Can Take, was just nine years old. It was hard to tell under his regalia, but he was almost exactly the average height for that age, if a little overweight. The robes of state did not so much build him up as broaden him, until he looked like a mountain dwarf. Rossacottan fashion relied upon mass, rather than elegance, for its effect.

In fact, Nimnestl had chosen the brooches the King wore; each was broad and heavy enough to deflect a blow at the throat, if anyone in Bekijn dared. Not that the King had disapproved her choices. His tastes had always run along butterfly lines. Nimnestl could remember when, not so many years ago, he had studied a clashing assembly of gold, purple, and green in the mirror, and turned to cry, "Oh, Nimnestl, I am perfectly gorgeous!"

Nimnestl glanced ahead, to hide her smile from those behind. They were nearing the line of trees that marked the southern boundary of the city lands. Here they would all stop. Then the King, with the escort he himself had chosen, would push on to Bekijn.

It had been a grand parade, winding through the streets filled with loyal, cheering souls, many of whom did not know the King's name, and some of whom would have been astonished to learn that Kings had names. For centuries the bureaucracy had kept the title of King powerful, encouraging its worship. In the end, this backfired; some of the Kings seized power for themselves. Over the centuries, the old style of government had crumbled, but the effects lingered. Merchants still bribed palace insiders to attend one of the quarterly Royal Haircuts and snatch a lock of sacred hair.

Those in the procession felt the same way, though their reverence was mixed with the prospect of personal gain. Anyone who could claim to deserve it had demanded a spot in the parade, in hopes that the King might drop some scrap of influence.

Nimnestl knew the name, profession, and really more than it was safe to know about virtually all these scavengers. Some followed in coaches, to display their wealth, and some came on horseback, displaying their horsemanship. Really important figures were surrounded by hangers-on, the hangers-on showing off how noble was the company in which they travelled, and their leader showing off how large a company he could muster.

Isanten, First Minister and theoretical Chief of the Council, rode alone; his term in office was nearly up. He affected not to notice this lack of support, providing a direct contrast to General Ferrapec, for whom a thinning retinue was as much a disaster as thinning hair. The general kept angling his horse toward the coach of General Kaigrol, so that his retinue might be confused with the larger one. This fooled no one: retainers wore their leader's badge, some colored sash or figured brooch. Nimnestl studied these to see which badges were prevalent, and whether they were the same ones that had prevailed the day before.

Colonel Palompec also rode close to Kaigrol, but he was reminding the general of some pressing requirement of the border troops. Haeve, the Royal Tutor, rode not far behind, herding the Royal Playmates and trying, without much success, to point out trees and land formations at the roadside. The Playmates were watching Morquiesse, Chief Figurer and Painter to the King, who had decided to ride next to the Minstrels' Wagon. A new brush he had invented for the occasion was being demonstrated. A metal prong that sprang from the brush lifted the shift of Arberth's assistant, perched on the edge of the wagon, so that the brush itself could be used to paint something amusing on her exposed back and buttocks. The wagon was so packed with the court's lesser minstrels and jesters that the girl could not move out of his reach without falling off. Her master, the painstaking but never competent Arberth, was, as usual, thinking of something else, and did not notice.

Behind the wagon, apparently oblivious of the scene and the noise of the Playmates, rode Kaftus, Regent of the Realm, in an open coach. The cadaverous necromancer owned both horses and feet, but always used his coach on excursions outside the Palace Royal. He said that if he rode, he could work en route, and thus not completely waste his time.

Behind him, serving as a divider between the VVIPs in front and the mere VIPs behind, walked a clump of riderless horses. They had the tiny, tiny ears of all Rossacottan warhorses, but were not the best of their kind. Still, they bore the marks of the Royal Stud Farm, and would be gratefully received by the winner of the lawsuit.

For this whole parade, which had turned the Palace Royal and the city of Malbeth inside-out, and which had been two weeks in the planning, was no more than a procession to see the King off to judge a simple land dispute.

The case was not unusual: the Duke of Bekijn was dead, and Bekijn was up for grabs. Buran claimed that the duke's only child, as an unmarried woman, had no rights under the law. Rimiar countered that as an illegitimate nephew (for his father had disobeyed the ancient law and custom forbidding any but the eldest son to marry before the father's death), Buran had no claim at all, much less a better claim than hers. What might have been an interminable lawsuit, and perhaps a small war, was distinguished by the unusual existence of a written will, in which the duke left Bekijn to his daughter, and a small estate to the nephew. In any case, according to the Court Lawknower, Buran was basing his case on nothing more than his sex and the presence of several relatives in high places in the Treasury Department.

The business could have been resolved more quickly, but Kaftus and Nimnestl had seized on the brangle as an excuse to get the King out of the Palace Royal, without either of them. The personal attention of the King would mollify Buran's relatives (who weren't all that interested in the young thug), while his taking a week or so to come to a decision would keep Rimiar from becoming too secure. Most important, this would give the King an entire errand to supervise on his own, bolstering his own self-confidence, and perhaps suggesting to some people that the King was more than a puppet in the hands of his guardians. He had their love and their worship, but their confidence had to be earned.

There was also an annual rent ceremony involved, in which the noble vowed to administer lands in the King's name and, at command, relinquish it all and go to fight penniless at the King's side, if need be. This oath was so traditional that it was generally performed with both the duke and the King represented by proxies, while the principals were dining at the Palace Royal, bare yards from each other.

The Palace Royal had always been the center of power in Rossacotta, the place to go for a piece of the action or a share of the loot. Duchies and estates were mere larders, not to be bothered with as long as the servants kept them running. As a result, Rossacotta held few castles and fewer cities in the lands between Malbeth and the mountains.

This atypical pattern had saved Rossacotta during several Holy Crusades against it, over the centuries. "There is naught to take and hold," complained the ninth-century Turinese general Lysan

Redleg. "It is like grasping an armful of water. But we must cleanse this filthy pool."

Rossacotta remained cheerfully filthy, giving shelter and encouragement to a whole continent's villains and thieves, in exchange for a large percentage of the take. The country was a blank space on most maps, an unknown land where brigands had the leisure to form into efficient bands of whom it had been written, "They left nothing inside the houses; they left nothing outside the houses. Then they knocked the houses down."

Royal revolts and governmental reorganization had muddled things. New kings instituted desultory clean-up campaigns. At the same time, neighboring rulers realized that Rossacotta was not only a very wicked country, but a very rich one. What couldn't be taken away in war, they reasoned, could be leeched out in trade. Brave merchants penetrated shunned borders, and enough came out again to encourage imitators.

Progress had been slow, but it did seem now that Rossacotta's long history was moving into a new chapter. Rossacottans strove to remake themselves in a more cultured image. Men who couldn't spell their own names were dictating odes to secretaries, and women who painted their faces because that was easier than washing them were also painting porcelain, that being a civilized pastime. "Civilized" was an omnipresent word of praise: merchants roared at customers, bullying them to buy new civilized boots, civilized beer, civilized garottes, and civilized turnips.

Even the law had been tidied up. A century ago, a lawsuit like the one in Bekijn might have been resolved through a less conspicuous procession, ending in the decapitation of whichever litigant was caught first.

King Conan's parade reached the trees and stopped, in sections. While the end of the parade was still cursing the front, Kaftus ordered his coach pulled alongside the King. Rising in his seat to tower several feet above his sovereign, the cadaverous Regent begged permission to give him advice. The King met his eyes, but urged his horse back a bit. Anyone who associated with Kaftus stayed alert and defensive; the Regent's law of ruling, indeed, his way of life, was "All people remember is being punished or being astonished."

The Regent was unpredictable, untrustworthy, and dangerously powerful on both mundane and supernatural levels. The only person who had not feared him was Queen Kata, who, dying, had named him Regent. "He has neither scruples nor morals," she had said. "But he also has no desire to be King."

His speech on this occasion was unobjectionable. It counselled the King to do justice and have a grave, good time. Conan was instructed to act in the best interests of his country, and to decide wisely, and to take his time, and to let his noble ancestry shine through, for blood would tell and the noble tradition of the monarchy would undoubtedly result in the fairest possible decision, and this was good because the eyes of Rossacotta turned to the King for guidance and so on and so on until the speech broke off in midsentence as Kaftus simply sat down again. Nimnestl shrugged; she knew Kaftus could stomach only so much verbal broccoli at one time. It might be good for everyone, but he didn't like it.

The formal farewell thus completed, the parade began to divide into two lines: one to go on and one to go home. This could not be accomplished without pushing and shouting. Fist and knife fights broke out all along the line. Treasury guards shoved members of the castle guard; dungeon personnel tried to knock down members of the regular army. This all took some time, and allowed those at the head a little time for last-minute advice and informal leave-taking.

Mardith fluttered to the King's right thigh and rummaged in the small pouch on the royal belt. "Got you the salt for the hungry goblins?" he demanded. "Don't lost that!"

Nimnestl leaned over to say, "Remember what we said about your royal dignity and not letting anybody get away with anything. You're the boss. And if it comes to a fight, don't kill them all. Leave some alive to spread word of what a terror you are."

The King licked a nervous smile, obviously feeling as little like a terror as he looked. He raised his left hand toward his face and, for one terrible moment, Nimnestl thought he was going to put that thumb in his mouth. But the King caught himself, and brushed a lock of hair off his forehead instead.

He seemed about to speak, but at that moment Nurse drew her horse abreast of his again.

"Put your hood up," she ordered. "You'll catch cold."

The King laughed out loud and, seeing that his escort was nearly assembled, turned his steed, Morsheen, away. He nodded to Nimnestl, who nodded back, and rode to the head of the new parade, Culghi close to his side.

Undaunted, Nurse strained forward. "And don't go riding like a courier!" she shouted. "Try to be civiliz . . . lintik blast that bird!" The target she had presented by leaning so far forward in the saddle had proven irresistible to Mardith.

Nimnestl ignored Nurse's tirade and Mardith's squeals of glee. The King was wiggling his ears, a trick he had learned from a quester who passed through the city last fall, as a private farewell signal. She glanced over at the Regent.

"Think the escort's all right?" she asked, for only the tenth time. "Do you trust them?"

Kaftus didn't even look up from his papers. "They are all knaves and fools. I trust the knaves. I can generally predict what they will do."

Nimnestl turned back. The Royal Playmates in the escort had caught up to the King but were still riding sedately, knowing they were observed. The Playmates who had to stay were calling useless advice from various vantage points. She counted them, absently, and came up one short. She studied the escort and counted the Playmates there.

Then she rode back to Kirasov, a big man with a huge lower jaw, which her uncle had always told her was indicative of pugnacious villainy. "Never," he had told her, "trust a man with a chin longer than his thumb." He had been betrayed and butchered in the Fall of Koanta by a man whose chin had been perfectly all right.

She waited until the Head Treasury Guard had finished whipping five brawlers apart, and then said, "I don't see Argeleb in the procession."

"Oh, ah," Kirasov replied. "I made him stay at the Palace. He's been, ah, fighting with his sisters again."

The movement of his jaw told Nimnestl he was uncomfortable. And Kirasov, at least within his family, was not known as a harsh disciplinarian, particularly not with his remaining son. The older boy, Anrichar, was still under ban for an insult to the Regent, and living in indefinite exile outside the country.

It did her no good, though, to know the man was lying until she knew why. And the personnel of the Royal Playmates had been altering without warning lately. This happened, but usually at the orders of Nimnestl or Kaftus. But Rentruan had disappeared, and then Macob. Argeleb might make three.

"One a week," the King had said, when Macob failed to turn up for a geography lesson. "They're working up to me." Neither Rentruan nor Macob had been particular favorites of his.

Kirasov moved off to break up another tussle. Nimnestl did not follow. She had enough to do just keeping track of the comings and goings of the adults. This was probably some petty matter, some interfamilial feud, and the kidnappings would work themselves out if she let them run their course. Kirasov, though he held a position of some importance, did not carry enough political weight to make an investigation worthwhile, either to annoy or gratify him.

Nimnestl, after all, was not charged with keeping order in the Palace Royal. Her involvement was only necessary in cases where there was a threat to the King.

She felt like turning to watch him go, but resisted the urge. Peace in the Palace Royal would not be enhanced if Nurse suspected she was uneasy. But she did wish she could have gone along. Culghi was good, but young yet. She snorted at the thought. He was only a year or two older than she was.

There was nothing to be done about it now. She turned and started back for the palace. The parade was splintering into smaller parades, some taking quick routes and some taking routes that led through the more entertaining parts of the city. Morquiesse was in the lead on the shortest road to the Palace Royal. He had from now until the King's return to finish his grand mural in the Great Dining Hall. Now that he would have the luxury of working without interruption, he wanted to get back without delay. There was no need to serve meals in the hall when the King was not in residence. People could dine in their own rooms, waited on by personal servants, in less grandeur but more comfort than among the paint fumes and official serving staff.

The bodyguard's hand swept down and caught a wrist, before the tug on her leg had even ended. It was a dirty wrist, but pale against the brown of her fist. The bundle of rags and whiskers attached to the wrist stammered, "M-milady, m-may I beg per-permission . . ."

"You have my permission to be on your way," she replied. She threw the wrist from her and wiped her hand on a lapel of her outer robe. One of the major benefits of her position was that all but the most aristocratic were too terrified of her to beg from her.

The beggar regained his balance and came back. "But, milady," he said, his voice heavy with the air of rotten parsnips, "I have information."

So he was trying to sell something. That was more familiar to Nimnestl, though just as annoying. She gave him the weight of her entire gaze.

He felt it, and his voice dropped to a whisper. "About Brown Robes."

Nimnestl turned away, without so much as a replying sneer. Nemmis had ridden up to see who was annoying his commander.

"Take this man into custody," she said. "Don't damage him if you can help it."

Nemmis bellowed orders to two underlings. As the bodyguards tied the beggar's wrists to their saddles, Nimnestl rode on. She turned up her collar. The weather would get worse before it got any better.

CHAPTER ONE
Polijn

I

TRADITIONALLY bad for the Feast of Arghast, the weather was holding off this year. Dark clouds, so low that it seemed they must rip out their bellies on the peak of the King's Bell Tower, had so far produced no more than a brief drizzle. Last year, Polijn recalled, they had cut loose with a blizzard, paralyzing the Swamp for six days, demolishing the planned festival, and eliminating her income, with disastrous effects on Ronar's temper.

Somewhere behind her, a wooden-soled boot kicked a shard of ice into a wall. Polijn ducked into the shelter provided by a stack of cartwheels that were rotted beyond repair or even scavenge. Two men, their knives out, passed the pile, too intent on something ahead to notice their young observer. After they had turned out of the alley, Polijn slid around the stack to hide in the leeward shadows. She listened for more footsteps, and heard none.

Polijn had never really been robbed while she lived in the Swamp. Everyone in her neighborhood (and she was careful about leaving it) knew that her money was her mother's, her mother's money was Ronar's, and Ronar's money belonged to Chordasp. Chordasp's money was his own, and anyone in that part of the Swamp could cite a dozen men dead in evidence of that ownership. What little money the girl made was not enough to merit attracting Chordasp's hostility.

But now Polijn was employed at the Palace Royal, and looked it. Her thin, tattered shift had been replaced by a heavy one, and her hooded cloak was a definite sign of prosperity. She had not been seen in the Swamp for months, and rumor had her attached to the harem of the King, able to command any luxury at the crook of a finger. Even those who didn't believe it knew that by leaving the Swamp, Polijn had forfeited the protection of Chordasp. So there was little to lose if one cared to find out how far rumor lied.

Her back to the wall, Polijn eased into the next shadow, behind a leaking rain barrel. Her right foot kicked into a lump of mud, still frozen at the center, and her sandal slipped off into a puddle. She stooped quickly and, retrieving the sandal, jammed it back onto her foot. It wouldn't be easy to get a replacement if she lost it. In truth, Polijn made no cash profit from her position as Arberth's assistant. Arberth was decidedly the worst jester at the court; the only fee he ever earned came in the form of copper coins thrown by the audience to damage, not reward.

He had been concentrating on a new song when Polijn went into their shared room. Like Polijn, he wanted to be a minstrel, but his qualifications consisted almost solely of knowing a lot of songs, especially classics from the books of Carnac and Estel. He taught these to Polijn, as well as he was able, and sometimes they had very professional-sounding arguments about whether Targon of Karef was a better writer than Ulan of Torfal.

When Polijn cleared her throat for the third time, Arberth had looked up. "The King is back?" he asked.

"You can hear the cheering, if you listen," she said, closing the door.

Arberth had glanced at his paper and thrown down his pen, rather recklessly, considering it was his last. "I'll never get this done for tonight's banquet!"

"Well," Polijn had answered, trying very hard not to look interested, "why not put it off?"

He turned watery blue eyes on her. "There'll be festivals all over the Swamp tonight. You could go there instead, earn a little extra money, and have a whole day before tomorrow night's feast."

Arberth, pulling at his mustache, had said, "You've been planning that, child."

"Well," she murmured, "I haven't seen my mother since the King's Birthday." That had nothing to do with it; they needed the money.

"Platform in the Swamp, eh?"

"Could you get off tonight's program without much trouble?"

His face had twisted with distaste. "You must be jesting. Oh, of course: you're a jester. Well, perhaps audiences in your part of the city are less persnickety. I can do some of my older numbers."

It had been rather quick agreement; Polijn had braced herself for more coaxing. On entering the Swamp, however, she had found that the jester, too, had a plan. Not forty yards into the slum district, he had found an excuse to stop at the Low Raven. There he had allowed three characters who admired his thick, green cloak to cajole him into a little game of chance. It was an even money bet, now, whether the game would break up in time for him to get a spot on a platform, and even money, too, whether it would break up because he remembered what he was here for, or because the indignant losers took him outside to be gutted. Clumsy on stage, Arberth was an adept at cards, and almost always won. He said this was because he "played the whole game." Having seen him play, Polijn felt she knew what he meant.

He would certainly not be pried from the game until he had won a few hands, and so Polijn had been left to her own devices. Rather than let Arberth see through her story, she had decided to actually drop in on Gloraida, at the Yellow Dog, and see what was new. She regretted her decision within moments of reaching her old neighborhood. But she was almost to the right building, and had suffered no serious mishap so far.

This was the dangerous part. She had to leave the alley and cross the street. She peered out past the rain barrel.

Unaccustomed homesickness swamped her. Everything was exactly as it had been at the last festival. Fried potato carts crisscrossed the street, exuding smoke and the smell of burning grease, pursued by children, dogs, cats, and rats hoping to snitch a bite when the vendor looked away. Sorei had his tattoo stand out, and was offering a free shave with every tattoo, since the clean chin was coming back into style at court. Sporrisch had set up a table to sell his rag liquor by the mug. He was doing good business, too, despite one customer writhing regrets in the gutter to which Sporrisch had kicked him.

Polijn slid out into the milling mob, holding her cloak to hide the hood, in hopes this would make it look like a respectable stolen blanket. She squeezed close to Sporrisch's customers, close enough for shelter, but far enough away that she wouldn't be taken for a cutpurse.

Busy with other attractions, no one paid her much attention. Salesfolk strolled with little trays, offering cheap merchandise that

was unexcelled in any part of this city, nay, in the country, and
which was only being offered at this obscenely low price because
the vendor had had too much festival and was out of her mind
drunk and you'd better buy now because tomorrow she'd have a
hangover and prices would triple. Anyone who got close enough
to these trays to buy something paid twice without knowing it.
Though business was brisk, the trays never seemed to get any
emptier.

A smoker, lighting his pipe, flipped a chunk of tinder at
Lothirien, who was at her usual corner. She had lost a few
teeth, and recently, to judge by the way she kept taking her
thumb out of her mouth to rub her jaw. Polijn thought of asking
her for news, but didn't know whether to trust her.

The biggest crowd shoved around and under the wooden platform on which various singers, actors, and jesters were playing
to the crowd. Khoss was dancing on the corner nearest Polijn,
undulating as if her body had never heard of morals, or bones,
while Edifryn played "The Last Lay of the Minstrel" on an old
lute. The dance was brisk, even hurried, for the sake of warmth.
She wore nothing but a dark smudgy handprint, carefully painted
on before she left the Thick Fleece, on the small of her back.

Those passersby not tossing coins or suggestions at Khoss
jostled and jabbed each other around the crowd, sizing up the
possibilities for robbery, sex, or a good fight. The rope pilers
had the only clear space on the pavement. These were good,
honest laboring men too busy for frivolity, looping rope into
circular piles. Passersby, touched by the sight of such dedication,
tossed coins into the centers of these piles. Those who failed to
be touched by the sight, and neglected the coin, found their legs
inexplicably tangled in the rope.

Polijn gave the rope pilers plenty of room, but to do so, had
to skirt the crowd at a small catbaiting ring. She caught a whisper
of, "That one in the blanket looks like Polijn."

She ducked into a small group that was bidding on a pair of
twins, but not before she heard a sportsman reply, "Polijn? The
one up to the Palace?"

Three men stepped away from the catbaiters. Polijn knew better
than to run, but she did speed up. The alley she wanted was close.
The three men were somewhat closer.

At that moment, a heavy body flew from the Bedbug. It hit
the street and didn't move. They didn't, once Ranbreyr was
finished with them. The three men knelt by this distraction to

see if Ranbreyr had left anything that could be converted to cash. Grateful, Polijn doubled her speed and gained the alley.

In refuge, under a flight of splintered stairs, she breathed out her relief. From here she had just three alleys to cover, and they were connected. Then her only problem would be getting into the Yellow Dog without being noticed.

II

POLIJN was in luck. From behind a frozen garbage heap, she could watch two early customers enter the Yellow Dog. Zhriacar was on door duty. The big man with the scarred pink fists and dimples in his cheeks was an old ally of hers. As soon as she judged the customers to be safely inside and away from the door, Polijn scuttled to the door and knocked.

Zhriacar looked out, and then down. Then he stared. "Well, ki . . . Polijn. Come on in. It's cold out there."

"It is," she whispered. "Is Glor in?" She slid inside, staying in the big man's shadow as he closed the door.

"Regular room, ki . . . Polijn," he answered. He cleared his throat and pointed down the corridor.

Polijn remembered the way. "I won't stay long," she promised.

"Take your time," he told her, almost bowing. Too intent on reaching Gloraida without attracting attention, Polijn did not notice an unusual tone in Zhriacar's voice. Nor did she glance back in time to see him whisper to one of the house runners. She trusted Zhriacar, and was devoting all her concentration to staying out of sight.

Karlikartis, owner of the Yellow Dog, and her righthand man, Torat, were deadly. Karlikartis was marginally more dangerous, with unpredictable temper and utter lack of humor. (When Torat was in the mood, he found strangling customers vastly

16

amusing.) There was a house rule against relatives working together; Karlikartis felt it engendered revolution. No relatives of employees were even allowed on the premises. The smaller the relative was, the better were the chances of immediate and violent penalties.

Most of the "rooms" in the Yellow Dog were cubicles made private by torn canvas over wooden struts. But, off to the right, down a short corridor, Gloraida had an actual room of her own. This was not issued to her because of her body, beauty, or talent. As star of the show, she had to wear a costume with rare, fragile lace from Silmarién. In this neighborhood, such a costume needed to be safeguarded in a room with a lock. Having the wearer dress in the same room was simply a matter of efficiency.

Gloraida sat naked on bare boards, shaving. The costume hung in its place of honor, far from the door and the leak in the ceiling. Gloraida's own clothes were balled up under the bench. She looked up when Polijn entered. Recognizing her daughter, she smiled, and turned back to concentrate on the leg she was scraping.

"Well, well," she said. "How are you? Are you getting enough to eat?"

Polijn shut the door and stepped to the right of it. She had time to say, "Oh, yes," before her mother went on.

"I'm getting fat," said Gloraida. She set down the old razor and grabbed a lump of thigh to demonstrate. "Things bounce when they're not supposed to."

Polijn thought her mother looked thinner, somewhere between haggard and gaunt. She did not mention it. "I was over at the Low Raven," she said. "And I thought I'd come over."

"You were always nice," said Gloraida. She picked up a brush and studied it. Then she peered into the mirror, hunching her shoulders as she shuddered. "I'm losing my hair, too. She's got to stop pulling it so hard. Look at my face. I'm getting old, Polijn."

Polijn knew her mother wanted not sympathy but prevarication, and that immediately. "What?" she demanded, walking up behind Gloraida. "Your back's just hurting you again. Want it rubbed?"

"No," answered her mother, shaking off Polijn's hands. "They can see the creases back to the fifth row now; I know it. Torat as much as said so."

"Well, I've got better eyes than he does," snapped Polijn. "Now, look." She pointed to the mirror. "You can see that you're older than I am." She ran a hand down the front of her overtunic until it was tight, and flat, against her body. "Other than that, you look as young as anybody. Younger. I saw Khoss on a platform on the way here: it hardly pays her to get undressed, the way her belly sags almost to her knees. And you should have seen Joliena waiting her turn. Her roots were three different colors, the bottom one grey. And it'll be another ten years before you sag so much."

"Yes, you're right," sighed Gloraida. She risked a glance at the mirror, decided to believe Polijn instead, and turned to face her daughter. "Just the same," she said, throwing her shoulders back, "I'm getting too old to simper and wince. I don't look the delicate maiden any more and I shouldn't have to do that part. I should be given something else."

Polijn bit her lip. Karlikartis would likely give Gloraida one of those cribs in the basement—a copper a customer—and Ronar would not object so long as he still got his cut.

"She can give that role to Purvlia," Gloraida went on. "She'd be good: that long neck, you know. She'll make it if she doesn't keep insisting on wearing her hair so long." Gloraida shrugged. Ronar had always said she had the most expressive shoulders in the Swamp.

Best to divert her before she did anything rash. "Who's been taking Harliis's rents, since he died?" Polijn asked.

"I don't know," Glor answered. To Polijn's raised eyebrow, she said, "My dear, we have so many of your Palace folk down here these days. They probably haven't yet decided themselves. We see a lot of that painter fellow, Morquiesse. He always comes in with Colonel Palompec. I suppose it's one of them."

Polijn rubbed her backside, still a little sore from vain attempts to scrub off Morquiesse's inscription. "I didn't know they were friends."

"Oh, they aren't. My dear, they always start a fight, which is what makes me think they're both trying for the rents. Torat had to ask them to leave, last time." Her mouth was open to explain in more detail, but she caught sight of the mirror again.

She studied it with growing doubt. "How old are you?" she asked Polijn.

"Um," said Polijn. "Nine." She knew this estimate to be at least three years short, but there was no need for accuracy at this point.

"Ooh!" said her mother, the shoulders hunching again. "But, of course, when you were born, I was a mere child selling cabbage."

It was a bit unfeeling to ignore the existence of Polijn's older sister, but Polijn knew it would be even worse to mention Mokono. She looked around for something else with which to change the subject.

"Stars and moons!" she exclaimed, staring at a stack of rubbish in one corner.

Protruding from the stack was a hapless face made of pink and grey rags, with an utterly filthy scrap of wool between the ears. That puppy had been around as long as Polijn, for all she could remember. She ran to pull it from the pile. After shaking some of the dirt away, she ran back, growling, to dash it at her mother's face.

Gloraida responded with the same horror she used on stage. "Beast!" she exclaimed, crossing her eyes and swearing with her thumbs.

"Mouse!" growled Polijn, flapping the puppy's ears.

"Rats and worse!" shouted her mother, grabbing Polijn and tickling without mercy. The women collapsed into shrieking laughter, and fell to the floor just as the door swung open. Karlikartis rapped on the jamb.

There were many small, bony women in the Swamp, but Karlikartis looked concentrated, rather than shrunken. She was already made up for the first show, with red lips and black lashes bright against a dead white face. Her hair was the same black as her gown. The intention was to make her look very cold, and very hard, to give the impression that there was nothing under her skin but bones and meanness.

Which was true.

"Glor," she said, "someone has to go out before showtime and . . ." She saw Polijn's face and recognized it. Gloraida crawled under the bench.

But Polijn had noticed three things. Karlikartis's hand was not on her whip. Karlikartis had knocked before walking into the room. And Karlikartis, who never, ever, called anyone by name, had used a nickname.

Her next words clinched it. "Why, Polijn, what a pleasant surprise!"

Polijn knew it was not a surprise at all, at least to Karlikartis. It surprised Polijn a bit. She had never known the woman was aware she had a name.

The bony woman actually stooped a little to look into Polijn's face. "You hardly ever have time to come see us," she said, "living up at the Palace Royal."

"Palace Royal" was the clue. Karlikartis thought Polijn might be in a position to get her something. Polijn decided to let her think that.

"We get so many customers from the Palace, though," said Gloraida, coming back up to the top of the bench, not without an uneasy glance at the whip. "The First Minister himself, now, he comes in and talks to Karlikartis himself, Polijn."

Green eyes flashed bright, and Karlikartis put a hand on Glor's shoulder. Red nails dug little trenches. Polijn cleared her throat.

"Oh, Isanten," she said, her voice rising a little. "Yes, we frequently dine together." They did, too. Isanten at the King's Table, while Polijn, as assistant jester, sat at a table yards away, where the food was frigid. But they did dine together, whether Isanten noticed or not.

As Polijn had hoped, the nails came out of her mother's shoulder. "I suppose you know the Regent as well?" inquired Karlikartis.

There was mockery in her eyes; Polijn decided not to let this story get too ripe. "I don't, ah, like to have much to do with sorcerers."

Karlikartis nodded. "Have you heard who might be taking Harliis's rents? We're always the last to know."

"No, they haven't decided yet," said Polijn. True, as far as she knew. "But since you know the First Minister so well . . ."

The woman bared her teeth. "Oh, hasn't he mentioned my name?"

It might be best to leave the subject of Isanten. "I don't know him that well," she said. "After all, his term's almost over. Perhaps the Chief Bodyguard would know."

Her audience gasped. "You know that black . . . that great guardian of our King?" demanded the smaller woman.

As a matter of fact, the Bodyguard did know Polijn's name, and they had actually talked to each other. "I'll ask her," said Polijn, putting a finger on her chin. "I can say I'm asking for my mother, the assistant manager at the Yellow Dog."

Gloraida gasped again. Karlikartis stepped back, her hand falling to her whip. But she forced a smile and said, "By the way, Glor, I wanted to talk to you again, to see if you'd change your mind about giving up the stage and coming to help . . . me . . . in . . . the . . . upstairs . . . offices." Polijn thought those last words would be bitten off, as slow as they were, and as close as the teeth were to each other.

"Oh, but . . . oh, yes," said Glor.

"Well," said Polijn, slipping the puppy into her overtunic and backing toward the door, "it must be nearly showtime and I have to let you finish dressing. Besides, I have friends waiting to escort me back to the Palace Royal. I'll visit you again."

Her courage stuck until she had passed the door. Then she turned and ran down the hall. She did not reply to Zhriacar's, "Good night, kid!"

She tried to catch her breath in the alley. Life had never changed this fast, right before her eyes. The woman who never called her anything nicer than "that filthy brat" had as much as asked a favor from her, had done her a good turn, in fact, in hopes of getting that favor. Polijn did think she had handled it rather well, even if she was still shaking.

But as she slid up the alley, another thought hit her. She'd have to deliver something now. If nothing came of the conversation, all the blame would come down on Glor. Maybe something was possible through Arberth; the Chief Bodyguard did seem to have a little affection for the stumbling singer.

Preoccupied, Polijn forgot the necessary precautions. A large and callused hand took hold of her hood.

"I knew it wouldn't be difficult," said a voice. "Here's one now."

Polijn knew better than to struggle; better to wait and find out first who had her and what was wanted. The hand dragged her into the middle of the alleyway.

There were three of them, Chorach-tai cultists with shaved heads and very little clothing. The goblin fanatics tried to imitate the fashions and hairlessness of the legendary monsters. These wore more jewelry than cloth. From brassbound belts hung feathered skewers, to be stuck into victims so those who found the body would know whom to fear.

Ordinarily, when cultists were contemplating an atrocity, they prefaced action with a proclamation to the victim: "We are the Brotherhood of the Ragged Ratbird," or "Broken Elbow," or whatever they called their gang. The man who had gathered Polijn in, however, said only, "Come along. You can be useful." Polijn stared up at him.

This man was slimmer at hip and shoulder than the others. His nose was broken and one of his ears was missing, but he could have done both himself, to enhance his reputation. He sounded like someone from a better part of town, who roamed in the Swamp for the excitement. On his chest there dangled a nicely carved wooden amulet that looked like two pears with wings. Polijn did not recognize it, but it gave her the shivers.

She did not wish to be useful to this man. After a glance at his free hand, to be sure it was empty, she turned to the one that had come down to her shoulder, and bit it.

The cultist had not expected that. He shook his injured hand and aimed the other one into her face. Polijn ducked. The fist passed through her hair as her head came down.

While she was down there, she caught at a rotted chair back. It splintered against the left thigh of the nearest cultist, but that was enough to distract him. Polijn dodged under the third cultist's outstretched arms and scrambled away.

Three more men, with clubs, stood at the end of the alley. Dark pear-shaped amulets were obvious against their broad white chests.

But this was Polijn's old neighborhood, and from frequent use she knew every burrow and hiding place. A quick look showed no one at the side door of the Bedbug. If she could get to that, run through the brothel to the far alley, and get around a corner, she'd be back at the Yellow Dog and (comparative) safety.

Sometimes on all fours, and sometimes on two or three, Polijn kept going straight at the armed men. She did not spare another glance for the Bedbug until she was right up to the door. Then she swerved and hit wood, her heart threatening to outdistance her as she felt for the latch. As usual, the door was unlocked, and she pushed inside.

Slamming the door behind her, Polijn braced herself for the briefest second of rest before going on. Then she spun and stared up into the faces of three more Chorach-tai cultists who had stepped up behind her.

Her last thought before the club came down was that she hadn't fallen for that one in a long time.

III

THE chamber was vast and gloomy, but Polijn was not aware of that right away. Her head hurt, and her eyes would not focus. The fact that there was very little to focus on made it all the more difficult.

She did not moan as pain and waking hit her. She didn't even move. She closed her eyes again and waited for her head to come clear. Instinct, not conscious thought, told her that if she made her presence known by sound or action, someone would hit her again. When she felt capable of thinking, she reopened her eyes.

An immense figure rose over her. It had no face, just a pair of eyes centered among five ears, or horns. A row of branched tendrils grew along its shiny, domed scalp. Long, sharp wings rose behind the monster. Loose skin hung in folds under the taloned arms. Spiky hair stuck out at its waist and between its legs. From among this hair snaked long appendages, some of which were tentacles and some of which were not.

Long before she had reached this stage of observation, the sheen of the creature's skin had told Polijn that it was no more than a statue. Relaxing, she rolled her eyes down to study herself.

She lay naked on what felt like polished stone. Slowly, carefully, she moved her fingers and toes. They seemed to work. She bent her elbows and knees the slightest bit, and felt no pain. Things could obviously have been far worse. The cultists must have meant robbery only, and, after taking her things, they had dumped her. But where?

Grey walls rose to a shadowy void wherever she looked. Beyond her feet, she could see another sculpture of the same monster above her. This one was kneeling, doing something with pincers under the figure of a shrieking horse. Polijn felt she would have recognized this had she ever seen it before. Farther along, there was only darkness, interrupted here and there by a shiny outcropping that might be another statue. The source of this reflection seemed to be coming from behind her, to the left. She rolled her head just far enough back to take a look.

The main statue stood there, alone and huge in a massive sanctuary. Before it stood three stone pillars, and a pair of dark, tablelike tripods. Several torches were lit in the walls on each side.

No exit there. Polijn was preparing to sit up when she took in two more vital details. The first was that each of the columns was engraved with a symbol that looked like two pears, with wings. The second was that one torch was moving, in the hands of the one-eared goblin cultist.

He stopped before the gigantic statue, his torch sending a thousand flickering shadows up the monster's protruding granite belly. "Soon, demon, soon," he whispered, the echoes carrying his words around the room and up the hall.

Another sound, that of footsteps, came back. There was enough noise to indicate the presence of several men with leather boots, a deduction verified when a sudden scream rang out of the shadows. The footsteps moved faster. Seven Chorach-tai fanatics dashed into the light.

"One of those lintik statues," gasped the one in front, "reached out and grabbed Kerslyk!"

The leader set his torch into a wall bracket. "Good," he said. "They are restless. If Suunwaduun is hungry, it is a good night for a sacrifice." He glanced up at the stone demon.

"Let's do it, then," urged the man who had spoken, "and have it done. I want out of this hell pit."

"We can't while the sacrifice is unconscious," snapped the leader. "You didn't have to hit her so hard."

Polijn felt everyone turn to look at her, and lay corpse-still. "You could put her on the pillar," said one of the others. "It'll save time later."

The leader shrugged. "No need for haste. Portentous things will happen tonight: things it would be better to take time over. Once Suunwaduun has told us how to dispose of Kaftus and the Vielfrass, we will have eliminated the only obstacles between our brotherhood and the person of the King."

"What of the ministers?" demanded one of his followers. "And the generals?"

The head cultist waved one hand in dismissal. "We can't kill everyone. Too much confusion, and the whole government will collapse, to become anyone's booty. Alive, the others can be bribed not to make trouble. Dead, they can't."

"What of the Brown Robe who led us here?" asked another. "He might come back."

"Odds are he's dead already," said the leader. "They're down on the Brown Robes, at the Palace. If he does come back, he will find us in possession of the temple, with Suunwaduun at our side. Even one of them can't do much about that."

"It's risky," grumbled a third. "If he's on our side, why not have him kill them all and set us up as Regents when he's done?"

"You think he'd do that for one sacrifice?" sneered the leader. "Either he'd blast us all to dust or else he'd do it and expect worship and payment for the rest of our lives. We'll do it my way: explain what they've built over his sacred temple, tell him we're on his side, and give him the girl. We ask him one little question and then we leave, sealing the door behind us. One quick deal, and the end of it is that Suunwaduun goes back to sleep and we take over."

The tallest of the cultists nodded. "A good plan. Risky. Truly worthy of a goblin."

Polijn thought so, too. She also thought it was time to go. Her head felt like last year's laundry, but there was no time for healing. She rolled to all fours and rose upright on her way down the corridor.

The cultists turned at the slap of bare feet on stone. The echoes of their shouting nearly knocked Polijn out again, but she was grateful for the light of the torches they brought. She tripped on the bottom step of a staircase, but recovered and hauled herself up and forward.

"Watch out for the statues!" someone shouted. A long scream told her the warning had come too late for someone else.

She found the top with her forehead. Turning around and bending over until her back was flat against the trapdoor, she heaved herself backward. Beyond the door was another flight of stairs, wooden and, as she discovered, somewhat splintered. She did not linger.

The room at the top of the stairs was the spare reception room of the Bedbug. Marvellous, she thought. The Bedbug was an all-male brothel, and now she had the establishment's bouncers to escape as well.

"I'm going! I'm going!" she shouted, flailing her hands above her head so none of the bartenders would mistake her for an employee and slow her down.

Outside, the festival was still in full fling, but only those merrymakers nearest the Bedbug turned as Polijn ran out. At this point in the evening, screaming people running naked from doors was part of traditional festival glee. Polijn turned up the street; there might be shelter at the Yellow Dog. Two strong arms caught her by the waist before she'd gone four paces.

She pulled away, striking out with one hand. This hand connected with a face, but her captor, grabbing her again, said only, "Polijn, hold still!"

She had no choice. The arms around her turned to wood, and wooden walls rose around her. Booted feet thudded down the pavement, one of them kicking the barrel in passing. Polijn shrank to the bottom and stayed there until the barrel dissolved.

"What was that all about?" asked her rescuer, leaning against a corner of the Bedbug. Polijn looked up into the vaguely foxlike face of Lady Oozola, the little shapeshifter who lived deep in the Swamp.

Polijn tried to think of a way to explain it. She took a deep breath and said, "Goblin cultists! The Vielfrass!"

"Oh, don't," shuddered Oozola. "Some evil spirits are summoned by their names. Faff! What did I tell you?"

Oozola flung an arm toward the street. Polijn looked over to see the dark spare figure of the Vielfrass striding toward them, his long cape twirling to snap left and right at the crowd. Passersby pulled away, leaving a good four-yard margin on each side of this cape.

Polijn had met him a few times. Fewer would have been better. Ronar, Chordasp, and goblin cultists alike were afraid of him. Arberth said, "He has eyes in the back of his head and probably elsewhere, and he knows everything except what he's going to do next." Some said he came from hell. Others, who had seen his rooms at the Gilded Fly, said that was redundant.

A rope piler, intent on his labor and bent double, did not see the Vielfrass. He saw only passing boots, unaccompanied by an agreeable jingle. His rope looped out and caught at one black boot. He tugged the rope to bring it back into line.

But that big, heavy boot didn't tug worth a tun. The rope piler looked up, saw the pale face of the Vielfrass amid the swirling mass of black hair, and turned green. The Vielfrass smiled. At this, the man's hand fell from the rope. It was too late for that. The rope also fell, breaking into a dozen individual snakes as it hit pavement.

The man dashed away, pursued by his ex-rope, and the Vielfrass moved on, his face gentle, benign. Polijn would have made a break, but the Lady Oozola had her by one wrist. The Vielfrass stopped before them and raised an eyebrow.

"Well, hibiscus, what would you?" he inquired.

"This little one," said Oozola, raising Polijn's wrist, "has large stories to tell."

"Come, then," said the sorcerer. "We'll listen in privacy." Knowing where they would take her, Polijn held back. "Oh, come, infant," he said, holding out one gloved hand. "We won't hurt you. Not unless it's a lot of fun."

Polijn had no choice, but she was fairly sure that Lady Oozola, at least, meant her no harm. The trio moved west, at the Vielfrass's pace, and were soon out of Polijn's neighborhood. Dressed as she was, she might still have attracted some attention, but all who saw the Vielfrass skittered away without even looking at her. It was like being invisible, and Polijn might have felt almost comfortable, but for the icy slush underfoot, and the fact that no one could be comfortable around the Vielfrass.

Roughly speaking, the city of Malbeth started at the Palace Royal, on its hill, and went literally and figuratively downhill, westward to the river. The Swamp was the section of the city farthest west and, hence, lowest. Honest people, it was said, went down there only with a large personal militia or a death wish. But even in the Swamp, there were divisions. Polijn's neighborhood was east of center, and safe enough for those who knew how to get around. Of her own free will, Polijn never went west of the Twisted Whiskers. For, beyond the places she knew, deep in the Swamp, was a tavern so low and ugly and degenerate that mothers used it to frighten disobedient children.

This was the Gilded Fly, the natural habitat of the Vielfrass and
the Lady Oozola. Polijn had come out of it safely twice, but she
could not suppress a shudder as they stepped up onto the sagging
porch. Every board gave an ominous creak; every board was half
rotted away. People said the only reason the whole building hadn't
fallen to dust yet was because the dust didn't want it.

Wedged between her escorts, Polijn saw little of the fabled
depravity. Under the stairs, there might have been a one-armed
woman reclining on a stack of bottles. But three men ducked
under the staircase as the Vielfrass led the way to the second
floor.

Upstairs, the sorcerer kicked open a door. Tossing his cloak
onto a large urn, he waved Polijn to a chair near what might
have been a broken eggshell. But why would an eggshell have
been green? And why so big?

The Lady Oozola sat behind a small table, and set her chin on
the stained top. "Do tell us all the news," she said. "What made
all those plug-uglies take off after you?"

Polijn looked to the Vielfrass for permission, but he was busy
wringing out the tassels in his boots. So she swallowed and said,
"They're goblin cultists. They didn't say which brotherhood. They
found an old temple under the Bedbug, and they want to summon
a demon called Suunwaduun."

The Vielfrass, his face blank, glanced at his partner. "Rings no
bell with me," said Oozola.

"They want his help," said Polijn. "They're going to ask him
how to destroy the Regent and . . . and the Vielfrass."

She was gratified at the sorcerer's little bow. "A large order.
Let me see." He strolled across the room to a wooden chest with
pixies carved in odd positions on the lid. From this he lifted a
copper-bound book.

"Suunwaduun," he murmured, flipping the book open. "I wonder how many apostrophes . . . ah. There is a demon with a similar
name. Class Y-27."

"Oh, Y-27," said Oozola, with a little yawn.

"What does that mean?" asked Polijn.

"Infant?" The sorcerer looked up. "You spoke? For convenience, we classify our demons by power and station. Not all the
demons imprisoned in days of yore were leaders and priests of
demon hordes, see. The vast majority were, oh, common laborers;
secretaries and assistant librarians and such. The big dangerous
types got all the attention, and everyone believes all demons

are equally powerful. Suunwaduun's a nobody, practically an apprentice demon."

"Oh," said Polijn. "Then he isn't dangerous?"

"Well, he's no one you'd care to have over for dinner," said the Vielfrass. "All that is white is not milk." He put a finger on the page he was studying. "A polyperverse imp with a vulgar sense of humor. He has some powers of prophecy, and is known to give advice, on completion of a complex ceremony and receipt of a human sacrifice."

"You were the sacrifice?" Oozola asked. Polijn nodded.

The Vielfrass snapped his book shut. "Very interesting. They have the right idea, basically, almost." He set the book back into the chest, and turned to look over Polijn.

"Well," he said, "they can easily find another sacrifice, so I don't think they'll come looking for you, particularly. But we'd better go back and check this temple, all the same."

"Me too?" demanded Polijn. "Why?"

The Vielfrass let his jaw drop. "Why, child, we have to find your clothes. You can't go through the Swamp like that." He paused. "Well, you could, but think of the delays."

It was ridiculous, of course, to expect him to lend her a shift and say, "Run along, infant; we'll deliver your clothes after we've slain the demon."

He had already turned to other matters. "We shouldn't go unarmed," he said. "Some of these demons will blow your soul to fragments first and ask questions later." He opened another chest. "I'll need my thyromantic devices, of course." He picked up a box Polijn could smell from where she sat. "Sacrificial wafers and sacred wine, in case a libation is necessary." He lifted a little tin horn and tooted it. After a moment's thought, he added it to the other supplies. "Some cultures have found noise of inestimable value in driving out demons."

Lady Oozola sighed. "You know, if you ever lose your mind, it'll be an improvement."

"Pay no heed to the floozy, Polijn," said the sorcerer, delving into the chest. "We have double duty. We must first halt the progress of whatever spells your blunderers have set in motion to waken the demon, and then we have to turn them backward. Shall I take the anti-demon masks?"

"No," said Oozola.

"You never let a fellow have any fun. No, I take that back. Justice must be allowed. All right, then I think this is enough to send Suunwaduun back to his place in the Great Blazing Ultimately. We're off!"

"Nobody knows how far," muttered Lady Oozola, rising from her place.

IV

AGAIN, Polijn hurried through the Swamp between her protectors, only slightly less uncomfortable. She did not trust the Vielfrass or his supposed mystic supplies. But hers was a philosophy of self-preservation, and, like most people who really believe something, she felt that anyone with any sense felt the same way, deep down. The cultists were enemies of the Vielfrass; surely he would not go down to that temple unless he had the power to defeat them. And he did have power. So she led them down to the basement of the Bedbug, and the stone temple beyond.

The sounds of a fight reached them while they were still on the stone stairs. "We shouldn't have to look hard," noted Oozola.

Two goblin cultists had Lothirien bent back against a pillar, while the rest tore at her clothes. Lothirien was giving a good account of herself, and had drawn blood. One cultist reached for his club. "Don't!" ordered the leader. "We need her awake!"

The bold, bad would-be goblin paid no attention, but in taking up his weapon glimpsed approaching shadows. "The Vielfrass!" he gasped, turning to stare.

His companions froze. Lothirien jerked loose and hurtled up the stairs. No one moved to stop her. Each cultist drew a knife or raised a club. Each also took three steps back toward the main altar.

"Quick!" hissed one. "Call him up!"

"I can't!" answered his leader. "No sacrifice!"

The Vielfrass failed to notice any of this. Taking Polijn by one shoulder, he strode forward. "I been looking for you guys all day," he announced. "Suunwaduun appeared to me in a dream last night and told me to look you up for fun times."

Before Polijn could take this in, he bent, lifted her, and tossed her to the cultists. "I brought this back," he went on, "and these." He pulled out his pack of supplies. "Wine, cheese, and crackers, some noisemakers: they're for your victory party, see. I'd've brought some funny masks, but the flimsy there wouldn't let me. Party pooper."

Gathering what remained of her wits, Polijn kicked at the arms that caught her and dropped to the floor. Before she could follow up on this, though, two cultists brought wet boots down on her back, pinning her to the floor.

That was enough for Polijn. Mutely, she let them take her to the central pillar. Her arms were stretched back around it, and fastened to a ring above her head. Her feet were also strapped together, and fastened to the front of the column. She threw one imploring glance at the Lady Oozola. The little shapeshifter seemed to sigh, and looked away.

"Well," said the cult leader, stepping a little nearer the Vielfrass. "Heh. With your help, we should be able to do the trick. If we make an error in the rites, you'll be able to correct us, eh?"

"Oh, yes," said the sorcerer. "I wouldn't have anything go wrong for worlds."

The cult leader glanced walleyed at him, not certain how this was meant. Giving up, the one-eared man strode to the braziers and cried, "Let the rites begin!"

Raising his chin, he took a torch from the wall and touched it to the brazier. Smoke dribbled toward the ceiling.

"Tsk," said the Vielfrass. "That's the worst of these underground abattoirs: your coals are always wet."

He snapped a finger and both braziers sprang to light, in yard-long streamers of flame. The cult leader jumped back.

"Oh, I am so damn good at this," chortled the Vielfrass. "Carry on."

The flames of the brazier on the right licked perilously close to Polijn's straining arms. She pulled away. Her heart rolled over as she felt the strap above her shift and slide.

The cult leader stepped back into his spot. "Oh, Suunwaduun!" he cried. "Your faithful worshippers call upon you! Avenge yourself! Modern men have forgotten your worship and built a den of perversion over your sacred altar!"

Polijn flattened against the pillar and strained to take the buckle above her between her fingers. Twisting gently left and right, she could tell the hole around the buckle's tongue was worn, and widened. She put a little pressure on the tongue.

"Oh, Suunwaduun!" implored the Cult leader. "Come from your deep home to give us aid and comfort!"

The flames ebbed, and smoke rose in obscene, rolling lumps. The strap slipped from Polijn's hands. She bit her lip and reached for it again.

"Oh, Suunwaduun!" cried the cultist. A turtle's face formed and vanished in the smoke, which rose into a massive cloud. Polijn tried to study the strap at her ankles. That buckle had to be located, too. If the top strap did come loose, she might be able to drop fast, unfasten that lower one, and run for it. Or she might just fall on her face.

The cloud changed color, swirling reds and yellows replacing blacks and greys. Polijn felt every muscle tighten and every organ quiver as the colors swirled into a ball, a glowing yellow eyeball with a red pupil. It turned for a moment on the awed cultists and then flattened, splitting into two dripping hands, one yellow and one red.

The tongue of the buckle slipped through the worn leather. Polijn caught at the strap and eased it free, not letting it flap, and guiding the tongue carefully past the other holes in the leather.

The hands vanished. A quivering orange mouth took their place. "What do you ask of Suunwaduun?" The voice was rough, as though the speaker was unused to talking, but it filled the temple.

"Oh, Suunwaduun!" cried the cultist. "We have little to ask, and much to tell. Sacrilege has been committed. Above your ancient altar, perverse mortals do business with catamites. May it not be long ere you punish these transgressors and take up your rightful place again! For ourselves, we ask only advice, and have brought you a sacrifice!"

The eye reappeared, above the mouth, and surveyed the scene below. "Not bad," said the mouth. "Nice belly."

It was time to go. Polijn released the strap and dove for her feet. A rough yank pulled her back, nearly ripping her arms from the shoulders. She realized in one agonizing moment that there were two straps: one to bind her hands together, and another to fasten them to the ring. She could go nowhere without unfastening the second strap.

And now it was too late. Three tentacles whipped out of the smoky mouth. Red and yellow, they shimmered in the air and then lashed down to encircle the sacrifice. Only Lady Oozola moved as they hauled the shrieking cult leader into the massive orange maw.

"And he's like this all the time," she complained, unstrapping Polijn's wrists.

The screams turned into thick sobs and then, with eye, mouth, smoke, and flame, were no more. The Vielfrass sighed.

"What a lot of trouble people could spare themselves with a little research," he said. "I'm sure it's a very interesting story how, over the centuries, the temple of Suunwaduun was secularized and turned into the Bedbug. But no one reads history these days: just out for the quick profit."

"I hope this all teaches you a lesson," he went on, bowing to Polijn. "Never trust anyone until you know what he's after."

Polijn slumped against the pillar, her chest heaving with mingled relief and fury. "I don't think she liked your little joke," said Oozola.

"She couldn't be so unreasonable," answered the sorcerer. "After I got her a front row seat and everything? But maybe we can make amends somehow."

As if in answer, a great rumbling voice demanded, "Now, what do you ask of Suunwaduun?"

"Ah," said the Vielfrass, snapping his fingers. "These things must be pursued to their natural ends." He bowed to Polijn again. "Ask something, if you feel you need more reward than my presence. Ask it for some new position unpracticed even at the Gilded Fly. Ask for a love balm to make you irresistible to the King. Ask, ask, child: fear not! We'll still come to visit you even when you're wrapped in red and green velvet and seated on a crotchless throne at the Palace Royal."

Polijn's mind was a bubbling froth of spiders, rats, and the bleached bones of the Vielfrass. She breathed at the sorcerer for a moment and then whirled to face the main statue.

"Where can I find my clothes?" she demanded.

It was not possible, but one shining stone arm lifted, and a taloned index finger indicated a shadow behind the pillar on her left. Polijn studied the shadow.

"There's nothing there," she snapped.

"Didn't say there was," grumbled the statue. "But that's where you'll find your clothes."

"Is he related to you?" demanded Lady Oozola.

"A faint imitator, fair frump," replied the Vielfrass, patting her hands.

Polijn felt her head swelling. Her vision grew hazy. But before she could explode entirely, a sandal flew over her head and landed in the shadow indicated by the statue. It was followed by her winter undershift, and then by the rag puppy.

The little group turned. Surviving cultists knelt by an iron-bound chest before one of the lesser statues. "It's all in here somewhere," whispered one. "We won't lose everything."

"If he had enough to bribe all those generals," said another, "there must be loads." Polijn's other sandal and her shift went up into the air next, followed by a garment she didn't recognize, from some previous victim.

"Someone's not paying attention," noted Oozola.

"Ahem, ahem," agreed the Vielfrass.

Recalled to a sense of their danger, the Cultists rose. The one who had spoken first put himself between the chest and the sorcerer, his knife out and trembling. "D-don't move," he warned. "Just . . . stay where you are."

"We didn't want to get involved with the demon," said another. "It was all his idea. We are the Mighty Brotherhood of the Wolf's Head." He was shaking.

"Don't try to stop us," ordered a third, backing toward the wall.

"Dear me," said the Vielfrass, pressing his hands together. "What a desperate bunch. Please, sidekick, oh, please don't try to stop them."

The Lady Oozola sniffed. "I should think not. In fact, this should help them along." Her head bobbed out on a long white neck and turned into the face of a snarling, slavering wolf. Its hideous grin exposed long, red teeth.

Dropping knives and booty, the cultists dashed screaming up the stairs. Oozola retracted her head. "Bunch of moonmen," she snorted.

Polijn had ignored most of this, dressing hurriedly. "Allow me," said the Vielfrass. He fastened her cloak around her neck and smoothed out the wrinkles with impudent fingers. Polijn submitted to this and then marched toward the steps without a word.

She had been used as many things in her life, and had learned not to complain, but she objected to being used as a complete idiot.

"You'll have to close off the staircase," she heard Oozola remark.

"Pity," the Vielfrass replied. "We could charge admission and make a nice pile. That statue over there, for instance . . ."

The bouncers did not approach Polijn as she strode through the Bedbug. They did not intend to interfere with the Vielfrass's friends, or even his enemies. Polijn, for her part, paid attention to very little as she marched eastward. She was still furious, as much with herself now as with the Vielfrass. He had made her so mad that she had acted like the idiot she looked. How could she throw away such a chance? The thousand paths to comfort and fortune that would have been hers to walk if she'd asked the right question now rose to her mind.

There would be no fortune for her this night. It was late, and dark, and snow was tumbling from cold clouds. With her luck, Arberth had lost life and all by winning at cards, and she would have to walk all the miles back to the Palace Royal, and find a new master.

She jerked her hood up, and a heavy fist slammed against the bruises the cultists had given her. For a moment, she thought she would black out again. Something hit the ground with a thud.

It was an object of bulk. Polijn stooped carefully, holding her head, and found one of those long bracelets that stretched from wrist to elbow. A shining fire burned at the wrist, and bright metal smoke wound up to go around the arm. By the heft and sheen of it, it was a solid piece. Even if it was just lead, it would have some resale value, and Polijn had a feeling it was not lead. Had the Vielfrass known it was in her hood? Of course: it was another little joke.

She nearly tossed it into the gutter, but told herself in time that she had thrown away enough for one night. She slid the heavy piece up her left arm, and hid this under the cloak. Glancing left and right, she slid into the shelter of a massive horse trough. She had all the more reason to keep to the shadows now.

V

THE clean neighborhoods were no safer than the Swamp for the small, the alone. The pavement was smoother, and the crime rate lowered somewhat by armed sentries who patrolled the streets at the request of the merchants who lived there. But these watchmen were recruited from the Swamp. A little extortion or plain robbery was not beneath them when enforcing the curfew palled.

Polijn could not shake off a feeling of being followed, though she avoided the sentries where possible. Most were asleep at their posts anyhow; this was a holiday and they had seen plenty of festival. Still she heard a background sound, which she could not swear was a footstep, nor swear it was not. When she turned around, there was only shadow, lit at wide intervals by a gleam from a window or sentry box. Once, a small girl stepped out of a shadow and begged for a tun or pennyetke. Polijn was so glad to actually see someone that she tossed out a coin. But as the girl dashed away with it, the footsteps were too loud, too noticeable to be the ones she thought she had heard.

A second coin paid the attendant at the Eastgate to let her out of the city. The third, her last, paid another to let her past the gate that opened onto the echoingly empty wooden bridge across the dry moat. Had anyone really been following her, the sound of the guards demanding payment or of feet on the boards would have alerted her. She knew this. Still she kept looking back.

She hurried. Her legs were sore. Too much sedentary Palace

life: her feet and legs were out of shape for an evening's walking. Ages ago, when she and Arberth left for the Swamp, she had hopes of perhaps making enough money to hire some transportation. When she returned to the Low Raven, she still had hopes that the jester might have won enough.

But he hadn't been there. "The lintik pizook won three hands and then said something about going to see somebody," a sour loser had said. "Went east."

It was odd, unprecedented even, for Arberth to leave a card game early, particularly while he was winning. But Polijn had given up trying to understand anything the jester did. Certainly, she didn't expect him to wait around for her convenience.

Her last hope left was that someone friendly would be working the Palace gate. Sometimes the guard would wave her through, without exacting payment. And sometimes a deal could be struck for payment in service.

But she would not have even bothered to imagine that no one would be on duty at all. Putting one shoulder against the big door, she pushed, fearing for a moment that there had been some kind of special order, and she was locked out. No one was behind the door either. She was just shouldering it shut again when someone bellowed, "Get away from there!"

She jumped away. A man wearing the oak-leaf badge of the Palace guard bustled to his post. "No one goes out any more tonight, understand?"

"Sorry, sir." Polijn backed through the corridor, stepping around the puddles. "Very sorry. I was just looking out at the weather, really."

She turned and was nearly rolled to the floor by the twisted figure of Measthyr, a retainer of the Duke of Bonti. In his day, the man had been a master swordsman, but a wasting disease, possibly of sorcerous origin, had burned away most of his strength. Like Torat he could speak only in a whisper, but Measthyr could make himself heard by singing, in a high, wheezy drone. Arberth made a little extra money by helping him develop his voice, a case of the tone-deaf leading the tone-deaf.

So the man recognized Polijn and, being a sociable type, put down a hand to help her up. "Where have you been?" he intoned. "There's been bladework aplenty. Morquiesse is dead, Borodeneth is wounded, and the new guard, what's-his-name, Ostage . . ."

"The one from Turin?" Polijn asked. "The one who comes up to talk about old times?"

"Aye," sang the swordsman. "He's been beheaded and they can't find the head."

A busy night, apparently: still, it was a festival night. "How did they know who it was if they can't find the head?" Polijn asked.

"His clothes," crooned Measthyr. He stopped to take a breath. "Only Arberth . . ."

"Hmmmmm?" asked someone strolling through the hall. "Excitement somewhere?"

Measthyr winked at Polijn and let the rest of the sentence fade. Arberth joined them.

The jester was smiling, but it didn't seem that his heart was in it. Arberth always looked depressed: something of a boon to the cardplayer but hardly an asset to the jester. His hair was sparse and sun-bleached, his eyes so pale as to be unnoticeable, and his new sidewhiskers long and bedraggled.

His clothes, however, as Measthyr had been about to point out, were as bright as his face was drab. But his eye for color was no better than his ear for music. He wore an overtunic of yellow, a blue tunic, and a red shift over orange trousers and scuffed brown boots. His cloak was a neutral green (the safest color, if you intended to play cards in the Swamp), but a pink scarf with peacock-blue spots set it off.

Measthyr pretended to shade his eyes as he replied, "Where've you been? Someone's opened Lord Morquiesse's neck."

Arberth's long mouth dropped open. "Ab . . . ab . . . Morquiesse?"

Measthyr shrugged. "Quite the tragedy, not?" he sang. "But it's a holiday."

"Morquiesse?" Arberth said again.

Polijn slid a hand down the back of her shift. "Did they just find him?" she asked. "What happened?"

"Just now," chanted Measthyr. "Everyone else in the lintik Palace is there now, I expect. Coming?"

Polijn looked to Arberth, who shook his head. "No, I, uh, it has been a long night, and one dead body looks much the same as another. I'm going to turn in."

Measthyr raised an eyebrow at Polijn, who shrugged in reply. She felt they ought to go see what was what. Morquiesse was important enough that there would be songs written about his death, and some detail of the scene might make a dramatic verse. But she was already tired, and there were all those stairs to consider. They could get the news in the morning.

So she nodded a good-night to Measthyr and fell in with the jester, two steps behind him and two to the left. Most of the corridors were empty, as Measthyr had suggested. They did spot Aoyalasse, Lynex's second assistant, slipping from Lord Arlmorin's chambers and into the shadows. Polijn wondered what Aoyalasse would say when she heard about the killing.

Otherwise, there was no one about, for which Polijn was grateful as she started up the seventh flight of stairs. The climb was bad enough without people sleeping on the stairs and in the hall to step over. The hall supervisors didn't bother to keep people out of the way at this level. Not many wanted to sleep up here, in this weather, but it was a secluded area, and secure hiding places were of prime value in Malbeth.

Arberth unlocked his door, and left it open so a little light could sneak in from the hall torches. He kicked his boots off and at the same time reached into his little oak chest for a folded nightshirt. An exile from the south, he had brought some of their civilized customs with him.

Polijn just slid her things off, working them around the bruises, and set them in a pile by the straw mattress. The shift went on top of the stack, to be grabbed up in case of some emergency. It also covered her overtunic, in which she bundled her treasures: a flute, a slide whistle, a mouth harp Arberth was teaching her to play, and, now, the heavy armlet and the rag puppy.

Once she had seen to this bundle, she hurried to the door. "Ready?" she called, shivering in the draft.

"Set," called Arberth, already under the blankets.

She slammed and locked the door, cutting off the light, and scampered to the bed. Just before the door had shut, she had noticed new bloodstains on the tunic Arberth had tossed over the chest. So she decided not to ask him where he had gone after leaving the Low Raven.

CHAPTER TWO
Nimnestl

I

THE granite passage was made for neither easy travel nor warmth. She leaned against the next chimney she reached, absorbing some heat before moving on. A pale, wavering wolf padded up to her. His jaws opened as wide as the passage, displaying three rows of steaming, daggerlike teeth.

Nimnestl grimaced and crawled in among the teeth. The wolf vanished.

By means of this recently rediscovered passage, Nimnestl had access to every room in this tower. Below her, it spiralled down to a tunnel that went right down to the river. Above, it reached to a small chamber just under the winter roof. The passage was ancient, perhaps older than the country.

Crude but effective murals were carved into the walls, showing a descent into hell. There were labels, and many of the faces had been carefully done as portraits. But Nimnestl was not here to study political satire two thousand years old.

She shivered. Kiermis's spell was taking a while to shake off. She hoped she wasn't going to be sick.

Her garments were not suited to the climate. Silence was essential, so metal armor would not serve her. Further, she could afford no cracks or wrinkles in her attire, for spiders to occupy. When Kaftus moved from his unlikely stronghold to the Palace Royal, he had accidentally brought with him a quantity of Bearded Spiders, which had bred with the local Stickleback Spiders to produce a venomous hybrid of startling potency. Palace inhabitants called them One-Step Spiders, since you could move just that far after being bitten.

So Nimnestl wore only a pair of leather gloves, a thick one-piece leather corselet, and a tight helmet that confined her hair, plus sandals. The abbreviated summer armor might protect her if Morquiesse lived long enough to strike back, but it offered little defense against spring temperatures.

A dragonlike worm, dripping slime, rose to greet her. Its claws were gold, its teeth silver. Obscene pink tentacles rose from spiky green hair along its spine. Nimnestl nodded. These shimmering colors had made Morquiesse famous, virtually the only artist of note to come out of Rossacotta in a thousand years. She pushed on. The worm blinked, and shook, and fell into vapor.

That bum in the Swamp hadn't known what he held: just a tale of Colonel Palompec, Captain Kiermis, and a little house in the Swamp where Brown Robes met. Not until Kiermis's interrogation had details come out, and even those had had to be paired with other scraps of information for the whole tale to become available.

Morquiesse was an Ykena, a Brown Robe, an adept in Ykena spells. That was why monsters patrolled this passage. The Ykenai could project defensive phantoms into any passage by which a foe might approach, even into passages unknown to the spellcaster. She hoped this one was still unknown to Morquiesse. Kiermis, under questioning, had denied any knowledge of it.

The monsters would have shredded her but for a fatal flaw in Ykena magic. Theirs was a sympathetic magic; it drew its force from magic used by the target. Since virtually everyone in Malbeth carried at least a good luck charm, it generally had some effect. Had Nimnestl not been wearing her poison detection ring when she tackled Kiermis, his spell could not have touched her.

All she carried now was a bowstring as thick as her thumb: not a very mystical weapon. And Morquiesse's monsters seemed less aggressive than the usual run of Ykena guardians. Maybe this was a mistake; maybe Morquiesse wasn't as important as they thought.

A monstrous ratbird strutted by, munching a dark-skinned woman. Nimnestl paused; that seemed to have been aimed specifically at her. She shook her head. Morquiesse might well guess that whoever came for him came from her, and try to startle intruders with this. Morquiesse, she reminded herself, did not know about this passage, or that someone would be coming tonight to kill him.

She hoped. Sneaking up to kill a man who was waiting for her did not strike her as appealing.

Neither did sneaking out to kill a man who was naked and asleep. As Chief Bodyguard to the King, Nimnestl was the one who generally ordered underlings out to do this kind of job. In fact, she had. Dilathys had failed, and was not in very good condition when the artist's servants had dragged him from the bedchamber. Nimnestl had felt honor-bound to take the next turn.

The strangling trick was one she had learned in the mountains when she was young. She had never tried it on a human before, but it was a favorite among denizens of the Swamp. Four of Morquiesse's servants had been recruited from that district. Swamp thieves, after the treasures the King had bestowed on Morquiesse for that new sundial; it was an easy story to tell. Nimnestl would have preferred something neater, something more nearly legal. But it had to be done this way if the past winter's work was not to be lost.

Once a small, reclusive religious sect, the Ykenai had developed political aspirations. These were discovered almost too late, but a spate of deaths on the King's Birthday had ensured that everyone in the Palace Royal knew about it when it did come out. Public opinion veered abruptly, violently, to the side of the normally loathed Regent and Chief Bodyguard. An office-by-office purge had been conducted through the winter; the gallows had been crowded for four months. Birds of a feather that flocked together made an easy target, and the court had something to think about through the long cold season. New feuds and interdepartmental wars, which burgeoned due to cabin fever, had this winter been at an all-time low.

But now bloodlust was satisfied, or at least bored. Courtiers grumbled that not all those high officials, surely, could be traitors. The Regent and Bodyguard were no doubt up to some private scheme. General Ferrapec, who had persecuted the Brown Robes diligently, had recently stood up in Council to suggest that the remaining sorcerers be left in peace for a few months, to allow them time to quietly deport themselves. Other plans for offering amnesty had been discussed.

And it was at that point that Nimnestl had finally been able to learn the name of the head of the sect. It was Morquiesse, Chief Figurer and Painter to the King.

The artist was popular: hearty, an accomplished flirt, a fine hunter, a good singer, and author of clever fescennine verse. More, he was a national treasure. Painting was culture, and of the most modern kind. It was intellectual, it was enlightened, it was chic. His paintings were sought by kings and collectors across the continent, which had helped bring envoys and ambassadors to a country everyone else had despised for centuries.

Morquiesse was a hero. If exposed as an Ykena, he could haul the sect back into popular favor. The Brown Robes could return to places high in the government and take control of the Council. If Morquiesse was executed as a traitor before he could appeal to the people, he would be of even more use to the Ykenai. Public sentiment would swing more violently, accomplishing the same goals much sooner.

But if Morquiesse died because he had been imprudent enough to hire scum from the Swamp, no one would ever know he was a Brown Robe. There would be rumors that the Regent or Bodyguard was involved—there were such rumors after every death in the Palace Royal—but without the fact of the Artist's membership in the sorcerous sect, no one could come up with a motive, and the rumor would disappear as soon as a more vivid one came up.

The trick would not be easy. The passage opened into Morquiesse's room through a door well concealed in the stonework behind a tapestry at the head of the bed. But there was no telling what Dilathys had said before he died. Morquiesse could know where the door was and how it opened. She remembered her own warning to her men: "Never let a bull have a second chance in the ring. Every fight he survives makes him smarter."

This was the door. Pulling her legs up under her, she paused for breath and rechecked the symbol on the stone. Then she slid the door up.

There was no sound, but the tapestry was a heavy one. Morquiesse and his men could still be waiting in a circle around it now, waiting for someone to drop out. Quite an accomplishment, to take the Chief Bodyguard.

She pushed the tapestry forward and dropped to the floor behind the bed. The room was dark and nearly silent. Only faint breathing disturbed the quiet. If they were really asleep, all she had to do was find Morquiesse's neck. She set her head around the carven bedpost.

A pair of eyes stared up into hers. Her bowstring came up. The eyes did not move. She looked down to the neck, and the position of the head. Someone had been here before her.

She shrugged. This changed things somewhat, but she could at least tidy up. If the unknown assassin had not made other arrangements, she could still implicate one of the servants, so the affair could be finished quietly. She was stepping around the bed when she saw that, not satisfied with taking the man's life, the assassin had also removed Morquiesse's arms from the elbow down.

II

PURSING her lips, Nimnestl stepped clear of the bedstead. No one sat up to say hello. She stepped across to the nightlight Morquiesse always kept burning, in case he needed to sketch something in the night. With the shutter open, she could view the whole set, scenery and all.

What she had taken for breathing was just the wind slipping past the window-covers. The servants were dead where they'd slept, their throats cut.

She walked back to Morquiesse. Dead bodies, by themselves, gave her no worries, so she studied this one without qualms. The neck was ugly, but clean. The rope had been removed before the arms, or there would be blood up there.

The chest beside the bed had been broken up. Inside sat a book open to a torn page. The murderer had wanted only that missing half-page; bottles of gilt and a jewelled knife had not been touched.

She knew without looking what the book must be. Part of the Ykena ritual was the keeping of elaborate records. Only once had such a volume fallen into the wrong hands, and that one had been destroyed before it could much harm the Brown Robes. Taking up this copy, she set it against the wall, just under the secret door, so she wouldn't forget to take it along when she left.

Someone's bare feet had left tracks from the bed to the next room. The arms must have been the last things taken. Nimnestl strolled across to the door and gave it a gentle push. When it swung open, she moved in, the arm with the bowstring in it across her chest, the other outstretched.

Less light reached the outer room, but there was little for anyone to hide behind. The footprints stopped; the murderer had his/her shoes/boots on again. But the arms had continued to drip a trail straight for the door that led to the corridor. Tilted against the wall was a large saw of southern design. Morquiesse had three or four like it. He said the Gilraën-made blade could not be matched in the north.

Nimnestl backed into the bedroom. In the pool of blood nearest the bed, she slipped out of her sandals. After tying the bowstring to them, she leaped to a clean space on the floor. She picked up her book, opened the secret door, and, with a jerk on the bowstring, brought the bloody sandals to her. Her bloody sandalprints would confuse the crowd, which was always to the good, but there was no point in letting the trail lead them right to the door to this passage.

Kaftus was waiting in his outer chamber. "So much blood!" he complained as she appeared.

She set the sandals on a pile of dry moss. "Yes, isn't there? And I have to go find some more."

"He is dead?" the Regent asked.

Nimnestl took up the basin of water she had left behind with her clothes. "He was dead when I got there," she said, rinsing her hands.

"Tsk." The Regent shook his head. "We'll have to schedule these things more carefully in the future. Who did the job for us?"

"That's what we have to find out." She took up her leggings and cloak. The rest of her clothes would have to wait.

"Here," she said, nudging the book toward him as she fastened on the leather leg protectors. "Something to read while I'm working."

The Regent clapped his hands softly. "How nice for you to have your theories confirmed. I'm glad I didn't waste the wine."

"Eh?"

"Among the rewards the King heaped on him for that wretched sundial," Kaftus replied, "there was a bottle of drugged wine."

Nimnestl let her shoulders fall slack as she stared at him. "And you didn't see fit to mention it to me?"

The necromancer shrugged. "A nice surprise for you," he said.

"It might make your job a little easier. And there was no guarantee he'd drink it tonight."

That was how the murderer had managed to go to work without complaints from the musclemen on the floor. "I'll see if the bottle's still there," she said, tying her cloak. "Any other surprises I should have known about?"

"Then it wouldn't be a surprise," said the Regent, picking up the hefty book. "Go play."

Nimnestl's glare of doom was ignored, so she pulled on her boots. She checked her hands for blood, picked up her hammer, and moved out into the hall.

On her way back to the artist's room, she passed a pair of men wearing the golden-branch insignia of the Treasury. Her errand was important, and she would have moved right on down the hall but for the way the men pulled back into the shadows when they saw her. That drew a second look. The men carried between them a large sack that was dripping at the bottom.

"What's in that?" she demanded, stepping forward.

Oryan, the guard on the left, swore, but his partner, Thiron, answered, "It's Ostage, ma'am, or most of him. Someone knocked off his head for him."

"Let's see," the Bodyguard ordered.

The men opened the sack. The body was headless, but recognizable as Ostage. The guard was an adherent of Korielar, Second Lord Treasurer, and, aside from his cloak and boots, wore nothing that wasn't of his master's colors, gold and black. The gold of the tunic was tarnished now, but the bright yellow trousers would have identified him anywhere.

"Very well," she said. "Carry on. I suppose a festival calls for some casualties."

"Yes, ma'am," answered Thiron. "At least he's the only one tonight."

"The night's not over yet," Nimnestl murmured, but she had turned away, and the men were also moving off.

As she neared Morquiesse's suite, she studied the floor for a trail of blood. There was none. Rounding a corner, she found out why. A woman with a green eyepatch knelt by a bucket in front of the artist's door, scrubbing away damp drops.

"What's this?" Nimnestl demanded.

The woman had not heard her approach, and tried to jump up, jump away, and jump over the bucket, all at one time. She failed miserably, and she and the bucket went rolling in dark water.

Without a word, Nimnestl reached down and heaved her into the air. "I didn't mean any harm!" wailed the servant, trying to get her feet on the floor. "He said he slipped and told me to go scrub the floor."

"Who?" Nimnestl asked, letting the woman down a bit.

"I did, Bodyguard," answered a voice from behind her. "I wish now that I hadn't."

Nimnestl let go of the woman, who collapsed onto the bucket. The speaker was Laisida, Morquiesse's one-legged brother. He held his free hand forward, wrist out, as he stumped up to her.

"On my artery, I wish I hadn't," he repeated. "I didn't see it was blood until I got back to my chambers." He put his crutch in front of Nimnestl and pushed past her to the door.

"Hoy there!" he shouted. "You awake?"

"Do you think something may have happened to him?" Nimnestl asked. The woman with the bucket had started to creep away, but returned on hearing that.

"You're so very clever, Bodyguard," answered the minstrel, without turning to sneer at her. He raised his crutch and hammered on the door. "Hoy there, brother! What's up? Is she any good?"

Laisida's belling voice was designed for attracting attention, and spectators began to ease into the corridor. "Break it down," called a dungeon guard.

"I'll find a key," said Nimnestl. She turned to survey the crowd, ostensibly to look for a member of the Housekeeping staff. Laisida, seeing that her back was turned, raised his crutch to a point just above and to the left of the lock.

"Here," he said.

Two booted feet landed next to each other at the spot indicated. Three hit the spot on the second kick. At the third, the door bounced open and the crowd rushed forward.

"Well?" called Nimnestl from the hall.

A thin smile crept across her lips at the first cries of horror. Things would move more quickly now.

III

A good crowd had assembled by the time Nimnestl left. She had put on a show for them, cheerfully measuring footprints and making wise sounds about probable intruders as she secreted the empty wine bottle in her cloak. As she left, she saw several people comparing their own feet with the prints on the floor. By this time, there was little chance of finding the original prints in all the clutter of new ones. The clotted saw was being passed from hand to hand.

Some few were arriving late; Nimnestl passed them on her way. Aoyalasse, second assistant to Lynex, emerged into the hall, yawning and blinking as if just awakened.

Nimnestl paused. "Seen Morquiesse this morning?"

"What's that to you?" Aoyalasse demanded, immediately wide awake, her eyes glaring up from the deep red shadows around them. A leading contender for the next vacancy among the Chief Housekeepers, Aoyalasse was one of those red and pale people who never looked completely healthy. Nimnestl felt there was something not quite clean about the bluish freckled skin, which had less to do with the pallor or freckles than in the way they contrasted with the bright orange hair.

Nimnestl shrugged. "If you don't know," she said, "you haven't seen him."

"What's that to you either?" Aoyalasse shot back. She tossed her head so the orange hair flew back. "What do you think, that I hang around his chambers?"

"Oh, no," the Bodyguard assured her. "That's not what I think you do . . . did around his chambers." She started to move on.

The little woman charged over to block her. "Did?" she demanded. A look in her eyes suggested a mood to murder anything within reach. "Listen, I have nothing to do with that idiot pizook."

"Other people don't think he's an idiot," answered Nimnestl, her tone one of gentle reproof.

Aoyalasse's fists were clenched near her ears, as if she were trying to tear down clumps of atmosphere. "He always has his arms around that chicken-breasted, cloth-tailed squirrel!"

"That's easily fixed," answered Nimnestl. "Just cut off his arms."

The woman slid back, her hands on her hips. Nimnestl saw the one hand slip out the knife, and waited. Aoyalasse paused, her anger slipping enough for her to size up the target and estimate how long she'd regret following through. The knife disappeared and she shoved past Nimnestl, toward the crowd.

Nimnestl shrugged and moved on. "So!" said a black shadow, falling to her shoulder. "So, so!"

"It was a small passage," said Nimnestl. "You'd have been slamming into walls."

"Don't messing around with me!" answered the bird. "What name you go alone?"

"Mardith, keep quiet," Nimnestl ordered, as they reached the door of the Regent's suite. As an old family retainer, Mardith considered accompanying his mistress on all missions to be his right.

"You not . . ." he began.

Kaftus glanced back from a bubbling pot suspended in mid-air. "Your crow is cross," he noted as Nimnestl closed the door. "Is he going to quit if you don't let him play?"

Kaftus was virtually the only inhabitant of the Palace Royal of whom Mardith was afraid, so the bird simply snorted and came to rest on a red skull, ruffling his feathers to let Nimnestl know he was annoyed. The Bodyguard grimaced and turned to the Regent.

"The crime is discovered, and has been duly reported," she said. "The King is less upset than I expected."

"Good," said the Regent, adding a toad to the pot. "We'll

have to go through the motions of an investigation anyway. The Council will demand it."

Nimnestl nodded and reached for the Ykena record book, which sat on an orange table. "All the usual sections," said Kaftus. "The list of members, snoopers to be eliminated, rituals. Flip to the snooper section."

Nimnestl turned to the black bookmark, expecting what she found. It was here that the half-page was missing. "Inconvenient. But suggestive."

"Doubly inconvenient," said the Regent. "The next page holds directions to a passage and secret shrine in the palace. The important part was on the missing portion."

Nimnestl checked the reverse side. Mardith, forgetting that he was ignoring the humans, flew to look as well. "No," she said. "I wouldn't know where to look either."

"Not knowing," said Mardith.

"The name Su'in Wa'du'in mean anything to you?" the Bodyguard went on.

"Vaguely," said the Regent. "A minor demon: I was unaware he had any shrines."

Nimnestl turned back to study the list of snoopers. "Well, we'd best find a culprit before the Ykenai decide to give us the credit. There are several possibilities."

Kaftus dropped a handful of leaves into the pot. "I am all ears."

Nimnestl held up a finger. "First, it could be someone who found out he was a Brown Robe, but was too zealous to inform the government before taking action. Second, it might be a rival painter."

Kaftus shook his head. "He was too fashionable. Everyone wanted to use his approval."

"It could have been one who didn't get it." She held up a third finger. "A disgruntled student or servant."

"Same problem," said the necromancer.

"And it could have been a personal enemy. I've been going over the candidates."

The Regent set the bubbling pot on the floor to cool. "Go ahead. You have plenty of fingers."

Nimnestl ticked these off on her other hand. "Haeve, Aoyalasse, Laisida, Ferrapec, Palompec."

"Colonel Palompec?" demanded Kaftus. "I wasn't aware of a grudge there."

The others were well known. Haeve resented the time the artist spent with the King, spinning tales totally at odds with the facts the Royal Tutor gave out. Aoyalasse had not forgiven him for transferring his affections to Maiaciara. Ferrapec, Maiaciara's father, despised all men of culture on general principle. He referred to them as "the men who can steal without once putting hand to knife." Laisida, who had lost a leg in one of his brother's practical jokes, was a man of intense pride and sudden anger. He might kill you for mentioning, in passing, that he was the greatest minstrel of all time, and would kill you if you suggested anything to the contrary.

"It's in the book," Nimnestl pointed out. She held it toward him. "The colonel is listed among the members, which we knew, but he's also on the snoopers page. The Brown Robes aren't as unified as they were last fall."

Kaftus took the book and checked the entries. "But he won't do. If his name is still there, he can't be the one who tore away the missing part. And, in any case, we can't afford to stress the Ykenai connection."

"A ruse," Nimnestl suggested. "Or Morquiesse might have been the only one with directions to the shrine, and Palompec needed that. I thought I'd question him with the others."

"He'd have taken the whole book." The Regent set the volume down and turned to consider the kettle again. "But find the best suspect and skewer him. We need a beheading quickly."

Nimnestl turned for the door. "Mind if I try to get the guilty one?"

"I'm not the warden," said Kaftus. "Do what you like. It's your funeral."

"Yes," said Nimnestl, nodding. "For you, it's always someone else's funeral."

"You not going with not me," said Mardith, flying to her side.

"Hush," she ordered.

"Yes, bird," said the necromancer. "You ruined her exit."

Nimnestl marched outside, right into the center of a procession of Royal Playmates. The King, turning to see what the disturbance was, ran to her.

"Oh, Nimnestl!" he said. "Did you find out yet who did it?"

"Not yet, Your Highness," she told him.

"Find him soon, so we can kill him," said the little monarch. "He told good stories."

Nimnestl glanced at Haeve in time to catch a vanishing sneer. "Where were you last night, when the Royal Painter died?" she inquired.

Haeve studied her with those little black eyes that seemed to see through bricks and discern souls. "I'm sure I don't know."

"Good," she said. "That would have worried me very much. I would like to discuss the business with you later."

"As you wish, Milady," the Tutor replied, with a partial bow. "But now we have a geography lesson." The Playmates moaned.

"You must draw maps of the places you've been," he told them, shooing them all down the corridor, "before you forget."

"What does that matter when a good man is dead?" the King demanded.

Nimnestl regretted that she could not stay to hear what Haeve said to that.

IV

MARDITH circled his mistress's head. "Where we go now?" he demanded.

"Oh," she replied, with a mournful sigh. "I've offended you so much, I'm sure I don't deserve to have you along."

If it is possible for birds to snort, Mardith snorted. "That don't matter damn. Where?"

Nimnestl considered. "The Dining Hall." Morquiesse had been unstable, but never stupid. He might well have known he was marked for death, and left a clue in the murals that had been his last work. In fact, it would have amused him to do so.

Possibly his greatest work as well (though the King would probably always prefer the fountain disguised as a sundial), the murals were a danse macabre painted on sixteen panels in the Great Dining Hall. Very chic, the theme was privately considered both foreign and morbid by Rossacottans. Not that they preferred to ignore death: many, particularly those of the passing generation, kept a few skulls as trophies among their possessions. But the danse macabre's insistence on death's regrettable features made as much sense as bewailing the dampness if you went out in the rain.

The hall was aswarm with servants. Men and women hammered up grandly gilded ornaments, while others hauled away debris and rotted straw. The major contingent was Iranen's retinue, being drilled in their duties for the evening.

"That's wrong!" bellowed the Fourth Housekeeper. "Back in line, my bitches, and start over!"

She snapped her whip and strode to a better vantage point. Nimnestl judged her to be in a good mood: the whip had hit no one. Two score women scrambled to their beginning positions, ignoring fresh, daggerlike straw under their bare feet. Those already in place shivered where they were.

"She's a good thing we're bitches and not cattle," whispered a thin, starved-looking blonde with tooth marks on her hands. "We'd be branded."

"Hush," said her lumpish partner, pinching her. "She hasn't thought of earmarking us yet."

Iranen reached the head table and turned, her unbound black hair slashing through the air. Even Nimnestl froze when the woman studied her army. She wore her "work uniform," a thick canvas gown splashed with blood. Incongruously, the soft dress slippers she had worn the night before showed under the hem.

Her eyes as she studied the assembly showed no sign of madness, only acute self-satisfaction. "Ready!" she declared. Lung power blasted the announcement through the huge room. "Joumb, you jade, keep those knees together! If they want what's there, they can find it without your help!"

Joumb blushed and quickly cupped her hands in front. No one over three was in any ignorance of the uses and abuses to which any part of the body could be put, but for two generations now it had been considered vulgar—uncivilized—to make any mention or display of them. Rossacottan propriety was not yet well developed, but the forms were observed. A loss of social value and respect followed any such exhibition, even under duress.

This did not, somehow, discourage a large crowd in the Great Dining Hall when it fell to Iranen's retinue to serve. Nimnestl wished the duty could have been switched out of rotation to, say, Lynex's followers for this event. The spectacle of Iranen's naked, terrified slaveys would hardly enhance respect for the government among those townspeople who came up for the King's jubilee. But the schedule was as old as the Palace Royal, and as unmovable. With a shrug, Nimnestl turned to a consideration of Morquiesse's handiwork.

Coming in by this door, she saw one of the eight large panels first, "Death and the Prostitute." It was masterfully executed, from the squirrels in the background to the heroine thrusting her hips at massive Death. Above her shrug, the face was covered in shadow and unrecognizable. Of course, everyone was guessing. Rumor had it that Morquiesse would produce special sketches of Aoyalasse for preferred customers. It would have been very like him to blazon one of these on the wall of the Great Dining Hall.

Every painting held some joke. The Maiden, choosing a dress from her wardrobe while Death proffered a shroud, was definitely Maiaciara, her face lifted in surprise and disdain at Death's presumption. Hers was the only surprised expression. The Soldier seemed relieved, the Executioner resigned. Recognizing his face in "Death and the Soldier," Ferrapec had protested loudly the suggestion that he would be glad to leave a battlefield. The only person who paid any attention was Laisida, who had composed an ode as insulting as it was brilliant. Ferrapec was unappreciative of the dual tribute.

"Death and the Executioner" held a good likeness of Mitar, the Lawciter, but the joke lay in the head of Isanten on the high platform Death was leading Mitar from. First Ministers held their position for life, which, by law, ended five years after they took office. The position was coveted because one could, theoretically, move up to safety by becoming Regent. Isanten had not supplanted Kaftus, and his five years had six months to go. Nimnestl shook her head at this nasty reminder.

Shrieking, an eight-year-old dodged around Nimnestl as Iranen's chicken-foot slashed through the air. "Back, you hazel-splitters! You're off again!" The three-pronged whip snapped back, just missing a woman's apron hem. (The older women were allowed aprons, but only in back. "To protect the diners, my bitches," said Iranen.) From her refuge, the small girl threw off a stroke-and-toss gesture that, had Iranen seen it, would have cost her her ears.

Iranen had been sane once, or so Nimnestl heard. The story involved a puppy and a fiancé who married someone else, but it changed with every teller. Dogs and women (particularly blondes) certainly figured in it somehow, for they had been reaping the whirlwind as Iranen rose through the ranks of the Housekeepers. When she was promoted to Fourth Housekeeper, the Council immediately transferred supervision of the kennels to Maitena, explaining that the kitchen department naturally needed access to the turnspit dogs. (Maitena had never used dogs as turnspits. Servants were cheaper and easier to train.)

Since the promotion, Iranen had been growing more dangerous. Deprived of the guidance of her sister, another casualty of the winter purge, she had turned increasingly erratic. She prowled the halls by night, and her personal servants disappeared at a rate of about five per month. Plenty of replacements were willing to take the risk in exchange for steady work. Iranen couldn't live forever, or even very long, at this rate; they wouldn't suffer interminably. And her underlings were always in demand in other departments, and for marriage, since everyone knew one of Iranen's bitches would have learned the price of incompetence or insubordination. Mere survival was taken as the seal of quality.

Nimnestl felt Morquiesse would have done well to use Iranen as the model for Death. But one could not leave out one's knock at the government, so Death in each panel was instead a perfect likeness of the Regent. This joke had rather backfired, Kaftus's sense of humor being as perverse as the artist's. The Regent let it be known that he was delighted.

"Death and the Clerk" was a dig at Haeve, anod over a dusty book, with spiders building webs between him and the desk. Nimnestl studied the pose for sinister signs, and saw none. "Death and the Artisan" was merely a Stonemason being shown to his guild tomb. The joke was perhaps intended for someone in Malbeth; Nimnestl did not recognize the face. "Death and the Priest" was more tantalizing. The figure stood in brown robes, but had his back to the viewer. Could that be Palompec's unruly mop of hair showing over the collar?

"Death and the Thief" was rather pat, just the Lord Treasurer shown as a cutpurse. One couldn't be screamingly funny in every panel, Nimnestl supposed. Then came "Death and the Soldier," a horizontal panel over the door, with "Death and the Prostitute" next. "Death and the Hunter" was a fine picture almost devoid of humor, with some excellently painted dogs the King had clapped his hands to see.

But these dogs were crowded into one corner of the panel, just above where Iranen would have to stand while waiting on the head table. She had been standing there, in fact, during the unveiling. At seeing nine massive dogs bearing down on her, she had leaped over that head table and rolled screaming in the straw. Everyone present had considered this one of the major successes of the evening.

The eight-year-old, now with six red stripes along her back and shoulders, dodged behind Nimnestl again, but this time was pulled out by the hair. "Back in line!" ordered Iranen, though it was uncertain from her gaze and the cut of the whip whether she was addressing the girl or the woman pulling her. "You want this across your saddle-shiners?"

The Council liked Iranen's sense of discipline. Illiterate and brutal, she was the overseer of the surgeons, minstrels, fools, trumpeters, chroniclers, and all other skilled laborers not employed by the Treasury or Department of State. Old-timers on the Council were especially afraid of the competition. Soldiers, treasury guards, and housekeepers rose slowly, step by step; a clerk or a minstrel who could juggle words and numbers well enough might be made Minister of State in a day.

Nimnestl and Kaftus did not interfere in Iranen's excesses, though they sometimes registered a protest. Let the Council have its fun, thinking it was thwarting the Regent: Kaftus did not really want any ambitious minstrels getting above themselves either. The King was largely unamused by Iranen's habits but, under Morquiesse's influence, had been developing a bloodthirsty sense of humor, and an acceptance of the Housekeeper's foibles.

The panels behind the head table were especially filled with Morquiessian humor, to the King's great amusement. First came "Death and the Housekeeper": Maitena caught in the act of tossing rats into the soup. This was positioned so that no one dining could avoid seeing it. So was "Death and the Fool," which showed Laisida in Bilibi's mouse-swallowing act. (Could Laisida have been involved in the murder? The footprints were not those of a one-legged man, of course, but his older daughters were well-muscled, and there would have been good motive for taking the arms back as a trophy in that case.)

Even Morquiesse did not dare suggest that Death would ever drop in on the King, so "Death and the Prince" was a portrait of Arberth, looking back at the glory Death was forcing him to leave as he stepped into the Royal Tombs. Morquiesse had the tombs done perfectly, those rooms to which everyone, seeing them for the first time, reacted the same way. "All those little boxes!" the King had cried, on his first and, so far, only visit.

Morquiesse had told Arberth for weeks that the murals would include a special surprise. The jester was late to the unveiling, but arrived in time to see the cloth pulled from "Death and the Prince." He had turned paper-white, and stumbled from the room. Pity to pull those tricks on Arberth, thought Nimnestl. He was a good, earnest soul who gave all he had to his profession. He just didn't have much.

The fourth panel, "Death and the Murderer," was just what would have been expected. The main figure was so shrouded in shadow that she looked dark from top to toe. The vultures seen in other pictures were here replaced by crows. Nimnestl did not bother to study that picture.

Up the next wall was "Death and the Peasant," which had apparently not interested Morquiesse much. It was just a farmer being tossed onto his own dungheap, picturesque enough for the dining hall, but otherwise not enthralling. "Death and the Lovers," another horizontal panel over a door, was more to his tastes, and the crowd's, to judge by the number of people with sore muscles from imitating the pictured pose. "The Executioner" was next, and then "The Maiden," and finally, because, like Iranen, Morquiesse was prone to spare nobody, came "Death and the Artist." Here Morquiesse put the finishing touches to a painting of a model who had obviously just received the same courtesy. It was a masterpiece of self-knowledge: the smile was perfect, the same one he had worn as he whipped away the covers to unveil his work. That smile—a grin of good-natured mischief with just a touch of utter lack of control—made you grin back, and assured you that whatever he did—pull a cat's tail, knife a treasury guard, burn down a house—was all done in a spirit of fun. He had probably joined the Ykenai from pure deviltry.

But there was not, Nimnestl noted, any real sign of impending doom, though Death reached in to take the palette away. The model's face was covered, but the body was probably that of Aoyalasse again, which was no clue.

"Show a little more life!" shouted Iranen. "Or I'll ship you all out as field mattresses for the border guard!"

"That might be more restful!" someone shouted back.

Both Nimnestl and Iranen, startled, turned to look for the speaker. But every servant was busy studying the floor or the ceiling, though neither of these needed further work. Iranen looked down the row at the head table, and then glanced at Nimnestl.

Nimnestl looked away, but it was too late. The Housekeeper had seen her watching. "Fausca!" called Iranen. "Come here!"

Fausca sat at the far end of the head table, a bowl in her lap. Come evening she would be posted there, shelling nuts as needed for the diners there. She was a Diarrian, long, lank, unself-conscious, with full, dark breasts but an otherwise youthful frame and face. She had had the misfortune to be pushing hair back from that face when Iranen looked around.

"You . . . you assigned me here, Milady," she said, half-rising.

"So I did." Iranen took two steps forward. "Now come here."

Fausca set the bowl on the table, very slowly. "I didn't say it, Milady," she ventured, without much hope.

The chicken foot snapped out and caught the bowl, knocking it up against Fausca's nose. Both hands over her face, she fell back into the sharp straw. Iranen charged forward and caught one outstretched leg. The Housekeeper dragged Fausca out into plain sight for the benefit of all bystanders.

"One moment, Lady Iranen," the Bodyguard interrupted.

Iranen did not relinquish her hold on the ankle, but turned, smiling. "Yes, Milady?" she inquired.

Nimnestl did not generally interfere with the torment of Iranen's slaveys, particularly not those from Reangle or Diarrio. For one thing, she knew Iranen singled out the dark-skinned women to annoy her; to object would be to admit the success of the ploy. And if she shielded Fausca now, the girl would only suffer worse later.

But it had occurred to her that Iranen was a perfect suspect. She was savage, she prowled by night, she had been humiliated at the unveiling of the mural. Morquiesse had been trying to convince the Council to create a new branch of government for the minstrels and artists, which would have subtracted from her prestige. Moreover, nobody liked Iranen. Now, if she could just be guilty, too . . .

"A word with you?" Nimnestl said, her voice bland.

Iranen started forward, dragging Fausca, who wisely made no complaint. "Without witnesses," Nimnestl suggested.

Iranen stopped and considered the body on the floor. She drove one slippered foot into it and then dropped the ankle. "Back to your place!" she barked. As Fausca crawled away, she swaggered across to the Bodyguard.

"What is it?" she demanded. "Have you more crimes than criminals, or more criminals than crimes?"

Nimnestl wondered, idly, why white people never noticed all the twitching veins and muscles in their eyelids. "Housekeepers," she began, "with so many keys to so many rooms . . ."

"Your pump is good, but the well is dry," Iranen broke in. "I wasn't anywhere near there, and all I know is it should have been done five years ago. Anything more you want to know, ask Morquiesse, if you can wake him up."

"Thank you for your assistance, Milady," Nimnestl replied. "I'll do that."

Iranen seemed to swallow, and took a step to one side, but her voice still rang of brass as she went on. "Such power in those arms of his!" She glanced up at the danse macabre, her eyes falling on "Death and the Clerk." "No cobwebs on those arms," she murmured. "And now he's missing his. Ha! Someone took arms against him!" She threw her head back and laughed, a howling "Aheee! Aheee!"

Two of her retainers collapsed at the sound. "Back to work!" she bellowed, turning.

"By all means," agreed a new voice, quiet and dry.

Forokell, the First Chief Housekeeper, was being pushed into the room by a member of her retinue, the thick wheels of her Farnum chair breaking straw as they passed. At the sight, Iranen moved to the right, as if to take shelter behind Nimnestl.

Forokell was an imposing sight, though a small woman, managing to convey the impression of ponderous age without wrinkles or shrivels. She had been a Chief Housekeeper when the parents of most present councillors were damp newborns, and commanded the respect of everyone in the Palace Royal (except Mardith, who had so little respect to spare).

She was not yet reconciled to being confined to the wheeled chair, but she used it to good effect. As she rolled through the Great Dining Hall, she kept her eyes ahead, sparing not a glance for Iranen, and barely deigning to look at Nimnestl.

"We are summoned to Council, Bodyguard," she said, in passing. "The rest of you have things to do."

"Make way, make way!" cried Mardith, perching on an armrest. "We mow you down!" He dodged the First Chief Housekeeper's fist.

Nimnestl followed more sedately. "I will speak with you again," she promised Iranen.

V

SOME two dozen men and women sat around the ancient brown table in the Council Room. Ferrapec and Adimo, somewhat rumpled, were settling into their seats as Nimnestl and Forokell entered. Some decision on seating precedence had obviously just been made, and the two men's bodyguards were being separated. There were no assigned seats, since there were no assigned Councillors. The leaders of the Palace bureaucracy were Councillors only if invited to attend a meeting. Otherwise, they were encouraged to mind their own business.

A seat at the end of the table was always left empty for Nimnestl. This was no official decree; no one cared to challenge her right to it since the day Wiolla tried it. She sat down and studied the assembly. Kaftus had summoned people of importance, self-importance, and importance to the case. Each had naturally brought sidemen to stand close at hand: retainers and bodyguards. Rarely did a Council meeting draw fewer than eighty people. Secrets were never discussed in Council unless they were secrets to be disseminated.

Nimnestl was the youngest person seated, but she was old enough to have heard or even observed the gritty origins of all these Councillors who resented her presence. First Minister Isanten, for example, was the son of a Lattinese exile who had turned to building locks when picking them proved unprofitable. His great success was a chastity belt with four locks, each requir-

63

ing two keys simultaneously. Closed, the belt could not be opened without all eight keys—unless one bought the combination to the lock hidden in the waistband. These combinations sold for slightly more than the entire belt, but business was so good that he was able to buy his son a post at court, not knowing it would lead to the First Minister spot.

Isanten's steady rise was attributed to natural ability and to bribery and blackmail, which, of course, took some natural ability. For all this, he had always lacked a solid core of loyal supporters. He tended to lease out all of his dirtiest work, which lost him some of his following. The use of agents was understood in Rossacotta, but a certain glamour was still accorded to men who occasionally took care of their own corpses.

The same rule applied to women. No one liked Akoyn, for example, who could decree the most memorable punishments to her servants and then walk away with a sigh of sorrow. Her underlings hated the pious sigh; her overlings despised the walking away, without the stomach to stay and watch. The daughter of a minor Treasury clerk, Akoyn had begun as one of the palace laundresses, and owed her rise to an incident that occurred while she was elbow-deep in hot water.

She was only present today because Kaftus had invited Aoyalasse to Council. One couldn't, without shooting rumors throughout the Palace Royal, invite the Second Assistant without also summoning the First. Akoyn's face (what there was of it; her lower lip was colorless and her chin almost nonexistent) showed that she realized this.

Next to her sat Lynex, Second Chief Housekeeper, in charge of all washing and cleaning in the Palace Royal, and of keeping the pious Akoyn and the volatile Aoyalasse in line. She was the daughter of a deceased count, far superior to either of them, and comported herself accordingly. A delicate woman of gentle grace, she spoke in soft, even tones that fooled no one who had ever felt the back of her hand. Her husband walked in terror of her.

As soon as Forokell was in place at the massive table, the Councillors looked to Kaftus, who rose from his seat at its head. Adimo, the current favorite, rose with him. No one joined the salute. Adimo had been on his way out for weeks and was the only one who didn't know it. Kaftus, his hands folded, waited silently until Adimo oozed back down.

"Council," said the Regent, his smile acid, "shall we begin?"

"Ayeh," said Grandfather Frog. "Get busy." First General

Kaigrol, a deaf and drowsy barrel of a war hero, was tolerated less for his white locks and service record than because civil war would erupt if he stepped down. Both Tollamar and Gensamar, the brothers who actually ran the Army, would try to step up. No major riots had broken out in the Palace Royal for some years, but that would bring on record-breaking ones. Every department had its private army, and an armory. And all the major bureaucrats had bodyguards and private weapons stores in case of major interdepartmental squabbles. On an average day, there were more armed men in the Palace Royal than on the border.

So the First General was tolerated. Kaftus gave him a little bow. "Council, our country's reputation has been endangered by the destruction of one of our national treasures." He paused, as if wondering whether to believe a word of that, and then went on. "The rest of Atfalas will be watching to see how Rossacotta deals with the murder of Morquiesse, Chief Figurer and Painter to His Majesty. The eyes of the world are on us, and we can choose today what parts we will play in the songs of tomorrow."

Nimnestl was too far away to hear what Maitena muttered, but it was probably uncomplimentary. The Third Chief Housekeeper, and Aoyalasse's mother, Maitena was a woman of generous, all-purpose figure, whose mind and body had been under great stress over the winter. She was capable of sudden violence, and might have considered Morquiesse's treatment of Aoyalasse a slight to the family. She was added to the list of possibilities.

"Has the Chief Bodyguard found anything?" rumbled Kaigrol, less because he expected it than because he wanted to hear her admit that she had not.

Nimnestl spread both hands flat on the table. "It is too early for definite conclusions. All we can say for certain at this point is that Morquiesse was murdered, no doubt by a person or persons with a long-standing grudge."

Laisida ran a hand through his straw-yellow hair. "What I can't see is how he could take out Morquiesse and all those guards as well."

Malaracha leaned over to remind him, "There could have been several. Remember all those footprints."

"By the time you saw the floor, half the palace had walked over it," snorted Laisida.

"What do you know about it?" Malaracha demanded. "I was the first one there and helped break down the door."

The First Minister broke in. "It was probably one of the outsiders: someone who knew him down south."

Patrak slapped the table. "I have been informing the Council of the need for more security restraints on the foreigners!"

Nimnestl had expected someone to set up the cry of "WE would not have done such a thing!" More foreigners visited the hitherto shunned city all the time. Rossacottans, though gratified, could not shake off the feeling that some massive plot was underway. Lord Patrak had been in the forefront of those demanding that these outsiders be quarantined, their dispatches and letters read, their activities monitored. But one had one's international reputation to consider, as Kaftus frequently pointed out. Besides, the Regent and Nimnestl knew opening their mail was to little purpose; between every line was the same message: "Buy Rossacottans."

"That jester, now," Isanten mused, "Arberth. He's from . . ."

"Now, now," objected Kaigrol. The general was constantly grieved by the antics of his younger colleagues. "It's no time to be naming names just yet. You don't rush into such things without proper investigation. There's this question of an attack on Chief Tax Collector Borodeneth. Might that not be related?"

Patrak, Borodeneth's immediate superior and closest ally, cleared his throat. "The Chief Tax Collector," he stated, "has no idea who attacked him, or why, but requests that the Council not use up its valuable time on the matter. He will handle the business himself."

There were nods of approval around the table. That private affair could be ignored, leaving them free to concentrate on the main event.

"It could still have been the jester," murmured Isanten.

"Shall we also disregard the murder of Ostage?" inquired Pammel, stroking the luxurious mustache that was braided into his beard.

"I doubt Ostage was close enough to the First Painter's quarters to be involved," said Nimnestl. "It is too early to eliminate any possibilities, however. The missing children could also be involved."

"Oh, come now!" protested Akoyn. "Who . . ."

"Then you will consider the jester," interrupted Isanten. "I think you should have found out if he, or any other foreigner, left the palace this morning."

"It will do them little good," Laisida announced, with a toss of his head. "When I have finished my song about this murder,

every cowherd in the sticks will be up in arms to catch the culprit."
More nods of approval greeted this. Laisida's self-confidence
was immense, but so positive and childlike that no one could
resent it.

"But this Arberth . . ." Isanten began.

Nimnestl did resent that. "Take up some other bone and chew
it, My Lord. The jester is still here; I spoke to him briefly this
morning."

The First Minister's mouth dropped open. "You d-did? Really?
Well, it was just an idea of mine."

Torrix adjusted two long horsehair cushions behind his back.
"Whoever it is," he said, turning toward the table again, "catch
him quickly. His punishment can be the climax of the festival; we
can put a platform in the Great Hall."

Nimnestl snorted. Torrix would think of that. Like a lord of
old Diarrio, Torrix kept two women chained in his rooms for his
private use. No one knew whether the current pair was the pair
he had started with. He was a Swamper, too.

Some courtiers ventured into the seedy end of Malbeth to
collect extortion, which was respectable, but a Swamper went
there for mere diversion. He preyed on the corn girls who sold
more than roasting ears on the western edge of the district, or
checked out the houses for thrills more dire than those available
from free-lancers at the Palace Royal. The current favorite was
the Yellow Dog, which was popular among foreign ambassadors
as well. Having visited it, they could say they had had a taste
of real Rossacottan degeneracy, without having to go into the
perilous west end.

The Swamp was also a good place to recruit bodyguards, as
Morquiesse had. Other Swampers included Isanten, Arlmorin,
Palompec . . .

Nimnestl frowned and looked around the table. The Colonel
wasn't present.

Laisida had started in on the plan for the new housekeeping
department for artists, while Patrak was talking, at the same
time, about setting aside a tower for foreign visitors, fruitful
topics which had little to do with Morquiesse's death, but which
could be counted upon to come up in any Council debate of any
length. Nimnestl had no compunction about breaking in.

"Is Colonel Palompec ill?" she inquired. "Or was he not summoned?"

"He's away," Ferrapec told her, glad, like many Councillors, for the interruption of Patrak and Laisida. "Taking a report to General Vetaki. Why?"

"When did he leave?"

The general's eyes narrowed. This indicated that he was concentrating. "Early this morning."

"Was this planned?" she asked. "Or was it his own idea?"

"What are you suggesting?" demanded General Gensamar.

Nimnestl turned to him, raising her nostrils. "Every convenient departure should be examined," she replied.

Kaftus, with as much dignity and more scorn, told her, "Woman, half of Malbeth was in and out of here once the cry of murder went abroad." In his eyes, Nimnestl could clearly read, "Forget Palompec."

The rather futile Yslemucherys cleared his throat. "Er, should the ball be cancelled in mourning?" he asked. "I think maybe it would be the most civilized thing to do." Every time Yslemucherys used the word maybe, he made bunny ears with his fingers and wiggled them, a gesture he failed to notice and would certainly not have considered amusing.

"It may be," Kaftus agreed. "What says Lord Isanten?"

Nimnestl let the conversation roll off in that direction. It would be best, she supposed, to ignore Palompec for now, and keep the Brown Robes out of public notice. If the truth were known, Palompec would die, but Morquiesse's membership could still revive the cult's popularity. A lot depended on how eager for martyrdom the colonel was.

For now, some other culprit, even a false culprit, had to be punished. That was how business in the Palace Royal was always conducted: another trap to be set, another web to be spun. This murder was, at the moment, so minor compared to earlier crises. What, Nimnestl wondered, must it have been like when Queen Kata lay dying, the infant Conan set to succeed? How had she managed to summon Kaftus before the end? What plots and subplots had polluted the air?

Morquiesse would have been newly returned from the south then. A fourth son, he had been sent to Gilraën to a minstrel's school. He was not much of a singer, but became an artist in spite of his teachers. (Treated as a hick, or worse, because of his nationality, he had had to kill a few of them to get any respect.) He came back by way of the fashionable cities of Turin, paying his expenses with drawings and a few tavern signs that needed repainting. Lattinese scholars had by now mapped very nearly the whole of his route, and were buying up tavern signs along the road for more than entire taverns were worth.

It might be worthwhile to find such a map; there might be clues to old grudges in it. But Nimnestl felt the murderer was more likely to be someone handy. If only Morquiesse had been less generous with his sense of humor. The new sundial had embarrassed a dozen court officials (including the Bodyguard) who, stepping up to it, found it was really a fountain. There were men in Malbeth who would kill for that.

But the King had laughed. Making the King laugh was an easy road to royal favor. Royal favor, at the moment, didn't count for much, but it might someday. Any scrap of influence had to be seized, the way the Palace bureaucracy was shifting. The Army, in the forefront for decades, was losing ground before those departments with literate employees, like Housekeeping and the Treasury.

In fact, it was Lord Treasurer Garanem who broke through the fragmenting debate to end the Council meeting. "I think for now we can safely leave further consideration of the matter to those whose job its investigation must be," he said, turning his head slightly toward Nimnestl. "A neat and ingenious solution will no doubt be soon forthcoming. In the meantime, I suggest that festivities go on as planned. It may serve to distract the people from their tragic loss."

The Councillors glanced to the Regent. "An excellent idea, My Lord," he purred. "One can see how you earned the esteem and high office in His Majesty's Council." A dozen Councillors who had been scalping invitations to the main celebration sighed in relief.

Lord Garanem swallowed and blinked. The First Lord Treasurer was pompous, arrogant, and greedy, but honest within his limits. In contrast to Ferrapec, whom anyone could bribe because all deals looked good to a man with no head for long-range planning, Garanem was almost unbuyable. Offered a copper less than he thought he was worth, and he was insulted. Offered a copper more, he was suspicious. Innumerable plots had gone to pieces on this rock, each solidifying his position. He knew only one fear: that Kaftus might judge him worthy to succeed Isanten as First Minister. But he did not reply to the dangerous compliment.

More ceremony was involved in leaving the Council chamber than in arriving, most of it concerned with not leaving any vulnerable spots open to the official behind one. Both safety and prestige demanded that one linger. Nimnestl and the Regent slipped into Kaftus's chambers as Councillors paused at the hall doors, smiling daggers down each other's backs.

Leaving Mardith by the door to watch for eavesdroppers, Nimnestl told the Regent what little she had learned. "Not bad for half an hour's work," he said. "What were you doing the rest of the time?"

"Well, don't that nice!" snapped Mardith, from his perch on the doorknob. "What you do all this morning while we walk, do your work?"

Kaftus ignored him. "We need someone to carry the bone in this. How about Measthyr? He won't be hard to take in, he has few friends to object, and his throat's too bad for him to scream if it comes to a trial."

"It wouldn't," Nimnestl replied. "But he wouldn't scream enough on the platform, then, to suit Torrix. Have you thought of Iranen? She had the opportunity, certainly, and no one would require much of a motive."

The Regent was considering a three-legged table shaped like a frog. "It might be considered too convenient. It's something for us to think about, though."

Nimnestl frowned. He didn't often imply that she was allowed to do any thinking. "Is there some other problem on your mind?" she inquired.

"I have sensed a new power in the Palace Royal," he replied, still staring at the frog. "A new sorcerer."

Unconsciously, she slid her hand down to her hammer. "Strong enough to pose a threat?"

Kaftus swept past the table and turned. "It's too new; I haven't had time to take its measure. But the power is there. A small amount will do if used properly."

"Then I will hunt murderers for the time being," said Nimnestl. " 'Powers' are your business. But find him fast. We have more sorcerers now than we need."

Kaftus's ghastly grin snaked up his face. "Well, don't that nice! Is this gratitude, Woman? After all, I got you into History."

"Fine," she told him. "Have you got a way for me to get out and still enjoy it afterwards?" Whistling to Mardith, she strode back into the Council Room.

VI

THE Bodyguard strode with a purpose, scattering the crowd before her. It was a fake. Though she was doing it at top speed, she was just meandering. She was a calamity about to occur, even more so than usual, and she knew it. All she could change about that was whom she would befall.

She had only to choose from an enhanced list of suspects: Laisida, his daughters, Ferrapec, Haeve, Maitena, Palompec, Aoyalasse, Iranen, Arberth, perhaps a couple more with immediate grudges. It would be easy. That didn't cheer her up.

Ferrapec would be easiest. Almost his entire bodyguard had deserted him for other officers, and his wife had been openly snubbed at the previous evening's gala. Motive would not be hard to prove. Nimnestl remembered now the affair of the portrait. Maiaciara had not paid for the painting, nor insisted upon owning it. "It is enough for you," Ferrapec's daughter had told Morquiesse, "that your painting will live forever because of my beauty, and it is enough for me that my beauty will live forever because of your painting."

Morquiesse used the full-length nude as a sample of his work. There stood Maiaciara, in all her glory, as beautiful as she was in life. And, after one glance, no viewer of the painting looked at her again.

Viewers were always too busy studying what the two men in

the background were doing. Her father had sworn revenge for that, among other things.

But why bother to eliminate Ferrapec, just now when he was nearly harmless? Far better, if one had to eliminate someone, to choose a person whose disappearance would strengthen the Regency. The most dangerous of the suspects was Palompec, who had the added advantage of being the man Nimnestl was mortally sure had committed the murder.

But Kaftus had the right of it, lintik blast him. If Palompec were formally accused, as was essential if he were to be held up as the slayer of Morquiesse, he would talk. And the winter's progress against the Ykenai would go like smoke. How convenient it would have been had he been found dead before he could answer questions. His quick departure had made that impossible. (How had he gotten away? The guards swore no one had been allowed out of the Palace once the order was given.) It could still be arranged; a message could be passed through the trustworthy bodyguards that Palompec was to be slain on sight. Or perhaps the Ykenai themselves would be shortsighted enough to bargain away his life for a period of peace.

For now, however, the one person she would have gladly had carved to death for the crime was the one man she didn't dare accuse. An innocent passerby had to be chosen for the knife and the pit. She growled at the thought. Two small boys who had been daring each other to sneak up and touch her tore off down the hall.

Coming to a halt by a high, narrow window, Nimnestl set one hand on the weapons bracket next to it, and looked out. Some green was trying to rise in the courtyard. It would be trampled as the season advanced and more people took outdoor shortcuts.

Ignoring the slapping sounds from Fiera's room, she let her imagination pass through the walls of the palace. Outside, she knew, there were green fields and royal forests, losing their winter smells for the spring ones. The smells were different in the Palace Royal. (Malbeth also lay in the direction she was looking, but as she was seeing only with her imagination, she could delete the city.)

Nimnestl was not yearning for freedom. She knew her job was a closed box, locked by time. Any day it would fulfill Kaftus's promise of early death: swiftly, violently perhaps, though poison or abduction were possible alternatives. If she resigned, she might make it as far as the gatehouse. Survival required that she stay, as long as she or the Regency lasted. After thirteen years, if she lived, if she did her job and raised little Conan up to be a king, she would have to leave him then to rule. She might retire to a royal estate near the mountains. She would think about that in thirteen years. In becoming a king, Conan could change his mind about her. She might find herself escorted to the border, her name inscribed on the tablet of exiles, or even escorted down the ramp into the dungeons.

He could be made dependent on her; she could become the ruler from the shadows. But massive as the old stone throne was, there was room for only one person behind it. Nimnestl had to admit that the Regent didn't seem inclined to want to rule that way, but he would hardly let anyone else do it. If it came to a fight between the Regent and the Bodyguard, the loser would not be the ancient necromancer.

Nimnestl shrugged and turned from the window. She had taken hold of a wildcat, and no one could help her let go. The power was hers for thirteen years or until she got careless, and the problems went with it. As her grandfather had said, "The larger the room, the harder to heat; the higher the tower, the fiercer the winds."

She started moving again, picking up speed as she thought. There were compensations: food, shelter, the companionship of the King. (The companionship of Kaftus was one of the things that had to be compensated for.) And she felt a few of the Royal Companions really did hold her in the admiration that all pretended. But they were impressionable, and liable to change.

She frowned. Other business besides the murder of the artist was pressing. Some pressing business was always being neglected, especially where the Royal Companions were concerned. It had been such a simple idea, originally: the King should not grow up alone, so they would collect a group of children his age and raise them all together. Members of the group would be chosen carefully; those who tried to lobby for their parents' causes could be disciplined or dropped.

Nowadays this band of small warriors played fierce and noisy games of war, or sack the city, to Nurse's fiercer and noisier complaints. Nurse felt this wild, violent element was all a result of allowing vulgar creatures into the privileged circle. Some of the Companions, like Merklin, were sons of ranking officers or bureaucrats, but others had sprung from mere soldiers, or even merchants who had regular business at the Palace Royal. Scions of anti-Regent families had been included, in fact: as many as could be without offending the pro-Regent parents. Everyone could see the advantage of having a child with direct access to the King. They had forgotten that, between now and the time that access would make a difference, all those children would be tutored by Haeve, watched over by Nurse, and frequently visited by both Kaftus and Nimnestl.

There were benefits to the King as well, besides the solidification of the Regency. He was learning things he would not have, surrounded by older lackeys. To Nimnestl's gratification Conan had developed an opinion that rank was no substitute for skill, and, better, that rank should be matched by skill.

"I'm King," he'd told her once, "so they'll make me chief on raids whether I'm good or not. So I have to be good." It gave her hope.

But there were difficulties. Courtiers resented the rapid climb of Ipojn, Merklin's father. Nimnestl worried more about the rise of Merklin. The King's decision in Bekijn had been based less on her opinion or that of Mitar than on what Merklin thought was a good idea. That Merklin agreed with her and with Mitar in this case did not change things. He could not, now, be removed from the King's circle. Changing the personnel of the Companions was becoming harder and harder; the King noticed absences or additions, and demanded explanations.

So far, Merklin was a wholesome influence, but there were others. To teach them about the diversity of religion in Rossacotta, Haeve had taken the Companions to meetings of every temple sect whose precepts allowed the presence of children and the uninitiated. Several of the Companions were offspring of Neleandrai, and the other children had become interested in the sect. Their parents did not object. A disagreement over some point of dogma, centuries ago, had split the Neleandrai from the Ykenai, and made them bitter enemies. In the last eight months, it had become very, very profitable to be a Neleandra. One could hardly, for example, be accused of being one of the treasonous Ykenai. When promotions were available, one's superiors obviously found it easier to choose someone known to be a foe of the Ykenai than risk promoting an unknown quantity who might have brown robes hidden in a closet.

Nimnestl had not been able to observe the Neleandra rites in person; the Neleandrai were apologetic about this, but rules were rules and their precepts forbade the presence of adult female foreigners at the ceremonies. Nimnestl had to depend on information passed on by Culghi, who guarded the Companions on visits to the Neleandra meeting room. Culghi felt the basic rituals and doctrines were harmless. They were certainly of a nature to appeal to children, with an emphasis on refreshments, loud noises, and games. It was entirely likely, Nimnestl thought, that this aspect had entered the ancient and sacred rites when the sect decided that the King, too old to be ruled by overseers, might be manipulated by friends. The Companions were being wooed; each convert was one more voice in the King's ear. If Merklin could be coaxed into membership, it would be a triumph; if the King himself, victory.

One rite particularly aroused Nimnestl's suspicions. Each week a complex game of cards, which could go on for a day or two, was played. A fresh deck was used for each hand of the game, a fact which had alerted her as soon as Culghi mentioned it. The winners of each hand were eliminated, and losers had to go on in competition. The ultimate loser had to perform some humiliating (but entertaining) act of atonement to pay for the misdeeds of the whole group. The King always seemed to run up a high score early in the game, and the loser was nearly always someone the monarch particularly disliked.

Culghi couldn't see any signs that this was engineered, and pointed out that once even the leader of the sect had had to doff all but the hood concealing his face, and perform that week's sacrifice. Nimnestl thought Culghi was strong and stalwart and brave and true. None of this had any bearing on his intellectual capacity.

Something had to be done about the Neleandrai. She had spies and agents of provocation in all the more important conspiracies disguised as religions, like the Rokila. Naturally, it was the unimportant ones like the Ykenai and Neleandrai that were making trouble.

She paused at the end of the hall, resting her back against a corner of the wall. This problem was the opposite of that in Morquiesse's death. The culprits, for all their hoods and mystery, were known. It was a matter of convincing anyone—particularly the King—that they had done something wrong.

Proof of cheating in their rites would help. Rossacottans thought nothing of cheating (as long as they weren't the ones losing), but they despised cheaters who got caught. The King, who retained some idealism, would be really shocked, and might even see that he had been manipulated.

The best way to do it, in fact, would be to have Conan discover the cheat. Nimnestl had meant to consult Arberth on the

CHAPTER THREE
Polijn

I

TWO voices—one high and wispy, the other low and ragged—
fought for the right to fill the dim little room with raucous
song.

> "But I couldn't guess what foolery
> Women take for the sake of joolery."

Arberth struck a chord that was two steps flat, and stopped.
"You're a little hoarse, Polijn," he said, pretending to adjust a
string.

Polijn swallowed and put a hand to her throat. "I'll be all
right," she told him. She recognized the signs. She would be
all right, after two weeks of misery. All winter she had avoided
catching a cold; why did one have to pop up just now, before this
performance?

Arberth cleared his throat. "Well, that'll be enough work on
that one now, anyway," he said. Polijn doubted it. "When we
finish that," he went on, "we'll go right into 'The Ram Forlorn.' "

Polijn barely restrained a cry of alarm. When she could do so
calmly, she said, "You did 'The Ram Forlorn' at the New Year
Festival and the judges gave it two-thirds of one point."

Arberth shook himself as if trying to cast off the memory. "Yes,
well, there are other people in the Palace Royal."

Yes, well, they're unanimous, thought Polijn. "How about . . ."
A faint scraping sound made her jump. "What was that?"

Arberth glanced up at the shadowy ceiling. "Oh, bats on the
next level," he supposed, "coming out of their winter's nap."

Shuddering, Polijn persisted, "Besides, there are those lines
about Morquiesse in 'The Ram Forlorn.' "

"Nothing worse than he ever said about me," Arberth replied,
setting down his ficdual and feeling around on the broken wooden
counter for a pick.

"While he was alive," noted Polijn.

"Alive?" said the minstrel. "Oh, while he was alive. Yes.
Hmmm. Well, perhaps we'd best try 'The Tattered Sails' in its
place."

Polijn nodded. It was, after all, her career, too, that would be
dumped out the window. She took a long breath, and expelled it
in a fit of coughing.

The air was cold in the high tower room. This chamber had no
fireplace, and the tapestry over the window was too worn to keep
out much wind. It did, however, let in a little light, very useful
since the jester had already used up this month's allotment of
candles.

Between the cold in the air, the cold in her throat, and the
shadows in the room at broad noon, Polijn felt like the burnt-out
wick of a dead candle. She had not slept much, either.

Arberth had made his scheduled morning joke about how had
the bed slept. Polijn responded traditionally, "The bed slept fine;
the fleas and I were awake all night." Of course, she had slept in
worse places than on this pallet with thin mattress and thinner
blankets. Once Ronar had neglected a payment and she, Gloraida,
and Mokono slept in a stable for a month. She didn't know why
sleep had been so elusive this time.

"Yes. 'The Tattered Sails,' " said Arberth. "Or maybe . . ." He
reached back for a manuscript case with a broken cover. His long,
pale fingers flicked among the torn and treasured songs he kept
there. Paper and manuscripts were rare, particularly for a minstrel
of his limited means and ability.

He delicately separated one ragged leaf and lifted it from the
rest. "Let me just step out into the light and check the wording
of this one. Be right back."

Polijn pursed her lips at the mirror as Arberth walked into the
hall. The minstrel would probably forget to come back. He was
perilously absent-minded. Sometimes he went out to sing and

forgot his pants, It didn't matter. He was funnier that way.

Arberth was a solo performer; everyone else left the room when he performed. It wasn't just his screech of a voice; he thought too much to be a good poet. He would sing that his lovely lady love was stroking a pony's nose and how he wished he was that pony, a perfectly acceptable concept if you sang it fast enough. Arberth slowed it down, and pondered what never should have been allowed to come up. Did he really want to appear before that lady love wearing nothing but a leather harness? And, if so, would he really want his nose petted?

Polijn had seen jesters who could have made that funny. Arberth could only wander around the subject for an hour, drawing nothing closer to a snicker than a snore. His turns of phrase were equally unfortunate; even Polijn could hear the problems in "My lover's buoyant gait is like unto a ship flying over the sea's rolling face."

Polijn did not feel that being this man's assistant enhanced her career prospects any. But she had very little choice. Slavery was not mentioned in Rossacottan law; to admit that some people were liable to sale would be to suggest that there were some who were not. Polijn was tied to Arberth the same way that everyone else was fastened in place; it was hard to climb alone, but easy to fall. You did not let go of what you had until something better was within reach, or you started to slide. For Polijn, this would have meant going back to Ronar, in the Swamp. Even being assistant to a maladroit jester was an improvement over that.

The maladroit jester pushed the door open. "Yes," he said, "I . . ." He looked at Polijn over the top of the page, and frowned.

Polijn realized she was curling again, sitting with her knees up and her head and shoulders forward. Arberth had been trying to break her of the habit. "Though a defensive stance is generally useful in our line of work," he had told her, "it can be overdone. They want us to look carefree. That makes it more satisfying when they catch us across the face with a handful of beets."

Polijn quickly unfolded. Arberth smiled. He smiled a lot. He was the smilingest depressed person Polijn had ever met. The smiles were apparently meant to uplift her spirits. His eyes said, "Yes, this is all pretty discouraging, but we must be optimistic." Or maybe he did it to encourage himself. Or maybe he really believed that, if he just kept hammering away, he would break through the wall of critical disapproval and earn the respect he knew he deserved.

Polijn's heart sank when she got a better look at the piece of paper he held. Optimism was again getting the better of experience. The page was new, no doubt another one of his own compositions, and probably, with her luck, "The Lovesick Bull." She sighed. She couldn't possibly talk him out of two songs in one morning.

A thump from the corridor brought her to her feet. Very few people ventured into the tower this high before the weather was warm; those who had apartments this high tried to find an excuse to sleep in those of more prestigious courtiers on warmer levels.

It was probably nothing, just nerves caused by that lump of gold hidden among her clothes, but she had to take a look. As Arberth admired his own handiwork some more, Polijn slipped toward the door.

It swung open before she reached it. A massive black form rose to cut off the light.

II

IT was the Chief Bodyguard, looking down with those eyes that demanded, "Well, what's your excuse?", giving you just that brief moment to justify blocking her view of the wall behind you.

Polijn fell back to give her room, and the Bodyguard strode inside, pushing the door shut. Arberth, smiling, set down his manuscript. The jester was one of Nimnestl's few admirers. In his case, admiration amounted to fanatic devotion and forlorn love. Polijn took it as another manifestation of the minstrel's determination to enjoy adversity.

Polijn herself had learned to take the big brown bodyguard on the same terms she took the Palace Royal: it was dark, massive, and dangerous, but you couldn't very easily avoid it. You had to live around it somehow, and hope for less than the worst. The woman was not unhandsome, in an oversized, overbearing way. Tall, high-breasted, somewhat long and broad of hip . . . she was too muscular, though. A woman might be allowed sturdy legs, but those thickly muscled arms were not very civilized. Gloraida would have said, "She'll make a good farmer's wife, she will. Or his horse."

The jester had his hands out, but Nimnestl did not take them. She never had, that Polijn could recall. She started to speak, but stopped, frowning. "You're not going to do 'The Lovesick Bull' again, are you?" she demanded. "You just did it on the King's Birthday."

"Oh, well, I was thinking about it, maybe," Arberth answered, sliding the page away a bit. "You can never have a good song too often."

To Polijn's disappointment, the Bodyguard did not answer that. Instead, she began an entirely different conversation. "I have come on two errands," she said, sitting in the only available chair, a bulky but broken piece leaning delicately against the wall.

The jester looked straight into the big woman's face. "Is one of them to ask where I was last night?"

The Bodyguard pressed a shoulder against the wall and crossed her ankles. "If it is, where were you?"

Arberth sat back against the worn counter. "I went out," he said, "having decided to try out some new songs on a Swamp platform." He made a delicate grimace at the mention of the Swamp. The Bodyguard mimicked it.

"Just so," said Arberth, smiling. "When I got there, I remembered that I had promised Lady Lynex that she could hear the words to the song her husband commissioned as a surprise birthday present. I dropped everything and came back."

"This was when?" asked the Bodyguard.

Arberth frowned. "I got to the banquet just as Morquiesse was unveiling . . . oh, one of the paintings. I forget which. Er, then I saw Lady Lynex seated near the head table. I went over and sang a bit, quietly, you know, in the spaces between the excitement. She didn't like it."

Polijn was not surprised. She had heard bits of the songs as it was composed.

"I brought it up here for some revisions and then I went back. People were leaving already, and Lynex was telling Akoyn and Aoyalasse how to take care of the pre-cleaning. I stood around and waited, you know. One of the women tossed a mop at one of the others and just missed me—with the mop, that is. I got a good spray of whatever was on it." He indicated the stains on his clothes. Polijn nodded.

"When Lady Lynex saw me, she took me off to one of her little reception rooms, you know? She had her own ideas about the song and we discussed them for some time." Arberth rubbed a sore spot on his arm and winced. "We finished up another draft. I came out, found this young one, whom I had left in the Swamp, and that's when I heard about the killing."

The Bodyguard was impassive. "And then?"

"Then we came back here." Arberth sighed. "It had been one of those long evenings."

One bored eyebrow went up. "You didn't rush over to see the excitement?"

Arberth shrugged again, "I hate crowds."

Just as well, considering his work, Polijn thought. But what an admission for a jester to make.

The Bodyguard made no comment on it. "Anyone see you with Lady Lynex?"

The jester shrugged a third time. When he shrugged, his head buried itself a little deeper between his shoulders. "Oh, there's always somebody watching. No one was with us; she saw to that. If I've followed the story all the way, she doesn't want Jontus to learn that she learned that he learned that she learned that he had commissioned a song."

He tried to shrug and smile at the same time. Failing, he went on. "But there was no chaperon. They know I'm a danger to only one person's virtue."

He got a frown for that, but the Bodyguard went on to her next question. "What did you think of Morquiesse?"

This time, Arberth tried for a casual shrug. But he was too jumpy, and it turned into a shudder. "His colors were a little bland. But he could draw armor so you could hear it clank, and as for his dogs and horses . . ."

"As a person," the big woman interrupted.

Arberth's shoulders drooped. He studied the Bodyguard for a second, and then said, "Polijn, come here."

Without a question, Polijn stood up and walked to the jester's side, trying to make her detour around Nimnestl unobtrusive. She looked up at Arberth.

"Turn a little more this way," he told her.

Polijn realized what he wanted. Grimacing a bit, she turned her back to the Bodyguard, and hiked up her shift. Though it had been scrubbed with some determination, day after day, the blue paint could still be read, blazoning the caption "A Better Singer Than Arberth" just above the arrow that snaked down between her buttocks.

"Now, I don't mind, so much, constructive criticism," said the jester. "But that's a bit uncivilized."

Polijn let the shift fall, and stepped away. The Bodyguard nodded. "Not close friends," she said. She didn't seem surprised, or even interested.

"My second errand is more important," she went on. The woman paused, and her lips drew in toward her teeth. When she went on, it was as if she spoke against her will. "I want you to perform a rather peculiar service for me."

All restraint, all diffidence, dropped from Arberth's manner. He leaned forward. "Name it," he implored.

The Bodyguard named it. Polijn turned away so they would not see how wide her eyes and mouth could open. This was a matter of state: vital, delicate. It was barely comprehensible that the Bodyguard would need help, and just within the realm of possibility that she should ask Arberth for that assistance. But that they could talk about it with a third person in the room was inexplicable, and unprecedented.

Perhaps they simply assumed she would not dare repeat the conversation. Not only would the Bodyguard's retribution be swift, but no one would believe the story in the first place.

"So," said the Bodyguard, when the bargain had been struck, "I can count on you for the facts of life?"

"I could do it with one eye closed and the other behind my back," Arberth replied. "Er, were you going to invite young Merklin, as well?"

The Bodyguard blinked. "I was thinking of it. Why?"

Arberth spread his hands in the air, palms up. "He's at that earnest, honest stage. If he has a part in this, you'll have a better chance at winning over the King."

The Bodyguard's head and shoulders rose, her astonishment obvious. Probably, thought Polijn, it had been years since she had been in a position to have to win someone over.

But the dark face quickly congealed again. "We'll see. Probably some time this week."

"I am at your service," answered Arberth. "Any time."

The Bodyguard rose and started for the door. Arberth followed much too quickly, and bumped his nose on her shoulder when she turned back.

"You will find us grateful," she said, not apparently noticing as the jester fell back into the seat she had just vacated.

"Oh," said the jester, weakly, "service to you is its own reward."

The Bodyguard yanked on the door and strode out. Arberth jerked from his chair like a puppet hauled to life, "She consulted me!" he crowed, clapping his hands over his head. "Me!" His long feet slapped the floor as he capered across the room.

Almost in echo, a loud smack resounded in the hall. Polijn knew this was only some sound incidental to the Bodyguard's departure, but she had to look. Sliding past the dancing jester, she eased the door open.

The Bodyguard had gotten as far as the stairs, where that eternally pouting red-headed housekeeper, Aoyalasse, stood panting, half bent over. She had slapped one hand against the corner of the wall for support. "I wanted," she gasped, "to talk to you."

The Bodyguard looked her over. "Obviously."

Aoyalasse pulled herself upright, still gasping. "I'm sorry about," she went on, "snapping at you. This morning. I was upset."

"People get upset," observed the Bodyguard. She shifted her weight, but did not move on. Even Polijn could tell Aoyalasse had to have more to say.

"I was out in the halls that night . . . and saw Lynex coming out of . . . of Morquiesse's room. And it was pretty . . . obvious that's where she was from right after dinner. She was carrying most of her clothes. That's what made me so angry. I don't mind so much if he . . . takes up with Maiaciara, but Lynex is old. And she's a prude, so why'd he want her? She wouldn't . . ."

"Where were you going?" the Bodyguard inquired.

"Oh, I don't know," Aoyalasse snapped, annoyed at the break in her story. She glanced up. Polijn could not see the Bodyguard's face from here, but apparently it inspired memory. "Oh, yes, I do so. I was on my way to the laundry to see if things were ready for tomorrow . . . today. Anyway, I've been thinking now, and I wondered if it might not have something to do with the murder."

"We'll look into it," promised the Bodyguard, and strolled to the stairs.

Polijn pulled back into the little apartment and shut the door. The housekeeper was just laying plots. Polijn herself, after all, had seen the redhead coming out of another room, the state of her bundled clothes testifying to her business of the evening. And Lynex had been with Arberth most of the night, conferring on that wretched song.

Polijn frowned. The Bodyguard had only Arberth's word for that. What if she questioned Lynex and the housekeeper claimed to be where neither Arberth nor Aoyalasse put her? Lynex wouldn't know why the Bodyguard was asking and, not wanting Jontus to find out she was helping with the song, she might say anything. That wouldn't hurt Lynex, and Aoyalasse's lie was simply straight opportunism, to be dismissed. But Arberth's story would collapse, and the Bodyguard knew the jester didn't get along with Morquiesse.

Polijn had seen it all before. When there was a fuss in the Swamp, men with clubs and spears tranquilized it and afterward, maybe, they tried to find out what had caused it. Morquiesse's murder meant a fuss. The easiest way to end it would be to accuse someone expendable and kill him publicly, intricately, officially. Once things were calm, the real killer could be found, if anyone was still interested.

Should Lady Lynex fail to support Arberth's story, the jester would become very expendable. It was now official knowledge, if verification were needed, that he had been offended by the painter. Certainly, no one would object to his removal on aesthetic grounds. He had no friends in high places but the Chief Bodyguard, and she might prefer life without her awkward suitor.

Polijn wondered if she ought to tell the Bodyguard about Aoyalasse. It meant attracting attention. It meant possibly setting her word against that of a housekeeper who far outranked her. But life with Arberth taken up for the murder of Morquiesse would be worse.

She glanced at her mentor. What excuse could she offer for running after the Bodyguard?

Arberth had settled back into the chair, his elbows on his knees. As she studied him, his eyes came to her.

"Um," he said. "Polijn, could you, you know, go somewhere and do something for about an hour? I have to consider how best to impart complex information."

"I guess so," Polijn replied, reaching for the door. She paused. "Just a bit."

She slid back across the room and lifted her sandals from the pile of her clothes, but she had really gone back to check the bracelet. It was still there. She ran one finger along a coil of smoke. Such a lovely thing: what would she ever do with it?

She tossed the clothes back across it for safekeeping, and hurried from the room. The Bodyguard was out of sight, but could not have gotten far.

CHAPTER FOUR
Nimnestl

I

NIMNESTL stalked away from the little room. That lovestruck
jester was a pathetic creature, and the limp he was trying to hide
today made it worse. Still, he knew what he was talking about.
Bringing Merklin along would certainly help turn the trick. Too
bad he was so intent on being a bad poet; he might have made a
middling-to-fair assistant for Haeve.

The girl had been satisfyingly shocked and attentive. For all
her odd features and underfed body (or because of them), Polijn
was bright, quick-eyed. She was also a comparative newcomer to
the court, not yet known to be on the inside of any schemes. This
made her useful; she noticed things that veterans passed over. Not
that Nimnestl trusted her, particularly; there was just no specific
reason yet to distrust her.

Someone was panting on the stairs. Nimnestl came to a languid
halt. She doubted that anyone was in that much of a hurry to visit
Arberth. When she saw Aoyalasse nearly fall against the wall of
the landing, she waited for the accusation that had to be coming.
It came.

Really, between the time of the murder and its discovery,
the traffic outside Morquiesse's room must have been no end
distracting. Fifty-six people had already confided that they had
happened by just about that time and chanced to notice someone
just leaving the room. Eneste, for example, claimed to have spotted Fiera sneaking away at the same time, according to Fiera, that

Eneste had been coming through the door.

Nothing was surprising in the accusation of Lynex by one of her underlings, so Nimnestl doled out a standard promise to investigate, and started downstairs. But Aoyalasse, despite a desperate lack of wind, hurried to keep up with her.

"Wait!" she gasped, reaching down into her bodice. Nimnestl paused, ready for anything from a love charm to a dagger.

What she got was a heavy piece of brown paper, with a column of names written down the left side. The housekeeper waved this in one hand, using the other for support.

"Take it," said Aoyalasse, gripping the rail. "A death list."

Well, that was novel, anyhow. Nimnestl detached the page from the woman's fist—keeping an eye on the other fist as well—and glanced down the list: Torrix, Gensamar, Ferrapec, Ipojn, Garanem, Mitar, Patrak, Borodeneth, Morquiesse. "Whose was it?"

Aoyalasse had to swallow a little more air to answer. "The Neleandrai."

Nimnestl was surprised. Surely her suspicions hadn't leaked out already, that plots were being formed around them. She flipped the paper over, and saw the entwined N and L that symbolized the sect.

"Ah," she said, and started down the stairs again.

"Lynex," panted the housekeeper, stepping down with her. "She's the high priestess. It's not really a religion: it's a plot! From the south. Her father was from Turin. Did you know that? They're eliminating all the southerners who might know the background of the cult."

Nimnestl strode across the landing on the sixth floor before answering, "Yes, I see that 'south' is written in after some of the names."

"Right," said Aoyalasse, with a quick smile up into the Bodyguard's face. This made her trip on the first step of the next flight down.

Nimnestl let the housekeeper steady herself, watching out of one eye. Literacy was not growing evenly everywhere. Only a few in the Palace Royal could read and write. Most could spell out their first name or initial, and at least recognize a name they had seen before. So Aoyalasse probably couldn't tell that "Morquiesse" and all those repetitions of "south" were in a different handwriting. It wasn't even quite the same shade of ink. The last "south" was smudged.

And a smear of ink could be spied on the inside of the house-keeper's right hand.

Nimnestl studied the sheet without comment, moving on to the fifth floor. Aoyalasse wasn't going to leave as long as this meal ticket was in any doubt whatsoever.

"How do you know it's a death list?" she inquired, moving around to the next flight of stairs.

They were getting into the areas where there was a better chance of encountering someone, so Aoyalasse moved in closer before answering. "They tried to kill Borodeneth, didn't they? And Morquiesse is dead. Then there's Ostage: he was from the south, too, and probably found out. So suddenly it's all holiday with him, too."

"Mm-hmm." For all they wore hoods, most of the officers of the Neleandrai were known to the Regent. Lynex wasn't among them. She could be a recent convert, but no power in the Palace could have made her high priestess while that job's functions were handled jointly by Colonel Tusenga and Akoyn. Pity Aoyalasse didn't know that. Having already put Lynex at the scene of Morquiesse's murder, she could have produced this list, unaltered, as proof that Akoyn had engineered the attempt on Borodeneth, putting both of her immediate superiors on the spot.

But the paper had to mean something; no one wasted paper just to make a list of names. "Where did you get this?" Nimnestl demanded.

They were nearing another landing, so Aoyalasse pulled in close to whisper, "In Kirasov's garderobe, behind the tapestry of the death of Ghurach. He had it fastened to the underside of the cloth." She paused for another breath and went on, "He's their hatchet man, the one who really does the killing. Lynex was probably just going in to see that he followed orders."

Nimnestl was polite. "Kirasov's a devout Kiarian. I don't see him turning to the Neleandrai at this point."

"That's why Lynex was checking, see?" Aoyalasse was out of breath again; she had to suck in some more to go on. "Let me tell you something: you know how everyone who joins the Neleandrai has to sacrifice something of great value?"

Nimnestl nodded. That much was common knowledge.

"So," Aoyalasse went on, "you haven't seen his son around lately, have you?"

Something about the woman suddenly reminded Nimnestl of the skin of a boiled dumpling. "Anrichar?" she demanded, deliberately misunderstanding. "Of course not; he was banished. He went to Turin."

"No, no," exclaimed the intrigante. "The other one—what is his name—Argeleb! Kirasov gave him up, and they've kept him. Either they've already killed him or they're holding onto him until they're sure his dad's following orders."

"Oh?" said Nimnestl. "You aren't sure?"

"I don't know all the details," Aoyalasse said, throwing one hand up into the air. "That's why I brought you the list! I couldn't denounce my own cousin before the Council without being sure. But you, who get around so much and see so many things, can easily, with your experience and intelligence, verify the last few details. It doesn't really matter which of us does the denouncing, so long as the government is served, and your benevolent supervision can be continued."

This was a long speech for someone whose lungs were still not carrying a full load, but Nimnestl was impervious to praise. She did suppress a sudden impulse to roll up the list, push it into one of the woman's ears, and pull it out the other. Somewhere in this list there was something important. So far as Nimnestl knew, Aoyalasse had no major grudge against Kirasov. The part about where the paper had been found might be true. That, paired with the fact that Argeleb was missing, suggested a different story to the Bodyguard.

The list could come in handy if she wanted to build a case against the Neleandrai for Morquiesse's murder. And if she was right about Kirasov's son, the Treasury would back her.

She came to a full stop on the third floor landing and turned to the housekeeper. "Lady Aoyalasse, the government cannot thank you enough for your exhibition of civic responsibility in bringing this to our attention. You have rendered great service to your country thereby, showing yourself a most loyal and intelligent servitor of His Majesty."

Aoyalasse had been fighting for breath, and this unexpected accolade took it away again. Her mouth hung open, but even in her astonishment, she was able to see through the words and find something lacking.

"Yes," she said. "But you will remember who gave you the list, won't you, if it comes to anything? That is, when Lynex is caught?"

"Oh, I am bad at forgetting," Nimnestl promised. "And she who feeds the horse deserves to ride. We had better separate now, lest Lynex suspect. I am going this way."

She turned and headed for the second floor. Those card lessons for the King had suddenly acquired new urgency.

II

NIMNESTL stopped at the doorway of the Royal Library, and risked one cheek and one eye far enough to peer inside. Haeve was standing by one of the bookpresses, reading quietly to himself. The King, sitting on one of his own feet, was staring out through a window. Nimnestl turned away; she could come back when he wasn't so busy.

Halfway back down the corridor, a shadow dropped from the ceiling and fell to her shoulder. "All in place, Missy," Mardith told her. "All busy with the party. Palompec still gone."

Nimnestl nodded. She hadn't expected Mardith's tour would find any of the suspects doing something imprudent, but there was always a chance that his surveillance would provoke the guilty to indiscretion. "Very well," she said. "Let's go visit Kirasov."

"What name we go see Square-Chin?" the bird demanded. "You pick something up again while I work?"

"You can't be there every time I hear people talk," Nimnestl told him. "Watch and keep quiet. We have to play this game in the dark for a bit."

Kirasov's chambers were on the fourth floor of a more fashionable tower than Arberth's. A clump of off-duty Treasury guards knelt around a massive chess table in the front room playing some game that involved dice and a great deal of shouting. The stakes, piled to one side, were fancy coats for the evening's wear.

"Hey, you know Fiera?"

"Which one? I know lots of Fieras. Every tomcat in the kitchens knows a Fiera."

Nimnestl couldn't see her quarry, and pushed the door all the way open with one foot. "Where is Lord Kirasov?" she demanded.

One of Kirasov's nephews, Eneste, glanced up at her and drawled, "Now, how would someone as young and lowly and white as I know the answer to that?"

"Oh!" exclaimed Mardith. "Now soon you be dreaming on you back!"

Another exclamation came simultaneously from Kirasov's wife, Namansi, who had just stepped out of the bedroom. "Oh, no!" she cried, running forward. "Eneste, you mustn't! Milady, Lord Kirasov is in the back room. You won't mind what my sister's son says? In the back room, Milady."

"One in my position learns to disregard the remarks of the young, lowly, and drunk," Nimnestl replied. "Eneste's observation was completely just. I had not expected him to know anything." Eneste's companions waited until she had passed to start hooting approval. Eneste had been winning with the dice.

In the back room, Kirasov was trying on coats for the evening, as two attendants lifted them from his wardrobe. Right now, he was admiring himself in a long blue jacket with gold buttons and no buttonholes. It was the sort of fashion to be found in a nation where men fastened dirty shirts with diamond studs.

He turned when the door opened. Nimnestl could read in the face of the Head Treasury Guard that he was annoyed at being interrupted, that he was embarrassed at being caught admiring his finery, that he had an aversion to the Chief Bodyguard, and that his teeth hurt him. His teeth always hurt. In his youth, he had filed the front ones to sharp points, the better to bite off bits of an opponent in a fight. Now the points were decaying and breaking off. Kirasov had a tendency to be irritable.

Nimnestl had little liking, but some respect, for the Head Guard. She had no illusions about his honesty: any government official not on the take or on the make was on the way out. But he ran his own little kingdom efficiently and well, seeing that it served not only his purposes but those for which it was paid. Many of his underlings were Neleandrai, but Nimnestl felt he was unlikely to risk his position to assist this once-negligible cult, even assuming he would disregard his own religious convictions.

She made no attempt to be sociable. Kicking away a few egg-shells that were in her path, she sat in the only chair available. "I want to talk privately. Your attendants may go."

One of the men started for the door immediately. The other lingered for some sign of approval from Kirasov. "Scat!" hissed Mardith.

The man slammed the door, hurrying after his partner.

"Well?" demanded Kirasov. "What is it? I have work to do."

"So I saw," the Bodyguard told him. "I think you look good in blue, myself." She let him sputter for a moment and then went on, "Your son is still absent from the Court, and I want answers."

"Anrichar?" demanded the Guard. "You, of all people, should know where he is."

Nimnestl crossed her legs. "And I do not want funny answers; the Court has more than enough jesters. There is reason to believe that the disappearance of Argeleb is connected to plotting of a higher order." She saw the big jaw lift, and went on. "Some claim Morquiesse engineered it."

"What you say?" demanded Mardith.

Kirasov's opinion was similar. "Are you so short of suspects that you have to nail that killing to me?"

Nimnestl ignored both responses. "Another story has the Ykenai involved. I hope that you would know enough to report to the Council any trouble with the Brown Robes."

He frowned. "Of course. But why should they be in it?"

"You are listed among the 'snooper' pages in their books. Their usual method is to kill spies outright, but they may have changed their ways in all the upheaval. Or perhaps they thought you could be more useful to them in some other way, and took the boy to insure your cooperation."

The points of three bottom teeth showed against Kirasov's upper lip, but he said, "This is ridiculous. You have nothing but guesses to give me, and I have important things to do."

Nimnestl, unabashed, took a folded sheet from one sleeve. "Another guess," she said, "involves this list." She unfolded it and held it up.

"Ho ho!" cried Mardith.

Kirasov's chin shifted, and his eyes jerked toward the door to the little triangle between the back room and bedroom. It was a brief lapse, but Nimnestl had been watching for it. When his eyes came back to her, she was no longer lounging in the chair.

"What is it?" asked the guard. "I've never seen it before."

Nimnestl's voice was cold. "My sword is out, Kirasov, and you are on its point." She had drawn no weapon. "This list was found, where you put it, by one who will testify that it is yours. You are to see that these die, that the Neleandrai may feel pleased with themselves."

"Take your guesses and go!" ordered Kirasov. "I am a loyal son of Kiaria; I would never do any killing for those . . . those . . ."

Nimnestl put the paper away, and dropped confrontation from her voice. "I thought not. Then you won't mind if I take this to the Council. Several are there who will be able to verify that this is not your handwriting."

Those lower teeth pressed against Kirasov's upper lip again. He stared for a second, doing nothing more demanding than breathing hard through his nose. Nimnestl took a step toward the door.

"No, Milady!" he said, taking two steps in her direction.

She raised an eyebrow. "Please," he said.

"The list?" she inquired.

"Mine," he said. The teeth dug into his lip, and then he went on. "I was checking the night watch and found twenty men where there should have been two. Three wore hoods. They were discussing people they would have to eliminate for their plans to go through. I came back and wrote them down. I heard most of the names they said, but there were some I didn't."

"Kaftus and Nimnestl, perhaps," she suggested.

"No," he told her. "It isn't that kind of a plot. They aren't going to take over by killing the officials; they just want to eliminate people who might object when the King started appointing Neleandrai to high spots. How they meant to do that was a plot I didn't hear."

"You ears too choosy," noted Mardith.

Nimnestl nodded. "And they found out you knew about the lesser plot when you tried to sell them this list."

Kirasov stepped down hard on another stray eggshell, grinding it into the carpet. "That lintik Tusenga said he'd pay; he'd think of something I wanted, he said. Ar . . . geleb didn't come back up here that night. We didn't think anything of it until Tusenga brought up his clothes the next day. They'll hold him, says the scum, until they're finished eliminating everyone on the list, or until they're beyond any power of mine to reach them." He crushed another eggshell.

"Too bad," said Mardith. "Where they took him?"

"We've looked," Kirasov answered, hunting for another eggshell to smash.

"How many of your men know the Neleandrai are involved?" asked Nimnestl.

"Only Eneste and Namansi," the guard told her. "The rest know my boy's gone; that's all." He looked up. "Every one has sworn to slay whoever is holding him."

"Even those who are Neleandrai?" asked Nimnestl. Kirasov's head dropped.

"Do you really believe they still have Argeleb?" she went on. "And that they'll give him back?"

The man turned away. "I don't know. Tusenga won't see me now. He's 'busy' whenever I try to get to him."

"Lord Borodeneth is on this list," Nimnestl noted. "Don't you feel it's my duty to report this all to the Council, since the attack on him?"

Kirasov's fists came up. "Milady, you don't know the Neleandrai; they're godless. They don't care what they do to a boy. Wait, at least; wait a while longer. Just because Lord Borodeneth's name is on their list doesn't mean that attack was any of their business." The fists merged into one. "Please."

Nimnestl saw no reason to torment him further. "You have not been the best friend of the Regency," she told him, "but if this is the truth, we have a common enemy. I will have to deposit this with the Regent, but I think, if I explain the circumstances, he will take no official action."

Hope lit the guard's eyes. "But watch the way you walk," Mardith cautioned, breaking into his thanks.

On that coda, Nimnestl moved to the door. She found Eneste waiting just outside, just lounging there to keep anyone not in on the secrets from listening. Kirasov followed her out to the corridor.

"I cannot thank you . . ." he was saying, when a jagged, rising screech broke through the sentence.

"They're up!" cried the voice, from a door around the hall to their right. Nimnestl turned and saw the elderly Jintabh charging at them, head down and forward, sweeping a sword he didn't have at enemies only he could see.

Both Kirasov and the Bodyguard started toward him. Hearing their feet, he stopped, and gazed at a point above their heads. "Eruquiesse!" he hissed, letting his sword arm fall. "They're on the wall! We're lost!"

"Crazy man!" scolded Mardith, taking wing.

Kirasov moved between the old man and Nimnestl. "No, sir!" he declared. "The gate is still secure!"

Jintabh squinted at Kirasov, obviously trying to place him. "The gate? Hombis still holds it? You're sure, man?"

"Yes, sir," said Kirasov. "If we can just hold our position, we'll have them running by morning."

"Ah," said the general. He glanced down his limp arm. "I've lost my sword."

"Go in and rest, sir," said Kirasov, taking his other arm. "It's being sharpened for the next push. All those rebel skulls left it sadly blunted."

The old general turned, but looked back suddenly over one shoulder. "Who's that?" he demanded, seeing Nimnestl. "No Brown-nosers in our troop, are there?"

Kirasov threw the Bodyguard a glance of entreaty and then answered, "No, sir, not us. That's just Bulton, blacked up to slip through the lines under cover of night. He'll get word to the others of the morning's attack."

"Ah." Jintabh nodded. "Ah, yes. Good man, Bulton. Wish you speed."

"Thank you, sir," said Nimnestl. "I'll get through."

"Good man," snickered Mardith.

Kirasov ushered the general back to his room, and returned shortly to the corridor. "I hope that business did not offend you," he said. "About . . ."

"Certainly not." She watched his face as he turned back to look at the old man's door. Odd to see courtesy like that between an Army veteran and a Treasury man.

"The hero of Southgate," murmured Kirasov. "And now . . ." He looked to Nimnestl. "His wife's over at Ferrapec's, you understand, and asked us to watch for him. It isn't often she . . ."

"Yes, I know," Nimnestl replied. "I have work to do, myself." She turned away.

"Where now, Missy?" asked Mardith, as they started downstairs. "The King?"

"To the King," she agreed.

"We tell him now 'bout them Neleandrai," gloated the bird. "Hoo, I always know . . ."

"No, we're going to wait," Nimnestl replied. "Not a word to him, understand?"

"Got a plot, eh?" demanded her old retainer. "What?"

"Later, later," she answered. "More than birds have ears."

III

IT might be best, Nimnestl thought, to check in with the Regent on her way, just to find out if any new crises had come up since she'd spoken to him last. Mardith was willing until he observed that Kaftus was in conference with the ambassador from Lattin. "Quick nap," he muttered, fluttering out to a torch sconce in the hall. "Or long one, maybe."

Both men, though, seemed glad of an excuse to break off negotiations. After ceremonious leave-taking, Kaftus settled into a chair. "The Lattinese have leathern lungs," he said. "Once more you have proven your ability at timely rescue."

She handed him the supposed death list. "Anything to do with the current crisis?" he inquired.

"No," she told him. "Next week's crises, maybe. Probably."

He set the paper on a black table, which swallowed it. "Then it can wait," he said. "I was able to finish questioning Morquiesse before My Lord Talkatlength stepped in."

"What luck?" said Nimnestl, leaning over him.

"Little. The spell had to be rushed, and all he saw before his death was hazy anyway, because of the drug. He fired a crossbow, then his throat hurt, then there was a tug on his arms. That's all. There was more than one drug in the wine. Someone dropped by early on and added a little something."

"Not all truly brilliant ideas can be limited to one brain," she told him.

"Don't try to be feline," the necromancer replied. "I have another game for you to play. Have you considered a little matter we'll need to resolve before we choose a scapegoat?"

"This is?" she inquired.

He lifted an eyebrow at her. "Where are the arms?"

Nimnestl frowned. That was a nice question. Any story they made up would have to include what would seem, to the uninformed listener, to be the most interesting feature of the murder: why were those arms taken, and where? She could think of several answers, but it would be helpful to know that the arms would not inconveniently turn up at some later date, to refute the tale. Had Palompec taken the arms with him?

"You are silent," the Regent noted, "How lovely. How novel. You may add to that a consideration which may be part of another crisis for next week, or part of today's. I have peeked into the research on the cult of Su'in Wadu'in, the demon whose shrine the Ykenai may be using."

"Yes?" said the Bodyguard. "Are they in the habit of cutting off arms?"

"Alas, no," the Regent replied. "The cult has been considered extinct for so long, however, that recent information is hard to come by. The last centers of it were suppressed in Keastone and Turin seven centuries ago. In its final, refined form, men were sacrificed to the demon Su'in Wadu'in, who would toy with the sacrifice, then create a mindless double which would be at the command of the high priest, doing his bidding and bringing him tribute."

Nimnestl started to set her hand on a nearby table, looked at the table, and changed her mind. "How many of these doubles could this high priest command?"

Kaftus shrugged. "As many as he had sacrifices. That may be the presence I've been sensing; some high priest is exercising command over semi-dead bodies in the Palace Royal. It would be nice to have the rest of that missing page."

"One of the Brown Robes?" Nimnestl demanded. "Palompec? But he's not here."

"He was here yesterday," Kaftus pointed out, "and I didn't feel the power then. Either someone has just arrived or the demon has just now chosen a high priest. Su'in Wadu'in preferred tricksters, but rewarded courage as well. In fact, he often chose a brave devotee as head priest and then consumed the priest as a special, prolonged sacrifice. Fairly acute, for a demon of his station."

"Just your type," noted Nimnestl.

The Regent bowed his head. "If you'd care to see a book that has some excellent, if hypothetical, illustrations of what Su'in Wadu'in did with the sacrifices . . ."

"Exactly your type," answered Nimnestl, brushing imaginary dust from one arm. "How comes it that you aren't a devotee?"

"Too young, alas!" the necromancer replied. "Had I been born a few decades earlier, perhaps . . . but the cult was already fading during my formative years. It was never a very cost-effective religion; the demon kept eating up his own profits."

Nimnestl fastened burning eyes on the man's face. He did not seem to be seared. "So, if you want to pursue it," he went on, "your best bet is a southerner or someone from the Keastonian Empire. This all may have nothing to do with our current crisis, of course. In fact, I'd have said Morquiesse would have been the demon's choice for high priest, out of all the Brown Robes. Su'in Wadu'in may have appointed someone to avenge the death of the artist."

"A pity we can't depend on that," said the Bodyguard.

"I can see you now, explaining to the Council that we aren't investigating the murder because we're leaving it up to a demon whose worship was banned even in Rossacotta," said the Regent, with a gentle smile. "I wonder what they'd do to you. I shall save that for one of my better dreams. In the meantime . . ." His tone became brisk. "We need that scapegoat, before tomorrow's Council meeting. Even a tentative one will do. It takes only a day to start the rumor that we don't really want to find the culprit."

"I have several possibilities in mind," she said. She explained briefly about the Neleandrai and the list he had filed for later. "The King will go to Arberth now. If this works, several leaders of the cult become expendable."

"Not so expendable as the jester," sighed the Regent. "Shame no one would ever believe it. Well, we shall contrive. Where do you go after Arberth's lesson?"

Nimnestl grimaced. "Top of the Grand Tower."

"One tower to another," Kaftus noted. "Do you feel a lack of exercise? Are you bored?"

"It's one sure cure for boredom," Nimnestl sighed. "But the pixies may have seen something that has to do with the murder."

"Very likely," answered Kaftus, with a shrug. "But I feel nothing short of full-scale massacre would make an impression on their . . . if you'll pardon an exaggeration, brains."

"Perhaps," Nimnestl agreed, turning toward the door, "but I prefer them to your Su'in Wadu'in."

"He isn't mine," the necromancer called after her. "And well you know that the only difference between him and your pixies is that he's bigger."

Nimnestl considered a supernatural being of demonic strength and mystic power, with the mental capacity and inclinations of a pixy. She shuddered.

In the hall, a short, grey-haired man stood studying the warning on the door of the Regent's suite. The sight of Nimnestl seemed to bring him to a decision, and he strode forward. Nimnestl strode too, but toward the stairs.

She didn't even look at him as he puffed up alongside her. "The Council ratified the decision, Buran," she said.

"Ungsyr!" grunted the would-be nobleman. "That Council's nothing but a bottleneck. Why don't you get rid of it?"

"Bottles need necks," she said, and kept moving.

A metallic scrape behind her said Buran was thinking of avenging the insult. Nimnestl made a half-turn, and watched him as he let his sword slip back into place. Mardith snickered.

"We will speak of this later," he growled, marching away with a dignity to match his speed. Nimnestl saw no reason to answer.

Sounds of a minor skirmish came from the Royal Library. "It isn't that I mind so much piling the books so you can jump off," Haeve was saying. "I didn't write them, so they can't be much good. But if you make a sound and Nurse hears it . . ."

"Oh, she isn't even around," Merklin answered. "She won't know we aren't taking our nap."

"What if someone tells her?" inquired Nimnestl, strolling in. "I don't speak for myself, you understand, but the bird here is a known snitch."

Both boys hurried to greet her, the King hugging her as high as he could reach, a token of affection which not infrequently indicated an approaching request. Haeve also seemed to regard her appearance as something in the line of reinforcements.

"See if you can add any testimony on the beneficial effects of naps," he suggested.

"Oh, how can anyone take a nap this late in the day?" the King demanded, looking to the Bodyguard for backing.

"And with so many things going on," Merklin agreed.

"There may be no point to a nap," Haeve answered with asperity, "but there might be some novelty in doing what you're told. I am not in the habit of making threats to royalty, but I can always remind the Council that it tabled the discussion of your prospective marriage."

The King wrinkled his nose. "Why don't I just marry you?" he asked, looking up at Nimnestl.

Merklin choked off a laugh. Nimnestl sneered amiably. "You're not my type, kirro. I only take men with mustaches."

"Don't move," he ordered. "I'll run get one."

Haeve snorted. "If you really have nothing better to do," Nimnestl suggested, "you could come with me to see Arberth."

Four sets of eyes, curiosity rampant in each, turned on her. "Why?" the King demanded.

Nimnestl shrugged. "He said he has something to show you. And, besides, when was the last time you were on the top floor in any of the towers?"

The King thought about it. Visiting Arberth was obviously not his idea of a treat, but it was barely preferable to a nap. He glanced at Merklin, who tried to imitate Nimnestl's offhand shrug.

"All right," he said. "Let's go."

"And if Nurse turns up while you're away," Haeve called as the party set off, "what message shall I give her?"

"Teach her some geography," Merklin suggested.

"Sing her a song," said the King.

Mardith's suggestion was cruder. "By no means," said Nimnestl. "Just say we're off to the tower."

"And don't tell her which one?" said the Tutor.

"I knew there was a reason we chose him as Royal Tutor," the Bodyguard confided to the King. "He's so clever."

CHAPTER FIVE
Polijn

I

TIME was drawing in the people of the Palace Royal. Anyone who wasn't still studying the murder room or getting in the way of the preparations in the Great Hall was off getting ready for the evening's exhausting festivity. Polijn saw no one until she reached the second floor, and stopped for breath. Then someone saw her.

"You!"

Polijn spun to see the lean, extended figure of First Minister Isanten approach. His doughy face was stretched into some emotion Polijn could not immediately identify, beyond that it was unfriendly. She glanced around to be sure the First Minister was talking to her. Her scant breath grew scanter as she saw she was the only other person in the little corridor.

"Where's Arberth?"

By gathering all her strength, Polijn was able to execute a sketchy curtsy and answer, "In his room, My Lord. I just now left." Her heart sinking, she realized this must lead to an order to go back up all those stairs and fetch him. "If My Lord wishes to see . . ."

"Why should I wish to see anyone like him?" demanded the First Minister. "Idiot!" He came to within three steps of her and stopped. He glared. Polijn resisted the urge to take a step back, which would be an insult, and simply lowered her head.

"Where was he last night?"

Polijn risked a look up, didn't like it, and looked at the floor
again. "I couldn't say, My Lord. He says he was working on a
song."

"You're lying!" snarled the First Minister. There was another
gap in the conversation. Polijn didn't move.

"Working on a song? Where? Not anywhere near the gatehouse,
was he?"

"I . . . I don't believe so, My Lord," Polijn replied.

"Ostage was found there, you know," snapped the First Minister. "No one seems to care who did it."

"No, My Lord," answered Polijn.

"Oh, be off!" ordered the minister. He aimed a kick at her, but
because Polijn was already in motion, it came nowhere near her.
Polijn wondered if it would have been safer to stay and be kicked.
Isanten was a desperate man, not yet without influence. He dab-
bled in sorcery, as well. Gossip put him among the chief suspects
in the recent disappearances of this and that extra child.

Polijn rounded a corner and started for the main corridor. The
first person she saw was Iúnartar, the youngest member of the
King's Playmates, and a messenger for Lynex. Polijn had a faint
hope that those heavy responsibilities meant the girl would be too
busy to stop and talk.

Iúnartar was never that busy. She came to a complete stop on
seeing Polijn, and turned to join her. "Oh, Polijn!" she cried.
"How are you?"

Polijn nodded. She knew from experience she wouldn't have
time for an answer.

"Have you been up to Morquiesse's room?" Iúnartar went on
after a quick inflow of air between "How are you" and "Have you
been." "It's terrible, isn't it? What will we do without him? It's a
terrible, terrible crime! Do you think they'll find out who did it
soon? I hope they do because it's horrible, just horrible! There
was blood all over, on the walls and in his paints, and even some
on the ceiling. Oh, it was dreadful!"

Iúnartar hadn't used the proper word yet. She lived for this
sort of thing, and the term Polijn felt would have more faithfully
reflected her shock and horror was, "Isn't it deliciously exciting!"

"I had my hair redone for tonight," Iúnartar went on. "How
does it look?" Halting in her tracks, she posed, one finger against
the mouth that was like a little rosebud when, as occasionally
happened, she had it closed. Her hair was drawn back on her
head, save for two massive curls centered above her eyes.

Polijn nodded again. Iúnartar changed hairstyles twice a month, at least, and was exhilarated for one day by the new look. Thereafter she decided it was depressing and horrid and hateful. Useless to express an opinion, whichever mood she was in: Polijn just kept moving.

The Bodyguard was likely on this floor. Certainly everyone else seemed to be. No one paid much attention to Arberth's silent lackey as she dodged around people passing on business, theirs or someone else's. But Iúnartar was not designed to go unnoticed. Those who thought she was just darling smiled down on her, and those who had daughters of their own frowned.

Iúnartar might have been cast on the world when her mother died. Her parents had never been able to marry, and Colonel Tusenga was not required to take responsibility for his daughter. But daughters of all kinds had experienced a sudden surge in market value. Prospective queens of Rossacotta were being groomed everywhere; Tusenga felt the motherless girl was an asset.

She had huge round eyes and a busy, bouncy lower lip. She was being taught to hold the lip lopsided and the eyes half-closed, to be coyly come-hither. Her front teeth could best be described as assertive, but would probably pull back as her face matured. Above all else, she was possessed of a ferocious perkiness, a conviction that all would be well if we all just started talking about something else.

Iúnartar would, as Gloraida would have said, make it in this business.

Polijn was virtually the only one in the Palace Royal with the leisure to listen to her. For one who chattered every minute, Iúnartar heard a great deal which she could not repeat to adults, who either laughed at her or scolded. Polijn, who hardly ever said anything, made the perfect companion.

Polijn's patience was not boundless, but it was easier to let the monologue flow than try to cut it off. At the moment, Iúnartar was repeating the tale of Kielda, married a month ago. Not sure about all the more technical aspects of the business, she had reportedly ordered one of the servants raped in her room. She hadn't liked the looks of it.

"So Tegaram says now she'll have the baby through her ear," Iúnartar said, looking wise. "That's how it works when you conceive through the mouth."

She had to break off to jump over Protuse, who was sleeping against the wall, snoring the alcohol from his system. Polijn, who knew more about it, said, "I see. That's why there are so many fatheads in the hall."

Iúnartar's mouth rolled into a disapproving bow. Then she laughed. "Oh, you!" she said, and launched into a story about Bothin. As Maitena passed, she was interrupted again. The Third Housekeeper's retinue was moving ahead of Maitena, keeping her path clear, though the housekeeper was oblivious of this. Her tiny mouth, almost lipless despite a long space between it and the nose above, was pursed in disapproval.

"Father ordered me to march clear of her," Iúnartar whispered. "She's planning the evening campaign. So Bothin told Ostage, you know, the one who was killed, that the red rooster was taller. See?"

She dodged suddenly, under a low-hanging elbow. Polijn had to jump to one side to avoid being bumped, and caught someone in the side. Black and naked, it was one of Iranen's miserable underlings, also trying to stay clear of Maitena's company. The girl glanced at Polijn, quickly taking in both fighting weight and the quality of her clothes.

"Get away!" she ordered, giving Polijn a push backward.

Polijn accepted the shove without remark, in an abstracted way. The story of Bothin's rooster had somehow merged with Lorore's new earrings, and she was wondering if there was a connection beyond the fact that Iúnartar was telling both tales at once. She took a step to one side.

So did the larger girl. "Just keep out of my way!"

Polijn was still not particularly put out; and took another step aside. Why did everyone want to get in her way just when she was hurrying?

She did, however, notice the dark fist with white knuckles plunging in at her face. Reflex took over. Her first step was backward, out of the path of the fist. Her second went in. She took a handful of the girl's hair and flung it at the wall. The girl's head followed.

The third step in the automatic process should have been to shelter, but Iúnartar was in the way. "Serves her right," she said, surveying the fallen girl with satisfaction. "Who's she think she is?"

Polijn reached to push Iúnartar out of the way, and saw her mouth drop open. "Polijn!"

She turned and saw the larger girl rising. A knife glittered in her left hand. Polijn wondered where she'd been hiding that.

Bits of the pushing throng fell in behind Iúnartar to watch. Nothing else happened for a moment. The naked girl was deciding how to begin; Polijn was waiting to see what would happen. She knew better than to move in haste when a blade was pointed at her. She did gather her hair into one hand; long hair could be a disadvantage in this kind of fight.

One smallish boy, crawling from under the legs of the onlookers, jumped up at the dark girl's knife arm. He was much too small for that. Twisting loose, she attempted to reprimand him with her knee. No stranger to this civility, he rolled and took the blow on his hip.

Iúnartar turned to more practical action. "Lady Iranen!" she shrieked. "Milady! Lady Iranen!"

Perhaps prompted by this, the servant launched herself at Polijn. The knife skimmed across Polijn's shift, stomach-high. Polijn's free hand came down on the knife wrist, fingers gouging at the center. The other girl twisted the blade up, aiming for Polijn's armpit. Polijn bore down, her nails biting through the skin.

At the same time, she planted one sandal in the middle of a system of welts across the girl's right thigh, just above the knee. Both combatants went down. The knife bounced free.

The crowd roared approval. "Ten on the one from the Swamp!" someone shouted.

Polijn looked for the knife or an escape route, and found neither. Then she looked up. The crowd had hushed, and her opponent let go.

A line of black crossed her field of vision. Rising, she took four steps back, and hit a solid wall of onlookers. Two of these took hold of her in case Iranen wanted her.

But the Housekeeper's attention was all on her own servant. Striding to the prone girl, Iranen delivered a swift kick to the nearest limb. It couldn't have hurt much; Iranen was wearing soft brown-and-white ball slippers. The girl glared.

"Fausca," said her mistress. "Up now, and stop annoying your betters!"

Immediate flight would have been the best response. The girl was too upset for that. "Betters!" she shrieked, rising on one elbow. "Betters! I am the daughter of long kings! Oyamnki! Ungielke!"

This use of epithets was all but suicidal. The crowd drew back five feet in every direction. Best to keep out of Iranen's way now. Fists clamped trembling lips shut.

Iranen's response, however, was one of glee, "The bitch barks!" she cried, drawing back her whip. "Let us see now if she can howl!"

Fausca, with belated comprehension, realized she had missed a chance to save herself. If she ran now, she couldn't get away. If she could get away, she couldn't hide. She did the only thing she could do; she rolled so she wouldn't have to take the first stroke across the face.

The first stroke didn't fall. Iranen craned forward. So too did the crowd. The Housekeeper squatted to lift the knife from where it had been under the girl's body. Polijn, her stomach churning, recognized it as one from the special set laid out on the head table for festival occasions. There could be hardly any escape this side of the grave for the girl now.

Iranen's voice, though gentle, throbbed with ecstacy. "Stealing a knife, then?"

"I didn't!" cried the girl. "I found . . . I saw . . . I . . ." There really was nothing to say. She put her head down on the floor and sobbed.

"She didn't!" someone put in. Iúnartar stepped forward. "We found it," she said, pointing to a shrinking Polijn. "We found it and we were bringing it back. She attacked us because she thought we stole . . ."

Iranen turned slowly, rising, very slowly. The whip was poised. The girl on the floor raised her head.

"Fiejin!" came a fierce whisper. "You've been careless with the silver again! Good for you then that the girl is there to take your stripes!"

Iranen's chief assistant had turned on one of the large, squarish women who wore her apron backward. The hiss was meant to be heard, and Iranen had heard it.

"I have spoken to you before," she said. The crowd parted to let the whip swing down on Fiejin. The ruse was obvious to everyone except Iranen, but no one felt like attracting the housekeeper's attention by pointing this out. Even Fiejin made no protest. There was no sense appealing to Iranen's sense of justice, since she had none, and to attempt to divert her again from a victim would be to volunteer to take the victim's place.

The changes of focus had loosened the wall of spectators. Prying free, Polijn looked for a road out, and saw her erstwhile opponent still sprawled on the floor. Iranen had nearly stepped on the girl twice.

Hauling under one arm, Polijn pulled her upright, and both got her out of sight and created a path through the crowd by giving her a shove and a kick, the latter to satisfy frustration more than anything else. She had some hopes of escaping her companion in the crush, but on reaching open space, she found Iúnartar waiting.

"I bet she put that knife there herself," huffed the little girl, "so she could catch somebody stealing it and whip 'em."

The boy who had made the imprudent grab for the knife was there, too. "I wasn't much help," he said.

He hadn't been, but of course he'd tried. Polijn felt that deserved some notice. "My thanks," she said, looking not at him but at the hall. She had come out on the wrong side of the crowd; she was facing back the way she'd come. "I don't remember your name just now, but . . ."

"To be forgotten by you, dear rose," he broke in, "is an honor, for it proves you knew me once."

She looked at him then.

He was one of Morquiesse's myriad nephews, an underfed boy with a high forehead and dark, eager eyes. Timpre was his name, now that she thought about it; he was Morafor's son.

"I know not where you may be going, Nimariel," he went on, with a little bow, "but I hope I may offer my escort." He made this reference to the fabled beauty with his face perfectly straight; he was as good at it as Morquiesse. Iúnartar giggled.

Polijn thought of pushing past the both of them, but paused to reflect. The Bodyguard could be anywhere in the Palace Royal by now. If she did happen to find the woman, she'd have two onlookers all the way, one of whom was a hanger-on of Lynex.

"No, no," she said. "I forgot something. I have to go back. Later, sorry." She ran back toward the tower, knowing that she could outrun Iúnartar, at least, if she couldn't dodge the girl. Maybe if she explained it all to Arberth, she could get him to take action on his own behalf.

II

ARBERTH did not look up as she came in. She doubted he'd noticed; he was flipping his cards onto the bed. Polijn liked to watch him manipulate the cards; it was something he was good at, for a change. Fingers too long or too short to ever strike the right chords became quick and nimble. His face lost its tightness, and his smile was smaller but more cheerful.

Once she had caught her breath, she walked up beside him. "Um," she said. He did not look up.

"The Bodyguard asked a lot of questions," she said.

"Yes," he replied, studying a seven. "She asked me to help her." He slid an eight from the bottom of the deck and set it down. "This might be complicated. You may wish to go somewhere, you know, and do something while I think."

Polijn licked her lips and tried again. "Do you think she suspects you of killing the painter?"

The jester snorted. "Don't be silly. That was just a pretext for coming to consult with me; she can't have the palace gossips spreading the word round. They'd say . . ." He sighed. "And, oh, how I wish they were right."

His assistant took breath for another attempt when the door swung open. "No," said His Most Reverenced Majesty, Conan III, "I didn't see him before, never. He had one ear cut off, and he was kind of stumbling around, with some flowers." A bird flew into the room, past his head.

"Probably drunk," said the Bodyguard, ushering the King and Merklin in ahead of her.

Arberth rose, hastily shuffling all the cards together. "Didn't know you meant to bring him so soon," he murmured, as Nimnestl came over to him.

Without waiting for her reply, he turned and executed a deep, rickety bow. "Your Majesty's Chief Bodyguard, the Lady Nimnestl, tells me Your Majesty wishes to learn some of the facts of life."

Merklin yawned. The King was too polite to do so, but stared silently up at the jester. Polijn knew what both were thinking: what could they possibly learn from Arberth?

The jester cleared his throat. "W-well, if Your Majesty would deign to have a seat, I'll see what I can do." He dropped his deck onto the bed. "We can discuss it over cards."

The King glanced at Merklin, who shrugged. The boys walked around to the seat Arberth had vacated. "We can play cards for a while, anyway," whispered Merklin.

"Maybe win all his money," the King whispered back. He took the chair. Merklin sat on the floor.

Arberth, meanwhile, had draped his best tunic over a broken wooden chest, and pulled it forward. "My Lady?" he said, with another bow.

The Bodyguard shook her head. "I must be about my duties, if Your Majesty will permit. Mardith, keep an eye on things." She turned for the door.

The bird, which had come to rest on Arberth's manuscript case, flew up like an arrow, just missing Polijn's head. "What, by my loneself? Oh, no, Missy! Where you go?"

"Out," said the Bodyguard, brushing him aside. "Stay and watch."

"I go also, too," insisted the bird.

"What are you going to do?" demanded the King, standing up. Merklin stood up with him.

"We ain't about to forgot how you go off to forest that time, and leave us back behind while you take the bandit," Mardith scolded. "What name you think we just sit where you put us?"

"You wouldn't be interested," the Bodyguard replied.

"That," said Mardith, "is nothing else but a lie."

The King mustered his dignity to add, "Remember, I just came back from holding a Royal Inquiry. I'm not just some kind of sort-of King now. I order you to tell me where you're going."

"Why, certainly, Your Majesty, if you're that interested," said the Bodyguard, with an obvious effort. "I'm going to make the rounds and see that the bodyguards on duty for dinner are in their places."

The King looked interested, but Merklin reached over to pull at his tunic. "My legs are tired already," whispered the boy. "Let's play cards."

The King sat down again, saying, "Very well. You may go." Mardith, deprived of allies, fluttered over to the counter to mope.

Polijn saw her chance to chat with the Bodyguard. Being busy with the King, the woman could in no way have interviewed Lynex yet. She started to follow the tall woman out.

"Polijn," called Arberth. She looked back.

"You're of an age to know these things," the jester said. He indicated a seat on the floor, next to Merklin.

Her teeth on her lower lip, Polijn dragged over to the bed. As people, Merklin and the King were just small boys, nuisances. As objects, however, they were repositories of power and even reverence. Polijn made her best curtsy, trying to smile just enough and not too much. The boys pulled over to one side. For her part, Polijn sat as far from the royal presence as she could, and kept her shoulder and back toward the boys.

Arberth, oblivious to this byplay, had evened up the deck. "Would Your Majesty care to cut the cards?"

His Majesty knew enough to answer, "Of course." He divided the stack.

Arberth took the cards and distributed them. The King arranged his.

"I . . ." His Majesty began.

"One moment," said Arberth. A hand was raised with authority; the nervousness had dropped from him. "Does Your Majesty have the two of stars, the three of eyes, the three of coins, the four of stars, and the six of axes?"

The King stared at his hand and then at the jester. "Yes."

"Here, I'd better do it over," Arberth said. "Something's wrong."

The boys tossed in their hands, sighing. The jester was so eternally clumsy.

Arberth shuffled and dealt again. Polijn tried to keep an eye on him, but those hands flipped out like fish at feeding time in the royal pond. The King picked up his new hand, and the royal eyebrows rose.

"Oh, yes," Arberth agreed. "Much better hand. The queen of axes, the queen of stars, the queen of eyes, the princess of eyes, and a blue jester."

The King gasped and threw down his cards. "You're cheating!"

"How could he?" demanded Merklin.

The King frowned, and flipped over his cards. "Yes, how did you? Or do you see through them?"

It was almost inconceivable to Polijn that the boy should have lived so long and yet know so little about touching up the deck. The only explanation she could think of was that he had, after all, led a very sheltered life.

Arberth gathered the cards and passed them from one hand to the other. "Creative dealing," he said, "has two missions. One is to make sure of what you get, and the other is to know what your opponent gets. The Chief Bodyguard, in her wisdom, felt Your Majesty ought to see how this is done, so as to be on guard."

"Oh, yes," said the King. "I don't want anyone cheating me."

"You just want to know so you can cheat someone else," whispered Merklin. The King elbowed him, and he giggled. Polijn hated the sound of giggling.

"How does it work?" the King went on.

Arberth raised his eyebrows. "I just showed you."

"Do it again," the King ordered. "Slower."

He did. The boys tried it. He showed them other tricks, one after another: how to render the cut irrelevant, how to shuffle, how to deal from the bottom or middle, how to hold the cards. The boys were fascinated as they tried and failed, or sometimes succeeded, in making the complex moves. Even Mardith settled on the bed to watch.

"That one I never see before," said the bird, as Arberth showed how to mark the cards with a little wax under one fingernail. "You ever run out the town in a hurry, man?"

Emotion flickered and was gone. "Twice," said the jester. "That's three times too many."

Polijn watched all of this in silence, storing information, and practicing with the cards when Arberth told her to. She was less interested in the tricks, really, than in the cards. They were old, worn, but they had been expensive enough once: the blues and greens and golds told her that. In the Swamp, what decks she had ever seen were cheap red and black decks.

She noticed, on glancing up from her cards, that although the King and Merklin were just as interested as they had been, Arberth was growing discontented. There was disappointment in his face; something was lacking.

"Another method," he said, taking a strip of grey-white cloth from his pocket, "is to get a small pin, or tack, and hide it in a bandage. This way, if someone brings in a fresh deck, you can mark them to your liking as the game goes on."

Merklin drew a sudden breath and glanced at the King. Arberth leaned back, smiling again. "Yes," he said. "I've known men who always seem to hurt a finger or thumb just before a game. Clumsy, or unlucky, or something, I suppose. But they always seemed to be lucky at the cards."

"Some . . . someone who knew how to do that," said Merklin, "they could win every time, couldn't they?"

The King brightened. The royal right thumb, which had slipped into his mouth, came out again, a little chewed.

"Well, they could," said Arberth. "But they wouldn't. Not if they were smart."

"Why not?" demanded the King.

"It's an old saying," the jester told him. "When you steal, leave a little for the heroes, and you'll prosper." He shrugged. "At any rate, if you win ALL the time, your opponent gets suspicious. When you lose now and then, you lull them into thinking it's just the luck of the draw."

"Well, that's a pretty lesson, I must say!" someone exclaimed, slamming the door open.

Polijn flattened her back against the counter and then turned to look. Entering the room was a round, greyed woman with a long mouth and no tact. Iúnartar said her name was Ponjen, but everyone in the Palace Royal called her Nurse.

"How is it, sir," Nurse demanded, charging forward, "that I find you in this nasty, drafty place without your scarf and without a single guard?"

The Bodyguard's big black familiar reared. "You have maybe a sip o' the nip, old noisemaker?" the bird demanded. "What name you say 'thout a single guard?"

Nurse ignored this and pressed on. Polijn dove across the bed and out of her way.

"But, Nurse," the King protested, "I . . . I . . . etchmpf!"

He had made a noble effort to suppress the ill-timed sneeze, but the game was up. Nurse allowed no nonsense about royal dignity.

Taking Merklin by the hair, she marched him away, declaiming on the responsibility of monarchs. The King ran alongside, exclaiming that he was perfectly all right; why didn't she listen to him?

The door fell shut behind the group. "Fhoo!" exclaimed Arberth. He glanced at his cards. "Anyway, it works best if you wear the punch on this side, and mark the cards around in this area, so the other players are less likely to find the marks."

"Oh," said Polijn, looking him over.

"Thought I'd finish the lesson," he said, shuffling the cards together. "They won't ever, you know, need to do this for their living. You might."

He got up and set the cards next to the manuscript case. "Where were we when all this started?" He flipped through the sheets and found his makeshift bandage in the way. Prying that off and tossing it on the bed, he checked the songs again. "Were we going to do 'The Ram Forlorn,' do you recall?"

"Um, no," she said. "We were going with 'The Tattered Sails.' Because of the bits about Morquiesse. You remember."

"Ah," he said. He sorted through the manuscripts some more.

Polijn took up the bandage, to throw it off the bed. It was not cloth, as she had thought, but twisted paper. It was odd for anyone, particularly Arberth, to waste paper that way. She unrolled it, and smoothed it on her knee.

A line of words along the top read, "To His Highness, Prince Ar," and broke off at the tear.

She looked over at the jester, fingering the heavy creased paper.

III

POLIJN was restless. She didn't know where she wanted to be or what she wanted to do except that where she was and what she was doing were not even close. She was moving, in a slow, general way, back to Arberth's room, but there was nothing up there that appealed to her at the moment. The flights of stairs made up part of it, but not all.

The noon meal had been hurried, sparse. Iranen stalked among the tables, whipping a cane down among the plates from time to time to encourage speed. Few people besides servants were dining; the others were saving their stomachs for the evening's spread. "But those of us with hard labor ahead need nourishment," Arberth had pointed out.

Afterward, the jester went off "to confer with someone." Just about everyone else had to assemble for last-minute instructions from Forokell, Maitena, Lynex, or Iranen. So Polijn was left to her own devices, of which she had none, it seemed, just now.

She could try to find the Chief Bodyguard again. It wasn't so urgent—if the woman meant to arrest Arberth, she would hardly have had him teaching the King—but it would pass time until the big show. She paused at the foot of the tower stairs.

Something, or things, squealed and sped past her left ear, one wingtip disarranging her hair. Whatever it was dropped something down the front of Polijn's tunic. She snatched it out quickly, feeling fur, but it was only a scrap of some old garment. It had been burned along one edge. She tucked it away, in case she thought of a use for it later.

She decided to go up to Arberth's room anyway, and maybe sleep away some of the time. She wouldn't be safe, exactly, from intrusion, but she'd be out of the way. With a sigh, she set a foot on the bottom step, and gazed up at all the rest.

At the sound of voices, she glanced back. Lord Arlmorin, the ambassador from Braut, was passing with Maiaciara. Polijn never tired of watching Maiaciara; she wondered what it must be like to have a complexion that perfect, that exquisitely dimpled. Not, she thought, that the dimples made much impact. They were too predictable. You looked at Maiaciara and told yourself, "Of course when this woman smiles, she will have one irresistible dimple here and another there." So when she smiled and the dimples appeared, they were hardly worthy of notice.

Arlmorin was a big, square, restless man with red hair that seemed to reflect some inner blaze. "Ah, Milady," he said, as they turned the corner, "could you try to live without me for a few moments?"

Maiaciara tittered assent, and moved on in the direction from which Polijn had come. Arlmorin came about and aimed at the stairs. Polijn stepped back to let him pass.

"Wait!" ordered the ambassador. Polijn set her back against the wall at the third step, and looked around to see if he meant her. Even from the third step, she had to look up into his face. He stopped at the bottom, one hand hooked into his gilded belt, the other around an ornamental walking stick.

"Is Arberth anywhere around here?" he demanded.

"No, My Lord," she replied, with a curtsy made awkward by the stairs.

"Ah." The ambassador nodded. "When you see him, tell him I would like to chat with him. It's about the possibility of using his influence to procure a few of the late Morquiesse's works for Braut." He leaned forward to add, in confidential tones, "The Maiaciara portrait, perhaps: you'll know the one."

"Yes, My Lord." She doubted Nimnestl's amiability toward the minstrel extended that far. What did the ambassador really want?

"Ah, the twists and tangles of an ambassador's life," he sighed. "Paintings by Morquiesse, and Rossacottan plums: I am become a merchant again. You may go, child. Remember the message."

"Yes, My Lord," she said again, with another curtsy. The man smiled and moved on.

In her hurry to depart, she nearly fell over the next step. Why, she wondered, was she so lintik nervous? Fear was nothing novel in her life, but she usually had some idea what there was to fear.

And she was so short of breath. She paused at the third-floor landing to catch her wind. When she saw Maitena and attendant retinue sweeping along the stairs, she squeezed against the wall until they had gone by, trying to keep out of the harried House-keeper's sight.

Allowing for a temper traditional in cooks, Maitena was not habitually hazardous. She neither schemed nor grubbed; she just held on with both hands to what she had. Any time she wanted it, she could easily force her way up to Second or even First Chief Housekeeper.

Rumors passed on by Iúnartar claimed that Maitena wasn't so efficient as once she had been. Two of her daughters had died in the Ykenai investigation, and their father, the man Maitena had hoped to marry once his father was out of the way, had died of a less political fever at about the same time. Her hopes now were based on a marriage to Colonel Tusenga, once his father died. Iúnartar hoped the colonel could do better; Maitena drank too much.

An unmarried woman, and her children, had no rights under Rossacottan law. Since Rossacottan law was, at best, iffy, one could ignore it and hope to override such technicalities through personal influence. But most women liked to make doubly sure. This was complicated by the fact that only oldest sons of a family were allowed to marry before the death of their father. One of the oldest of Rossacottan laws, its original intent had been to avert blood feuds among grandchildren/heirs of wealthy landowners. The obvious drawback was that there could be only so many oldest sons to go around. And the new push for civilization had lengthened lifespans; old men were not dying as soon as they had in previous generations.

So the court was being entertained by the spectacle of women of fifty or sixty, possessed of considerable wealth and position, courting untasseled young men in hopes of attaching them once they reached marriageable age. (Sixteen was the absolute mini-mum for marriage, and then only by Royal Charter.) One could try to catch a young son and hope his father would be short-lived, but there was no financial advantage in that. Widowers of mature age, of course, were constantly beset with propositions.

"I had rather be a purse of silver in the Swamp," ran one of Laisida's songs, "than a bachelor in the Palace Royal."

Polijn watched the last of the Housekeeper's suite move past. That almost looked like Chordasp, skulking in the rear; he always carried a bag like that. Silly: why would anyone import a thug, no matter how experienced, from the Swamp when so many were available right here?

She had turned for the stairs when a heavy hand dropped onto her left shoulder. Had the hand not been so heavy, she'd have jumped to the fourth floor in one leap. Instead, she was spun around to look up into the drawn face of First Minister Isanten.

"Where is Arberth, drudge?"

Polijn swallowed. "I don't . . ."

He let go of her and backed away, his face a mask of naked fear. "You! You're supposed to be . . ." Polijn crouched to run, but threw one glance back to whatever he was seeing.

All she saw was Arberth, coming down the stairs. "Something?" he inquired, as she stared.

"Lord Isanten was just . . ." The First Minister was no longer on the landing. "Was just here, asking about you."

Arberth gave his head a little shake. "Funny. Ardita just told me the same thing. What could he want with me, I wonder."

"And Lord Arlmorin wants a word with you," she added. "Something about getting him some of Morquiesse's paintings."

"But I don't have any," said the jester, frowning. "Except you, of course, and in all due courtesy I can still not say you're some of his better work."

"I think he wanted you to use your influence with the Bodyguard," she suggested.

"Hmmm," he replied. "Have you seen Measthyr?"

Why does everyone think I'm keeping track? thought Polijn crossly. "Not lately."

"He wanted to squeeze in another voice lesson before tonight," Arberth said. "Well, all right. I'll see if I can find him, or Arlmorin, or Isanten, or anyone else who wants me. My, but I'm in demand, of a sudden."

He hurried past her, stumbling a little at the second step. Polijn moved up. With any luck, everyone was congregating on the lower floors, and she could reach her destination without further interruption. She didn't feel particularly safe out here, even when, panting, she reached the sixth-floor landing.

Between apprehension and the climb, her heart was pumping mercilessly. It did not quicken perceptibly when she saw the crumpled body crammed under the other stairs. Bodies were always being hidden there.

This one lacked a head, but she knew its weapons. A blade was still ready in each hand, bloodied, of course. Though he tired easily and would have been especially winded after climbing this far, Measthyr was still a swordsman. In his heyday, it was said, he could keep himself dry in a storm with just his flatchet, fending off raindrops with the point.

Polijn stepped over for a closer look. Measthyr himself was no longer there: this was just a random collection of limbs attached to a crumpled bag. The head was off to one side, its eyes looking out at nothing.

Polijn peered at the hair, which was not quite the right color. Stepping to one side to peek into the face, she understood why.

This was Ostage's head.

She turned and hurried up the last flight of stairs. She raised no outcry; she knew better. Reaching her floor, she ran off the landing to the hall, and up to Arberth's door. A sound of quiet footsteps seemed to follow.

Something lying at the door made her pull back. A little clump of dandelions, the symbol of the royal house of Rossacotta, had been dropped there. Polijn had not been raised in a flower-conscious neighborhood, but she did know dandelions. For a second, her fears were pushed back by a wave of nostalgia. She lifted the flowers and brushed them with one finger.

Then she threw them back down. Even the dandelions in the Palace Royal were different. They had blood on them.

A voice cried, "No no no no." There was no other sound around her. The footsteps had stopped, had perhaps not existed save in her imagination.

Self-preservation battled in her mind with one of the most perilous of basic human needs: the need to know what's going on. She turned and stepped back out onto the landing.

The double staircase stopped at the seventh level, but above it was the crown of the tower, a guard post. A small wooden roof above her could be removed in time of war, so that weapons could be hauled straight up the stairwell to the top of the tower. It had not occurred to Polijn, looking up at the towers from ground level, but the ceiling above the stairs was flat, while the tower roof was conical. So there must be a room up there.

She found the rungs set in the wall. Moving up, not without many a glance below, she wondered if she were allowed on the crown of the tower, and, if not, what the penalty was.

A hand on the trap door produced nothing. She climbed another rung, which brought her back and shoulders against the wood. She shoved up as gently and quietly as she could, considering that her whole weight was involved.

The door started to fall back. Grabbing the ring in the center of the wood, she kept it from falling, though the weight of the door pulled her up and onto the walkway. No one shouted at her as she got up from her knees. The walkway was empty, as far as she could see. Where was the guard? There was always a guard; the shift seemed to change every night just as Polijn was falling asleep.

She left the trap door open in case a quick exit was called for. The high stones around her were streaked and pitted, rough and cold to the touch. The sky was grey and the wind that whipped her hair across her face smelled of oncoming rain. A few heads, still attached to spikes after two generations, rattled as the odd breeze hit them.

Polijn moved aimlessly around the circle until a muffled whimper and a flicker of light hit her senses. Both seemed to have come from within the peaked roof. She eased forward and set her face against the wood, her eye to a crack.

Two men stood in the small chamber. The guard on duty was lighting his pipe from a small brazier at his side. The other man, who wore the badge of a Treasury guard, was fastening a strip of bloody cloth around a mouth already filled with wadded fabric.

The small boy, naked, with knees and wrists bound up against his chest, tried to complain. His eyes were wide with terror.

"Bored, kitling?" demanded the Treasury guard. He put both hands on the rope that circled the boy's waist, and hauled his captive into the air. The boy tried to kick, but his legs were too securely bound. He dangled head down.

"Let's see what we can find to keep you busy." The guard brought a knee up under the boy's shins. This released one hand so he could reach into the shadows among the slanted beams of the roof.

"Ba-a-a-ad place to keep an arrow," he noted, drawing a long, dark shaft from the container fastened there. "It might rot. It might be overrun with spiders. And sometimes they fall down, and people try to steal them to cut themselves loose. Now, where

CHAPTER SIX
Nimnestl

I

NIMNESTL considered, down all the stairs from the jester's apartment, whether Mardith should be fried or boiled. Both seemed so pleasant. She did not slow down on reaching the right floor, but marched across to the Grand Tower. This was the shortest of the Palace Royal's high points, and it took her very little time to reach the peak. She paused as the wind hit her. Surveying the broad, flat roof, she found a blur of multicolored objects clustering around the fish pond. Steeling herself, she pushed forward into the wind. The wind was not what made her grit her teeth.

The air was cold, and smelled of rain. The harness-pull in the courtyard, designed mainly to coax some of the crowd outside, would no doubt have to be cancelled. But the pixies didn't seem to notice. None wore any more in the way of clothing than mushroom skirts and socks of cat fur. Some had high, winged helmets. These fell off when they used their own wings, but that apparently didn't matter.

The colony had settled here for the winter (she hoped that was all) and had proclaimed Chicken-and-Dumplings, who had found the place, their queen. Nimnestl couldn't make out the monarch in the blur, but followed the sound of voices to a small wicker house next to the pond. Outside, a chorus of males had linked arms and was singing, "Oh, we'll all have chicken and dumplings when she comes."

"Get away!" shrieked a bundle of fury, zipping from the house. "We're makin' plans! Whoop!"

She had seen Nimnestl. "Hi there," said the queen, flying up to the level of the big woman's eyes.

Chicken-and-Dumplings was a perfectly formed orangish-pinkish woman somewhat shorter than Nimnestl's foot was long (though Nimnestl had unfortunately never gotten in a kick to be sure). She had short, dark hair and dark, wicked eyes, and she was never, never still.

"We're making plans for our Great Springtime Glee," she confided, fluttering back toward Nimnestl's ears. "It's for the first day of Spring."

"Um," said the Bodyguard, repressing the instinct to bat away anything that buzzed near her ears. "On my calendar, that's today."

"Well, hoop-tee-doo for your calendar," answered the queen. "Break your calendar in half and it'd still be just as dumb."

The other pixies considered this sally a masterful example of royal wit and spiralled into the sky, a cloud of giggles. Nimnestl let remark and pixies pass her by. She did not know what a Great Springtime Glee was, but it sounded ominous. "You will warn me about this Glee, won't you?" she asked Chicken-and-Dumplings. "Before?"

"Warn you?" demanded Chicken-and-Dumplings. "We'll invite you!" She fluttered down to straddle the roof of her wicker palace. "Can you get any fairer than that?"

Nimnestl's reply, whatever it was, was cut off by two pixies screaming, "Mine! Mine! Mine!" They carried a strip of yellow cloth between them. One flew to Nimnestl's left and one to her right before she could duck, plastering the bounty across her face.

"Excuse these lumps," said Chicken-and-Dumplings, as the Bodyguard spluttered. "That hasn't been quite distributed yet. Someone threw it away last night." She watched impassively as Nimnestl threw it down, and then added, "Puh-robably because of the bloodstains." Nimnestl picked it up again.

The roughly torn fragment was of heavy fabric, slathered with small but hideous green lilies. Nimnestl looked from it to the pixy queen and, careful to show no interest at all, anywhere in her voice, said, "Oh? I don't see any bloodstains. Where's the rest?"

The queen threw a hand across her forehead and cried, "Alas! I had to cut it up to satisfy THEIR childish longing for pretty things."

"Fox pong," remarked one of her subjects. "I notice you kept all the fur collar for your own self."

"Except the burned part," added another, who was trying to ease the fragment from Nimnestl's hand.

Nimnestl's hand didn't ease. "Burned part?"

The queen turned completely upside-down and dragged a sodden but very rich strip of brown fur from her chimney. "Somebody was trying to burn this neat thing," she said, kicking away acquisitive underlings. "Can you imagine?"

Nimnestl could imagine. Bloodstains could have come from many places, but to burn this valuable a garment at night was encouraging. If the burning had occurred before the murder was discovered, it could even be useful.

"Horrible," she agreed. "What wastrel did such a thing? And when?"

"Oh, who brought that in?" the queen asked herself, "Oh! It was good Sir Tell-You-No-Lies. I knighted him for noble service."

"Oh, is that what you call it?" squealed a pixy nearby.

As the queen took off in hot pursuit, a red male with green spots fluttered before Nimnestl's eyes. "I'm Sir Tell-You-No-Lies," he said. "Ask me some questions."

"Very well," said Nimnestl. "Who was burning this fine garment?"

The pixy scratched his thigh thoughtfully. "It was a big person in a hood," he said. "Or a person in a big hood."

Chicken-and-Dumplings whizzed to a landing on Nimnestl's shoulder. "You didn't peek to see?"

The pixies gasped. "Well," said Tell-You-No-Lies, drawing his head down, "I was busy. I was playing leapfrog."

Despite some nods of approval from her kingdom, the queen snapped, "That's no excuse. I revoke your sirness and I intend to lock you in a box with hungry mosquitoes."

"Oh, yeah?" demanded Tell-You-No-Lies. "I'll lock you in a box with . . . with horny toads!"

The queen snorted. "How many? Better be at least five."

Nimnestl felt, somewhere behind her wisdom teeth, that the pixies were not going to be of much further help. Folding the cloth, she said, "Thank you, Your Highness. I'll keep this."

Chicken-and-Dumplings relinquished her hold in Tell-You-No-Lies's hair and spun back to address the Bodyguard. "You will, will you? What've you got to trade for it?"

Nimnestl rolled up the bit of fur, too. "How about a bowl of punch for your own at the festival tonight?"

"Pooh-pooh-kachoo," answered the queen, wrinkling her nose and knees in disdain. "I can steal all the punch I want to drink, from the big people."

But by now Nimnestl had some experience with pixies, and answered, with equal scorn, "Not for drinking: for swimming in, and washing off the frosting from when you sit on the cakes."

Exclamations of awe rose from the crowd, which had not expected such insight from a big person. But the queen hesitated, so Nimnestl added, "A big bowl, big enough for all your subjects."

The queen's head tipped to one side, and her tiny mouth puckered. "With a slide and little boats," Nimnestl went on.

The whole colony was screaming approval. Some members performed indelicate somersaults. The queen flew closer to the Bodyguard and, with a fierce glare, declared, "And marsh-mallows!"

II

AS Nimnestl started down the spiral stairs, a dark shadow spiralled up to meet her. "What you do?" it demanded, settling onto the shoulder recently vacated by the queen of the pixies.

"I thought," Nimnestl snapped, "I left you with Arberth."

"Oh yes," the bird replied. "He playing cards. Very pretty cards, Missy. You know half are one color and half are one other color? Yes, yes, very interesting, Missy. Best job, no scare, I have in long days. You do something more dull, I think, like kill somebody?"

"Mardith," said the Bodyguard.

"Just to ask," he replied, polishing his beak on his shoulder. "I need no fun after all that whee with cards."

"You're so sweet when you're trying to make a point," she told him, taking another step down. "Why aren't you with the King?"

The bird shifted his feet. "Nurse find us. Want to hear more?"

"Not really." Something was eventually going to have to be done about Nurse. She was always scolding: at table, for example, she made the King take more if he took a little, less if he took a lot, regardless of what was being served. The King, having figured this out, took liberal helpings of turnips and passed up the meringue shells, knowing he would have his choices reversed.

Still, it must affect him to be constantly belittled. The trouble was that Nurse was not only devoted to her charge (though it didn't cause her to rate his judgement or intelligence very high)

127

but also filled the positions of Chamberlain, Keeper of the Royal
Wardrobe, and many lesser posts that it would be a regal pain to
fill if she vacated them.

Mardith had never learned to distiniguish his Missy's contemplative moods from being ignored. He pecked at her nearest ear
and redemanded, "What you do?"

She swung up one hand and pushed him away. "If you really
wanted to talk to the pixies, you can go up now. They're playing
Hide the Feather, no hands."

"I love pixies," Mardith confided. "That's a lie. What name
you want to talk by them?"

"I'm sure I don't . . ." Below them, on the third-floor landing,
a small figure crossed a swatch of light. The shadow carried a
bundle just the length of a man's arm, and scuttled through the
light as if afraid of it.

Nimnestl jumped the last steps to the next landing, took a long
stride forward, and let her right hand fall on the figure's neck.

"What you do?" Mardith said again, this time to the captive.

Nimnestl pulled back into the light, and found that she had a
grip on the Second Assistant to the Second Chief Housekeeper.
The woman had a big saw from Gilraën, raised to strike at her
captor.

"Oh," she said, recognizing Nimnestl. "Oh, it's you." Aoyalasse
lowered the saw. "I was bringing this to you. I found it in Lynex's
chambers. I was afraid for a minute you were Dorvyan. She had
this hidden in . . ."

"Walking backward, were you?" Nimnestl broke in.

"Eh?"

Nimnestl let go of the housekeeper and started across the
landing for the next flight of stairs. "Lynex's room is this way."

"Well, I had to sneak around the other direction," Aoyalasse
snapped. "Someone might see me. This could be the telling piece
of evidence."

Mardith snorted. Nimnestl recalled that Aoyalasse had not made
it to the murder room until later, and couldn't know the saw that cut
off her lover's arms had already been well seen and handled before
it disappeared. Every saw from Gilraën had disappeared from the
Palace Royal within an hour, as servants cached them away to take
into town, to be sold as "the very saw used in this heinous and
bloody deed." This saw could be that very saw, or another. There
was even a chance that the little pale woman could have really
found it in Lynex's chambers. It still meant nothing.

Nimnestl, who had an inner core of fair play that Rossacottan living could not remove, was on the verge of advising the house-keeper to go easy on finding so many clues when the railing under her hand swayed. Nimnestl let go and slid back, expecting a trap. Aoyalasse had been running to keep up, and bounced to the side barely in time to avoid a collision.

"Down there!" cried Mardith.

Aoyalasse looked first. "It's a big bag," she noted. "Some-body's loot."

The railing that generally sufficed to keep anyone from acci-dentally dropping five stories down the stairwell was wavering from the strain of a rope that had been tied to it so that someone's cache would be out of sight. Nimnestl and Aoyalasse put their hands to the rope at the same time.

The Bodyguard's hopes were immediately dashed. The bag was too heavy to contain a pair of arms. At any rate, it could not have been hanging there very long; someone would surely have noticed anything that big.

Aoyalasse gave up even trying to pull along with the larger woman, and watched the rising of the prize. "A little more. The light from the next landing's going to be on it in . . . Ah!"

"Ah?" echoed Mardith, who had been watching to make sure no one was coming at them from the corridor.

"What?" demanded Nimnestl. She had nothing to brace against but the railing, and she knew that wouldn't hold her weight. She could only keep pulling, or let go, and wanted to know which was better.

Aoyalasse's face, turned up toward her, was paler than ever before. "Let it drop," she whispered. "It . . . it's too terrible!"

"No do, Missy!" called Mardith. "No!"

Nimnestl would not have let go at this point, for any reward, but suddenly the weight at the end of the rope lightened. Maintaining her grip, she eased to the railing and peered down the stairwell.

She had assumed someone on the next landing down was haul-ing in the booty. But the booty, with a little help, was pulling itself in. Lynex, her pearls and the rope around her neck, blood and fury all over her face, was clinging to the arms of an assistant, and climbing over the rail.

Nimnestl turned to Aoyalasse. "You would have liked to see me drop her, wouldn't you?"

Aoyalasse fiddled with the handle of the saw. "Is . . . is she still alive?"

"Go away. Take your saw with you."

"But . . ." said the housekeeper, raising the saw.

"You go!" spat Mardith.

Aoyalasse sniffed at him, started down the stairs, thought better of it, and started up instead. Nimnestl continued down.

Hanging someone in a stairwell had worked in the past, but never in the Grand Tower, where there was so much traffic. This was an incredibly clumsy attempt, almost designed to fail. In fact, Nimnestl would have assumed it had been designed to fail, had there not been another equally clumsy attempt in the past twenty-four hours.

Finding five people in Borodeneth's bed, the assailant, instead of killing all five, had struck a light. This had roused the Chief Tax Collector. When Borodeneth raised the alarm, the assassin had chosen to attack rather than flee, and lunged across the bodies of the other sleepers. This hampered him so much that Borodeneth, among others, had been able to exchange blows with him. He was wounded several times, in the leg or in the stomach, but was able to get away, successfully concealing his identity. That was the only thing that had gone right.

As Aoyalasse had pointed out, there was considerable mortality among those in the Palace who had connections to the south. And most of it had exhibited a clumsiness not generally associated with the experts in the Palace Royal: why take time to cut off Ostage's head or Morquiesse's arms? If this was all to be attributed to the Neleandrai, to work against them was redundant. They were plotting against themselves.

She shook her head. Why should the members of a conspiracy clever enough to woo the King the way they did become suddenly chuckleheaded when it came to their killing? Who else did she know who was so inept?

"Make way!" ordered Mardith, as they reached the throng comforting Lynex. "Make way!"

Nimnestl forced her way forward, but felt a tug on her sleeve. The coded tug was one she had taught her own men.

She turned to find Culghi. "Ma'am," he said, up close to her so he could say it low, "we've just found that swordsman, Measthyr. He's had his head knocked off and Ostage's put in its place."

His superior turned away, making no response. Behind the blank face, she was thinking, "Well, the festivities have started early."

CHAPTER SEVEN
Polijn

I

"AH, what do you want to do that for?" Polijn heard the guard with the pipe say.

"Teach him to try to get away," growled the Treasury guard. Polijn put her eye back up to the peephole. The guard on duty was Alohien. He was new to the Palace, only staying until a murder or two blew over in Gilraën.

"I heard what his old man called you this morning," Alohien told the other man.

"Nobody puts a name like that on me," snarled the Treasury guard. "Slugged me, too. Besides, the brat probably knows all the old man's secrets: where the keys are, what code words to use, things like that. We could really pile it up."

Alohien shrugged. "I could wait. Their Worships say we'll be piling it up soon enough."

"Not soon enough for me," answered the other man. "You got a splinter? Between that and a little fire, we could start piling right now."

"Could be," said Alohien, looking around on the floor. "Be better later, though, in the laundry room."

"Laundry room?" demanded his partner. "What do you mean, the laundry room?"

"You've seen it, haven't you?" answered Alohien, pointing one thumb toward the floor. "Thick walls, plenty of fire and water to use. Nobody'll be near there during the party, if he yells."

"He can yell if he wants to," the guard replied. "Nobody around for four levels down; they're all inside, drinking, while we got duty."

"Heavy duty," noted Alohien, puffing on his pipe.

Polijn felt a dangerous idea growing. She tried to shake it from her head, and failed. Well, if it worked, Kirasov would be financially grateful; that was one thing. She took a deep breath of cold air, and sneezed.

"What was that?" demanded Alohien. "Oh, put the sprat down."

Polijn stepped back. She had meant to cough a little later, once she had this all set up in her mind. But perhaps if she'd thought about it, she'd have given up the whole idea.

A section of the wooden cone fell back and a man stepped into the wind. As Polijn had hoped, it was Alohien, the guard.

"Hey!" he shouted, in his best intimidate-the-trespasser voice. "What are you doing?"

Polijn set her hands on her hips and cocked her head to one side. "Trying to make a little money. Got any?"

"How make money?" Alohien demanded.

"Oh," she replied, putting her right thumb to her upper lip, "I'm just sure you can think of something!"

"Hmmm-hmmm," said Alohien, looking her up and down. "Well . . ."

"I can stay longer," Polijn said, "if it's warm." She took a step toward the door.

"Get back!" ordered Alohien. "We're busy in there."

Polijn leered at him. "That's what I saw. Trying to make him tell something, huh? Why don't you try the Wooden File?"

"You got one, I suppose?" sneered Alohien.

"It isn't what you got; it's what you do," Polijn informed him. "Don't tell me you never heard of it."

"I never heard of it," Alohien replied. "Get inside. I guess I can't let you leave now anyway." He stepped back to let her pass in front of him.

Polijn swaggered through the door and stepped down. "What's that?" the Treasury guard demanded.

The light admitted by the door was cut off as Alohien pulled the wooden hatch back behind him. "What's the Wooden File?" he asked his partner.

"Maybe it's that jester's new song," answered the guard. "That's his wiper you've got there."

"That so?" said Alohien. "Maybe you're right. You're from the Swamp, aren't you?"

"Sure scare," said Polijn, with three scornful strides toward the center of the chamber. Brrrr, but that man had loglike arms.

"This should be something to watch," said Alohien. "I've heard of the Swamp."

The guard nodded. "Maybe we'll learn something new." Polijn hoped so. She also hoped they wouldn't learn it before she was ready.

"Well, you want to open a mouth," she said, "your best bet's a Wooden File. That arrow'll do." Alohien handed her the arrow while the other man, at Polijn's gesture, flipped the boy over, bringing one knee up under his back to present Polijn with the broadest target area.

She had been right about the ropes: just the way Ronar used to do it. The right arm and leg were tied in one bundle, the left arm and leg in another. Cinch ropes were used to pull the loops tight. The cinch ropes were then tightened by being tied to a loop around the boy's waist. Cutting the main cinch ropes should loosen the rest just enough, she prayed, for the boy to pull his limbs free.

"Here's how you go on," she went on. "Let me see." She stepped to one side and inserted an index finger between the boy's calf and thigh, just behind the knee. He turned his head to watch as she slid the arrow into this opening; the point was bare inches from his nose.

Gently at first, and then faster, she slid the arrow back and forth, just barely keeping the arrowhead from pulling back into the flesh. As the friction started to burn him, the boy struggled, trying to straighten his legs. His eyes watered, then widened as he saw the arrowhead nicking a knot at each stroke. The eyes rolled to Polijn.

She mouthed the words. She didn't even breathe them. "Kick when I say go."

She hoped he caught it. She hoped he had the strength. He couldn't have been tied up all the time he was missing, surely?

This knot couldn't be cut any farther; it might break before she had the second one cut. She slid the arrow out. The shaft was hot.

"Like that?" she inquired. "I can do the same on the other side."

She tapped the arrowhead lightly on the boy's shin and moved around to the other side. She paused to see if the Treasury guard, watching her, had noticed anything overripe about the knot.

All he said was, "What are you waiting for?"

She put out a hand, palm down. "Just let him think about it. The water's hotter when you dip back in." She looked to the boy. "No? Well, just lift your thumbs when you want to tell the news."

Polijn slid the arrow in under the other knee and started to saw again. The boy was in obvious pain, but doing his best to hold up. She thought suddenly of a dozen worse things she could do; he could really be made to squeal. This was a real novelty, having someone at her mercy. Usually she was the one inside the ropes.

Still, there was business to be taken care of, and she'd best keep her mind on it. There was no Vielfrass around to make magic if she failed this one.

When the second knot was frayed enough, she took the arrow out. "So?" demanded Alohien.

"So?" she repeated. "We're working up to it. There's more things, some of them more tender, you can get an arrow between. Now he knows what the Wooden File feels like there, maybe he won't like to think about it between his toes, or under his arms, or someplace else. You take these now." She reached between the bundled legs. "I hear they're kind of delicate." Swinging the arrow above her head, she went on, "This gives a man get up and GO."

The arrow came down hard, on a hand angled to keep anyone from noticing that what the arrow hit was her own index finger. The boy jerked and kicked in the same motion. Polijn knew one knot, at least, had given away when his foot hit her in the chest.

II

"HEY!" Polijn shouted. "What?"

She fell back, swinging her arms so wildly and unerringly that the arrow sank deep in the arm of the guard. That worthy dropped Argeleb and, bellowing incoherent obscenities, tried to grab the arrow and Polijn at the same time.

Polijn, at least, was not within grabbing distance. Catching up one of the ropes that flailed free from Argeleb's waist, she was on her way out. The captive, still attached to the rope, started to complain, but Polijn hurled him against the door. Once outside, she bounced him ahead of her and kicked the wooden cone segment shut on Alohien's face and fingers.

This would not slow him much, so she dove after Argeleb. She slid, rather than climbed, along the row of rungs, and landed straddling her fellow fugitive's neck.

"Move, you dolt!" she ordered, dropping over him to the floor.

"Eeyagh!" shouted a voice above them. Alohien had tripped headlong on the open trap door. With a wrenching twist he had managed to fall across the opening, rather than through it. His knife landed between Argeleb and Polijn. The boy made a grab for it, but Polijn hauled him away. They had to get under cover.

Arberth was not in his room. Polijn couldn't decide whether that was good or not. She pushed Argeleb down on the bed and hunted up her oldest shift for him. It was a little damp, for cold rain was starting to slip in past the tattered tapestry, but it would do.

"I had it all figured out," the boy panted.

Polijn turned to see him spitting the last pieces of the gag from his mouth. "I could have gotten away," he went on, "but that filthy . . ."

"Hush!" she hissed. She tossed him the shift and started to hunt for her old sandals.

"I had it all figured out," the boy began again. "I was only tied by one leg, then, and I got the arrow . . ."

Where were her brains? Those were the sandals Morquiesse had snatched off her feet the night she was dancing to Arberth's rendition of "Fur Gloves." He'd tossed them in the fire, getting a bigger laugh than the song. Well, running was quicker in bare feet. She kicked off her own sandals.

"But Syncrats came in and caught me," Argeleb was saying.

Polijn heard footsteps and dove across the bed. She shoved one hand under Argeleb and forced him up into her other hand, which was flat against his lips. Though he bit down, she did not let go until the footsteps had moved on.

"That hurt," he complained, rubbing his mouth. "If you do that again, I shall scream."

"Do and you shall be kicked," she told him. "Put this on. Get up."

Argeleb seemed neither surprised nor offended. "What are you doing?" he asked, as his head came up through the shift.

"Quiet!" she ordered. The blanket was too thin. She tossed it to one side and rolled up the mattress instead. "They'll search the rooms next."

"How?" he demanded. "Won't the people complain?"

Polijn did not bother to answer. The boy had grown up on a much lower floor. "This way!" She hauled the rolled mattress under one arm. "And be quiet or I'll throw you down the stairwell."

Argeleb put a cold hand in her free one. "You saved me," he said.

Polijn expelled a long breath, and walked to the door. She both pushed and pulled on the door, letting it open only a tiny space with each move. The hall was dark. Many of the torches had been taken to supplement the illumination in the Great Dining Hall. Others, untended, had gone out. Or the men had taken them.

"I don't know which room," called one. "I'll check these."

Pushing the door wide, Polijn darted for the stairway opening farther from the voice. A sound of booted feet came louder, faster. Polijn glanced back, and, realizing that now her pursuer had seen her face and could be sure, sped up.

At the fourth stair, she dropped Argeleb's hand and turned. There was no time to arrange the mattress; she could only throw it down and hope it didn't unroll too soon. Then she ran up to Argeleb, who had gone on two steps and turned to look, slapped him on the arm, and ran ahead with him.

Alohien reached the top of the stairs before they completed the first turn. "Syncrats!" he shouted, descending after them.

He got as far as that fourth step, where his foot hit a roll of cloth and straw instead of the expected stone. The mattress flattened and spread under his weight, and the momentum unwound it. Before he could hit the stairs, however, the guard twisted, throwing himself away and to his left to save himself. Instead, he succeeded in throwing himself over the railing.

Argeleb, Polijn, and the remaining guard watched as he disappeared into the gloom. He struck, with a crack and a groan, at least two floors down. There were no further sounds. No one cried out at the sudden appearance of a body. Polijn wondered if the whole tower was deserted by now.

Syncrats was the first to recover. Stepping carefully (he could not see what his companion had fallen on), he bellowed, "You brats are carrion! Right now!"

Polijn was willing to believe that, but she wanted to give him a run for it, at least. Catching hold of her old blue shift, she spun Argeleb around. Their mad dash continued without pause until they reached the next landing. There, Polijn risked one glance back.

The Treasury guard was perched on the low concrete wall into which the railing was set. He was poising for a jump, and she felt it was not meant for a suicide. He intended to take a shortcut to the landing. If he made it, there would be nowhere to run.

She drew a long, shuddering, and not very helpful breath; and moved on. Argeleb didn't follow.

"I want to see this," he said, slapping away her hand.

Polijn got hold of him anyway and pulled. This had taken too long. After a clang and four heavy footfalls, a hand landed in her hair.

This jerked her head back so that she was staring up into the bared teeth of the Treasury guard. He had his injured arm wrapped around Argeleb's neck. The boy was kicking. The man didn't appear to notice.

"After I finish with you," he said, shaking Polijn by the hair, "you'll never lift your chin out of your lap again."

Polijn pulled away and down, willing to relinquish some hair in the name of survival. Syncrats let go of the hair, but got a hand wrapped in her tunic instead.

Polijn was also willing to lose the tunic, but was frozen in the act of tearing free by the apparition forming out of the shadows. A long, pale face coalesced and hung for a second above Syncrats's head. Then both face and Syncrats vanished into a dark corner of the landing.

As the Treasury guard struggled with whatever had him, his captives turned away, electing by silent mutual consent not to wait and find out what it was.

III

THERE was no sound of pursuit. This did not mean there was no pursuit. Polijn and Argeleb continued their headlong flight along old stairs worn slick. The only noises around them came from occasional thunder outside. One yowl when Argeleb kicked a straying cat did not slow them down.

But when Polijn saw straw, she came to a full stop, throwing out one arm. This caught Argeleb in the stomach and would have knocked the wind out of him if he'd had any left.

"What's . . ." he gasped, "that . . . for?"

Polijn pointed to the straw, and a scrap of cloth nearby. "What?" demanded the boy. "Oh. The matt . . ."

Polijn had enough breath by now to shush him. She looked at the stairwell, and followed the line of the railing where it reflected the light from one dim torch. There was a long gap between two of the stone uprights, as if the railing were missing or displaced.

Argeleb, following her eyes, looked up at her. "Maybe he just . . . bounced there," the boy panted, "and went on down."

Polijn nodded, and backed toward the wall without taking her eyes off the railing. Argeleb, going back up one step, flattened himself next to her. She took a step down, and he followed. She paused, listening for any sounds of breathing besides hers and the boy's. She wasn't sure whether she heard any.

Polijn took another step down, and glanced up for the ceiling. It didn't seem to be there. Somewhere above her, she knew, was

139

the underside of the stairs, but the shadow just seemed to reach up forever. In the rumble of another cascade of thunder, she risked another step down.

More straw, but not an entire mattressful; maybe Argeleb was right. Alohien and the mattress might have just stopped briefly here. The guard probably grabbed for the railing or the concrete base and hit the stone upright instead. Trying to kick the mattress from his feet, he could have shaken it to pieces.

But who could say he hadn't tried again and succeeded on the next attempt? They advanced another step. Polijn leaned forward just a little to consider the landing they would soon reach. That was the place for an ambush. Alohien could wait there in a shadow until they moved down past him. Then he could grab them from behind.

"See anything?" whispered Argeleb.

Polijn rolled her left hand into a fist and brought it down on the boy's shoulder. "Sorry," he said.

She thumped him again and moved down another step.

The doors that opened onto the landing would be great places to hide. She watched them particularly. Who had rooms on this floor? What floor was this?

Her head jerked back, pulled up by a sound of soft, padding footsteps. The footsteps stopped. Or had she really heard them?

Polijn shook her head. She wasn't used to all this silence; her mind was just creating sounds to fill the void. She moved down some more.

Dark, motionless tapestries cushioned the walls down on the landing. They looked flat, but in this light she could only guess. What if someone did jump out? Her legs were tired. She didn't think she could run much farther downstairs, and she knew she couldn't run back up. Diving over the stairwell would be easier.

There were only two steps to go when Polijn's nerve snapped. "Come on!" she whispered. Taking Argeleb's outstretched hand, she dashed down and across the open space. Anyone who jumped at them now could easily miss and go right over the edge. If Alohien was injured, they might even be able to outdistance him before he realized what they were up to.

Nobody showed any interest as the children covered the space between one flight of steps and the next.

Polijn kept up that speed for the first few stairs of the next flight, but discovered in time the large, dark mass spread across the sixth. Not about to be caught in her own trap, she jerked to a halt. Argeleb, unable to see the obstacle, banged into her from behind. They slid down, coming to rest with Argeleb on top of Polijn and Polijn's feet on the lump of cloth.

They rolled back toward the stairwell as the lump moaned and moved. Feeling the stone of a support column at her back, Polijn got a hand on Argeleb before he could slide under the railing. The lump tried to sit up.

The scarred, battered face turned up at them was not Alohien's. But Polijn recognized it. In this environment, she took a second to put a name to the face. She had dismissed the notion that Chordasp could be in the Palace Royal before. There was no mistaking that grim, ugly face, though.

The burly thug swore feebly and raised one hand. It fell back; he studied it. Polijn had seen Chordasp covered in blood before, but it was obvious this time that most of the blood was his.

"Lintik under him," growled the crumpled man. "Heard him singing; thought I had him. Ahglish! Didn't think he hit me so deep."

"Who hit you?" demanded Argeleb, before Polijn could stop him.

Chordasp's eyes rolled up. "You won't go telling tales of me, back in the Swamp," he growled. "Little stemmed squirrel. Wouldn't sit there laughing at me if I got my breath. Lintik under him, shuptit singer. A singer! Pfah!"

The thug shuddered and turned to his left, looking up the stairs. "Who's there?" he demanded.

Argeleb and Polijn followed his gaze. Shadow stretched uninterrupted behind them except where rare torches sent down flickering fans of light. At one of these points, the shadow had developed a lump in the shape of a man. No feature was visible beyond a glowing amulet showing two winged pears in its center.

Polijn shoved back against the column and, getting her feet beneath her, plummeted down the stairs. Argeleb followed. They did not pause until they had put another flight of stairs and another landing between themselves and the dying thug.

Now Polijn could see they were nearing the main floor. More torches here: they shone on more decorative carvings and thicker tapestries. That made for more hiding places. Long shadows wavered in the not one but three doors that led from the landing into the hall that proceeded to the Great Hall.

Polijn's plan was to get Argeleb to Kirasov, or Arberth, or the Bodyguard: anyone who could be trusted with him. Once free of her hazardous prize, she would be safer. But which way to go? The central door led to the main access corridor, where there was more light, and also more chance of meeting people. If there was more than Alohien and Syncrats to this plot, someone could reclaim Argeleb before she found someone she could trust. A stab or two in passing would be all that was necessary.

She came to a stop behind a gilded replica of a rearing horse. Pulling Argeleb close enough that her lips brushed his right ear, she whispered, "You look up the left-hand hall and I'll check the right. Then come back here."

Argeleb glanced back up the stairs. He was shaking and, now that Polijn got a look at him in the light, alarmingly pale. But he panted, "Okay," and hurried away.

Polijn was as quick as the need for silence allowed. Keeping her eyes shifting from the stairs to the central corridor to the corridor she was scouting, she slid into the shelter of a thick, soft wall hanging. She peeked around this, glanced back, and then stepped up into the little hall.

No one was there but Yslemucherys, with his back to her. He was tuning a small hand harp, probably planning to try his luck with a new song in honor of the King. Polijn stepped quickly backward. From all she had heard, Yslemucherys was probably not included in anybody's conspiracy. This was probably the corridor to take.

"Ah!" cried someone on the landing. Polijn turned and saw no one.

From her right came sounds of a scuffle, and then the slap of a hand against bare flesh.

"Ow!" cried Argeleb.

IV

POLIJN eased up and around the corner. She peeked into the central corridor. There was a distant babble of voices, but no sign of Argeleb.

"Where have you been, you little catamite?" hissed the voice.

"I . . . I . . ." stammered the boy. "Upstairs. But . . ."

"Quiet!" ordered the voice. There was another slap.

Polijn shot across the corridor opening and ducked behind a heavy table on the other side.

"If you know what's good for you," said the voice, louder now, "you'll tell everyone the Neleandrai had you!"

"But, Lady Aoyalasse," protested Argeleb, "they . . . ow!"

"And that I saved you," the voice went on. "Do you hear me?"

"Don't do that!" wailed the boy. "I was . . ."

Polijn put her head into the third corridor. The little house-keeper had a dagger out, with a blade as wide as her hand. The fist holding it came down hard on Argeleb's head.

"Maybe a few days in a laundry tub will give you the idea," Aoyalasse said as the boy crumpled. She knelt, wrapping one hand in the cloth of the shift the boy wore, and looked around for witnesses.

Polijn did not move back fast enough. "Arung!" swore the housekeeper. "Two of the brats!"

It wasn't too late to run, and Polijn gave it a try, but the housekeeper was spry enough to jump over the boy's body. Polijn was halfway down the central corridor when an arm swung around her windpipe. The dagger came in at her face. Polijn caught the wrist, but the housekeeper's muscles were too thick for Polijn's fingers to force a release.

"You won't make a liar out of me," muttered the housekeeper, dragging her captive backward. "I'm losing ground already."

Polijn took no further action until the housekeeper stepped back onto Argeleb and stumbled. Then she twisted and bit down hard on the bare wrist that was within reach.

Aoyalasse swore again and kneed Polijn in the back. Without letting go, she moved her arm up over Polijn's chin and forced a velvet-covered arm into her captive's mouth.

"Bite on that," she ordered. Polijn obeyed, but the thick cloth, heavy with silver decorations, gave her no satisfaction.

"It'll be easier to kill the both of you," muttered Aoyalasse. "Found you both too late, the victims of Neleandrai plots." Just as Polijn thought of kicking, the housekeeper brought one leg around to pinion her ankles.

"The boy might be of further use alive, though," she murmured.

Polijn could not get a handhold in the dress behind her, and she wasn't in position to try to reach up backward at the woman's face. She could see the worn spots in the dagger's wooden hilt as it came at her again. Involuntarily, she raised her hands toward the blade.

Twisting, she heard muffled footsteps. Fearing them less now than the dagger, she wrenched her head to the side. Silver thread cut into her lips, but she gained space enough to yell.

Aoyalasse pulled Polijn's head back into place. In the same moment, the shadows at the staircase end of the corridor parted and a face stood out from them with alarming clarity.

"Skbook?" it said.

Aoyalasse stepped back. "Party games, children?" the Vielfrass went on. He came forward, and a cloaked body appeared under the head.

"Mmm. Yes," said the housekeeper. "It's just a little joke."

Polijn raised her hands in entreaty. The Vielfrass blinked, and went on, "If it was a joke, it's over. Let the little bit go." He took one more step forward.

"Get back!" the housekeeper ordered. "And mind your own business, or I'll cut you!"

"With what, my dear?" asked the sorcerer, holding up a dagger.

Aoyalasse stared at the dagger and then at her own empty right hand. Polijn was surprised to see he'd left the fingers.

"Give that back!" demanded the housekeeper.

The Vielfrass tossed it into the air and caught it on the tip of one finger. "I will," he promised, studying the balance. "How soon you let the kidling go will determine where I put it."

The housekeeper reached for another knife, but Polijn jerked to one side, nearly knocking her off her feet. "Lintik!" cried Aoyalasse.

She threw Polijn to the floor. "I'll remember this!"

"You will, to be sure," the Vielfrass agreed, still looking at the knife rather than the woman. He took a silver toothpick from inside his cloak and balanced that on top.

Polijn sat up and saw Aoyalasse backing away. But one foot was hooked inside the armhole of the tunic Argeleb wore.

"Oh, you can leave that, too," said the Vielfrass, not taking his eyes from the dagger. "You couldn't carry anything that size anyway, not with your hip so sore."

The housekeeper looked up at him, her mouth open to ask a question. Then she closed her mouth, raised her skirt, and started to run. Only when she had rounded the corner at the end of the corridor did the Vielfrass move. He dropped the knife, straight down at Polijn's outstretched legs. Polijn pulled away, but the knife fell forward instead of down. It vanished in the corridor's shadows.

Polijn stood up. Somewhere way down the hall, Aoyalasse howled. There was the sound of a body hitting the floor.

The Vielfrass wasn't interested. He swept past Polijn and, taking the boy by one wrist and one ankle, tossed him up like a cloak. "Let's take this back to its rightful owner."

Polijn rubbed her bruised mouth. "She wanted him to say the Neleandrai had him. He was up under the roof in this tower. Alohien . . ."

"That's pretty funny," said the Vielfrass, adjusting the boy's legs. "Pity you aren't omniscient, or you'd appreciate just how funny it is. Come." He turned away.

Annoyance rattled at Polijn's nerves. All her running and hiding would be lost in the Vielfrass's sudden appearance, carrying the boy. Absurd to think he'd give her any credit, not that anyone would ask him how he'd found the boy. The Vielfrass could apparently do anything, be anywhere . . .

She ran to catch up with him. "Say, have you been following me around?"

The sorcerer stopped in his tracks. The head turned slowly back, eyebrows raised. "Here, here!" he implored. "Let's not give ourselves airs. I have better things to do. In fact, I have better things to follow around."

While noting that he had not exactly admitted or denied the crime, Polijn recognized the truth of the statement. "Well, somebody's been following me," she muttered.

"Some secret admirer, I have no doubt," he replied. "Better get used to it. You're of an age for the long hunt."

Before Polijn could comment, a shimmering flash of flesh sped through the air. "Oh, you ARE here!" it cried. "Let joy and rapture be unconfined!"

"My sentiments precisely," the Vielfrass replied. "Yet so few agree with us. Tell me at once what infernal devilment you've been perpetrating."

"Say please!" ordered the pixy queen, settling demurely on Argeleb's uppermost thigh.

"Your Majesty," said the sorcerer, "let's have a drink."

"That's close enough," said the pixy, fluttering into the air again. "But we'll have to find some place that serves pixies."

"A place that isn't fussy, eh?" said the Vielfrass, rubbing his chin. "How about the Gilded Fly?"

"The Gilded Fly?" shrieked the pixy. "The Gilded Fly? You know what they did to me once at the Gilded Fly?"

"No, but I'm dying to find out," the sorcerer replied. "Tell me about it immediately. I didn't know they did anything just once at the Gilded Fly."

Polijn had been dragging somewhat in the rear, keeping out of sight. The Vielfrass was unpredictable but he was, as far as she knew, restrained by gravity at least. Pixies, being airborne, were even more difficult to keep track of. Besides, her legs were all but crumbling.

She was several paces behind the pair, therefore, when she emerged from the corridor into the Great Tower, and a hand fell on her shoulder.

She twisted to see her newest assailant. Arberth smiled down at her.

"Time to go back to work," he said, cheerfully turning her in the direction from which she had come. "Fun time's over."

V

POLIJN reached the room breathless and clammy, having tried to keep up with the jester's long strides. Maybe when tonight was over, she thought, leaning against the door, she'd be allowed some rest.

Arberth didn't seem to have noticed her discomfort. "Lucky you didn't go on that way," he told her. "They'd have grabbed you to set up chairs or something." He lifted a ficdual from the counter.

"I set your clothes out for you," he went on, gesturing to the bed. "So we'd match."

Polijn staggered to the low wooden frame and clutched at the wall for support. Had she not already been in agony, this clashing array of glory would have left her breathless. No use complaining; she would never be able to explain why that shade of yellow should not be worn over that shade of green. She wouldn't even try to spell out how the tunic she was to wear had nothing in common with the tunic he was wearing, or that she had no overwhelming desire to match Arberth.

She started to sit on the bed, remembered that the blanket covered only a net of ropes, and straightened. She gladly threw off her cold, wet shift.

Arberth, meanwhile, tried to force the old ficdual to tune. "Were we going to do 'The Ram Forlorn'?" he inquired, striking two strings together.

147

Polijn let the cleaner shift slide down over her. "No!" she answered. "It was . . . 'The Tattered Sail.' "

"Hmmmm," noted the jester. He struck a few more chords, obviously unsatisfied with "The Tattered Sail." He was not, of course, alone.

She fastened her tunic as Arberth crossed to his meager supply of manuscripts.

"Do you know all of 'Someone Stole the Moon'?" he asked her.

Polijn frowned. "Maybe."

He slipped the pertinent page from his collection. "Let's run through it."

She slipped on the overtunic and tied it. This was not a bad choice. "Someone Stole the Moon" was no better than his other compositions, but he had chosen to add an incongruous clapping section into the chorus. An audience that was clapping along could not throw things.

Arberth propped his backside on the counter and struck three notes on the ficdual. Then he started in, just a little more than an octave above the third note.

"Do you recall the moon, my dear?
I'll never forget it myself, no sir!
The clouds were all gone; there was no storm a-brewing
As we swore our love by the silvery moon."

A small white box sat on the blanket; Polijn wondered if this was some ornament she was expected to wear. She did not usually wear jewelry, but, knowing Arberth's taste, the idea held no excitement for her. She stooped to her own bundle of things and plucked out the slide whistle and mouth harp. The tattered puppy lay near the top of the stack; she was sure he had been at the bottom.

Her hand struck cold metal, and she slid aside another shift to reveal the glistening armband from the demon's temple.

Arberth was swinging into the chorus. Polijn cleared her throat; it had been lintik cold on the roof.

We swore that our love, like the moon, would go on;
We swore as we lay there from dusk until almost dawn.
Why is it now vanished and lying in ruins?
All I can suggest is someone stole the moon.

Clapping in rhythm was harder when the rhythm kept shifting.

Should she wear the armband? This would hardly clash with any of her ensemble, any more than any part of it clashed with any other.

A spider strolled across the floor. Polijn would have said it was early for spiders, but this was her first spring in the Palace Royal.

Do you recall the moon, my love,
That night in the fall when you wandered off?

She reached now for the box on the bed. It was open. A picture of a red spider decorated the side. A real spider sat on top.

It was misty and cold, quite devoid of heat,
But the moon was still there. At least, I thought I could see
  it.

Another white box with a red spider on the side sat by the manuscript case. She couldn't remember having seen it before, but the boxes were small enough for the jester to have had them stashed away somewhere.

We swore that our love, like the moon, would go on;
We swore as we lay there from dusk until nearly dawn.
Why is it now vanished and lying in ruins?
All I can think of is someone stole the moon.

Polijn wished the jester could resist the temptation to rewrite during a performance. It hardly ever improved the song, and it made singing along even more difficult.

Another white box sat next to her bundle. These boxes had surely not been lying out while she was here with Argeleb. Arberth must have set them out while he was changing his own clothes.

How well I remember the night of the storm!
It was cold, it was damp; no one was feeling warm.

Polijn stiffened. That spider on the bed had prickles. But there wasn't enough light for her to see whether the prickles were red. Another spider crawled out of the box.

I learned from a friend you were not coming home.
The moon was not seen. I was chilled to the bone.

Something tickled the top of her foot. Polijn took a long breath
before looking down. She was correct. Furthermore, those prickles
were definitely red. And the red dot up by the head verified that
this was actually a Two-Step Spider, a distinction without a
difference. If it bit down, this meant she just might live long
enough to warn the jester.

We swore that our love, like the moon, would go on.
We swore as we lay there until dusk was almost dawn.
Why is it now vanished and lying in ruins?
All I can suggest is someone stole the moon.

How fortunate, thought Polijn, that it was impossible to tap your
foot to "Someone Stole the Moon." The Red-Spotted Stickleback
was not so malevolent as the One-Step Spider, but it could be
nasty if annoyed.

She considered, and discarded, a quick jerk of the foot (the
spider was too light, and might not be dislodged), a swat with
the hand (what did it matter whether the spider bit her foot or her
hand?), and a mad dash across the room (one more mad dash, and
her lungs would burst from her body). The idea of asking Arberth
for help was eliminated as soon as it came up.

In spite of our vow, you'd decided to depart.
There were clouds in the sky, love, and more in my heart.
And all I can think of, as I sit here and moan,
Is "Our love is deceased, and someone stole the moon!"

Arberth reached for a climactic high note and, squeezing it out,
made it crack. Polijn, forgetting the spider for a second, cringed.
The spider, stunned, gathered its legs into a ball and rolled down
her foot.

Polijn could just barely wait until it fell clear, and then smashed
it under the sole of her sandal.

"No," said Arberth, "I don't believe I'd stamp there. Let's wait
for the final chorus and clap and stomp all at once. Big finish,
you see."

"Can we just go?" demanded Polijn, her voice rasping against
her throat.

Arberth gave her an indulgent smile. "I get that way before a big performance myself," he said. "By all means."

Polijn reached for the box, but, on his way to replace the manuscript, Arberth kicked it out of her reach. It bounced against the far wall.

Only the jester could be so clumsy. Polijn shrugged. Just as well: whoever planted those boxes in the room could easily have put more than one spider in each box. She could ask around without taking a box to exhibit.

She grabbed up her armband as the jester neared the door. Shaking it first, just to be sure it was uninhabited, she thrust it into hiding inside her overtunic. The sleeves were long and, once she got the piece in place, it would be hidden from observers until she got up to sing.

If she did sing, of course. She studied the stairs and wondered how she could possibly survive another descent.

CHAPTER EIGHT
Nimnestl

I

"YES, well, next time leave thinking to the horses. They've got bigger heads."

Nimnestl marched in to join the throng. Culghi knew better than to be taking bets while on duty.

Mistun and Dyveke were backing toward her, dragging a struggling page. The Chief Bodyguard drew a dagger at her leisure and rapped Mistun on the back of the head with it.

"It's early for that," she said. The trio broke up and dashed away, the page faster than the older men.

Nimnestl surveyed the vast room. Already there were more merrymakers than the allotted space would hold. The room was hot, stuffy, crammed full. Guests jostled and jabbed on their way to the food and drink. The noise level made her ears throb.

Taken as a whole, the celebration was a perfect triumph.

The wary gave her as wide a margin as possible as she passed. Nimnestl, usually impressive and deadly, was now impressive, deadly, and splendid. The King had ordered her to wear the deep green suit that flattered her, along with her emeralds and chrysoberyl belt. The King was getting quite puffed up with his latest boost in responsibility; she dreaded the possibility that he would order her to sing at the celebration. He was entranced by her singing, but the songs he liked best were hardly consistent with her public image.

Neither were the dandelions pinned near her collar, but these

he had insisted upon. For the fifth year, the King had scanned
the grass and snow for the first blossoms of the year. These
had come from the yard of an inn on the road to Malbeth. Once
the Tumbled Mug, this inn had quickly changed its name to the
King's Dandelions.

Just now, the King stood on an ornate platform at the royal end
of the room, out of reach of visitors in the gallery. The platform
was meant to keep the King higher than anyone else in the room.
This would have been ridiculous even without the new gallery,
fifteen feet up. The King was still shorter than many of his guards
standing on the floor.

He and Kaftus were busy receiving the compliments of the
foreign ambassadors and town notables, neither bothering to show
much interest in the bows and curtsies that the visitors had practiced in private for days. But each courtesy was measured to the
inch by all onlookers, to be recorded in the fossilized gossip
that surrounded such occasions, and was hauled out for each
new one.

The King was resplendent in purple and silver, the outfit he and
Nurse had agreed upon only after long, loud debate. Nurse had an
eye for color, and His Majesty had an eye for effect, so from the
grey-silver fox fur to the purple boots with silver bows, the King
was dazzling. At his throat he wore the Unicorn Sapphire. When
the light hit this gem from the proper angle, a white unicorn's
head could be seen blazing in the center. Each of the notables
was trying to bow so as to get a glimpse of this and revel in the
good luck it was supposed to portend.

A bevy of girls giggled and goggled from the steps, waiting
a turn to try their fledgling wiles on the King. Conan rightly
regarded this as a tremendous nuisance. "Couldn't they go and
seduce someone else for a change?" he would demand. "Just to
practice?" They couldn't, of course; they had their orders.

Nimnestl noticed that it was Iúnartar, Tusenga's girl, who had
pushed her way to the spot nearest the King. She was trying to
hold her mouth small and demure, but she hadn't done it often
enough: the lips kept sneaking shyly up her cheeks. She would
never be very pretty, but when she smiled, she was worth looking
at. Nimnestl surveyed the entire would-be harem. Kaftus had been
holding out a possible marriage with a foreign princess as bait for
ambassadors, but it might be a good idea. Certainly none of this
lot was suitable.

Nemijan was singing an innocuous ballad and dancing with a

fan taller than she was. Later, people would be singing broader
ballads in broader accents. Tonight's celebration would be more
boisterous than last night's; the weather would keep everyone
inside. Nimnestl absently noted the fan for future reference; it
was big enough to serve as a weapon.

The festival had been divided into assemblies in the Barracks
Auditorium, the Great Dining Hall, and this one, in the Great
Hall and Royal Reception Room. Here the entertainment would
be more refined, or at least more expensive. Traffic between halls
was snail-paced. Added to the servants bearing provender were
masses of guests shoving from one assembly to another to be sure
they were missing nothing at the other places.

The poor and uninvited were held to one end of this particular
assembly by a specially decorated beam in the ceiling, matched by
a death line on the floor. This kept the crowd down, and massed
the unwashed near the entrance, which controlled the drafts. A
few were risking mutilation or worse by sneaking across the line
to beg, or sell cheap goods. Most had come merely to see the
legendary figures they heard about, prayed for, or prayed to.

Nimnestl eased her way along to the tables of food. Passing up
heavy delicacies like the fried goose liver and the sheep's tails,
she settled for a small roll. Her ring gave her no warning, so she
ate it. Setting her back against the table, she turned to study the
crowd.

Dirty handprints could already be seen in indiscreet places
on expensive robes and tunics. The fashion this month seemed
to be running to high collars and ornamental hoods for men,
with low backs and bare shoulders for the women. Besslia and
Tyell passed, their necks and shoulders corked and marked with
symbols giving an opinion of the Chief Bodyguard. Nimnestl let
a passing notion, to brand those symbols permanently in place for
greater convenience, pass.

All ages were gathered in festival. An effort had been made to
herd the younger ones into the Great Dining Hall "where they'd be
more comfortable." But all the Royal Playmates and their families
had to be in here, and those children who were officially part of
someone's retinue were here as well. This had also been planned
for. Although all Palace inhabitants could see that sliding down
the bannister of the gallery stairs made more sense than looking
at that big stone urn on the end, it could not be allowed when
there was serious celebrating to be done. So, in one corner, Imidis
was running the cards, telling fortunes to avert boisterous games

of Toss the Great Stone. Tucked under the stairs, grey-bearded Yvelen was holding them quiet with a story.

"Once," he was saying, "there were three giants: Gog, Magog, and Demagog." The children hugged their knees and waited to hear about the young undaunted orphan who killed the giants. Some were pages, in neat but gaudy suede suits. Others were naked and gilded for a spectacle later in the evening. These last were children of no particular importance, and had been selected for looks rather than lineage. They would probably, after their appearance on stage, be auctioned off in some deeply hidden, highly secret room. (No doubt, thought Nimnestl, Therat's office again.) This was technically treason, though Nimnestl hardly considered it high treason.

The clothes showed just as easily who was who among adults. Iranen's shivering slaveys were the bottom layer, of course. Forokell and Akoyn had deftly arranged tables and screens to keep most of these out of sight, but some screens were rearranged when Iranen came through. Next up were the servants in clean work shifts, and then the servants in livery.

Hand-me-down ball clothes were worn by higher servants and lesser relatives. The farther up the scale, the newer and heavier the clothes. Weight showed status: the minimum required for the highest class was five layers, not including the mail often worn underneath. Some layers would be discarded in the course of the evening, if only because of the heat. This was why many servants were not drinking even when they got the chance; they had to see that the clothes got back to the right owner, or highest bidder.

Consumption of alcohol wouldn't suffer. Plenty was being stashed in nooks and niches for later. Cups and plates were being stowed under tunics and gowns, and not just by servants. The King might be sacred, but it was okay to steal from him. He was too rich to notice.

All had been budgeted for. This was Rossacotta, after all: one did not ignore facts. Everyone knew what Rossacotta was. It was the wife of the First Lord Treasurer spitting beer into the face of Raiprez, a sleek sophisticated woman whose gown was cut low enough to reveal the VV branded on one shoulderblade. It was the vast, beautiful inlaid table, on top of which were shining trays of expensive food, and under which were squat ceramic pots (or ceramic squat pots, as they were known). Rossacotta was Illefar drinking directly from the pitcher, and then blushing when his mother pointed out he had wiped his mouth on his sleeve instead

of his handkerchief. Guests who had not yet chosen sides in
the debate between forks and fingers were carrying books and
toothpicks to show their civilized ways. Cleanliness was highly
civilized. So Iranen, after finishing off a turkey leg and tossing
it to the floor, beckoned to one of her servants. The woman,
dragging a broken leg, struggled over with ewer and soap to
wash her mistress's hands.

Nimnestl moved away from the food. She didn't have much
appetite.

A scuffle at the far end of the table brought her head around.
The envoy from Domiscket had bumped the wife of the ambassador from Anganai. They didn't even recognize the existence of
each other's country, so an amicable resolution could hardly be
expected.

But these foreigners were slower with the knife than Rossacottans, so before violent words could become violent deeds, Seitun
was there, tripping over the woman's train and spilling a large
mug of cossetted beer all over everywhere. Joining in abuse of
the clumsy bodyguard, the ambassador and his enemy's wife were
all but chums by the time they parted. Nimnestl wondered how
Seitun's little stratagem would alter politics, or even geography,
in the Northern Quilt.

So many countries had ambassadors in Rossacotta that only
half the plotting done tonight would have to do with affairs
there. It was comforting to reflect that, in all this haze of plots
and counterplots, there were a few Nimnestl wouldn't have to
worry about.

Most of the ambassadors and their retinues were edgy tonight.
Someone had leaked word (probably to Arlmorin, a rumor net-
work in himself, as if the Palace Royal needed one) that the Council was looking for a foreigner to take credit for Morquiesse's
murder. Most of the envoys had brought little tokens of appreciation for each Council member, to encourage the Council to look
in other directions.

Nimnestl looked around for her own suspects. Maitena, sober so
far, was talking urgently to Nuseth, one of her daughters. Nuseth
was very pointedly not looking at her mother or her husband,
Avtrollan. Avtrollan had painted his chin in swirls of blue and
gold, which clashed with her gown. (Chin-painting, started by
men who missed their beards, amused the King very much, and
threatened to become the prevailing style.) The quarrel was a
petty one, but two of Laisida's daughters and a niece of Kirasov

were at the man's side, building a mountain of it. Every divorce meant one more eligible male in the Palace Royal.

On the high stage behind them, five acrobats were going through a series of leaps through barrels and over flames, but the real show was beyond this in a corner, where Iranen's seldom-seen assistant, Aliquis Split-Tail, was supposed to be supervising three young apple-peelers. She was doing her best to attend to business. Her face showed concentration in every line. In fact, her face was mostly lines: narrow eyebrows, thin lips, dark slots for eyes, and a nose so small as to be nonexistent.

Aliquis was a woman of some importance, who dealt with accounts and other matters for which Iranen was constitutionally unsuited. She was also Iranen's chief project, and had been specially prepared for tonight's display. Shaven from head to toe, she was unclothed but not naked. Iranen had hung her with little brass bells which jingled as she dodged the rolls and old plums tossed at her. The short chain which usually attached her to her desk was now fastened to a heavy stool. When she was forced to jump far enough to make the chain pull tight, all the horizontal lines in her face shot down into painful slants.

A glorious creature stood jabbing her with a long knife to see her jerk. He wore a travelling cloak. Several guests wore cloaks, adding a layer to their consequence, but none had one made entirely of feathers, feathers of eight colors and forty shades, obviously useless as a travelling cloak. Nimnestl wondered who it was, and where he'd found the money.

She almost released a whistle when he turned enough to show his face.

Nimnestl ignored the dozen questions that leapt to mind, and turned away. Let her rush up to Palompec here and now, and she would destroy any chance of keeping his role in the artist's murder quiet. She hoped no one had seen her face at that second.

No one had. Everyone was turning toward the entrance. Nimnestl felt a moment of unease. Then she heard a whisper of "The Vielfrass!"

Some few people in the Palace Royal had a presence one could feel before one saw them. Kaftus projected the power and terror of old bones; she could identify him blindfolded at thirty yards. Lord Arlmorin's vigor made him another impressive presence. Iranen's madness, Forokell's unquestionable authority, all had the power to impinge upon the senses.

The Vielfrass had all those characteristics and more. He was a

II

"I suppose you couldn't have gotten there earlier and saved us some trouble," said Nimnestl.

The sorcerer turned to watch as his accomplice, Oozola, carried the boy away, followed by Kirasov, Kirasov's entire retinue, and a large contingent of onlookers. "I don't see why I should have to do all the work around here," he replied.

Nimnestl blew out a long breath. If the boy had been hit too hard, and didn't wake up, she'd have no direct evidence against the Neleandrai. She whirled away from the sorcerer. In the blink of one eye, the time it took her to take stock of her surroundings, her face smoothed out into a mask of utter indifference.

Two women with expensive gowns and hair nets of silk and gems were approaching. Lynex nibbled daintily at an almond cake while Akoyn, moving energetically so her sandals would peep out from under her hem and exhibit her toe rings, carried two massive tankards.

Nimnestl did not wait out their approach, but charged forward to put large hands on the Second Chief Housekeeper's arm. "I am so glad to see you up!" she exclaimed. "How are you? I was afraid you might have suffered severe damage."

Both women were taken aback; Lynex choked. This had been Nimnestl's intention; alternating hostility with warm affection kept the Councillors off balance.

When the Housekeeper could speak again, she claimed to be in

good condition. "I don't think he knew the trick of it." Her laugh
was brittle. "Do you know who it was, yet?"

"Ah, folly, folly," reproved the Vielfrass, who had followed
the Bodyguard over. "When there are so many real murders to
avenge, you can't expect the poor woman to pay any attention to
mere attempts. It will probably turn out to have been something
innocent, some neighborhood improvement program."

Akoyn moved up to try to cover the silence that followed
that. "Here," she said, pushing one of the big mugs toward the
Bodyguard. "This is for the fund to buy chewing tobacco for
disabled veterans."

"A worthy charity," nodded the Vielfrass, putting both hands
behind his back. "I'll spread the word. I feel I can afford to give
it a plug."

Akoyn frowned. "So far, most of our donations have come from
the courts of the foreign ambassadors. I hope the message gets
around that this is an approved way to spend money."

Nimnestl had trouble remembering where her pouch was in this
outfit. Finding it, she took out three silver coins. "Try again
later," she advised, "as the ball goes on and the cheerful word
spreads."

"It is a cheerful evening," Lynex said, looking back over the
massed nobility. "His Majesty is enjoying it."

"There is that," Nimnestl admitted. "I meant the news that
Argeleb, Kirasov's son, has reappeared."

"Oh?" said Akoyn, her voice perfectly level. "I hadn't heard."
But her head moved just a fraction toward the door Kirasov and
the others had used in leaving. "When?"

"Just now," said Nimnestl.

"How long has he been missing?" demanded Lynex. "I really
hadn't noticed."

"Oh, you must have seen how worried the Head Guard has
been!" Akoyn rolled her eyes to the ceiling and sighed. "I hope
Kirasov will keep a closer watch hereafter. Who knows what kind
of devilment the child has been up to, all these weeks? I'll swear
he was the one tossing gravel up through the windows during
chapel."

"Argeleb?" Lynex demanded. "I thought you were saying
Hevylet did that."

"Hevylet?" the Vielfrass demanded, with a good imitation of
the Housekeeper's voice. "Why, he couldn't hit the broad side of
a laundress!"

He followed this by craning his head to one side, looking around behind Akoyn. She swept the train of her gown around and stepped away.

"Ah," sighed the sorcerer, "do any of us understand how difficult it must be to be a laundress? Look around the room. See all the long hoods? I hear that's getting to be the fashion. How can a laundress cope?"

At the words "long hoods," Akoyn shot a glance at the Vielfrass, and then another at Nimnestl. Not sure what she saw there, she excused herself from the conversation.

"I believe I must go see what Kirasov has to say about where the boy was during chapel," she said, trying to work her way around the Vielfrass without presenting her back to him.

"He left," Nimnestl informed her, "with his retinue. The boy looked unwell—too many sweets, perhaps—so they carried him away." The Bodyguard stared out over the heads of the two Housekeepers. "Just as well. Relieves a bit of the pressure."

This sounded sinister to both Akoyn and Lynex, who made uneasy departures. The Vielfrass sent them off with a serenade. "I am a happy launderer; I scrub the pants and shirts, and rub the soap into the cloth, 'til it's so clean it hurts. Val-de-ri!" He stopped, and sighed. "Oh, I am a man after my own heart!"

Nimnestl gestured him over to his side. When he didn't come, she stepped over to him, murmuring, "These long hoods you mentioned . . ."

"Sssssh," responded the sorcerer. "We can't miss this."

He was looking up into the air. Nimnestl refused to take the bait until she saw that several people on either side of her were doing the same. She put her head back.

Chicken-and-Dumplings and her multicolored retinue had deserted the massive punch bowl Nimnestl had set up for them in the Great Dining Hall, and now clustered around the chain of a massive chandelier.

"Back, back!" ordered the queen, kicking her subjects into place.

The Bodyguard stared at the gaudy bodies, trying to divine what their plot was. The queen appeared to be trying to force her entire nation into hiding behind that chain. Finally, Chicken-and-Dumplings took a place at the top of the populace, her glistening rump as bright and obvious as the candles themselves.

"Hush!" shrieked the queen of the pixies. "Quiet!"

The mass of bodies looked nothing at all like a chandelier chain, and was far from inconspicuous. Yet the entire group fell instantly silent, as if this would hide them.

What were they hiding from? wondered Nimnestl, gazing around the ceiling. "Oh!"

Mardith was a dark harbinger of ill, the familiar of the Head Bodyguard. He was apparently pleased and unsurprised at the hush that fell as he entered the Great Hall. He soared with an extra vigor, turning his beak up at a proud angle. He was mighty impressive.

He was also headed directly into ambush. Nimnestl did experience an urge to call out to him. Somehow the impulse was very easily mastered.

Mardith had reached the center of the room, and was in full view of everyone present when he happened to look down toward the chandelier. An old, experienced bird, he saw his danger in an instant. His advance halted; he dove desperately.

It came too late. A whirlwind of flashing wings tore down with a screaming squeal that seemed to be made up of the words "Moogly moogly moogly!" Nimnestl lost sight of him in the tempest, but he reappeared, plunging dangerously close to the heads of the earthbound spectators. Ferrapec ducked, knocking a mug from the hand of his mother. A cat that had managed to climb up to the table while attention was diverted turned away from the plate of cold meats to swat at the bird.

Mardith knocked the cat to the floor and sped out through the nearest window. The pixies, all whooping, some waving black feathers, followed with cries of bliss. The crowd's cheers followed them. Nimnestl herself felt like laughing, but did not. You never knew who might notice: Mardith, for example.

The only person not pleased by the discomfiture of the Bodyguard's ally was Meugloth, who was in charge of keeping the evening's entertainment on his painstakingly organized schedule. In pushing around for a good view, the mob had disordered portions of the main platform. He signalled to Laisida, who ordered up a series of dance figures until the platform could be reassembled.

In the crush as the center of floor was cleared for dancing, Nimnestl tried to return to the Vielfrass's seeming reference to the Neleandrai. But as she opened her mouth, he raised his hands as if to push her away.

"Nay, nay, dear lady!" he implored. "Don't beg! I must sit this one out; I really must. No, say no more. Your broken-hearted eyes speak volumes."

He paused. "There's one I can sell to Arberth. Ah, my girl, if only my sleazy sidekick weren't present to witness it! We'd make such a lovely couple. But even illumined by my splendor, you could not hope to compete with the young buck who's wearing those purple boots."

He waved to the assembled dancers. Nimnestl glanced at the dancers, and then up to the Royal Platform. The little figure seated next to Kaftus had pulled up the hood of his fur cape. The short figure on the floor had also raised his hood. But he had not had time to change his boots when he and Merklin exchanged capes.

Nimnestl was more annoyed by the oversight than by the imposture. She nodded to Seitun, and then jerked her head toward the King. Her subordinate understood in a second, grimaced, and moved in, quietly rearranging the dance to clear a space around the King and his partner, Iúnartar. Nimnestl felt a little sorry for the girl, who was no doubt following orders and didn't know what she was getting into. Rossacottan dancing was none too civilized, and tried to make it up in vigor. The King seemed to feel that the point was to whirl your partner so madly that she got dizzy and landed on her back. He was not so far wrong.

Nimnestl looked over the crowd near the King's platform. Haeve was arguing with Nurse, gesturing madly to keep her attention away from the dancers. Lynex had no doubt been sent to perform that same function with the Chief Bodyguard. Kaftus was probably in collusion with the others.

"Thank you," she told the Vielfrass. "I might not have noticed that."

The sorcerer shrugged. "We can't all be perfect."

The Bodyguard glanced at the Royal Platform again. The Regent, noticing her, beckoned.

"I . . ." Nimnestl began, turning to the Vielfrass.

"I know," sighed the sorcerer. "Stood up again. Running off with another man at the dance. Women are endlessly fickle. And so lacking in confidence. That they should all prefer other men to the challenge of dealing with one of such overpowering masculine appeal! But pay no mind; I'm used to it."

Nimnestl had no idea how long this soliloquy was likely to last, and left him addressing the air.

The crowd had concentrated to make room for the dancing couples, and though people still tried to make way for the big Bodyguard, Nimnestl had to do some pushing and shoving on her own. En route, her ears collected snatches of conversation, recording them for further use in case anything said became useful later.

"I don't know who it was: just grabbed 'em out of my kid's hand, like to ripped his arm off. I ever find . . . oh, yeah, the kid marked him. Pretty good, too; big gouge in one hand."

"See Lestis over there by Imidis? They say he stole her practically from under Ferrapec. Says she's doing some sewing for him."

"He's stitching her legs to her belly, I suppose."

"Hey, I hear he uses a pretty big needle."

"Isanten could be right. Arberth's only been here two years; what do we really know about him?"

"Oh, Fiera's a sport. She came to Patrak's last masked party."

"So did a lot of women."

"But she wore a mask without any eyeholes."

The Bodyguard finally reached the Royal Platform and climbed the stairs past the makeshift garderobe tucked into a corner. "Yes?" she inquired, reaching the Regent.

"If you think you can keep the King here," said Kaftus, with a long, slow blink on the word "King," "I will slip out to have another chat with Morquiesse while the sightseers are busy elsewhere."

Nimnestl nodded. There had been a procession all afternoon to view the body of the dead artist, to hunt for clues or check certain rumors about the man's anatomy.

"The ambassador from Keastone is imbibing a little freely," the Regent told her. "And see that Merklin down there doesn't overtire himself."

"Indeed," the Bodyguard replied. "And you saw Palompec?"

"I did," Kaftus replied. He stepped around behind her, and murmured, "Do you feel his removal from our little circle will subject Rossacotta to any great cultural deprivation?"

"You will let me talk to him first?" she replied.

The Regent raised his eyebrows. "I intend to leave the whole thing in your hands. Practice should make perfect."

He swept toward the stairs and Nimnestl started for his place. She stumbled. "Already?" demanded the Regent, not looking around.

"It's this lintik gown. I can't walk in it."

"Naturally not," Kaftus answered, stepping down. "The object of high fashion is to emphasize the uselessness of the wearer. Fine feathers make mediocre birds, as your crow will no doubt tell you if he has enough left to fly back."

III

STEKHEN, bored, was leaning against the wall to the left of the stage, picking at the stones.

"Stop at once!" ordered his mother, dealing him a clout on one shoulder. "You'll have the castle down!"

Children had been picking at the stones for centuries, and the Palace Royal still stood. Of course, Nimnestl allowed, this might be because for centuries their mothers had been clouting them for it.

Many more things could be seen and heard from her vantage point beside the "King": Iúnartar, barely balancing herself on one leg as the real King swung her into Seitun, the Vielfrass propositioning Fiera as Lady Oozola returned, and all sorts of plots in progress. Lord Dabren, from the western empire of Keastone, was indeed drinking heavily, but he was chatting with Prabeo, who never let any man leave his company sober if he could help it.

Near the Royal Platform, behind the food tables, sat Fausca, tied to her chair, with her wrists bound above her head to a torch bracket, and her ankles fastened to the legs of the chair. She seemed unwounded, but uncomfortable as well. She bounced in her place, trying to dislodge some of the early spring flies that had gathered.

"Oh, my dear, don't do that," cried Iranen, noticing. "You'll shake them off!" The Housekeeper reached back to the bowl of

165

honey and brought up a dollop on the server. "That will help," she said, dribbling the thick goo across the flies and Fausca.

Turning to replace the server, she murmured something to Lord Garanem about a saucy piece. "Ready for you by the end of the evening," she concluded.

Across the room, Garanem's daughter, leaving her clothes in the arms of her best friend, was slipping behind a tapestry showing the Victory at Drawziw. The secret passage behind that particular tapestry led to several rooms. Nimnestl thought she was most likely heading for that of Tollamar, whose eldest son was eminently eligible.

People were moving in and out through all the doors, open and concealed ones alike. The traffic at some secret passages was almost as congested as in the regular halls. Nimnestl could understand the traffic; what she couldn't figure out was why everyone was pushing and shoving and climbing over each other to join it. Why hurry when there was nowhere to go? Each room offered the best and worst of the celebration, in equal quantities.

She had to remind herself that these were not figures from her imagination nor puppets she had set in motion. They were not even, in most cases, actors reciting lines. These were separate beings, with their own lives and opinions. They believed what they said and considered what they did to be as rational as she did her own actions.

Nimnestl had not so far convinced herself. It was the truth; she just didn't believe it.

Laisida was taking his place among the musicians, a signal that the dance would soon wind to an end so Meugloth could return to his sacred schedule. "Ahem!" called someone, over the sound of music.

Nimnestl had seen her coming, and didn't look down. "Isn't it a lovely evening for a party?" called Aoyalasse.

Nimnestl didn't answer. "I heard you had some excitement," the Assistant Housekeeper went on. "I missed it. The, er, pixies, I heard. They're all mad, completely mad."

This was too obvious to require a reply. Aoyalasse cleared her throat and spoke more loudly. "I was out changing my gown," she said, "and couldn't get back sooner because there was a little accident. I ran into some brat and knocked him down. While I was trying to see if I'd hurt him, that sorcerer—the Vielfrass, you know?—he came by and misunderstood everything. And you can never explain anything to him. He's probably plotting something."

The logic of this left Nimnestl unmoved. "Oh, well." The woman shrugged. "You know no one ever knows what he'll say next. He had that slut of Arberth's with him. I wonder what they were doing in the dark doorways."

She still went unanswered and, to all appearances, unobserved. Aoyalasse aimed at another target. "Have you learned anything about, you know, the list?"

Nimnestl accorded this a shrug. Encouraged, the Housekeeper went on, "You know, I like you. I really do." She looked as if she'd have liked to put an arm around someone and talk confidentially at this point, but she couldn't reach any higher than the Bodyguard's foot. She put one finger on this, experimentally.

Nimnestl moved the foot. Aoyalasse jerked back from the platform.

"I have no desire to chat," said the Bodyguard. "I really don't."

The Housekeeper merged reluctantly with the crowd. A case could be made against her, Nimnestl thought. The list could be brought in evidence that the woman was plotting massive plots, and all the Neleandrai, at least, would support the accusation. But Palompec should be dealt with first.

Laisida was singing a gentle love song, and the dancers were dispersing. Some carried swooning partners, fashionably overcome by the civilized nature of the melody. The "King" snorted and moved to the sheltered niche behind his seat. Seitun was following "Merklin" at a discreet distance as the little figure approached the King's Platform, one eye on Nimnestl. Iúnartar limped into the mob, breathless but glorified.

Seitun and "Merklin" disappeared under the platform. Seitun returned as sounds of slight commotion came from the little garderobe.

"Nails out of two planks, Ma'am," he reported. "I'll have 'em fastened back?" Nimnestl nodded.

The King popped out of the cubbyhole, his hood thrown back, his face flushed. "My!" he said, seeing Nimnestl's eyes on him. "It's hot up here!"

Nimnestl raised a hand. "You probably need a drink."

"Oh, yes," he said, grateful.

Nimnestl struggled with her conscience and then added, "Dancing is thirsty work."

The King was listening to Laisida and didn't take that in at once. Then his head pulled back between his shoulders. To Nimnestl's pleasure, his first question was, "Did Nurse see me?"

"The Tutor had her to one side," she told him.

He sighed with relief, then frowned. "You mean the Tutor knew about it?"

Iranen stepped up the stairs, bearing a large golden cup. She was dressed to appear almost civilized tonight, barring the belt of dog's heads. Her gown was all of black feathers, with a large spreading collar turned up in back. She looked like a severed head floating in a dark closet.

She fell to one knee, showing a face of pure reverence that she gave to no other being. The King took the cup, drank noisily, and handed it back. He nodded.

With lowered head, the Housekeeper backed down the stairs, taking slow, measured steps. On turning, she saw that Lotilia had moved two feet from the tray of cakes. She set the King's Cup down, took up the Regent's, and brought two of the gilded putti on the handle across the bridge of the servant's nose.

"Why didn't you say you were deaf when you came to work here?" she roared. "I told you to stand over there." She indicated her belt. "If you can't listen, maybe your head hangs here next."

"I am sorry," gasped Lotilia, as blood ran down her chin.

Iranen swung the cup again, nearly taking off an ear. "Don't bark 'til I rattle your chain, bitch!" She put a slippered foot up into a bare, bruised thigh. Nimnestl saw she was still wearing those same off-white slippers.

The King noticed none of this. "How many other people saw us?"

At that moment, Laisida brought his song to a shuddering close. As was customary, he looked to the King's Platform for approval.

"That was a new song," said the King, his high, piping voice carrying across the room.

"Yes, Your Majesty," said the minstrel, with a bow. "I call it 'The Gentle Cat.' "

"I like it very much when you sing about cats," the King called. "Do you know other songs about cats?"

This was reasonably close to a command, so Laisida said, "I know this one," and took up his harp again. Meugloth kicked at a table leg, but there was nothing else he could do. He waved the athletes back from the stage platform.

The King turned to continue his discussion with Nimnestl, but a flittering form interposed itself. "I like cats, too," it said. "They eat birds."

"Hi!" said the King, always happy to see the queen of the pixies. Chicken-and-Dumplings basked in his smile and put up a hand to smooth her hair.

"Would you care to do something amusing?" asked Nimnestl.

Both the King and the Queen looked up into her face. "What?" asked Chicken-and-Dumplings, with some suspicion.

Nimnestl nodded toward the crowd. "Fly out and get me one of Lady Iranen's slippers. You do know which one is Lady Iranen?"

"Certainly," sniffed the pixy. "The one with heads on her belt. Why do you want a slipper, huh? I could get you her chest straps."

The Bodyguard shrugged. "Well, if you don't think you can get a slipper," she said, "those would do."

"Ploof!" answered the pixy, flying up to kick amiably at the Bodyguard's nose. "I can get a slipper as easy as pulling out a feather. You just watch: I'll have her feet in the air faster than General Ferrapec."

The little woman turned, but Nimnestl caught at her wings. "Don't bring it to me here. It isn't politic for anyone to know a queen is running errands for a mere Bodyguard. Bring it over to that doorway next to the Birulph tapestry. I'll meet you there."

The Queen nodded. "Okay. Oh, look! That man with the blue cheeks is . . ."

"You will remember, won't you?" said Nimnestl. "Bring me one of Iranen's slippers, over there. This is an important errand, which I could entrust to no one but the true sovereign of all the pixies."

"Oh, yes!" Chicken-and-Dumplings rubbed a bright red mark across her left thigh. "You wouldn't trust, huh, that . . . that boord!"

Nimnestl let her go, and she zipped up toward the ceiling. "What do you want a slipper for?" asked the King.

"Ssshh," she replied. "Later." She beckoned to Seitun.

"Nimnestl," said the King, more loudly. "Not later. I order you to tell me now. I am the King."

"I have to hurry," she replied. "You know how fast she is. I'll explain when I get back."

The King stamped his feet, but she had already started down the stairs. The crowd was less concentrated now, particularly when Laisida finished his second song and the audience turned to the stage platform to watch "The Flying Scarves." On her way, she passed Iranen, who was thoroughly slapping Ginder, the servant in charge of drawing corks as bottles and jugs were brought to the table.

Ginder was one of the few male servants on his level in Iranen's department. Most of the men who served under this House-keeper were specialists, persons who could not be damaged. She also commanded the prison guards, but these, too, had to be maintained, to give Housekeeping its private army. So the few expendable men who did come within Iranen's command were guaranteed personal attention.

Iranen had started slapping him across the face, and was work-ing her way down. He finally stepped back when she reached his midsection. "I don't have to stand here and be abused!" he snapped.

He was incorrect. The fifth son of a very minor bookkeeper, he had no prospects whatsoever outside of this position. And Iranen knew it. "You'll take what I give you, cur," she said, "and come back for dessert."

Someone had left an eating knife on the table nearest her. Iranen picked it up and wiped a bit of apple from the nicked blade. "Do you know how they take care of incorrigible hounds?" she inquired.

Nimnestl was fairly certain this was only a bluff; it was too early in the evening for serious violence. Ginder was less secure. He reached for a full jug. Iranen advanced.

"Yeeeack!" she exclaimed, throwing her head and shoulders backward. She grabbed at her spine, throwing the knife to one side. Ginder, afraid the knife was coming his way, ducked, knocking empty bottles off the cart behind him.

So far, Nimnestl felt Chicken-and-Dumplings was doing a good job. Diving down the back of a gown was calculated to unnerve anyone. She did feel it was rather in poor taste to start barking.

"A dog!" shrieked the Housekeeper. "Another dog!" She threw herself onto her back.

The pixy must have been crushed, but, in a flurry of black feathers, the human bauble bounced out. She snatched off the right slipper and sped into the air, crying, as one word, "Heeheeheeheeheeheeheehee!"

Everyone had the sense to duck except Iranen, who sat up. "Bring that back!" she bellowed.

Chicken-and-Dumplings was easily persuaded, when she was in the mood. She swept down through the crowd and landed the slipper hard across the Housekeeper's mouth. Iranen fell back. The pixy snatched the slipper up again and was out of sight in instants.

Nimnestl proceeded to the doorway she had indicated. The pixy joined her, after several seconds of suspense.

"Ah, at last!" said Nimnestl, as the pixy arrived.

"What?" demanded Chicken-and-Dumplings. "Did you think I'd forget? I am mortally and fatally affronted!" She zipped back as Nimnestl reached for the slipper. "Ah ah ah," she said. "How bad do you want this?"

"How badly would you like to know where Manikitani went, leaving her clothes back here?" the Bodyguard countered.

"Ooh!" breathed the pixy. "I must have been out of the room." She settled to Nimnestl's shoulder. "What's the story?" she demanded, crossing her legs.

She utterly declined to believe a single word of it, it was all a lie, and she would just go check on it to prove what a black-faced prevaricator the Bodyguard was. After she had swirled her exit, Nimnestl raised the tongue of the warm slipper and peered inside. She nodded.

The slippers were thick; blood wouldn't soak through. One could slip around in one's bare feet in a murder room, and then step back into these, leaving without a trail of blood following behind. The bloody gown, even with its expensive fur ornamentation, could be burned, but the slippers made a good souvenir. Until the furor died away, one could simply wear them so the curious did not see the inside.

So. This would open several new cans of worms. At least no one would need to be convinced. Her nature was too well known.

Nimnestl slapped the slipper against one open palm. It was wrong. Iranen's nature was well known, and because of that, anyone could see she was not Morquiesse's killer. Iranen was capable of cutting the arms from a drugged and helpless man. But she wouldn't have strangled him, too. She would have been content to watch him bleed to death.

Palompec, or whoever it was, strangled him first. Then Iranen, on her nightly prowl, happened upon the body and decided to take the arms.

She slapped the slipper down again. Morquiesse kept his door locked, and everyone knew about the thugs who guarded his room. One couldn't simply stroll in, past the anteroom to the bed-chamber. And even Iranen wouldn't be rattling every doorknob she passed on the prowl; she'd get her head knocked off. So something must have drawn her attention to that room, and its unlocked door. The most likely something was the exit of the murderer.

So, during that morning interview, Iranen knew who the killer was. Nimnestl pushed her lower jaw forward. She took a step and then gave the order to relax. Of all people, the Housekeeper could have a good, if hardly innocent, reason for a bloody footprint inside her slipper. Iranen might never have been in the room at all, at least before the news got out.

All the same, a second interview was in order. She turned to see what had become of the Housekeeper. Her elbow bounced off the nose of General Ferrapec, who was trying to peek inside the slipper.

IV

"IS there any particular trouble you wanted, General?" she inquired. "Or would I do?"

One of his aides snickered as Ferrapec pulled back. His expression of affronted dignity was marred by a wince as his irritated neck rubbed on his collar. The general's collar was very fashionable, fastened by an azurite pin that was the only break in a straight column from his cleft chin to his chest. Above this he wore a noble plumed hat really unsuitable for wear indoors (or perhaps anywhere).

His face was stiff again when he answered, "I wished to inquire for the Regent. I intended to consult him about the order of salutes in the awards ceremony."

The order of salutes was a matter for the likes of Meugloth and, say, Colonel Tarrisol, not for the Regent and a general, even this general. The excuse was so feeble as to insult Nimnestl's intelligence, and she was barely able to refrain from offering four better ones.

Instead, she said, "Can it be postponed? There are things I wish to ask you."

This was no request, but a command. Ferrapec didn't like it. "My time is very important, woman," he said, his face petrified.

Nimnestl made a quarter-turn toward the nearest exit. "We can save some of that time by talking on our way. The Regent is in his chambers. Come."

The general glanced toward his aides. Not one offered any suggestion. Two, in fact, were easing over to where Lord Gensamar stood.

"Let's go, men," he said.

Nimnestl held up one finger and a thumb. "We'll do better to chat by ourselves."

For a moment, the stiff lines in the general's face shook. He knew he was a suspect; he knew his lack of prestige made him a good target. But there was no route of escape that wasn't riskier than consenting to go along.

"Very well," he snapped. He stepped forward and then glanced back to say, "Stay here, men." No one bothered to pretend the command was necessary.

Nimnestl and Ferrapec were nearly to the nearest door when a weary, tattered black form dropped onto Nimnestl's shoulder.

"Whoo-ee!" it panted. "I fly all the way clear plumb to the stables."

"Here," said the Bodyguard. She held up the slipper. "Just take this back to Lady Iranen before she tears apart the crowd looking for it. Our little joke is over!"

Ferrapec, no matter how he twisted, could not get a look inside that slipper. But Mardith could. "Little joke, ha?"

"Just go," said the Bodyguard. The bird grumbled and took off. The general and the Bodyguard moved on into the corridor.

Neither made any comment until they were free of the crowd. Nimnestl had feared the general would make a break, but he was apparently perceptive enough to know what kind of target his hat would make him. There were not many places he could run, even without the hat.

Too, he had no hint so far what the Bodyguard wanted. Nimnestl didn't give him one. Soon he would have to start probing.

"You know," he said, aiming at nonchalance, "it's a pity that artist had to die just now. Maiaciara was starting to cool on the rascal."

Nimnestl jerked her head up, as if startled out of deep musings. "Oh, Maiaciara!" she said. "Ah, yes; I was thinking of something else. Yes, she was seeing him regularly, wasn't she?"

The general's upper lip pulled in and moved out as he cursed himself for bringing it up. "Ye-es," he said, "But the affair came to nothing. He was just looking for influence with the Army."

"Ah." Nimnestl nodded. They were marching past the Regent's door, but Ferrapec did not bring it to her attention. "Now, I, myself, would have said that Morquiesse never had much use for the Army."

"What do you mean?"

Nimnestl shrugged. "He never, ever painted a picture really lauding the Service. It must have been a great irritation to our soldiers."

Ferrapec passed her a walleyed glance. "We bore it. There are worse . . ."

"I wasn't thinking of you, of course," she hurried to add, "but there are men on the general staff whose tempers are less certain. Copper-haired men can erupt into violence."

"Aha!" The general was silent then; they pressed on to the door to Nimnestl's rooms. "Do you know," he whispered, stopping to look up and down the hall, "there are troubles ahead, from copper-haired men."

Nimnestl did know it, which was why she had mentioned it. Both Tollamar and Gensamar had red hair.

"Copper-haired man, I should think," she urged. "The one in the Palace was the one I had in mind."

"There isn't a copper's width between them of difference," said the general. "Thank you."

Nimnestl had swept aside a bundle of empty scabbards so Ferrapec would have a place to sit down. "Well, there's only enough room in this murder for one," she told him. "Would anyone believe it?"

Ferrapec considered at length. "I think so . . . if . . ."

She gave him a nod. Finding the Bodyguard amiable was all the general required. He was more than willing to be helpful. Ferrapec detested the Regent and the Bodyguard, but needed every friend he could find. His daughter's dalliance with Morquiesse had been of more benefit to him than to the artist. Now even that sliver of prestige was gone.

Rumor had it that his half-sister Maitena was bribing the Regent to have him sent away. He was heir to a dukedom, rumor had her saying, let him go take care of it. This would promote him to a position of honor and trust, and also keep him away from court for at least six months at a time. When he returned, he would be a duke, but a duke who had lost all touch with affairs in the Council.

Nimnestl liked the idea, but Ferrapec still had one or two allies who, though they had no real interest in Ferrapec, would complain of the insult to the Army if he were sent away without obvious cause. If his father, Jintabh, died, there would be no excuse to keep him in the Palace Royal. He was safe while his father lived, but his father was an old man.

So he was eager to tell the Bodyguard anything that might give him a boost. The main theme of his remarks was corruption, in the Army specifically, but covering all departments of the government. He had been checking into it of late, he mentioned in passing, hours of studying papers long after dark, every night, even after celebrations like the one the night before. Nimnestl smiled at this subtle insertion of alibi. It was possible, of course, though the general's reading skills were almost nill. He might have had a clerk checking the books with him.

The regular bookkeepers, he stated, were incompetents and thieves, though competent thieves. Tollamar and Gensamar allowed massive rake-offs, with much of the money going into the pockets of artists and singers, so that they would paint and sing the mighty accomplishments of those with the price. That this was allowed was not only the fault of the two red-headed generals, but also of that doddering old housekeeper, Forokell, too senile to properly oversee the singers and painters under Iranen's command. Surely one or the other woman ought to be replaced by some competent courtier, a woman from outside the department, a woman who was uncorrupted and competent, a woman like, oh, just for example, Raiprez, Ferrapec's wife.

Nimnestl set her ears on sift; she had heard much of this speech before. After a while, even the general's attention began to wander. Discouraged by a lack of response, he started leaving out details and hurrying to a conclusion. "And there's no need to repeat the business of those battering-ram heads," he said. "Everyone says they were faulty because Palompec is as fat as a hen in the forehead. Well, he's in on it, too. Anyone can tell he . . ."

"Those were the ones with clay for lead?" Nimnestl broke in.

"What?" said the general, losing his place. "Oh, er, yes."

"Palompec was involved? We've had our eyes on him for some time now. Perhaps that would serve as an excuse to look into what he and Gensamar have really been up to."

"Oh, ah," the general began. "Er, yes, Milady. Yes, indeed. Many's the time I've said . . ."

"I think so," she agreed. "Can you find him and bring him here? Quietly? We can question him now, while Gensamar is celebrating, and can't prompt him."

"We shall work together," Ferrapec promised, "to clean up the Council." He rose and, saluting, turned away. He would not be back. Nimnestl knew all about the faulty battering rams, and knew how much Ferrapec had made out of the deal. He wouldn't risk being around for Palompec's counter-accusations.

Not much time passed before Palompec arrived, his feathered cloak sweeping the ground behind him. He also wore feather gloves, attached to the cloak by jewelled chains. The face didn't match this glory. The colonel was an amiably stupid-looking man, of medium height, with a broad, good-natured nose and ears that stuck out from under curly hair. His smile was easy and infectious. He was wearing a faded version of it now. He was alone.

"Er, Milady Bodyguard," he said, on entering. "You asked after me?"

"I did, Colonel," she replied, not rising from her seat.

"Um, er," he stammered, turning red, "if it's, er, about those battering rams that General Ferrapec . . ."

"I am not interested in rams," she informed him. "I am interested in General Ferrapec. Sit down."

He obeyed. "Now, speak quietly," she said, leaning across the table, "and tell me what you know about the general and Morquiesse."

The smile blazed and the big brown eyes glittered. "Morquiesse's death doesn't make you very popular, does it?" he said softly.

"I am here to guard the King, not please the crowd," she informed him. "Someone who could pass Morquiesse's guards and kill him is a threat to all in the Palace Royal. The culprit, no matter who it is or how high his rank, must be brought to justice."

Brown eyes flared. The speech wasn't fooling Palompec. The Bodyguard obviously wanted help throwing the blame all over Ferrapec. He was happy to oblige.

"Would it help," he inquired, "to recall how he got a sleeping drug from Keili? I asked what he was doing, and he said he was going to get a Brown Robe with it. I'd bet that's what kept the guards so quiet, and Morquiesse, too, while he was lying in bed."

He looked to the Bodyguard, and pulled way back on the seat as he saw her face chill. "Keili will swear to it. Er, what do you think?"

Nimnestl rose. "I think you're coming down to the Questioning Room."

The colonel nearly fell over backward. "What? Why?"

"To see what else you can recall." Nimnestl unhooked her hammer and swung it suggestively.

"Too much detail," she told the colonel as he came to his feet. "Who but a Brown Robe would have known Morquiesse was one?"

"But that's what Ferrapec said, Milady," said Palompec, raising his hands. "He must . . ."

"And the sleeping drug," she went on. "Who knew Morquiesse was drugged, besides someone who planned to kill him?"

The colonel put both hands before his face. "Rumor . . ."

Nimnestl swung the hammer to her shoulder. "Tell the truth and save your life."

Palompec dropped to his knees. "I am an Ykena," he said. "If you find the book, you'll see. But I wanted to quit; I . . . I haven't got the stomach for treason. Really, Milady. But they couldn't let me go: I was too deep in their secrets. Morquiesse was going to kill me for that, but I never killed him. I didn't."

Signs of doom appeared at the ends of Nimnestl's mouth. "I didn't," the colonel insisted. "I was going to run last night, and I put the drug in his wine to keep him from sending someone after me. I was halfway to the lake when I heard he was dead, and came back! Please, Milady, it's true! You must believe it! I can show you our secret meeting place in the Palace, and . . . and everything!"

He leaned forward, his hands clutched before his throat. "You can get it all in one raid! Then cut my head off; that's all I ask. A quick death will be better than anything I could get from the Ykenai!"

It was such a tidy story. It explained everything. But Nimnestl did not feel much inclined to believe it, beyond the part about the drug. What a jolt that bottle of wine must have given the drinkers! Maitena would be asking for the recipe.

"Get up!" Nimnestl ordered. "Show me this secret meeting place and I'll show you whether I can be grateful. Signal or speak to anyone . . . anyone . . . on the way and you'll never know what became of your head."

They stayed to the less-travelled corridors, and met no one until they reached the massive wooden doors of the dungeons. No one questioned the Bodyguard's entrance. She kept her hammer raised and let Palompec unlock the doors. This would make a good place for an ambush, but everyone was busy at the celebration. Even so,

Nimnestl walked more slowly now, and looked around her rather more often.

The dungeons were ancient, evil, deep. The main corridor wound down in a wide spiral. Only the first half-mile, which had been Royal Apartments in the bad old days, was still used. Guards patrolled this area in pairs, and only in the daytime. Prisoners cried out in terror as the colonel passed, holding a torch.

No one had been beyond the three-quarter-mile mark in living memory. They were nearing it when Nimnestl demanded, "How much farther?"

"Just a short ways, Milady," answered Palompec. "Here."

He pointed to a cell, and drew a key from inside his tunic. Over his shoulder, Nimnestl could see into a dry, clean room, its floor clear. Having seen maps of this area, she thought she recalled this as being a Royal Exercise Room.

The colonel swung the door open and bowed. Nimnestl replied with a face of great disgust. "You will walk in front of me."

He did so. "This isn't the meeting room," he noted. He stepped across to a wall covered with metal brackets and shallow holes. Nimnestl, following his footsteps exactly so as to avoid boobytraps, spotted a metal disc with four holes in it, attached to the wall. She knew what this was for.

Palompec flipped his key around and inserted the end with four metal pins. When these pins were locked into the holes, he twisted the disc three times to the left, once to the right, and four times to the left again. Nimnestl took hold of the feathered cloak with her left hand, holding the hammer before her with the right.

Nothing dropped on her; the colonel did not try to run. Instead, as the door pulled open, he stepped down. A flight of stairs descended into the darkness. Nimnestl let go of the cloak and walked behind him. This would be a nice, remote place for someone to die; she wondered which of them it would be.

The stairs were steep, with false steps set off at various angles. Palompec explained that these staircases ended at dead ends or long drops. In other places, the stairs would move up for two or three steps, to slow anyone who was charging down them.

After what Nimnestl judged to be about eighty feet, they reached a landing. Palompec took an unlit torch from a stack there, and lit it from the guttering one he carried.

"Now, this is the tricky part," he said, leaning against the wall to catch his breath. An echo carried his whisper up the stairs.

Nimnestl poked him away from the wall with her hammer. "Keep moving."

"Yes, Milady." He started down, and stumbled as the trailing hem of feathers caught under one boot. "Lintik blast these stairs!" he said. "You may wish to lift your robes a bit, Milady. These are specially designed steps."

In the brief second that Nimnestl turned to look down the next flight, Palompec reached for an empty torch bracket. It had not been designed to hold a torch: only visitors.

The Bodyguard didn't even feel the steps as she hit them.

V

LIGHT flickered behind her. She was lying down. Trying to get up hurt so much in so many places that she decided to give it up.

Her chest and shoulders sat hard against a block of rough stone. Only her toes touched the floor. She seemed to be almost kneeling. She tried to lower her knees and kneel all the way. That hurt, too. She let it go.

Action was doing no good, so Nimnestl turned to observation. Her head drooped over the edge of the stone block. She turned this head, slowly, right and left. There was nothing to see but dark stone and the cast-iron feet of some kind of furniture. Bracing herself, she pulled her head back and looked up.

A contemplative face looked down at her. Nimnestl lowered her eyes, taking in all the details of the body beneath the head: twisting tendrils, talons, wings, and other unsavory features. She could remember now what she had been doing when last she was doing anything. Palompec had obviously brought her down to an altar of the demon. She spent a few seconds cursing him and then herself.

She knew she had to do better than that. No killing tools were in evidence, and the Ykenai would score a coup by exhibiting the Bodyguard alive. But the way she was tied to the altar suggested other ceremonies. The time to take action was while she was still, apparently, alone.

Nimnestl wiggled her fingers behind her back. At any rate, she had escaped the fate of Lodoth, one of her predecessors, who rotted away in a small room no one visited. That was the occupational hazard she feared most: one good thump on the head, and forty years' drooling.

She struggled experimentally, less to break free than to find out how she was held. She did not ignore the pain; she analyzed it. No broken bones were immediately evident. There were superficial wounds on her left arm. She was still lightheaded, despite a head that felt leadbound.

Her wrists were tied together, and fastened to a cord wound tight around her waist and between her legs. The hands would move an inch in any direction she chose. She wondered at them leaving her that much.

She was not actually attached to the altar. Her knees were tied to opposite ends of a long wooden bar which spread them too far for her to plant her feet on the floor. To keep her from lowering her knees, another bar, perpendicular to the first, was fastened to the granite altar. The knee-spreader rested on that, and was prevented from sliding off by a vertical bar at the other end. This vertical bar was attached at the top to a horizontal bar which had been forced into a position that discouraged any movement of her torso right, left, up, down, and especially backward.

Nothing kept her from moving forward, so she did, taking little jumping steps with her toes. Each bounce sent her scraping an inch or so forward. At the fourth step, however, she found that that lower horizontal bar slanted up toward the altar. When her toes came off the floor, she had too little weight on the altar to hold her position, and slid right back to her previous place, the knee-spreader smacking the vertical stop. Nimnestl gasped and cracked her head down against the altar.

When the room came into focus again, she licked her lips. She stepped forward again, just those two little toe-steps. She paused. She tried the third step. She chewed on her upper lip a bit. This was going to hurt whether it worked or not.

Throwing all her weight forward, she jerked her legs up as far as she could. Before gravity could claim her, she kicked straight back. When the knee-spreader hit the vertical connecting rod, the whole temple seemed to shudder.

Nimnestl's teeth were clamped so hard together she thought she'd break a few. But when the earthquake settled, the top horizontal bar had a wobble it hadn't before.

Sweat and tears poured onto the altar as she repeated this maneuver two times. After the third impact, the vertical rod cracked loose and clattered across the room. The top horizontal rod pulled from her body and fell. Then she fell, too, face and shoulders scraping along the granite. She got her feet under her before she came completely free of the block, but couldn't muster the strength to rise. Straddling the lower bar, she slid to a seat on the cold stone floor.

Nimnestl rested a bit, but there was little time to spare. She slid around to get her back to the altar. Bracing against this, she rose far enough to sit on top. After letting herself breathe twice, she pulled herself upright.

The statues around her looked entirely too real. She didn't like the idea of getting close enough to cut her bonds on that spiky hair. But the bars on the floor were wood; there were no convenient sharp edges there.

Still hobbled by the knee-spreader, she staggered toward a pile of rubbish under an incense burner. She was very careful. If she fell, she would not be able to catch herself.

The pile was, as she had hoped, made up of her clothes, armor, and weapons. She tried to kneel next to it, and instead fell face-first into the bundle. She had seen the handle of her hammer, and was able to twist enough to miss the head. One of her daggers lay right under her nose.

The sheath was still attached to her belt, so the blade was easy enough to draw with her teeth. Getting it situated so she could work at the ropes was trickier, but it was a trick the had practiced, expecting to need it. She freed herself without shedding much additional blood. Once the knee-spreader was cut away, she was ready for action.

The action she took was to fall backward and lie where she was among the tumbled clothing. Her head was heavy, she had scraped away a lot of her outermost layer of skin, and she was exhausted. Yet, all her effort was just the beginning. The stairs waited. They would be challenge enough even if Palompec and the Ykenai were not on their way down to meet her.

Rolling over, she forced herself to her knees. A look at her armor and all those clothes nauseated her. She picked up her cloak and tucked it around herself. The belt and sheath were probably necessary, but she decided that was as much as she cared to do. Booted feet bumped the door as she fastened the buckle.

Time was up. She put her back to the wall and rose for a fight. It would not, at least, be a long one.

"Ah!" someone said. The door slid open.

Any chance she had lay in surprise, but Nimnestl's body would not leap. She had only enough energy to glare, and hope that terror would work where muscles would not.

The little man was a bit startled, but intelligent eyes picked out the blood and the state of the Bodyguard's clothes. "Well," he said, leaning on the door jamb, "and here I thought I'd get to rescue somebody."

As far as Nimnestl knew, and she knew pretty far, Haeve had no connection to the Ykenai. He was one of a dozen men she was almost prepared to trust. He might be a demon worshipper, of course, but she was not presented with a choice.

"I must see the Regent," she whispered.

"Are you the only one here?" asked the Tutor. "Let's go, then." He came to her side, but didn't touch her.

She let her dagger drop. The less weight she had to carry, the better. She took two steps forward and, with a "Why is the floor so slippery?" expression, started to slide down.

Haeve threw an arm around her waist and forced her semi-erect. "You're a dead weight, Bodyguard," he gasped.

"Not yet, Tutor," she whispered. "Not yet."

They wrestled over to the door and then the stairs, Nimnestl leaning alternately on the Tutor and on the wall. She forced herself to take at least two steps between each rest stop.

The little man was stronger than he looked. On the stairs, Nimnestl found breath to pant, "Why did you have to leave Keastone, Tutor?"

Haeve glanced up and smiled a little. "I was a horses thief."

Nimnestl started up the stairs again. "Horse thief," she corrected.

The Tutor braced himself under her elbow and said, "I never stole a horse, Bodyguard. I stole herds. Just an exercise in political science, really."

Nimnestl lost track of the times they stopped to rest. They gained the secret door and stumbled out into the small cell. After that, it was the twisting ramp, which was almost harder. They met no Ykenai.

Voices could be heard from the far side of the massive dungeon doors. Haeve stopped, but Nimnestl, recognizing them, tottered forward.

"So there I was," Culghi was saying, "with the slips in one hand and the cash in the other, giving Jansiesse odds. Brother, didn't she rake me into the garden and spread me on the tomatoes!"

"Go on home," retorted Sixlift. "You sure it wasn't just because you wouldn't let her kiss you?"

Four of the King's Bodyguards looked around when the dungeon door opened. Shock, anger, and terror showed in equal parts on their faces as they recognized their commander.

It took effort, but Nimnestl had an iron reputation to uphold. "Just Brown Robes," she said, in response to frantic questions. "To the Regent, now. All of us. Move quickly; move quietly."

The route they took was long, but they were able to reach the Regent's chambers without meeting anyone conscious. Kaftus was inside. He watched, entertained, as the weary band pushed through the doorway. Nimnestl did not stand on ceremony, but collapsed into the handiest seat.

"Told you not to mix your drinks," the necromancer said.

"Palompec," the Bodyguard panted. A grey cloud drifted before her eyes. She shook her head. That hurt.

When she looked up, there was nothing to see but grey stone and little black dots. Stone was pressing on her chest. Breathing hurt.

"Here, woman, wake up!" ordered a rough voice. Someone shook her shoulder.

CHAPTER NINE
Polijn

I

ONE eye and a fraction of Polijn's attention were on the crowd,
watching for Aoyalasse or other foes. But the grand assembly
took all the rest. There had been other parties, over the winter,
but Polijn had never worked the main room before. This time,
though Arberth had again been relegated to performances in the
Great Dining Hall, the jester had arranged for her to make her solo
debut here. Meugloth wanted minor, unobtrusive acts to take up
spaces between the major exhibitions, giving the crowd something
to watch during rearrangements on the platform. So Polijn was
to sing while his men cleaned the stage after Jarmory's dancing
horses, but only if the platform needed cleaning; Polijn hoped the
horses had been well fed and watered.

The Great Hall glittered with magnificence. Polijn could see
Hansil, sweeping up thrown food and broken glass, but had no
mind for him. Iranen's servants were passed over, too: nudity and
brutality had no novelty to offer. What filled her eyes were the
glittering garlands wound around ceiling beams, and the little dogs
in page suits, rolling in the laps of women whose back cleavage
was outlined in silver braid and whose arms jangled with bangles.
Polijn put a hand to her own armband, to be sure it was still there.
It hung heavy on her arm. How heavy, she wondered, were those
fashionable conglomerate costumes?

A great peacock pie, long feathers spread behind it like a fan,
sat in the middle of the buffet, accompanied by an array of dishes

186

exciting for variety as well as quantity. Polijn would not be eating anything here—she had to save her throat for singing, and the attendants knew well who was entitled to eat at this table—but it was almost as good to just look.

She wasn't hungry anyhow; there was too much to look it. (And look for? She backed against Arberth, but the woman drawing a fortune from the vendor's hat was not Aoyalasse after all.) A flying scarves act was finishing up on the platform, looking much more thrilling than the ropeskipping exhibition in the Great Dining Hall. Back down there it was all stale wine, cold potatoes, and those death's heads in Morquiesse's mural, grinning down. Much better to be here, near the Banner of Kairor, the Holy Throne, and other relics: each with a story, and half the stories forgotten already, so used were these people to having them around.

Polijn was not blind to the danger that accompanied this magnificence. She and Arberth dodged under a table, joining a dog, two cats, and a Treasury guard, as Iranen passed in pursuit of the Bodyguard's raven.

"You need get more close nor that!" called the bird, waving something just beyond the woman's reach.

The crowd closed behind them, laughing as loudly as was consistent with personal safety. "I wonder what that was all about," said Polijn, as she and Arberth rose from shelter.

"At one of these affairs," answered the jester, wiping his forehead, "you never know what will happen next."

A hand fastened on his left arm. "Murderer!"

Polijn and her employer turned to face Kohoontas, one of the Palace midgets. "And thief!" added the little man. "You've killed a rat and stolen its face. How much did they throw at you down in the Dining Room?"

"Oh," said the jester, with a shrug, "I just hit them at the wrong time. They're grieving too much for Morquiesse to care about good music."

"I'm sure that's it," said the midget, nodding. "Come, let's get a jug and you can show me that card trick again."

Arberth, Polijn had noticed, did not care much for cards at the Palace. He had said something to her about preying outside one's neighborhood.

"I don't have any cards," he told Kohoontas.

The small man nodded again. "I have cards," he replied, in a voice of patience. "Come along."

Arberth shrugged again. "One moment."

He turned to Polijn. "Keep an eye on Meugloth," he told her, pointing the man out. "If I'm not back, he'll give you the signal when you're to go up. Be alert, or he'll pass you over."

"I will." Polijn doubted she'd be able to relax.

The jester limped away with his smaller counterpart. "Have you heard what Isanten's saying about you?" Kohoontas demanded. "It's a real chiller."

Once they were gone, Polijn found a nook among the furniture, from which she could watch Meugloth unseen. She had, as well, a good view of the platform, where the jester Bilibi was doing an act with skulls and his small daughter. Polijn settled back to watch and pick up pointers. Her view was immediately blocked by a spectator who turned to cry, "Polijn!"

Iúnartar's cheeks were puffed out as if she'd been running. She probably had been. She ran everywhere. Polijn wished for some of that youthful energy.

The girl wore earrings bigger than her ears, made of nine hoops to symbolize nine magic waves. Those not tangled in her hair jangled against her cheeks as she turned to point at the assembly and then back at Polijn.

"Did you see me dancing with the King?" she panted.

"No," said Polijn.

"I did," she said. "He was in disguise as Merklin, but I knew who it was, of course. But don't tell anyone, not anyone. It's a secret!"

"Mm-hmm." The story was possible, but that it would remain a secret was unbelievable.

"And I have new shoes," Iúnartar went on. "He liked them." She put out a foot to show off her slippers. They were cut off across the front in the shape of a mouth, and had cat's-eye stones farther up to make a face. Iúnartar pointed this out twice, and went on to explain her frilly overdress, which bounced whenever she took a step, and which was cut lower in back than in front: her first adult dress.

Polijn murmured proper appreciation and Iúnartar soon turned to what everyone else in the room was wearing. The little girl was fully versed in all the technicalities of chokers, combs, ribbons, ribands, headdresses, chin straps, scarves, fans, kerchiefs, handkerchiefs, neckerchiefs, sashes, gloves, purses, and a hundred other additions and accessories on display. Polijn didn't even know the names of some of these, but Iúnartar was more than willing to supply any information that was lacking. She was also happy to pass along who had embroidered shawls and whose were merely appliqué, and whose jewels were paste and whose doublets or triplets.

She pulled Polijn up and forward, the better to point out this or that example of true style or false pretenses. So much for remaining inconspicuous. Iúnartar's high, chipper voice (and perhaps her dance with the King) naturally drew attention. People parted for her as she dragged Polijn through the crowd. Even those people who always stopped right in the flow of traffic to chat moved aside and smiled as the little girl passed. Others, striding past, turned to look, not stopping, but letting their heads swivel as they moved, ready to pause if the girl returned the glance. Iúnartar never did, but Polijn could tell she was aware of her audience. Whenever she thought eyes were on her, she would drop her smile and replace it with a silly sultry expression.

Fine men and women, some arm in arm as couples, passed on every side. Polijn wondered what it was like to be that way: fancy as a toll gate, Ronar would have said.

What would they be doing at home, just now? Ronar, having supervised the departure of the others, would have settled in for the evening's drinking. Gloraida would be making up at the Yellow Dog. And Polijn and Mokono would be outside, Polijn near the alley behind the Thick Fleece and Mokono, carrying lunch, around from the apothecary's.

Polijn felt she was coming to understand Mokono better and better. Even being apprenticed to a bad jester was better than ever going back to the Swamp to stay.

Iúnartar was in the middle of a discourse on the pros and cons of decorative armpit shaving when Polijn realized the little girl was pulling her toward the benches of the Royal Councillors. This was, in its own way, as bad as the Swamp, but maybe the benches were too exposed for anyone to risk attacking her. And by listening to conversations among the VIPs, she could maybe decide to sing about Haddanto, about Derwan and his dogs, or turn instead to one of the songs popular at the Yellow Dog.

"I like the vegetables crisper, myself," said a bored-looking colonel. "Oh, yes, Morquiesse was a mighty marksman. He could shoot an apple off your head at ninety paces."

"I've seen him do it. I've seen him shoot off an ear instead, too, if he thought it'd be funny. Remember Laisida?"

"Oh, a mad wag he was."

Polijn coughed. If Alohien and Aoyalasse weren't anywhere near her, why was she still so jumpy?

"What do you know about it?" demanded a man at the shuffle-board table. "Lord Neinceiuns of Lattin . . ."

"Oh, those Lattinese just like to hear themselves talk."

Jonsert was unconscious under the table. A giggling Treasury guard poured something from a mug into the man's ear. For a minute the guard had looked like Haeve, but such amusements were beneath the dignity of the cool Royal Tutor. Haeve was really up near the Royal Platform, chatting with the King's Nurse.

Iúnartar detected a lapse of attention and repeated her previous statement more insistently. "And she may have a birthday party for me when I turn nine. Did you ever have a birthday party, Polijn?"

"Um," said Polijn. "No."

"When is your birthday, anyway?"

Polijn coughed again. "It's past."

"How about your next one?"

"It's coming."

"How old are you, anyway?"

"Twelve, or something like it." Perhaps Iúnartar could be interested in the fine art of tying a cherry stem with one's tongue. It might keep her mouth closed.

Those VIPs not pushing among the sights sat in a civilized manner on long benches, with small and exceedingly civilized little tables pulled up before them. Behind them were representative selections from among their retainers, prepared to guard their backs, fetch the wine, and add to their consequence. Flanking Lynex, Iúnartar's obvious target, were Laisida on one side and old Duke Jintabh on the other. Jintabh seemed to have no retinue besides his family. Scads of young men were, however, attending on his granddaughter.

Polijn knew even before Iúnartar whispered it that Ferrapec was taking another slide. Every time he lost prestige, Maiaciara was deluged with offers, young men hoping she'd accept them out of desperation. Maiaciara flipped long lashes at them all; she was not the one who was desperate. Her gown showed no fashionable back cleavage; her eyes said, "You know what's under here; I don't have to show it off. Your problem is how to get at it." In a place where eligible men had to be fought for, she could have had a hundred admirers to use as a pillow.

Ferrapec joined his family. He was smiling, and this smile attracted followers as he moved through the room. At the same time, the crowd before his daughter melted, leaving only a few diehards. He patted his wife on the shoulder, and nodded assuringly to his mother.

"In my next life," declared his father, to no one, "I'm going to make it shorter."

One of Laisida's seven daughters also meandered by. Her father didn't seem to be paying attention but, as she passed, he whirled, snatched up her skirts in back, and gave the exposed flesh a smack with his crutch.

"I saw you with young Illefar over there," he replied to her shocked exclamation. "You keep your knees together and your dress over them."

"Oh, Daddy!" she snorted.

Lynex's eyes were disapproving, but they warmed when they fell on Iúnartar. "Do come sit up here," she called. "You'll be able to see so much better."

Polijn couldn't even see where they were expected to sit. Lynex and her most trusted attendants were leaning all over each other on the bench. But Iúnartar walked straight forward. The Housekeeper swept her lap of crumbs and elbows, and lifted Iúnartar to it.

"Oh, Lady Lynex," said the girl, "this is Polijn, my friend."

"I see," said the Housekeeper. Polijn squatted in an awkward curtsy. "Do find a nice place to sit, Polijn." Her manner was cool but not cold. Even the Second Chief Housekeeper didn't care to offend the assistant to a friend of the Head Bodyguard, even though that connection showed no great potential for benefit right now.

Polijn knelt on the floor, rather out from the bench and somewhat in front, so as not to offend those of the Housekeeper's retinue who wrinkled their noses. One or two slid away as Polijn sat back on her heels. Iúnartar didn't notice; she was explaining to Lynex how Lady Ysela had changed the pattern of her oxters.

This was a good spot from which to watch the platform, but Polijn didn't like it. Part of her training in the Swamp had been to know when someone was looking at her. Someone was looking at her.

She slid her eyes back and forth. The Housekeeper's women weren't interested; they were averting their eyes from the grubby assistant jester. She glanced toward Laisida's retinue. No one there paid her any attention.

Turning to Jintabh's crowd, her eyes met three pairs of deep, black eyes aimed at her. Ferrapec, Raiprez, and even tall, cool Kodva, with that nose just built for looking down on the presumptuous, were studying her. Polijn looked away, watched the movement on the platform. Until they spoke, it was none of her business why they were studying her, and insubordinate to stare back.

She did check to be sure her armband was still well hidden. It was, so perhaps there was no more to their scrutiny than the clothes Arberth had picked out. She should have known better than to think she could stay inconspicuous in those.

II

IÚNARTAR, oblivious of Polijn's discomfort, chattered on, picking up speed and increasing in volume now that her audience was enlarged. Lynex directed her attention to Veira, over by the buffet, and began to discuss the finer points of flirtation through manipulation of gloves and handkerchiefs.

"Oh, yes!" said the girl. "See, Polijn? Raising the hanky that way means 'My lips could be yours.' And look! Lord Kercia recognizes it!"

"Mm," said Polijn.

"And the gloves folded across each other in that manner?" asked Lynex.

"That's 'My love . . . ' No, wait. That means 'I Would Speak With You.' "

Unfortunately for the civilized but fledgling art of silent messages, Lord Kercia was distracted by Joive. Passing, Joive gave the ambassador from Dongor a nice smile and then, as she turned the corner around the buffet, flipped up all her skirts in back. Lord Kercia followed, brushing past Veira as he whispered something to the other woman. Joive's mouth opened in apprehension as one of her eyes closed in comprehension.

Veira threw her gloves on the floor and pushed past two men laughing into their hoods, nearly knocking over Buran, who had been approaching her with a proposition of his own. Buran pulled his elbow up out of the tureen he had fallen back against and came

193

face to face with Mitar, the Court Lawknower. The Lawknower
was either preoccupied or deliberately ignoring the would-be
nobleman, and failed to raise his hat. Buran reached up, grabbed
the broad velvet hat and smashed it into the Lawknower's face.
As a matter of self-defense, Mitar snatched up a fork from the
table and ripped down through Buran's chest, scattering dusty
woolen padding. Two bodyguards by that time were able to force
themselves between the two men before violence could spread.

Iúnartar was helpless with laughter; Lynex's ladies tittered. The
business simply annoyed Polijn. Whatever Reival was singing
sounded as if it might be a pretty good song, if one was allowed
to hear it.

One of Jintabh's great-nephews reached up from under the
bench, tickling the duke's nose with a long, stolen feather. Kodva
reached down, caught his wrist in a hand like a vise, and whispered, "If you wake him up, you can sit here and amuse him for
the evening."

This chaos had its soothing side, too. She might not have to
worry about the audience for her song. No one would be paying
any attention. Those who happened to glance at the platform now
were interested more by those fascinating poles and bars being
assembled behind Reival than in the minstrel's performance.

Whatever was being erected was proceeding on schedule, for
Meugloth was leaning contentedly against the platform, moving
only when his assistance was called for in securing a pole. Behind
him, his daughter Lefeald watched in awe as a castle of iron bars
rose. An older girl, realizing Lefeald's attention was elsewhere,
reached up slowly for the doll the child was dragging on the floor.
A long arm encased in black silk shot out of the crowd.

The older girl was jerked back and dealt a slap that could be
heard even over the sound of construction and Iúnartar's shrieking
laughter. Meugloth whirled. A woman all in black smiled amiably
at him. The master of ceremonies pointed to a chair and barked
an inaudible command at his daughter.

"Oh, I ayam!" piped the girl. She climbed into the chair knee
first, her ruffled skirts flying up in back. Two or three men
leaned in, but pulled away when Meugloth turned again. The
older girl, meanwhile, pulled loose of her mother and stomped
away. Like other lower class children, she wore a skity, a skirt
of multi-colored strips hanging from a waistband. At each step,
she bared her legs nearly to the waist, but no spectators turned
to look at her.

Reival finished, bowed, and retired to a smattering of applause and old potatoes. The crowd was all but silenced, studying the high castle of wooden bars, metal joints, and canvas elements. A ruffle in the tapestry depicting the Victory at Drawziw attracted some attention, but this, it developed, had nothing to do with the act. Manikitani, looking both hurt and disgusted, came out from behind it, jamming herself into the clothes handed her.

Meanwhile, a company all in black silk mounted the platform. Two boys walking in the rear jumped up and over the rest of the company, and the audience sat up. A knot of card players off behind the throne platform arrested their game, and even Chymola and Iúnartar were quiet for a second. Only those who were too far back to see kept up the background roar, as did Colonel Palompec and a little group by the buffet.

The oldest woman in the company nodded to a slim girl, who stepped forward with a bounce and a skip.

"Ladies, Gentlemen!" she cried. "Your Sacred Majesty!" The two boys rolled and tumbled behind her. "We now p-present the tale of Derwan. B-but first, have all the dog and cat doors been closed? We can have no drafts during our p-performance!"

Iranen rose and, murmuring something about going to see, rushed from the room. The story of Derwan was definitely not one of her favorites.

The girl closed her eyes, swallowed, and introduced the company. The tremor in her voice had nothing to do with the danger of tumbling, and Polijn guessed this must be her first time on stage in such a tight, brief costume. The others were not conscious of it at all; the boys strutted back and forth, to be sure everyone noticed the black fringe that ran up the cloth tight around their calves and thighs. Some of Lynex's attendants were drooling.

But the girl, though her voice was strong and her tone brazen, was terrifically embarrassed. You could see it in the way one hand kept slipping behind her, and how she kept bending her knees as if to hide the inevitable.

The Royal Tutor pushed past, blocking Polijn's view. He had not meant to stop just there, but was stopped by a bodyguard who whispered, "My Lord, a lady over there has admired your cloak and thinks your costumes would match perfectly if you but bought her a necklace from that vendor by the door."

Haeve worked his way around the man. "Tell her ladyship that the cloak is not paid for, and neither will the necklace be."

The girl had turned a bit when Polijn could see her again. She was wearing, Polijn realized with a shock, underpants. And in front of all these people, not to mention the King! It was no wonder the girl was upset. Oh, the boys wore something under their tights, and one of the women had straps to hold her buttocks up, but these were complete pants.

Polijn was not the only person who noticed the garment, so recently introduced that decency crusades were being preached against such things. The crowd grew more interested, drawing nearer the platform. Hands came up, and fingers began to point. The girl backed up. The oldest woman, probably her mother (the same woman who had averted the theft of Lefeald's doll), put a knee up behind her to halt the retreat. Then the woman nodded to someone among the minstrels.

When she sang, some of the age marks vanished; you could almost mistake the mother for the daughter. Polijn could tell the older woman was the more practiced performer. Her head bobbed merrily on each beat, and her smile could easily form a pout or pull back in a coy smile, depending on the expression necessary for the story. The girl just sang along.

The rest of the company presented an acrobatic version of the tale of Derwan. In this version, Derwan was a prosperous bandit chief, whose outlaws naturally rolled around a lot and did somersaults while bouncing balls, tossing scarves, and ringing little bells. The oldest man in the group, his long red cape swirling through the assembly of black figures, was meant to be Derwan, a bandit of such venerable splendor that he could do a double twist in the air and touch the back of his head with his calf.

The story of Derwan was known to the audience, which found this prologue uninteresting. Everyone was poised to pay attention the moment things turned exciting, but saw no reason to suspend conversation indefinitely.

"Aren't those pretty pearls Lady Chymola has?" Lynex asked.

"Oh, yes," said Iúnartar, in a languid tone that did not fool Polijn. "It's marvellous what they can do with glass and fish scales."

Lynex was as impressed as Iúnartar had hoped. "Oh, isn't she precious!" the Housekeeper exclaimed.

Everyone laughed, though Chymola's laughter was a bit brittle.

Several bandits on the platform sneaked back behind the castle, donning gold capes and helmets to become soldiers of the Duke.

Conversation gave way, but the noise level did not drop. The audience screamed and cheered as Derwan leaped up into the air and arched a tremendous two-handed swordblow down on a soldier. Derwan rolled over the soldier as the soldier dropped stone dead, only to scramble up again and become a new soldier. Lynex's ladies joined the rest of the crowd in screeching advice, betraying what was now considered for ladies an uncivilized knowledge of swordplay.

Derwan was carried away and "locked up" in the castle at last. His bandits slunk away and returned on all fours, barking out their new roles as Derwan's loyal dogs. These last supporters of Derwan made plans carefully (and at the tops of their lungs, but perhaps the Duke's soldiers, all of two yards away, did not speak dog languages), and then hauled a length of rope, or wire, to the top of a high pole. One dog leaped from there to the castle, the rope in his mouth. He fastened it to a high tower, and then tumbled away. As the dogs discussed the next phase, the rope pulled tight. Polijn noticed that the girl was no longer singing, and made out another figure inside the castle with Derwan.

Now the dogs leaped to the attack and a new battle began, all barking dogs and swirling gold capes. It was fortunate that Iranen had left. They fought not only on the platform, but on the sides of the castle, bounding up and falling away as their roles demanded. Derwan, a long pole in one hand, appeared at the top of the castle, a good twelve feet, Polijn estimated, above the platform. He took a step onto the rope, and the audience was silenced once more. Dogs and soldiers continued to roll up and down the castle.

"Oh!" cried Iúnartar, grabbing Polijn. "He's shaking! Look at the fringe!"

"That's why he wears it!" Polijn snapped. "So you can see how hard this is."

Someone nearby applauded her lightly and said, "Bravo!" but Polijn was too intent on the show to pay attention to Laisida. How did he arch his leg that way? Did he always keep two points of contact with the rope, in case one slipped, or was she seeing wrong?

As the fight went on, Polijn began to detect a pattern in the barks of the dogs, a rhythm in the falls and attacks. A moment's consideration told her why. Every time someone fell, they shook the castle, and the rope. Derwan had to know when the rope was going to tremble. So each fall, each bark, was planned, part of a system. It was inspiring.

Whether the rest of the audience could see this, it thundered its approval as the act ended. Dozens of people pushed forward to congratulate Derwan, his dogs, his bandits, and his other assistants. A large crowd gathered around the girl who had introduced everyone. Her mother stood behind her, a wary old cat watching those who would tease her kitten. Reival stood by, looking from the girl to one of Iranen's naked slaveys and then back, measuring, estimating.

The crowd was forcibly thinned by workers forcing a way through to disassemble the castle. Among the musicians, Tarobbin stood forth and began to sing a song he said was new. Beside him, one of his assistants blew a note on a luron, and called out the title, "The Wolf and the Lamb."

Three lines into the song, Lynex, who had been discussing calf muscles with her attendants, sat up straight, dislodging two ladies and greatly discommoding Iúnartar. She threw one glance at her husband, Jontus, who had his hand over his wolf tattoo. This was worthless, since everyone knew what picture was on his arm.

Chymola, sitting nearby, golden-haired and glowing, blushed prettily, hugging her elbows. Polijn understood in seconds why Lynex's smile had taken on the air of rigor mortis. Jontus had commissioned a song for his wife from Arberth, but for his mistress he had called on Tarobbin, one of the King's Minstrels.

Some spectators understood this too, and turned to laugh into the seclusion of their hoods. Others pretended they were just listening to a pretty song. (It was very good, Polijn thought.) Others made no pretense, but just looked from Jontus to his wife and back again. Jontus had the expression of one who has just put a half-eaten peach down someone's blouse and is pretending he knows nothing about it. Lynex's smile was firm and wavering by turns. Her hands went to the raw rope marks on her neck.

Iúnartar started to slide down, a second too late. The girl crashed onto Polijn as Lynex, leaping over them both, went for Chymola. Seeing a knife in the older woman's hand, Chymola screeched and covered her face. The Housekeeper caught her up by the hair and hauled her out of her seat, half-tearing and half-slashing the bright golden curls.

Nuseth and Avtrollan were the only ones who dared intervene; she being one of Lynex's assistants and he one of Jontus's, they saw their livelihood in danger. Slapping and scolding Chymola, Nuseth managed to get an arm across the terrified woman's head and face. Avtrollan gauged the moment and then shot out one hand to twist the hand that held the knife. It fell to the floor among the bloody curls.

Jontus, who had hitherto wavered on the edge of the spectacle, fondling his sword, now moved in, talking to his wife at a hundred words a lick. His wife screamed back at him about pet squirrels.

"What's going on?" demanded Jintabh, opening his eyes.

One of his attendants, a square, hulking soldier, bellowed for his wife. A small, pale woman in a golden dress hurried to his side.

"Sit down," he ordered.

Her eyes widened, but she turned to look for a spot on the bench.

"Sit down," he repeated.

She stared. He took a step forward.

She sank down onto the floor. Something among the straw made a squishing sound as she settled there. She winced, but did not take her eyes off her husband. He nodded with satisfaction, and turned away.

III

AN indication of how impressed Iúnartar was by it all was that the only word she could pronounce for the next several seconds was "Wow!"

But the little girl was thinking all the time, and rose to plant herself on the bench she had just tumbled from. The Housekeeper's entire retinue had followed Jontus from the room, leaving lots of space. Tugging at Polijn's shoulder, Iúnartar urged her friend up next to her.

"It's all right," she announced to the attendant who came to protest. "We are holding Lady Lynex's seats until she returns."

The attendant, possibly recognizing her as the girl who had danced with the King, bowed and withdrew. Polijn was impressed.

This interlude unfortunately loosened Iúnartar's tongue again, and Polijn found herself getting a not very condensed version of Chymola's entire life, and Tarobbin's biography as well. She was not listening. Meugloth had signalled to men who moved in to assemble a large ramp. Polijn had an inkling of what this was for, and she was right. A shiver shook her as she saw the first horse come forward.

"Oh, we aren't that bad," said Iúnartar, feeling the shiver. "Only one person loses."

Polijn frowned, having lost the thread of the conversation.

Iúnartar nodded toward the doorway that had been opened for the horses. "You should come to the next rites. And don't worry about meeting Maitena; we never even invite her. She wouldn't like it."

The girl seemed to be indicating her father, playing cards with two men, and two children. Polijn recalled, suddenly, that Iúnartar and her father were Neleandrai. Playing cards had some important role in their rites, she'd heard. Iúnartar had told her a few dozen times, with the result that, right now, Polijn could remember none of it.

"The King is really interested, though," Iúnartar went on. She nodded now to the monarch on the Royal Platform. He was leaning far over one arm of his seat, watching the cards flip into piles. "We think he might even join, one day."

The King was not the only one leaning out of his seat. Members of Ferrapec's retinue and some of Laisida's had begun to tip alarmingly toward the empty spaces on the bench. Those seated slid closer. Little pitchers had big mouths.

A trembling, half-fed girl in a red skity picked up her cards and blanched. Iúnartar jumped a little, crowing, "Masalan must've gotten a red seven! She always does that when she has a bad hand!"

The girl put her cards, and then her head, on the table. Colonel Tusenga gently drew the cards from under her. He checked them over and then raised his hands above Masalan's head.

"The King hates Masalan," Iúnartar confided. "She talks too much."

The King was sitting back now, apparently watching the horses file up the wooden ramp. His mouth was thin, set, and his eyes looked a little pinched. He said nothing. The King could seldom afford to speak ill of anyone, for everyone was listening.

The boy who had sat next to Masalan, having tossed his cards in with the others, left the group and ran to the Royal Platform. It was Merklin, so he was allowed to pass. He said something to the King, who glanced once at Masalan and then away.

Colonel Tusenga was drawing the girl over to the steps at the front of the platform, far from the horses but close to Polijn's seat. "Just wait until you get one," she heard him say. "A fresh one."

The horses waited in an uneven circle on the platform. Masalan dragged herself up the steps. Her foot caught on one of the strips that dangled from her waist, and she nearly fell flat on the stage. Landing on her knees, she stared up at the big, solid animals and shuddered.

Iúnartar sat up straight and released a long, pealing laugh, considerably startling both Polijn and her father. "I know what she's supposed to wait for!"

Her father raised sardonic eyebrows. Those nearest Polijn laughed with the girl. Polijn did not laugh. She hoped the girl would not be required to keep the entire stage clean, or there would be no need for a song between this and the following attraction.

Seuvain stepped up onto the platform and, not seeing the nearest spectator, called to the horses to form their pyramid. One had to take two steps closer to Masalan to get into position. The girl crawled toward the steps, but Tusenga was there. She backed away.

A horse reared. It had not seen her yet; this was the point at which it was supposed to rear. But Masalan, turning to look, saw massive raised hooves, and doom with them. She ran to the back of the platform now, covering half the distance in a headlong fall. A woman stationed there grabbed her by the shoulders, stood her up, and pushed her back toward the horses.

"Stop!" someone shouted.

All laughter, all hooting, all shouting, all noise of any kind, stopped. Even the half-conscious were startled out of their euphoria. The King had spoken.

He seemed to have no inclination to speak again, but stood before his chair, his lower jaw jutting. He stared at Tusenga.

A member of his bodyguard leaned forward to whisper. The King turned, and Tusenga stepped back and over the bench his daughter sat on. In moments, he was gone, invisible in the sea of spectators.

The King was giving his bodyguard definite orders, but all Polijn heard, even in that unlikely silence, was, "It isn't funny!"

"Eru!" whispered Iúnartar. "I didn't think he even liked her!"

The bodyguard strode down from the Royal Platform, across the floor, and then up to the stage where the horses stood, restlessly awaiting the rest of their orders. The big man ignored Seuvain, the horses, and the crowd. Masalan, who obviously regarded a Royal Bodyguard as a peril on the same level as a warhorse, darted away, but he caught her by the waist. He set her on one shoulder and bore her away to the Royal Platform. Merklin offered her his chair.

"Thank you, Culghi," said the King. He turned to Seuvain. "The horses will not be injured now. You may continue."

"Do you think he really likes her?" whispered Iúnartar. "Or does he just have a headache? Or what? What if we made him mad? What do you think I should do, Polijn? Polijn?"

Polijn had no advice to give. There was enough to occupy her mind just thinking of what she would do next. Meugloth had beckoned.

Dashing around the platform, keeping well away from the stairs just in case someone thought she was an imitator of Masalan, Polijn hurried to the master of ceremonies. Meugloth had lost all his good cheer. "Be ready, girl," he growled.

"Yes, Master," she replied.

"They're cutting this dodge short. Lintik, and we were doing so well before Tarobbin . . . And now this. Ah, do what you can."

"I will," she promised.

He scowled at her. "And listen. When they throw things at you, take them. That way we don't have to clean the stage twice!"

He stalked off a few feet and then looked back. "Well? You can't go up that way, with the horses coming down!"

"Oh," said Polijn. She trotted after him, improvising apologies. He answered none of them.

Which song? Derwan had been taken; she couldn't bring it out so soon after that performance. She could still do the one she knew about Haddanto. It was a good hero tale, with a strong, robust chorus.

They passed a short bench where a very young man she didn't know was helping Veira's mother on with a glove. They were having little luck, and giggled about it. Polijn thought, for no particular reason, of the first time she had been drunk.

She sighed. Best go with one of the songs from the Yellow Dog.

IV

POLIJN thought she'd have to sing without an instrument, but as she reached the stairs, Arberth caught at her sleeve. Breathless, he passed her the ficdual. Polijn wrapped one arm around the wooden bell-shaped body, and one around the neck.

"Stand up straight," he panted. "Breathe. And remember, at base, none of these people are any better than the ones you're singing about. Each has moaned over a lover. Or under one."

She giggled. He seemed to expect her to, and there was no harm in humoring him.

Starting up the stairs, she remembered her clothes. She wasn't prepared to humor him that far. Setting the ficdual on the top step, and keeping her eyes on it, she shuffled out of everything but her shift and her tunic. Red and gold: they didn't clash so badly, and the armband went with them.

"Hot in here," she said, handing the extra clothes to Arberth. Before he could object, she took up the ficdual and hurried to the platform.

The horses were making their final turn before filing down the ramp. A chair left over from the second pyramid had been set to one side. Polijn claimed it, and turned to face the Royal Platform.

A shiver she hadn't expected rattled through her as she looked out at the audience. Her spot on the platform was chilly, exposed. Most of the spectators were still concentrating on the horses, but a few turned toward the newcomer. Polijn's throat tightened; she gave a little cough.

Everyone in the Palace Royal was a qualified music critic because everyone in the Palace Royal sang, if only along. It was a sign of civilization, a mark of status, and a way to while away time. There were love lyrics, story songs, patter songs, nonsense songs, and everybody knew a dozen of each, not including old songs that everyone knew as a matter of course.

But people who sang professionally, the minstrels and musical jesters, were not allowed slips that would have been overlooked in, say, a colonel of the City Guard. Polijn knew she would be judged by the exacting standards of dabblers listening to a professional. She could gauge current sentiment by the number of people strolling back to the buffets and selecting the pieces of fruit no one had chosen to eat. They knew whose apprentice she was.

Clearing her throat once more, she focussed on a tall, dark laundress with a pierced nose. She stepped forward and tossed the audience a long, red grin. Some grinned back, and a few applauded, less in expectation of any talent than in appreciation of the way she winked and propped one leg on the chair. Hitching back the hem of her shift, she stuck the ficdual against the inside of her left thigh. The strings would have to be tuned to the crank; they always needed work after Arberth had used them.

"It isn't far now, friends," she announced, in a husky whisper she hoped would cut through the room. "That inn to which we all go at night, though we know some never come out again."

The riddle was old, but a young and moderately tiddly soldier in Ferrapec's retinue shouted, "Sleep! You mean we go to sleep!"

Nodding, and pointing to her assistant, Polijn shouted, "Excellent! It's a scholar!" The crowd laughed some, the soldier himself louder than the rest.

"As a scholar," she went on, "he knows Rossacotta's history was not made by people who used inns at night. Even that inn can be passed by, when necessary."

The ficdual was now tuned as well as it could be, under these conditions, so she struck her opening chords. These were recognized by people who jumped and then did their best to pretend they had to sneeze.

Arberth had naturally suggested that she do one of his songs. She had pointed out that everything he wrote dealt with lovesick men, which would not fit her at all. So she swaggered across the platform and tossed out the first verse of "Talking With My Mouth Full." She threw her shoulders forward and let her head drop back, giving the audience a wink before the first punch line.

Oh, the crowd laughed! Some laughed delicately and some bellowed into their hoods while others blushed and tittered. They had to. To fail to laugh would suggest that one had heard the joke, and the song, before. To admit an acquaintance with the entertainment at the Yellow Dog was to fall to the depths of uncivilization.

Eru, which verse came next: the horse or the sausage? Polijn pulled her lower lip back and let it hang as the upper spread in a wholly abandoned, and slightly vacuous, smile. Would that she had one of Iúnartar's dimples to go with it! But three men over in Garanem's retinue were clapping their hands more or less in rhythm, which showed they had dropped the rotten potatoes. Maybe she wouldn't need dimples.

"He spread my thighs with his eyes," she squealed, and pranced back across the stage, taking the audience's attention with her.

Arberth sat on the ramp, greatly impeding the efforts of the workmen carrying rolls of ribbon to the stage. He was nodding to the music, half a beat behind Gensamar's lackeys. His smile was as bright and incongruous as his wardrobe, broadening and flattening his face. The wolfish aspect this gave his features rather startled Polijn.

She swung her head around to chortle at another portion of the audience. When she looked again toward Arberth, Alohien was limping up behind him.

She nearly missed a beat, and had to swallow quickly before she went on. After that fall down the stairwell, he should have been dying, or at least severely damaged. Now there was no way for him to miss seeing her, and nowhere for her to hide.

The guard's smile showed all his teeth. Polijn danced to a far corner of the stage, dodging the workmen setting up stakes. When she glanced down, Alohien was prying a little wooden block from under the ramp. Polijn strutted to the stairs, but found Meugloth there.

"Keep still," he growled. "And out of the way. Do four more verses."

If Alohien didn't hit her with the first toss, he could try a second. And the sentiment of an audience in the Palace Royal could shift with amazing speed. Everyone had come to be entertained. If they decided that stoning the performer was more fun than listening to her, there was nothing to hold them back.

She checked again. Alohien had started to limp up the ramp, still smiling, still holding his wooden missile. Apparently mistaking him for another workman, Arberth slid to one side. The guard smiled a little broader, and sat down next to the minstrel. He nodded to Polijn. He was going to let her wait.

Polijn looked over at the Royal Platform. The King and Merklin were talking to Masalan. They probably hadn't heard any of her song at all. Foolish to have expected a rescue from that direction anyway; who would repeat a moment like that so soon? Her only hope was Arberth. That was no hope at all.

She slid so that a couple of stakes, at least, stood between her and the guard. She had not intended to give him the satisfaction of seeing her look back again. She had hoped that if she didn't see the projectile, it couldn't hit her. But she couldn't help it. She had to see where the woodblock was.

She did not see it. Both Arberth and Alohien were gone.

Turning slowly around, emphasizing the key words of the chorus as if expecting the audience to sing along, she surveyed the crowd. Some members sang along and some did not. This didn't matter so much as the fact that none seemed to be holding a block of wood.

She expected a sharp shock on any note of the last verse. It never came. Finally, Meugloth raised a hand. Polijn nodded, and wound down the final chorus.

There was a little applause, and some cheering, as she curtsied. One or two men near the steps called out suggestions that shocked Polijn only in their lack of originality. Then everyone turned to see what those long avenues of ribbon on the platform could be for. This was not exhilarating, but, considering how many plums had hit the floor instead of the platform, it was encouraging.

She ducked under a ribbon and tripped downstairs. "Nice job," said Meugloth, looking over her head at the platform. "Now we're ready for the fat women's race."

V

FORTUNATELY, a dispute broke out almost immediately about the contestants, and whether someone who was merely pregnant was eligible for a fat women's race. This distracted the crowd, allowing Polijn to force her way to the door past those spectators who wished to congratulate her, among other things. The rule was that unless one was on the level of Laisida or Tarobbin, and entitled to be in the Great Hall, one got out as soon as one had performed. A lot of people ignored this rule until forcibly reminded, but Polijn was glad to retire. It would be no safer, she thought, but it might take Alohien longer to find her again.

She took a long route, with more shadows to hide in and fewer passersby to hide from. Many of those she did see were in hiding themselves. Daverna was back on one of the window sills, her dress tossed up over her shoulders in back, paying off a gambling debt. Polijn hurried by, but noticed in passing that the woman was cheating, thighs pressed tightly together to give her partner a false impression. Polijn wasn't shocked, particularly. She did wonder where a Palace lady would have picked up the trick.

Two of the smoking rooms were in this corridor. Tobacco was banned from the Great Hall on major occasions: there was no sense taking chances. As Polijn sidled past the second, she felt a hand brush her sleeve. She jerked away, but two fingers were caught up under the fabric, and she was pulled back.

For the shadow and smoke, Polijn could not make out a face. The figure was bulky for Alohien, but there were others in his plot. He was no more than a minor figure, and could have alerted his superiors to her spying. On the other hand, it could be someone who had noticed her golden armband and just wanted to make a profit.

Flight wouldn't help. Her best bet was to hand over the heavy ornament and be done with it. Encouraged by her good fortune on stage, as well as by the fact that the man hadn't tried anything so far, Polijn thought she'd mouth her way out of this one.

"It's not for you, friend," she announced, her voice ringing. "I'm savin' it for somebody prettier. He's big, too, and he won't like your thumbmarks on my clothes. Why don't you go off and mind your own personal business for a while?"

Polijn held her breath as the head inclined down. Then he let go and shuffled down the corridor. Just a drunk after all: pity to waste the performance.

She found her breath still short. Why was she so lintik nervous tonight? Her big solo was over, so there was nothing more to fear from that. At least two people were hunting for her, mayhem on their minds, but that was not so new to her either. She did think it appropriate that the first thing she saw inside the Great Dining Hall was the painting of "Death and the Cowherd." The peasant's expression of confusion and terror as he landed on the dungheap matched her sentiments precisely.

Polijn studied the crowd for a second before plunging in. She wanted to stay inconspicuous, but she wouldn't mind being inconspicuous next to the food. Maybe she could find that team of acrobats and ask a few technical questions.

But when she moved forward, her sleeve was pulled back again. "I've had a goblin's own time finding you!" exclaimed her latest captor.

She looked up into the face of a man she didn't know. "Lord Laisida sent me," said the man. His mouth jerked up at one side. "He wants to talk to you some time, if you aren't tied to that swampstained jester somehow."

"Oh!" said Polijn. "Oh. Yes, I . . . I would be . . . glad to. Tomorrow? Tomorrow afternoon?"

The man let go of her sleeve. "Not early. Maybe tomorrow night's better. Keep it in mind." He turned back up the corridor.

Keep it in mind? One of the King's Minstrels wanted to talk to her, if she wasn't required to go on working for Arberth, and that lackey thought she'd forget about it. Polijn whistled.

Calm, she told herself: stay calm. Laisida might simply need a new attendant for one of his daughters, and preferred someone musical. Or this could be some intrigue of the assistant's. Other schemes started to occur to her.

In any case, she'd better talk to Arberth first. She looked around as much of the crowd as she could see. The jester was not in evidence, but other people were. What was Lord Isanten doing in the Great Dining Hall, when he was clearly entitled to better places? And there was Lady Raiprez. The entertainment could certainly not be the attraction. It was a mere group of contortionists, and not especially good ones, though creatively clad.

"Isn't she underdressed a bit?" demanded a woman Polijn was trying to work around.

"She's wearing a whole quart of whipped cream," shrugged a soldier.

Arberth was probably tucked in some inconspicuous corner, back at his cards. She aimed at a corner equally inconvenient to the platform and the buffet.

"By the way, you haven't said how you like my new furs."

"Lovely, my dear, but did you hear the furrier's wife wailing all day?"

"Whatever for?"

"Can't find her cats."

Polijn succeeded in attaining the corner, only to find a stack of discarded tunics and two small thieves shuffling their way through them. She looked for another corner.

Lady Raiprez was still in sight. Polijn was turning away when she realized the woman's eyes were fixed on her. One flawless eyebrow rose to show that Raiprez was also aware that Polijn had understood. For Polijn to move anywhere now would be flagrant insubordination.

"You were the girl singing that song just now," said the general's wife, reaching her.

Polijn admitted it and took up a defensive stance. If necessary, she could dodge past the woman, under that bench, and down behind the buffet.

"Your name is Polijn," Raiprez went on.

"Yes, my lady," said Polijn.

Raiprez stretched her upper lip back across her front teeth. Polijn thought this was very likely meant for a smile, but was unsure what a smile from Raiprez might mean.

"If you are not bound to that jester in any way . . ."

A hand took hold of the lady's arm. The tall figure of General Ferrapec was right behind her. Pulling his wife slightly to one side, he said, in an undertone, "There's no time for that now. He's having a bad one."

"I thought Janeftox was taking him to his room," she replied, her lower teeth showing.

"He was. But on the way they tripped on a head and now he's on the battlefield again."

While saying this, he had turned and started away, confident that his wife would follow. She did take two steps, but stopped abruptly and demanded, "A head? Whose head? Where?"

The exasperated face turned on her indicated that this was a wholly irrelevant consideration. "Nobody's. No one's. A Treasury guard: Alohien, somebody said."

He moved off again. His wife followed, pausing only to stretch that smile at Polijn again. "We will speak more of this later," she said.

Polijn's cheeks puffed up as she expelled a long breath. More to worry about! There had to be a quiet spot where she could think things out.

She looked to her left and her right, and found her face covered with bilious orange cloth. "What?" she demanded.

"Get back here, you bacon-eater!" someone shouted. "No one leaves the game until I have all his money or he has all of mine!"

Polijn fought her way free of the cloth. "Lucky I saw you," said Arberth. "Take these back before Kohoontas insists I stake them. Was that Raiprez talking to you? What did she want?"

"I'm not sure," she told him, taking the armload of clothes.

"You did a good job with that," he told her, jerking his head toward the more prestigious room. "Pity it wasn't a nobler song, but maybe you had the right idea. Win them over with a loud song first and then move on up the scale. If there's room on the program, maybe we'll try another duet later, on the strength of your reputation. 'The Lovesick Bull,' maybe."

Polijn coughed. " 'The Lovesick Bull'?"

"I'd like to go with 'The Ram Forlorn,' but I can't seem to turn up the manuscript," said the jester. "Maybe . . ."

"Back to the cards, jester!" shouted Kohoontas. He was apparently sitting down, for Polijn couldn't see him anywhere.

CHAPTER TEN
Nimnestl

I

NIMNESTL shook her head to clear it. Despite the discomfort of her position against the gritty altar, she kept drifting in and out of a dangerous drowse. The pain in her arm still throbbed enough to keep her from getting too far under. She was glad of that; she wanted no more dreams in this place.

She tried for the thousandth time to find a more comfortable pose against the pitted rock. She did not find one. When would the Brown Robes come and end this miserable game?

When she heard the rustling sounds from the stairs, she closed her eyes and forced her muscles to relax. The bar that held her knees apart slid a little along the lower horizontal bar.

A door opened. "By the Burning Bone!" an Ykena exclaimed. "The Bodyguard!"

Many feet scraped along the floor. "She's still out? How hard did you hit her?"

"Don't worry," said the owner of a hand that slid across the Bodyguard's buttocks. "I know how to wake her when the time comes." Nimnestl clenched her teeth.

Palompec strode up past her to stand before the massive statue. "Brethren of the Brown Robes!" he called. "Thou hast seen what I have done so far, unaided! Is it not?"

"It is!" chorused the Ykenai. Nimnestl estimated two dozen.

"Now," the colonel went on, "when the sun is farthest from us, we shall call Su'in Wa Du'in to finish the job. Then the Ykenai

213

will rule this land and its many armies!"

"Will he take her?" demanded one follower. "A woman?"

"That thing?" called another. "She's two-thirds man as it is!"

"Not from my angle!" shouted a third.

Palompec clapped his hands for attention. "Our demon," he announced, "has an historical appetite for the stalwart, the strong, and, above all, the dignified. And we have carefully restricted his diet to untasseled youngsters this far. I promise that before this night ends, we shall see the Bodyguard twist and weep in the demon's embrace."

Nimnestl promised him something as the group applauded. She risked letting her eyes slide partially open.

Palompec lit the braziers on each side. As tinder leaped into flame, he cried, "Oh, Su'in Wa Du'in, your faithful worshippers call!"

The flames shot up. "Hear our plea!" Palompec shouted. "In your deep home beneath the earth, attend to our cries! Rise! Give us your counsel and strong arm!"

Light died. A faint rumble, like thunder at a distance, grew out of nothing. A blast of heat burst from the altar. Nimnestl had to strain to lie still.

"Master!" the colonel called, his head enveloped in billows of grey smoke. "Accept another sacrifice from your followers! Come forth!" He raised a long metal wand from the pedestal of the statue and directed it at the naked captive.

Nimnestl would have been granite herself to remain unawed by the mighty grey-beaked bird that formed from the hot grey clouds. She felt as if she had turned to stone when the bird fluttered free and, seated on one shoulder of the still, cold statue, raked her from head to foot with empty eye sockets. A laughing screech of approval shook the iron braziers as the bird rose to the ceiling.

Another wave of heat blasted the room and the bird was gone, clouds dropping in hoops around the demon statue. These rose into an orange cylinder, glowing brighter, growing higher. Palompec had to step back.

The cylinder vanished with a resounding roar. All Nimnestl could see now, and that through a haze, was the statue. She bit her lower lip as the spiked hair rustled, and a tentacle rose. The Ykenai were silent.

That great granite head rose and turned toward the altar. A smile oozed along the face. Nimnestl looked away, and was thus the only one in the room to see Kaftus step from behind the statue's base. Dwarfed by the demon, looking oddly vulnerable, the necromancer raised his arms. He used no magic of his own, which would have exposed him to the Brown Robes. He let the growing force of the demon flow through him, and directed it to his own purposes.

Su'in Wa Du'in stretched like someone roused from a comfortable nap by the smell of an agreeable supper. "This," he said, running one hand over his stomach, "is the finest morsel I have seen in centuries."

One bulb-tipped tentacle snaked down toward Nimnestl's face. "You have done very well," the demon went on. "What do you . . . eh?"

The tentacle jerked back; the statue frowned toward its feet. Two tentacles slid down toward Kaftus.

But the necromancer had finished. Human forms rose from the brazier and the pedestal. Nimnestl could see them clearly: long, grey, apparently boneless bodies oozing up toward the leg of the granite demon. Tight, dry lips were drawn back against teeth in permanent snarls. The noses were flat, collapsed, but the rest of the features showed dead sacrificial victims from all races: aristocrats from Diarrio, ranging warriors from Reangle, bearded minstrels from Keastone, sacrifices from all edges of the continent. Some were young, some were old. But most were warriors in their prime: the demon's favorite.

The dead caught hold of the demon's tentacles and hauled themselves up. Su'in Wa Du'in shook them off, but dozens rose to try again. "Get away!" bellowed the statue. All the stones of the walls seemed to rattle an echo.

The demon's victims rose in grey masses and streamed into the hair at his waist. The demon's eyes, and his stomach, grew very wide. "No!" screamed the demon. But soon all the dead had vanished.

Light and heat surged through the room in an explosion that was no less violent for being completely silent. When Nimnestl's face cooled, and she could open her eyes again, the statue was gone, the demon burst from within. Only a few wisps of orange smoke trailed from the victorious dead.

They did not stop to cheer. Now they turned on the necromancer.

"Go down!" he ordered.

They did not go down. Two reached forward and took his sleeves.

Kaftus drew back as if offended and, in the same motion, pushed a hand inside his robes. When the dead continued to advance, he drew out a glowing blue gem.

The blue light cancelled the greyness of dead skin. For a moment, faces were reborn in the shapes and hues they wore in life. The victims blinked, a few smiled, and then all of them collapsed into dust, which glowed for a second and also disappeared.

Sweat dropped from the necromancer's domed head. He thrust the gem back into its hiding place and collapsed against the granite pedestal.

Palompec was the first to regain the power of speech. "Don't run!" he barked at those of his followers edging toward the stairs. "He's exhausted! We have him and his black dog both at our mercy! We can kill them both down here, without being indebted to the demon!"

The Ykenai saw the sense in this. Cheering, they charged. Kaftus sat up and waggled his fingers at them in an amiable way. The surge stopped in its tracks. Kaftus winked at Nimnestl and pulled up on the pedestal to sit.

Nimnestl planted her feet square on the floor and rose. Loose loops of cord dropped, as did the bars lightly glued into their original places. One horizontal bar, really her hammer, rose with her and caught the leading Brown Robe in the belly. He arced away over the heads of his followers.

The Ykenai halted in the wrong place. Haeve dropped from hiding, left leg extended and a sword raised above his head. A Brown Robe fell back, breathing through his ribs, and the others turned for the exit. Culghi and five gleeful bodyguards awaited them.

Nothing to do now but fight: glittering swords came from under brown robes. Culghi took the advance, and the headless body of Aizou walked three steps before it dropped. One or two of the traitors turned back and were met by Haeve and the Bodyguard. The hammer sent a head flat against its owner's back and, on the backsweep, threw an Ykena back to be impaled on the spiked hair of another demon statue. Haeve's thrust finished Colonel Palompec, whose last expression was one of outrage.

The remaining Ykenai had conquered panic, and were concentrating on those men between them and the stairs. A few Brown Robes could not resist the expanses of dark skin shining in the dim light daring them to come in and cut it. These learned quickly the dangers of temptation. A hasty sorcerer leaped up to the altar, seeking the advantage of height and completely forgetting Kaftus. The necromancer's face was contemplative as a glowing axe swept from nowhere through the man's shins.

Quarter was not asked nor offered. This was a battle for life and death, and, incidentally, the kingdom. A bodyguard, his sword broken on an Ykena's collar, reared against the stairs and then dove among the crowd, his hands tensed for tearing.

A Treasury guard, Adrom, turned from the battle of the stairs and saw a chance. He ducked under Nimnestl's swing and brought his blade up as hard as he could on the handle of the Bodyguard's weapon. The head of the hammer snapped away, dashing another demon statue into fragments.

The Bodyguard shoved Adrom back with the splintered handle and pulled up a dagger that had hung from the cord knotted around her waist. She beckoned, but the sorcerer, appalled, backed away. The hammer had been death, too, but at least it kept her at a distance.

Kaftus, seeing without difficulty how this battle would end, shouted, "Take one alive, at least!"

Haeve dropped his sword and tore a rope from around his waist. A loop of cord snaked off after Adrom, who had dodged to put the altar between himself and the Bodyguard. He dodged again on seeing the rope, only to have the rope jerk sideways and come after him. He mouthed the spell that would turn the magic back on the Tutor, but the rope was unaffected.

Nimnestl finished the last of the Ykenai before her and looked inquiringly at Kaftus. The necromancer shrugged, shaking his head.

Adrom stumbled, but the rope overshot its target by a good two feet. The Ykena slashed at it from below, whereupon the loop swerved, dropped over his wrist, and pulled tight. Adrom stabbed and then clawed at his wrist, but Haeve gave a jerk. Adrom was pulled back across the bloody altar, and rolled onto the floor. Haeve was over him at once, looping more rope around the fallen sorcerer.

"Kill me!" Adrom demanded, as Nimnestl and Kaftus joined the Tutor.

"Tut," said the necromancer, as Haeve forced a gag into the prisoner's mouth. "Our Bodyguard has the matter of a broken hammer to discuss with you, and there are questions I'd like to ask, myself."

He turned to Nimnestl. "Speaking of which, why are you tat-tooed right there, particularly?"

"Tradition," she snapped.

She turned to the panting bodyguards on the stairs. "Well done," she said. "Culghi, take the prisoner to the Regent's rooms. See that no one knows of it until we give orders." She pointed to their own casualty. "The rest of you, see that Caluar is properly set out."

"What about the others?" asked Bonti, gesturing to the dead Ykenai.

"Leave them here to rot," said Culghi.

"Off with you," Nimnestl ordered. "We have our own purposes here. You have your orders."

The bodyguards departed, with the two bodies. Once they were gone, the Regent inquired, "Our own purposes?"

Nimnestl surveyed the battleground. "We may have to sort them out, or move them," she said, "depending on our story. One of them has to be picked out as Morquiesse's murderer!"

"I thought you had decided Palompec had done it?" the Regent replied.

"He'll do, for a story," said the Bodyguard. She turned to the Royal Tutor. "But you did it."

II

HAEVE didn't answer. Turning her back on him, Nimnestl walked over to fetch her clothes.

"I suppose," she said, "that the Royal Tutor might, on a Festival night, decide to take a stroll near the three-quarter mark in the dungeons. Once there, he could have happened on the right cell, found the secret door, and remembered a combination he had read in some ancient volume of lore he'd seen once in the Royal Library. And I suppose he could have known he would find someone tied to an altar at the bottom of the stairs. But there are other supposes."

"There must be," said the Tutor. He reached under the slashed tunic. "I'll try to come up with some, one day. But you'd better take this."

The paper was bloodstained now, but Nimnestl could still identify it as the missing half-page from the record book of the Ykenai. Kaftus nodded as she passed it to him. Without looking at the Tutor, she then crossed the room to fetch the head of her hammer.

"Arlmorin told me Morquiesse was taking an interest in Rentruan," Haeve said, for once not irritated by seeming inattention. "I had caught the ambassador in factual errors before; I doubted he'd waste any true rumors on me. But Rentruan disappeared, and so did Macob. I had seen Macob chatting with the painter. Morquiesse spoke of the boy's artistic talent. I'd had him in my classes for over a year and hadn't seen any. Morquiesse dismissed this as a layman's blindness."

A tinge of emotion almost forced through the neutral geography-lesson voice, but he went on. "After Argeleb vanished too, I kept an eye on the artist. While he laughed at your expression when the sundial gave you a faceful, I saw the amulet tucked way back inside his sleeve. They call the demon Soan Wadoyan in Keastone, and his worship has been banned for decades, but we still know his symbols. And I know how he handled his victims, too. My students are not to be wasted in that fashion."

Haeve paused; his nose went up exactly as if this were a lecture on geography. "I stopped at his rooms later, and drugged his wine. And I saw to it that he and his guards all had a drink before I left. He drank cheerfully enough, planning his next trick. I was coming back later, and he knew it."

"He was pretending to be asleep when I went in, but after I'd closed the door, he pulled back the covers and fired at me. When the arrow missed, I knew the drug had him. He shouted for his men. They couldn't answer. He muttered something about the wrong antidote."

Nimnestl shook her head. That had to be the most potent wine in the country at this point.

"I had to kill him now." Haeve shrugged. "But there was no rush. I took a look around the room. That's when I found his book and tore out the page of their enemies. That got my name out of his records and, at the same time, gave me directions to a room I had never known of. It appealed to my antiquarian interests, and there was a chance that I might find the boys there, still alive."

He shrugged again. "Then I went back to Morquiesse and finished the job. I can't say that part of it bothered me much."

"What did you do with the arms?" asked Kaftus, who had not changed expression.

"Nothing." The Tutor held up both hands, palms out. "I'm telling the truth. His arms were intact when I left. I didn't kill his guards, either. It was better to let people think one of them had done it."

"A ruse worthy of a master's mind," said Kaftus. Haeve bowed.

"And that's the lot. I meant to search the room tonight, when everyone was preoccupied with the festival. I had it planned for later, but when I saw Palompec looking so pleased with himself, I wondered which of my students was to be sacrificed next. And that's all I can tell you."

Kaftus's smile made even Nimnestl's blood a little chilly. "You're quite sure you couldn't tell us something about the arms?"

But the Tutor shook his head.

"Don't imagine that we're not grateful," said the Bodyguard, buckling on her belt. "We can still get you off with a whole skin."

"If we feel like it," the Regent put in.

"Perhaps I'll throw myself on the mercy of the Throne," mused Haeve. "The King might be merciful. Still, I made him memorize all that geography."

"May be merciful for what?" piped a voice from the stairway.

The King stepped down into the shrine, following a triumphant black bird which cried, "There! That teach you, maybe, to go off adventure without Mardith!"

The King, studying the corpse-littered floor, could say nothing but "Wow!"

Nobody else said anything. Mardith came to rest on Nimnestl's shoulder and was thwacked away by a heavy fist.

"Yeah, yeah," grumbled the bird, fluttering to a perch on a fragmented statue. "Sorehead."

"More Brown Robes?" demanded the King, taking three steps farther into the carnage.

"Your Tutor led us to them," Nimnestl replied. "With his help, we may have finished the last of them."

The King studied Haeve with new respect. "That's good work. Why didn't you tell me? You ought to tell me things, now that I'm a real King, you know."

Nimnestl didn't know what to say next. Haeve snatched a piece of paper from the hands of the Regent and pushed it into those of the King. "That's true," said the Tutor. "Being a King is not all triumphs and trumpets. These are the directions for finding this place. None but the Ykenai seem to have known about it before this."

The King was taking a deep breath to say "Wow" again. The Tutor added, "I found it in Morquiesse's room when I killed him."

The King swallowed the "Wow." "Morquiesse?" he demanded.

"He was the new leader of the Brown Robes," Nimnestl told him. Kaftus, seeing that this was likely to take some time, pushed half a body off the altar and sat down.

"Morquiesse was . . . one of them?" said the King, frowning. He looked up at Haeve. "And you killed him?"

"Yes, your Majesty," said the Tutor.

"But that's terrible!" The King turned to Nimnestl. "What are you going to do?"

"You're the King," Kaftus told him, with a yawn. "Remember?"

Conan stood silent, obviously struggling. His thumb started up, but stopped. "Well," he said, his voice a little thick, "it'll be okay, I guess. I can pardon you." He looked to the adults for approval.

"The people won't stand for it," said Haeve, shaking his head.

"They want blood," Nimnestl explained, taking a step forward. "They loved Morquiesse as much as you did, and they don't know Haeve at all. Not many still think the Ykenai are dangerous. If we say that Haeve killed him, they'll want you to decree punishment. You could banish him . . ."

"Never make it to the border," said the Regent.

The King was shaking a little. Nimnestl wanted to put her arms around him, but instead she looked away, and said, "It could have happened another way, of course."

"What do you mean?" Conan demanded.

"Maybe the Ykenai killed Morquiesse," she said. "Maybe he was looking around and found out about this place, about the demon. He was killed for that, but not before he got word to Haeve, who told us. That makes Morquiesse and Haeve heroes, and look." She gestured at the strewn bodies. "We've already killed most of the culprits. A tidy story, and one that people will like much better."

The King studied her. "But it's a lie," he said, wishing to be reassured on this point.

"It's a lie," Nimnestl told him.

He stood where he was, stricken, all eyes on him. It was a terrible thing to ask of a nine-year-old king. He could avenge one friend by killing another. If he didn't, he could tell thousands of people who worshipped him a story that he knew was completely false. Nimnestl could see the future of Rossacotta twisting in the wind.

Thugs and thieves had thronged to Rossacotta for centuries, swapping booty for a chance at the top of the heap. Many succeeded. Rossacotta was very old, very rich, and very ugly. It stood now between the old ways and the new ways, run by pirates who dealt in vice but considered themselves civilized because they dabbed at themselves with napkins. All the cruelties and vices of an underdeveloped country were wrapped up with those of an overdeveloped one, and none of the virtues of either.

The only reform that had not come unreformed was a result of the strength and determination of Rossacotta's ruling family. But the monarchs had wrested power from the ministers too recently. It would take just one weak or vicious ruler to throw everything back to the cesspool days of the past.

Whatever the King decided now would alter his personality, and that of the country, for decades to come. And, for the life of her, Nimnestl could not tell which way he ought to decide.

Conan clamped his hands together, tucking the thumbs inside. "Nimnestl," he said, "may I whisper?"

The Bodyguard didn't know whether to laugh or cry. "Yes," she said. "Of course, a real King always holds Secret Councils."

The King didn't smile. She bent down to hear what he had to say. "Why don't you just tell me what I should do?" he asked. "And I'll do it."

She shook her head, and waited. The King was silent for a moment. Then he said, his voice even lower, "I'm going to let him go. Nobody needs to know. We'll tell everyone . . . what you said. Is that all right?"

Nimnestl didn't know. But she stood up and replied loudly, "The murderers of Morquiesse shall be displayed as you have ordered, Your Majesty."

The King's eyes were a little moist, and now the Bodyguard did take his hand. She was leading him to the stairs when Haeve coughed.

"And I?" he inquired, when they turned.

"Publicly," said Kaftus, "the Tutor has committed no crime, but he can still be tried among us. As a murderer, is he still fit to be your Tutor, or shall we send him away?"

The new complication sent the King over. "I don't know!" he shouted, tearing his hand loose. "Leave me alone!"

He dashed up the stairs. Mardith swooped after him, pausing only to tell Nimnestl, "Very sorry, Missy."

Nimnestl said nothing. Haeve walked over to the door.

"I wouldn't have been the one to teach him that lesson," he said, "for thrones." Nimnestl didn't say anything to that, either.

III

THE room was dead. For just that reason, the Head Bodyguard's office was so effective for preliminary interrogation. It was cold beyond mere temperature; the walls lacked that warm patina acquired by rooms that were lived in. Nimnestl herself made use of the rooms only as a temporary and occasional base. Her place was with the King. This office was mainly for storage: weapons and armor for the members of the bodyguard, and now and then a body that had to be held until disposal. Caluar was probably lying in the back room now.

Nimnestl unfastened her upper armor and loosened the rest of her garments so that they slid down to her waist. Stepping over to a basin of icy water, she dipped a sponge in and began to swab her face and neck. Every few seconds, her eyes turned to the mirror in front of her, not to see herself but to watch the door at her back. She had conditioned herself to do this, and now never saw her own face in the mirror at all. Rumor had it that she avoided mirrors, being a witch.

She grimaced as she reached around to moisten the back of her neck. The drug Kaftus gave her had numbed the pain and restored strength, but the body still needed time to heal. Hardly a muscle failed to register discomfort. Nimnestl felt like stretching out on a mattress and not moving for two days. If one of the feather beds from her youth were available, she'd make it two years.

A breeze from the window made her shiver. Striding to it, she pushed the heavy tapestry aside so the wind could hit her full in the face. There was nothing to be seen from the window but a dismal, dripping fog. She wished she were out in it.

Tossing the sponge back into the basin, she turned and went to the chair from which she had questioned Palompec. She sat down, her arms dangling. Not thinking, not feeling much, she was just a pile of person, waiting for the energy to sigh.

Somebody knocked at the door. Wearily, Nimnestl put a hand under the tunic crumpled at her waist and brought out a dagger. "Come in."

Light poured in from the corridor. With it came the King, with Mardith on his shoulder, and Culghi three steps behind. Nimnestl rose, and bowed her head. "Your Majesty," she said.

"Culghi, you may go," said the King. The lesser bodyguard backed out of the room, showing in his eyes abashed admiration for the iron woman standing before him. He closed the door.

The King glanced at the guttering candles, then at Nimnestl. He pushed Palompec's chair over to the table, climbed up, and sat on the table, his feet on the chair. Nimnestl could now be seated. She sat down.

Mardith flew up to his mistress, considered perching on a bare shoulder, and then thought better of it. He went to a rack of spears instead, and took up a place in a vacant notch.

The King and Nimnestl looked at each other as best they could in the dim light. Finally the King said, "I shouldn't have run off like that. But it isn't fair."

"No," said Nimnestl.

"You know what I mean?" the King asked.

Nimnestl knew what he meant. When she was nine or ten, she had had a favorite cat. She also threw seeds out for a chipmunk that sometimes came to her window. One day she saw the chipmunk go by in the mouth of the cat. "It isn't fair!" she had said to anyone who would listen.

Those who listened shrugged and said, "That's the way it is. A cat has to eat, and they catch little animals."

And Nimnestl never meant it that way, not that it was unfair to the chipmunk. It was unfair to her.

"Anyway," the King went on, "if Morquiesse really was a traitor, then we ought to let . . ." He swallowed. "Let him stay on as Tutor. He helped us."

Nimnestl nodded. "Fair enough," she said. She watched the King wind one foot through the rungs at the back of the chair.

Then she said, "I suppose I shouldn't make things difficult, but you ought to know."

The King's shoulders slumped and he turned imploring eyes on her. "Now what?"

"Haeve didn't kill Morquiesse."

The King's mouth dropped open. "What?"

"A dead man wouldn't have bled so much when his arms were cut off," she said, looking away. "I'm a little surprised the Tutor didn't know that, but maybe it's not his field."

"Who did kill him?" asked the King, angling around to face her. "I thought Haeve took the arms, too."

"No," she said. "The one who took his arms, so that he bled to death, was the real murderer."

The King leaned forward, his feet in her lap. "Who?" he breathed, his eyes bright.

Nimnestl told him. "Really?" he demanded.

"Think about it."

He nodded almost immediately. Then he frowned. "But what are we going to do about that?"

"It might be best to let Haeve believe he did it," she replied. "It will certainly impress him with your magnanimity. Anyway, he meant to do it, and thought he did it."

"But to cut off the arms and let him die that way!" the King exclaimed. "And the guards, too!"

"Remember," Nimnestl said, "officially, the Ykenai killed Morquiesse and the guards. We'll have to consider the whole thing and figure out how to manage affairs quietly. Once we tell everyone the Brown Robes killed the artist, we don't have to hurry."

"All right," said the King. In the moment of silence that followed, Mardith fluttered to a perch on the mirror, a little closer to the table than the spear rack.

"While we're thinking," the King said, his head coming up slowly, "there's something else."

It was Nimnestl's turn to demand "Now what?" but she simply waited.

The King put his hands on his knees and looked down at them. "You probably know how the Neleandrai—the ones with the hoods—have been inviting me and Merklin to their rites."

"Missy know everything," ventured Mardith.

"Yes," said Nimnestl, ignoring the bird.

"You know how they pick out a lamb? How they have all the members play cards and the last one to lose has to do something as a sacrifice for all the things everyone has done wrong?"

"Yes," said Nimnestl, preparing to be shocked and surprised by what she knew was coming. "I remember when one had to try and steal my hammer."

"Well," the King said, measuring his thumbnails against each other as though to see which was growing faster, "they always . . . the loser was always somebody I didn't like." He looked up at the Bodyguard. "I thought it was just the way things happened. But they planned it that way."

"They had the cards all picked out?" asked Nimnestl.

"Yes," said the King. "I was watching them tonight, and Tusenga was doing just the way Arberth showed me, with his thumb in the deck."

Nimnestl had hoped for this, but not tonight, at the festival, when neither she nor Kaftus had been on hand. "So what did you do?" she asked, hoping there was no war going on in the Great Hall as she spoke.

"I couldn't come right out and accuse them right there," he said, looking at the toes of his boots. "I wanted to, but everyone was watching."

Nimnestl closed her eyes and breathed three long breaths. There was hope.

"I just made them stop bothering Masalan, and let them get away without saying anything." He looked up and saw her eyes tightly closed. "It was all I could think of!"

Nimnestl opened her eyes. "Why, you showed prudence," she said, "and a very proper concern for not spoiling the festival for everyone else. I must say you acted like the King you are. Kaftus and I could hardly have done better."

"Really?"

"I doubt that even Nurse could have objected." She slid forward in her seat and took his hands.

The King was breathing hard, though whether from relief or anger she couldn't tell. "They didn't really care about any true religion or whether I was a member," he said. "They just wanted me as their yes-master."

"It must have been part of their plan." Nimnestl told him about the list Aoyalasse had turned in.

"They're just as bad as the Brown Robes!" cried the King. "I know who they all are, too, so you can catch them!"

Nimnestl already knew most of them, too, but let the King go through his list. Akoyn, Colonel Tusenga, Seuvain, and many lower-level Treasury officials were mentioned. Nimnestl was proud that he was so observant, but a bit worried about what he meant to do next.

"We should kill all the leaders," he concluded, answering her question, "and banish the rest."

"Um, yah!" said Mardith.

"Careful," Nimnestl intruded. "There are a lot of them, and some have powerful friends."

"Well, I'm the King," he told her. "And I'm not their friend. And Merklin saw them cheating, too."

Nimnestl supposed it was overly optimistic to think he could learn the lesson the first time, that having the power of life and death over one's subjects still didn't mean one could do anything one wanted. "Maybe I can think of a better way," she suggested.

"Oh, very well," said the King, with a jerking shrug. "You take care of it."

"She do good job," Mardith put in, sliding to the nearer end of the mirror.

"We'll take care of it," she told him. "Do you remember that quester—his name was Roiphe—who told you how he used to catch monkeys in Gilraën?"

The King looked a bit confused, but said, "Yes. He said they put out boots. The monkeys would put them on and walk around in them and be so proud they'd forget they couldn't climb trees with them on. Then they'd get caught. You said you didn't believe it."

"I still don't," she answered. "But it can work that way at court. Let's give the Neleandrai some boots."

The King tipped his head to one side. "I don't know what you mean."

Nimnestl held up a thumb. "Take Tusenga. Now, if you banish him, he can take his case to his friends on the Council, and complain, and raise a fuss, and make things difficult. He wouldn't do that if you made him a general."

"No," said the King. "But why should I do that?"

"Because," she went on, "if you make him a general in the border guard, and have him report for duty right away, you're really banishing him just the same. You promote the other soldiers you mentioned, only you send them to different parts of the border. You're rewarding them, but you're sending them so far away that their plots are ruined, and so far from each other that they can't make new ones. You'll break up the Neleandrai, and they won't be able to complain because they're getting all those rewards."

The King frowned. "I think I understand that."

"A lot of the people you mentioned are in the Treasury," she continued. "Who would be better to send along if you made some valuable gift to another King? It would be a long, dangerous trip, and many of them wouldn't . . ."

"Nimnestl," the King broke in.

"Yes?"

He shook his head. "No, forget it. It's silly."

"Go ahead," she said. "Kings don't get to be silly very often."

"Well," he went on, bouncing back and forth in his seat, "isn't that a lot like cheating at cards?"

Nimnestl couldn't see where this had come from. "Is it?"

"Well, isn't it cheating?" he demanded. "Yes, it is. Instead of telling them they're going to be punished, we make them think they're going to win something. And all along, we have everything fixed so they're going to lose. It's just like the way they picked out who would get good cards and who would get bad cards. And we're cheating them because they cheated us. Or isn't it the same?"

"Not the same," said Mardith. "Not the same a bit."

"We are playing a nasty trick on them," said the Bodyguard. "It depends on whether you think that's cheating. But you have to remember two things. First, we aren't playing cards. We're running a country and they want to do it instead. It's no game: it's a matter of one side going on and the other side dying. Second, keep in mind that we are not punishing them because they cheated at cards."

"We aren't?" the King demanded.

"We aren't," said Nimnestl. "We're punishing them for trying to use the King of Rossacotta to get what they want. And there is no law against that. In fact, it has a long and honorable precedent. So there's nothing we can truly arrest them for. They could even claim that what they did with the cards is an ancient rite, and we just don't understand. We have to do it another way."

The King did not look entirely convinced, but Mardith chimed in, reinforcing the Bodyguard's opinions until Nimnestl told the bird to shut up.

"All right," he said. "Can we do it tonight?"

"As soon as possible," she told him. "Just let me get my clothes on."

IV

IT was decided that there might be less suspicion if the King and the Chief Bodyguard arrived separately. Nimnestl opened the door and found Culghi just outside.

"Do you know where Seitun is?" she demanded.

The bodyguard had sprung from his waiting place across the corridor at the sight of her, but now leaned back. "Not nearly."

"Mardith!" Nimnestl called over her shoulder. "Go get Seitun. Tell him he's to escort the King."

"Ma'am," said Culghi, "I can . . ."

"You're too busy," his superior told him. "You're finding out who was on duty at the gatehouse and at the door last night and this morning. Take them all into custody and find out which let Palompec through."

"Yes, ma'am!" Culghi exclaimed, and set off.

"Have you left yet, Mardith?" Nimnestl demanded.

"Now yes, Missy!" called the bird, and shot over her head.

"You tell people what to do and they do it," said the King, coming to the door.

"Sometimes," Nimnestl replied. "You heard how Culghi was going to whimper because Seitun was escorting you? He's as bad as a Royal Councillor; he really is."

Seitun appeared in due course and followed the King toward the Great Hall. Nimnestl, Mardith on her left shoulder, took the longer way around. She was passed by Joive, running along in

230

no more than a black velvet ribbon, shouting something about a shovel.

The festival had apparently progressed in her absence. On the stairs, Fiera was shrieking as she was tossed down the stairwell to someone who would probably catch her but who had, after all, been drinking quite a lot.

Nimnestl therefore walked with her hand on a dagger, ready for surprises. When a door slammed open in front of her, Mardith sped up into the air, prepared to dive at any assailant.

But the slammer of the door had her own problems. A whip cracked over Fiejin's head as she ran into the hall five steps ahead of Lady Iranen. "Out! Get out!" shouted the latter.

"But I sleep there!" wailed Fiejin.

"Out!" Iranen repeated. "The stables are not yet full!" The whip cracked again.

"Lady Iranen," said the Bodyguard, her voice low but carrying.

The Housekeeper whirled, her whip ready to fly again. Instead of standing clear, Nimnestl moved in. "We were just wondering," she went on in a conversational tone, "what you did with those arms."

The whip hand came down slowly and a long smile eased across the Housekeeper's face. "They were in the urn on the Grand Staircase for a while," she said. "Now I have them aging in my room. I thought some of my bitches would like the bones later."

Mardith settled to his mistress's shoulder. Nimnestl forced a little smile and went on. "We would like very much to have them back, if you could bring them to me quietly. The Regent will be very grateful."

Iranen's smile grew. "How grateful?"

With an effort, Nimnestl stepped even closer to the little woman and whispered something. Fiejin was gone, but the whisper made it seem more official. Mardith whistled. The Housekeeper's face looked a little less mad as surprised gratification blossomed there.

She pulled away from the Bodyguard. "I'll take care of it," she whispered. She started off at once, but paused to look back toward the Great Hall.

"Right away," she assured Nimnestl, and bustled back into her chambers.

Nimnestl braced herself to enter the orgy in the Great Hall, but found that things had not degenerated quite that far yet.

On the performance platform, a magician from the city was decapitating himself. "Notice," he commanded, "that I speak no spells, summon no demons."

Nobody noticed. Overhead, Roucek's son was attracting their attention. He had unwound one of the garlands from a ceiling beam and was now swinging back and forth, swearing that he could so reach the next beam from here, if only his page's jacket weren't so tight. On each backswing, his father gave him a healthy swat on the rump, not for chastisement, but to add momentum.

Meugloth's three-year-old daughter was dancing in Nimnestl's path. The Bodyguard stopped. Lefeald wasn't dancing because she was drunk, or because she had stolen something particularly valuable, but simply because she was feeling good, and because a three-year-old often has more energy than she can comfortably contain. A high-pitched, tuneless happy song went with the dance. It was like a splash of cold water against Nimnestl's hot, dry face.

Through a swirl of hair, Lefeald suddenly noticed the dark bulk towering above her. She rolled to the floor and scampered for safety under a bench. From that shelter, she watched with wide eyes as Nimnestl passed. Nimnestl wished there was a way to be proud of this.

Tucked away behind one corner of the food tables, small naked boys, their gilding a little spotty now that they had completed their appearance as fire from the mouth of a papier-mâché dragon, were being held in place until the auction could begin. Oozola, the Vielfrass's half-clad, half-human companion, had taken over the storytelling duties.

"Being a ghost," she was explaining, "Weino had to drink blood. Not being accustomed to that kind of diet, she was naturally cranky."

Kaftus stood nearby. Unless he had suddenly taken an interest in gilded boys, he was loitering to hear the story. He raised an eyebrow as Nimnestl approached.

In an undertone, she gave him the gist of what had happened and what was underway. "You manage these things so well," drawled the Regent. "I may just retire. I would naturally hesitate to add anything to a tapestry of your weaving, but may I recommend Lord Oidon to you?"

Nimnestl glanced across the room. "That isn't very far."

"You've been listening in on the geography lessons," Kaftus replied. "The route does, however, pass through much of southern

Rossacotta. Your guards will have sufficient work to hold their attention and, rather than come back the same way, some may be persuaded to desert to Turin. And it would obviate the necessity of my listening to Oidon's presentation to the Council tomorrow afternoon."

She nodded. "Always a worthy cause. I'll talk to him now."

"Do so. And I will find out what became of Weino in this version. You should have no trouble chatting privately with him, the way the festivities are expiring."

The crowd had thinned. Many guests had collapsed and been carried off by their retainers, hopefully to their own rooms and not to dark niches under the stairs. Others had left under their own power, realizing more was being drunk to the King's health than was good for theirs. Some had realized the scheduled entertainment was drawing to an end and the heartier partiers would soon reach the furniture-throwing stage; they had slipped out for shelter.

Those who had stayed were either waiting to hear the King's announcements, traditional at the end of a festival, or were simply in no condition to leave but too feisty to be dragged out. Lord Patrak had retired under a table with two jugs, and sat there sneering at the crowd. Yslemucherys, in contrast, was drinking and laughing as fast as he could to keep up with two of his superiors, neither of whom would remember, the next day, having told him he was the best of all fellows and overdue for promotion.

An uncomfortable cluster of foreign ambassadors also waited, grimly intent on hanging on through the festivities, just to show how interested they were in Rossacotta's ways. They had drawn closer together, forgetting wars and other quarrels, as the night grated on. The veneer of Rossacottan manners was eroding; more baleful glances and mutters of "murderers" were being flung their way.

Nimnestl sought out Oidon, the cadaverous greybeard sent north as ambassador from Cahoots. Rossacotta's southern neighbor was a great producer of gold and silver, much of which travelled to Rossacotta by unconventional means that neither country ever labelled "plunder" or "smuggling." Though not as civilized as some, Cahoots was a very virtuous nation. The main tenet of their religion was peace of mind, to achieve which they ordered that those things which would not respond to persuasion and could not be remedied by force should be ignored, lest such provoke unwise action. Sending

Lord Oidon as ambassador was the closest thing to ignoring Rossacotta.

"Greetings, Lord Oidon," said Nimnestl, bowing her head a bit. "My Lady Pheryn."

"G-good evening, Lady Nimnestl," said the ambassador, his eyes shooting left and right. Some of his retainers drew away from him, and his wife came up closer. Rossacottans leaned in to listen.

"Your unsparing efforts have brought fruit," she told him, her face saying nothing. "It would be imprudent of me to speak of the outcome until the King makes the formal announcement, but I wished you to know now that you may rely upon me if you require advice."

"I see," said the ambassador, frowning. The speech could mean anything, or nothing. A couple of retainers came up behind him, not sure whether they were coming to share the wealth, or the blame for Morquiesse's death.

"Madame Bodyguard . . ." But he was cut short by a trumpet blast.

The King reappeared on his own platform, behind two almost sober trumpeters, and followed by Seitun, eight other hastily gathered bodyguards farther back. The room fell silent as the procession moved up before the King's chair. The magician finally gave up and jumped down next to Meugloth.

"Hey!" called a voice.

Nimnestl and Lord Oidon turned. Aoyalasse, her pale face showing an unhealthy flush, marched up to them. She had stripped down to a tunic and overtunic and, as she raised a hand to hail the Bodyguard, she spilled a mug of wine over an old silver brooch that was blackened at the top, not as if the silver had tarnished, but as if the silver had chipped off.

"M-my list!" she stated. "Am I g-going to g-get a reward or not?"

Nimnestl nodded to the King. "That you will hear. There are to be many rewards forthcoming."

She scanned the room for the other major actors. In the wake of the King's procession, other members of the Bodyguard Royal had entered, to be ready for attempted escape or assassination. Many of those to be honored were in evidence. Nimnestl missed Lord Arlmorin from the assembly. Pity: he'd love this spectacle.

V

THE severely intoxicated were only momentarily diverted, but others pushed forward as the King took his place. He had obviously run into Nurse on the way, for his hair was freshly brushed, and every pin and lapel of his costume was perfectly positioned. He maintained a solemn pace and a serious face, but Nimnestl could see he was enjoying himself.

Kaftus joined the procession, Seitun and four bodyguards moving to let him in, and then returning to position. They were studying the crowd, ready to close in in front of the King if anyone objected to being promoted.

Word had already spread through the festival. Crowds at the doors had become big enough to become dangerous. Guards posted there were busy, knowing who could be allowed in and who was not. Nimnestl thought she saw First Minister Isanten among those massed at the East Door, but even he couldn't plead or bluster his way in.

The King raised his hands to attract attention, a needless gesture, but one he always felt was dramatic. "Children of the Panther!" he cried.

"Ah, pop him on the head and shove him under a table," someone said in the silence that followed.

Nimnestl turned and knocked Dyveke's hands from Illefar's throat. "We need him yet."

Dyveke backed away. "I'm . . . sorry, Milady. D-didn't see you there."

"Hush youself!" croaked Mardith. "Your King, he talk!"

"There are tidings for all!" His Majesty was saying. "The murderer of our painter, Morquiesse, has been found and named!"

The audience leaned forward as one body. Nimnestl frowned to see Kaftus's lips moving. The King could do this without prompting.

"This murder was another plot of the Ykenai traitors!" he called.

Fierce joy gave way to a fear-tinged caution. More than one courtier glanced at the Regent, or the Bodyguard. The King himself, a little surprised at the lack of enthusiasm, rolled his large eyes back toward Kaftus.

Then he leaned out and shouted, "It is true! Their leader, Colonel Palompec, whom we had trusted, had such evidence in his hands as proved it. Morquiesse stood in the way of their plans, and so Morquiesse died. Tonight, while trying to accomplish his evil plot at a time of festival, Palompec and all his aides died as well. The investigation of the Ykenai is at an end now, for all the Brown Robes are dead!"

Since the King seemed to expect it, everyone cheered. But this glee was guarded. What the monarch said and what his Councillors might be planning behind his back could differ.

The King frowned a bit, not happy with this limited response. But he went on, "Now that punishment has been dealt out to traitors, we can openly and without misgivings reward those we know to be faithful!"

The clamor was more heartfelt now. Greed could overcome caution almost any time.

Nodding, the King glanced to Kaftus for approval. When the Regent bowed, he took a long breath of relief and raised his arms for silence again.

"In honor of the end of the Ykenai plot," the monarch announced, "I declare tomorrow to be another day of festival and rejoicing!"

Nimnestl wondered if the Palace Royal could take another day of festival and rejoicing. She glanced at Mojira, who sat under a table on her right, exposing damp white thighs. Every few moments the woman would pause for breath and then go off on another cascade of mad giggles.

"There is double cause for rejoicing," the King went on, "since we also celebrate our new treaty with our neighbor to the south.

Tomorrow morning, a caravan departs to bear gifts to our brother monarch of Cahoots. A number of trusted servants of Rossacotta will accompany the treasure, suitably attired and fit to represent us there."

He then recited the names of those members of the Treasury guard who would move south with the gift (much of which was gold looted from Cahotian traders in the first place). Some of the names he mentioned were of men only suspected of being Neleandrai, but Nimnestl felt the possibles as well as the definites could be sent. They weren't cutting heads off, after all.

Lord Oidon beamed, ignoring the glares of his counterparts from other countries. With any luck, he'd be promoted too, and not return from the trip south. Or, more likely, Nimnestl thought, the Cahotians would have him beheaded once they saw what he had encouraged to enter their country. Those Treasury guards who did return would likely bring back more than they took down.

The King went on through the other reassignments and promotions, with an occasional reminder from the Regent. Other Treasury personnel had to be promoted, to cover for those who were going south, and also so that anyone who suspected this trip was banishment would get little sympathy. General Tusenga was sent to the north, in company of a rigidly monarchist aide. (Who, at this moment, was crawling on all fours under the buffet, stalking a piece of sausage that Queen Chicken-and-Dumplings kept pulling out of his reach.)

"Since Lady Akoyn has requested that she be allowed to travel with the caravan, and watch over those wives and families that will be accompanying it, we have found it necessary to name a successor," the King announced.

This was the first Lady Akoyn had heard of her request. She closed her eyes, and her lips appeared to be moving in prayer. It was also news to both her immediate superior and her immediate subordinate. Lynex and Aoyalasse gazed up at the King, one in apprehension and the other in anticipation.

"Hereafter," he went on, "Lady Aliquis shall be First Assistant to the Second Chief Housekeeper."

Aoyalasse was confused for a second. Then comprehension dawned. She cast a long, appraising look over Lynex, whose concern was now even more pronounced.

"That leaves the Fourth Chief Housekeeper without a First Assistant," said the King. "For her services, Lady Aoyalasse shall take that position."

Aoyalasse greeted this promotion with utter lack of facial expression. Then her chin dropped and her lower lip slid in. Lynex, her smile sweet, leaned over to her sometime assistant and whispered something, perhaps congratulations. The red-headed woman turned and pushed her way into the crowd. A scream escaped her, bringing echoes of laughter from the crowd.

Nimnestl turned away and headed for the door. The crowd parted for her, and the guards made no demur as she left the room.

"Milady Bodyguard!"

Nimnestl looked over to see Lord Arlmorin, the ambassador from Braut, striding up to her. She braced herself. "Yes, Ambassador?"

The big man stopped before her, perhaps unaware that he was blocking her path. "I felt you must know at once," he said, his eyes meeting hers.

It was not comfortable, but Nimnestl held the gaze. "If it is about Lord Oidon's . . ."

"I am afraid," he broke in, "that I have been guilty of an indiscretion."

The Bodyguard glanced at Umara, who, with a gathering of friends in a niche in the corridor, was bobbing for apples, her skirts much higher than her mother would have approved. Fortunately, her mother's skirts were over the bald head of Menixa, back in the Great Hall.

"Surely one indiscretion can go unnoticed tonight," she suggested.

"Perhaps," he replied. He raised his hands, fingers outstretched. They didn't come within two feet of Nimnestl, but she could have sworn she felt something as they rose.

"Do you know the girl who sang 'Mouth Full' on the stage a while ago?" he asked. "A nice girl; dark hair, interesting face. Her voice is rough, perhaps; she should breathe more."

Nimnestl could not immediately identify the person he meant. "It may be I know her," she said.

"Arberth's servant."

"Ah," said the Bodyguard. "Yes, I know the girl. I didn't hear the song. I was likely out of the room. What about her?"

"She wore a heavy metal armband," said the ambassador. "I am afraid I pointed it out to the wrong person. She may be in danger."

"If the ornament was valuable," Nimnestl told him, "the indiscretion was hers. Someone else would have seen it, if you had not. In any case, I fail to see that this involves me."

As the ambassador explained how it did involve her, Nimnestl felt a growing alarm. At last she raised a hand to cut him off.

"Follow me," she said.

They started for the Great Hall. She hoped she could get Kaftus away from the platform without attracting too much attention.

CHAPTER ELEVEN
Polijn

I

THE Great Dining Hall had abruptly lost half its population, leaving behind only those who couldn't move or didn't care. In the rush to hear the King's pronouncements in the Great Hall, the scheduled entertainment had been replaced here by impromptu performances. Mistun was singing of the intimate injuries suffered by a bear who had found the Head Bodyguard sleeping in the woods and had been overcome by lust. (The Bodyguard, he claimed, had slept through the assault.) No one was overly interested. Maitena, trying to change her slippers on a bench near the platform, was attracting more attention.

Nuseth and Avtrollan were making up, noisily and thoroughly, under a table. The only person who noticed, particularly, was Polijn, and it was of significance to her only because she had intended to take a shortcut under that table. Now she had to back out and pick a new route. Glancing behind her, she found an inconspicuous spot beneath the painting of "Death and the Huntsman." She pushed a dislodged bowls table into a more convenient position, and sat down on it. It rocked a little, for the game pieces trapped under it, but Polijn didn't intend to stay long. She was restless, uncomfortable, dwarfed by the huge room.

Her chief worry, at the moment, was that Laisida might be drinking too much to remember his invitation tomorrow. Her second worry was that he wasn't, and would. The prospect of trading herself off to another master didn't bother her; everyone in Rossacotta was merchant, customer, and merchandise.

But she didn't know what to do about Arberth. He had been a decent master, and she didn't want to offend him by desertion. But there was no doubt she'd learn more as even a servant of Laisida than she would as the jester's assistant. One side of her said, "Grab what you can" while the other said, "Don't let go of what you have." And she couldn't grab anything with her hands full.

Polijn stood up and took a few aimless steps, stopping behind an upturned bench. Her decision was already made; it was only a matter of telling Arberth. But that speech was hard to compose; the thought that someone was watching her kept pushing in.

There was almost certainly nothing to worry about now. Alohien was dead and Aoyalasse, according to reports from the Great Hall, had been carried off to Iranen's offices by no less than the Regent and the Bodyguard themselves, Mardith plucking out most of her hair and one eye en route. There was perhaps a bit of inflation involved in the story, but it did mean that all she really had to dodge in the Dining Hall now was random violence. And she'd dodged that for years.

Probably, she thought, her fears were no more than the sudden emptiness of the Dining Hall and lack of shelter. She couldn't go back to the room in the tower, not with all those spiders still waiting. Iúnartar would probably give her a place to stay. But Polijn had heard about Tusenga being sent to the border, just when his daughter was on the brink of great social success. This was a good time to steer clear of Iúnartar. The girl was just as tedious unhappy as happy, and a whole lot damper.

"Ah!" she said. The Palace apothecaries were always dealing in poisons. Maybe one would pay for a crop of spiders like the ones upstairs; maybe there was also an easy way to harvest them. Polijn left her hiding place and looked around for a druggist, preferably Ronzini, who stayed sober at these affairs so he could be the first one out in the morning to sell his hangover cure.

She stepped over and around debris, keeping one hand at least on the wall tapestries for added security. These were horrendously greasy; diners had been coming by all night to gaze on the paintings above them, and wipe their hands on whatever was within reach. All the Dining Hall tapestries needed extensive repairs and cleaning after a major festival. Polijn's hand slid into a long tear, the latest effort to separate the two legendary lovers depicted on the cloth.

Polijn slid her hand out and started on. Then she stopped and reached back inside. That had felt like paper.

It was paper, and immediately recognizable paper. Someone had no doubt stolen it to use against Arberth in the matter of Morquiesse's murder. She refolded it and started to slip it back into its hiding place. If she never had to sing "The Ram Forlorn" again, the omission would not throw her into deep despair.

Something was written on the back of the sheet, so she pulled it out once more and unfolded it. What song could be so bad that Arberth would disregard it, and write another on the back?

No song, apparently; a letter. The text seemed to be an offer to overthrow a government for the recipient, if the recipient, an exiled member of a royal family, would lead the revolt. Not all of the words were in Polijn's reading vocabulary, and there were no names in the letter except the partial one at the top. But Polijn got the idea right away, and without any trouble about who "-berth" might be.

How like him to scribble a song on the back of such a piece of treason! Even if this was a forgery, one more of Morquiesse's jokes, it was too dangerous to leave around in the Palace Royal, where extensive schemes had been built around less. The thing to do was dispose of it right away.

Polijn looked around for a torch or brazier within her reach. One eye was also open for the gaudy garments of the jester. Arberth might have objections to losing "The Ram Forlorn." And she held some respect for his right arm, which he had proven he could use with efficiency when faced by suspicious card partners.

She stopped to think about that, tapping the manuscript on her arm. Could Arberth have killed Morquiesse? The painter might have known about the letter. Yes, and painted Arberth into "Death and the Prince" because of it. And Arberth would have known the painter had to be kept quiet. On his budget, there was only one way to do that. Polijn glanced up at the painted faces of Arberth and Death.

She was troubled. This was surely just a product of her mind, which had never needed much to wind up with a story. But it was entirely too plausible. Arberth had let her coax him into the Swamp, and started playing cards. Once he was sure his assistant would be busy for the evening, he had excused himself from the Low Raven and run back to do the killing. He had, after all, had those fresh drops of blood on his tunic, and he had refused to go see the body.

Measthyr could have seen the paper during a lesson, stealing it for Morquiesse. That was why Arberth had been looking for the swordsman, and why Measthyr had died. It explained, as well, the jester's limp. Of course, Chordasp could have done that, too; he said he had wounded his assailant, a singer. Admittedly, it was stretching things a bit to call Arberth a singer, but Chordasp had never been a man of refined sensibilities.

That wolfish grin of Arberth's: he had been sitting close to Alohien, and later Alohien turned up dead. And Polijn knew she was not the only person to be suspecting these things. She had seen it in the way Lord Isanten kept asking for the jester. The story that blamed the conveniently dead Ykenai was only a coverup, a ruse to keep the First Minister quiet. The Bodyguard would naturally want to shield one of her few friends.

Polijn shook her head. Arberth? A stumbling bumbler to work out so many killings? Still, he was a skilled and underhanded card player. Who was to say he couldn't do it? Was the kidnapping of Argeleb part of it, too?

Polijn ran over the details, turning them into rhymed and rambling verse, and considerations of politics and safety slipped from her mind for almost a full minute. They were not gone long. In her proto-song, she observed that those who had held this manuscript died. It occurred to her that the manuscript was now in her right hand.

She was looking down at it when someone passing between her and the nearest light shouted, "You! Here!"

One glance at a green-and-orange sleeve was all she needed. She was off.

Polijn knew she couldn't outrun those long legs; she would have to lose him. Right under "Death and the Fool," she took a sharp turn and slid under the table there. Anyone of Arberth's height would have trouble following.

Once free of the table, she aimed for the opening under Death and the Lovers. If she could reach the Great Hall and find Lord Isanten, he might know what to do. Or Laisida, if he hadn't left yet, or Raiprez. If they were interested enough in her to offer employment, they might help save her life. The Bodyguard, if she wasn't busy on the Royal Platform, might lend some aid.

But she couldn't afford to run straight at the door; he'd realize where she was going and move to cut her off. So Polijn dove around benches and between tables, keeping in what cover she could find. It was not only Arberth she had to dodge. Anything running in the Palace Royal was worth a grab to anyone, just to see who was chasing it and what they'd pay.

Nothing seemed to distract her pursuer. She heard heavy footfalls behind her all the way, and not so far behind her, either. He was practically breathing on her when she heard him slip, curse, and, unfortunately, not fall. But she took advantage of the distraction to dive between a pair of housekeepers blithely unaware of the whole drama, having smuggled three jugs of the good liquor from the Royal Reception Room. Polijn had a view of green shins dashing past her.

She waited for Arberth to get six or eight footsteps away and then leaped from her hiding place, zigzagging for the door. She saw a bench between her and the goal, and jumped over it. She did not see the discarded fan until she was coming down. By stretching one leg a little too far, she cleared this, too, but then it was impossible for her to do anything about missing the greasy roll beyond, even if she'd seen this in time.

She hit the roll and skidded. Throwing herself ahead to avoid falling backward, she fell forward. Her fingers could get no hold in the tapestry that hung under "Death and the Executioner." Stubbing the fingertips on the stone did break her momentum a bit before she hit the wall.

A pair of hands caught her under her overtunic. The cloth tore, but she was twisted around. "It's not you I want, you fool!" growled her assailant.

Polijn looked up into the glowering face of First Minister Isanten.

A grey hood dipped in between her face and his. "Hey, tajos," said the wearer, alcohol all but flowing over the words, "inside and outside for us, eh? Looks good. I'll hold the arms and a leg for you and then you can do the same for me. We . . ."

Isanten pulled one hand from under his captive's outer garment, reached inside his own, and thrust the knife he found there up into the face under the hood. The man dropped without a word. Isanten kicked him out of the way.

"Now," the prime minister went on, shaking Polijn a bit, "I do not intend to be foiled by a drudge worth three coppers, at best. Hand it over."

Polijn immediately held out the letter. He knocked her hand away.

"I never want to see that thing again! That wretched jester's head was to be my ticket out of Malbeth, out of this lintik ministry. But the idiot's unkillable!"

He pushed Polijn back against the wall, banging her head into the tapestry, and then let go. "I hired the best man in the Swamp, they told me," he snarled. "I wanted but one head. The shuptit jester wasn't around; I had to describe him. So first the idiot brings me the head of a Treasury guard who wore mismatched castoffs, and then the head of that singing swordsman. Measthyr killed him, anyway, which saved me the trouble."

The First Minister clenched his fists. "Narindahl thought the spiders were a grand idea," he went on, "until he went up to check and got himself bitten to death. Something certainly upset those spiders. I saw the jester myself, later, and sent Orfuy to deal with him. The idiot brought me the head of another Treasury guard! They thought I was collecting them, perhaps."

Polijn, thinking these reflections were diverting his attention, slid a little to the left. She was wrong.

"I should have known," Isanten growled, winding a hand in the fabric of her overtunic, "that any scheme involving that lintik jester, even as a corpse, even as a bloody head, was doomed to fail. But give me that bracelet now and I will command legions!"

Startled, she put a hand on her armband. "This?"

"The power of that is all I need," said the First Minister. "We'll see whose term of office ends in six months. Give it to me, drudge, and you may live to see another Regent."

Polijn looked down and started to slide the ornament from her arm. But a wary eye flicked back to the First Minister. Not knowing this, the man was slipping out a broad dagger.

"Um," she said, trying to think of anything that would prolong the conversation, "are you the one who's been following me, then? To get . . ."

Isanten knew a stall when he heard one. "Give me that bracelet!"

Polijn dropped and the dagger went through the cloth of the overtunic. She tore to one side, but the waiststrings still held. The First Minister took hold of these with his free hand and pulled her to him.

"Somebody!" she screamed.

II

ISANTEN jerked backward. Huge hands pulled at his throat, the thumbs pressing on the joints of his jaws and all eight fingers hauling under the chin. The First Minister flailed behind him with the knife; this did him no good. His head was drawn back; he couldn't even open his mouth to shout.

Polijn was not inclined to linger. She recognized her rescuer's broken nose and shaved head, and didn't want to wait to express gratitude. The last time she had seen that face, it was being sucked up, with the body, by that statue of the demon.

She slid along the wall until she was clear of the combatants. Turning to make her break, she tripped headlong over the fallen drunk. Her face hit rough, fragrant cloth. This was no tapestry. When she looked up and found that she'd walked into the Regent, she fell back, landing hard on stone, next to the hooded corpse.

Kaftus paid no attention to this diversion. He fixed the Chorachtai cultist with a glower and drew a blue crystal from within his robes. Blue light hit the First Minister and his assailant. In moments, only the First Minister remained. Isanten dropped to the floor, one outstretched hand barely missing Polijn's arm.

"Why didn't he come up with the others when you called them in the temple?" demanded the Bodyguard, stepping up behind the Regent.

"He was still committed to service of the master of the armband," the necromancer replied. "Or, in this case, the mistress."

Isanten had been no more than dazed. He rose now to his knees. The first thing he noticed was Polijn, who shrank back as he raised a hand. It took but a second for the First Minister to remember they were not alone. He looked up at the Regent.

"Get that bracelet away from her!" he panted. "It's a demon's talisman!"

He rose to his feet. Turning, he found himself being studied by not only the Regent and the Bodyguard, but by the more sober members of the Council as well.

"Neddertrechticha!" he growled, looking around at Mitar, General Gensamar, Laisida, Meugloth, and Lady Forokell.

"You saw what she did to me!" he cried to them. "Who knows how many more of those demon-spawn may be waiting in the shadows?"

Polijn could feel their gaze as it passed over her head. She knew it well, having sung so often beside Arberth. It said, "You are failing to amuse us."

Isanten threw up an arm to point. "She's in with them! With that lintik shuptit sorcerer and his black dog! They'll kill us all!"

He looked around the group for support. Once he might have found it. But during his five-year administration, the fanatic anti-Regency officials had slowly and painfully been replaced by those who were willing to tolerate Kaftus's regime as long as Kaftus was so powerful. It was the most basic law of Rossacotta: follow strength.

Isanten did not represent strength. He knew it.

The First Minister's nostrils flared. All his teeth showed in his grin, and all the whites of his eyes. He reached for his sword. Gensamar and Mitar did the same. There was no chance of escape for him; even Polijn could see that all he wanted was a quick death.

Just before battle was joined, however, the corpse of the drunk rolled over and caught at Isanten's left leg. At the same moment a figure pushed through the circle to tap the First Minister on the shoulder.

Isanten whirled to face the new arrival, stiffened, and dropped.

"Just a little premature rigor mortis," said the Vielfrass, reaching down to help the recently dead body to its feet.

"Thank you," noted the Regent, who had not moved throughout the confrontation, except to tuck his sorcerous gem back into its hiding place.

The recently deceased sot blurred and became the Lady Oozola. The little shapeshifter turned and put down a hand to Polijn, telling her, "If you'd stay out of places like the Gilded Fly and the Palace Royal, these things wouldn't happen to you."

Polijn got up and then handed Lady Oozola the crumpled song manuscript. "You'd better . . . they'd better . . ."

"For shame," said the Vielfrass. "Stage fright at this point in your career."

Polijn lacked the courage to glare at him, but Oozola handled that for her. "I heard the whole story," said the shapeshifter. "I'll start and you correct me if I miss something."

Between them, Polijn and Oozola outlined the First Minister's schemes. "Who'd have thought the jester would be such a prize!" exclaimed Laisida. "What do you suppose Isanten wanted with him?"

"We shall have an answer to that," answered the Bodyguard, "as soon as we have a very frank visitor."

Forokell twisted around in her chair to look up at the Bodyguard. "Are we to have a very frank visitor?"

"He should probably be fetching . . . Ah!"

Lord Arlmorin broke into the little group, pulling a reluctant Arberth behind him. "Alas!" said the ambassador, looking over the body of the First Minister. "This is my fault!"

He let go of Arberth, who eased over to stand by his assistant. "I will be very frank," said Lord Arlmorin, looking at the Council members. "None of this would have happened had I not failed to report Lord Isanten's conversation with me. Foolish of me, I now know. But I could not feel, at the time, that his efforts to escape beheading were so very treasonous, after all."

"Possibly not," Mitar replied, considering the question. "There are a few points in the law. . . ."

"What was the nature of this conversation?" the Bodyguard broke in.

"He hinted that he would not be averse to taking a position in the government of Braut," said the ambassador. "He was willing to offer us his experience and expertise at a somewhat lower salary, but, of course, without such a fatal retirement benefit. At present we had no need for a former First Minister, but I did mention that there had been some ruckus in Turin over an exile, one Arberth, who had gone into a different line of work."

Everyone turned to the jester, who stammered, "S-see, my grandfather . . ."

"There's no need for that story," the Bodyguard broke in. "Not tonight. We wish to hear about Lord Isanten."

Arlmorin shrugged. "That particular revolution came to nothing. The exile declined to participate."

"Erugarn!" exclaimed General Gensamar. "Didn't you care to be King of Turin, man?"

Polijn looked up at the jester. His head shrank back into his shoulders some, but he answered, "There have been more Kings of Turin hanged than jesters, My Lord."

"At any rate," Lord Arlmorin went on, "Isanten took my suggestion and apparently decided to take the exile's head as well, a gift for the Turinese government, in the hopes that they would express their gratitude in a suitable fashion. When this scheme went all awry, and he heard about the Armband of Mastery there, he decided to try for that instead."

Polijn cleared her throat and said, "Please, what is this?" She passed a hand over the shining ornament.

"Oh, nothing much," the Vielfrass told her. "Only an armband worn by the high and mighty plum pudding of a demon cult. While you wear it, you have command of all revived sacrifices deceased since the demon voted you into office."

"So," Polijn said, "that goblin worshipper . . ."

"Was waiting for orders," said the sorcerer. "When you didn't wear the bracelet, he wandered, watching for you but not making any contact. He was confused and stumbled around, looking like three-quarters of the population of the Palace Royal the day after a party."

"Very useful," said Gensamar. "Why didn't Isanten just plug her with the knife and take it?"

"It cannot be taken," Kaftus told him. "It must be bestowed." The Regent rubbed his chin. "I wonder if this small mistress of the undead can be persuaded to bestow it on me. The thing must have some residual power, if it can still control a dead man after the demon's destruction."

"I'd give it to him," the Vielfrass whispered. "He likes pretty things, and he has a tendency to pout when he doesn't get his way."

Polijn would not have withheld it for all the thrones in Turin, Cahoots, Braut, and Rossacotta. She slipped it off her arm and raised it in both hands.

The Regent took it, looked it over, and slipped it, too, under his robes. It didn't even make a bulge.

The Bodyguard cleared her throat. "Thank you?" she prompted.

"Oh yes," said the Regent. He raised an eyebrow at Polijn, who shrank back. "Many thanks. You have done Rossacotta a signal service."

"She didn't have much choice," said the First Housekeeper, her tone and her expression very dry. "And if she also likes pretty things?"

"There ought to be a reward," Gensamar agreed. "She's helped ruin a mighty pretty plot."

"I always said Isanten was as smart as any three people," said Laisida. "Provided two were fools and one was a madwoman."

"I suppose this constitutes a decision of the Council," sighed the Regent. "Is there anything we can feed you, infant? Don't open your mouth too far; you have earned no feast."

"They have an opening for First Minister," whispered the Vielfrass.

Polijn ignored that and thought it over. Then she said, "There's a place in the Swamp, called the Yellow Dog. You . . . you've probably never heard of it."

The Councillors gravely denied any knowledge of a place called the Yellow Dog. "Oh, come now!" exclaimed the Vielfrass. "Such memories!"

"It's late," suggested Oozola. "And they're tired."

"Can it be exempted from the tax?" Polijn ventured. Her eyes were on the Bodyguard. She thought she saw contempt in the great, dark face, so she added, "My mother works there."

"Is your mother the one . . ." Gensamar began, but broke off.

"It can be done," the Bodyguard put in, covering his confusion. The contempt, if it had really been there, was gone now. "Tomorrow . . ."

She jerked, as if bumped. Mitar, standing next to her, stepped aside. Yslemucherys, flushed, stumbled into the circle. "Council meeting?" he demanded. "Why . . . why wasn't I . . . sh . . . summoned? The Keeper of the P-p-p-privy p-p-p. . . ."

He turned to survey the Council members. "Ah, isn't this a pa-pa-party? Who's for a game of cards?"

Yslemucherys was not. His legs folded under him. He looked thoughtful as he rolled down and fell across the body of the First Minister. He closed his eyes.

"Is your bird around, Woman?" the Regent demanded. "Send for a man with a broom, to sweep all this trash away."

"My good sir!" exclaimed the Vielfrass, shocked. "What a way to talk!"

Everyone stared at him. He put his hood up, and then swept it off. "Bow, gentlemen, now, and you, child, make your curtsy. I won't expect manners from that revolting shapeshifter, but the rest of you should know better. Show respect! Mitar, your hat is still on, and yet we stand in the presence of the next First Minister of Rossacotta!"

Everyone looked at the fallen body of Yslemucherys. Gensamar glanced at Mitar. Mitar shrugged. Everyone looked to Kaftus. Kaftus shrugged. Mitar raised a hand and removed his hat.

The Vielfrass rubbed his hands together. "And won't he be livid when he finds out!"

Polijn saw smiles on the faces of the other Councillors, but Forokell was unmoved. "If this concludes the evening's entertainment, I shall be off to bed. Your leave, My Lord?"

Kaftus bowed, and the Housekeeper backed out of the assembly. Mitar and the Regent then stepped aside to discuss drawing up papers to regularize all these decisions. A large black bird joined the group.

"What excitement now, Missy?" it demanded.

Laisida took advantage of the distraction to take Arberth's arm. "That assistant of yours is a resourceful piece, jester," said the minstrel. "I have an ambition to employ her."

"Do you really?" Arberth demanded, as if pleasantly surprised.

"Yes," said the minstrel, pivoting on his crutch. "Let's chat about it over some warm wine in my quarters."

The two men moved to the door. Polijn looked around and then followed. She had not been invited to join the discussion, but she did feel she had a right to be curious.